PRAISE FOR *IN THE CARDS*

"Infused with . . . fresh detail. Between the sweetness of the relationship and the summery beach setting, romance fans will find this a warming winter read."

—*Publishers Weekly*

"Fans will love the frank honesty of her characters. [Beck's] scenery is richly detailed and the story engaging."

—*RT Book Reviews*

"[A] realistic and heartwarming story of redemption and love . . . Beck's understanding of interpersonal relationships and her flawless prose make for a believable romance and an entertaining read."

—*Booklist*

PRAISE FOR *WORTH THE WAIT*

"[A] poignant and heartwarming story of young love and redemption and will literally make your heart ache . . . Jamie Beck has a real talent for making the reader feel the sorrow, regret and yearning of this young character."

—*Fresh Fiction*

PRAISE FOR *WORTH THE TROUBLE*

"Beck takes readers on a journey of self-reinvention and risky investments, in love and in life . . . With strong family ties, loyalty, playful banter, and sexual tension, Beck has crafted a beautiful second-chances story."

—*Publishers Weekly*, starred review

PRAISE FOR *SECRETLY HERS*

"[I]n Beck's ambitious, uplifting second Sterling Canyon contemporary . . . Conflicting views and family drama lay the foundation for emotional development in this strong Colorado-set contemporary."

—Publishers Weekly

"[W]itty banter and the deepening of the characters and their relationship, along with some unexpected plot twists and a lovable supporting cast . . . will keep the reader hooked . . . A smart, fun, sexy, and very contemporary romance."

—Kirkus Reviews

PRAISE FOR *WORTH THE RISK*

"An emotional read that will leave you reeling at times and hopeful at others."

—Books & Boys Book Blog

before
I knew

ALSO BY JAMIE BECK

In the Cards

The St. James Novels

Worth the Wait
Worth the Trouble
Worth the Risk

The Sterling Canyon Novels

Accidentally Hers
Secretly Hers
Unexpectedly Hers

before I knew

A CABOT
NOVEL

JAMIE BECK

Montlake
Romance

Text copyright © 2017 Jamie Beck
All rights reserved.

Published by Montlake Romance, Seattle

www.apub.com

Amazon, the Amazon logo, and Montlake Romance are trademarks of Amazon.com, Inc., or its affiliates.

ISBN-13: 9781477824443
ISBN-10: 1477824448

Cover design by Diane Luger

Printed in the United States of America

To every reader who needs a second chance in life and in love.

I have been bent and broken, but—I hope—into better shape.

—*Charles Dickens*

Prologue

Two Years Ago

Of all the dilemmas Colby Cabot-Baxter had faced in her twenty-nine years, none had tortured her like this one. It didn't help that, unlike many spring mornings in Lake Sandy, Oregon, the sun peeked through the clouds now, causing the fine mist coating the grass to glitter. Normally she'd appreciate a reprieve from the dank air that settled beneath the skin, but today she would've welcomed its bite.

Although warm inside the car, Colby shivered. Through the passenger window, she watched the mourners entering the church. Heads bowed, shoulders hunched, looking as if the weight of their grief might tip them forward.

A fleeting image of Joe's rugged face flashed—one from days earlier, just before he and her husband, Mark, had set off on a hike.

She'd grown up trading smiles with Joe across the backyard fence. His broad grin had showcased the gap between his front teeth. The gap he'd used to squirt water at her sometimes, just to be irksome. Her buddy—coconspirator, even—sneaking into the tree house their fathers had built in the nearby woods to spy on or torment their older brothers, depending on their moods.

Five years ago, Colby had been tickled when Joe welcomed her then-new husband into his circle. Of course, now she rather wished Joe hadn't liked Mark so well.

Her eyes misted again, like the dew-covered earth, as her throat tightened.

Mark's movement beside her snapped her back to the decision she couldn't put off any longer.

"Wait." She clutched Mark's forearm as he prepared to open his door. "This is a mistake."

"I need to pay my respects." Mark's baby blues widened in defiance beneath thick, straight eyebrows. Innocent-looking eyes that belied his often-convoluted thoughts. Thoughts that, when left unmedicated, had contributed to why they were here today.

"He was my friend, too." She loosened her grip but left her hand resting on his arm. Her marriage might be running on fumes, but she wouldn't compound his misery by arguing. At least not today. Gentling her voice, she added, "But maybe we shouldn't add to his family's grief by showing our faces."

Mark's jaw clenched. "You mean *my* face, don't you?"

Reflexively, she shrugged, then wished she hadn't. Mark's eyes dimmed at the silent accusation.

"Mark," she said, her voice barely audible, but then couldn't think of what else to say.

Heavy silence, the kind weighted down by unspoken judgment, consumed the car. In the trees near the church, she noticed a black-headed grosbeak eating from a bird feeder, acting as if the world hadn't been indelibly altered.

If only that were true.

"You can't blame me more than I blame myself," Mark finally muttered. "But it's done. I dared, he jumped, and here we are. I can't hide from it, and neither can you. I have to say goodbye to my friend, Colby, and I'd like your support."

Tears welled in her eyes while she imagined Joe's cocky grin just before he jumped off the cliff above Punch Bowl Falls in the Columbia River Gorge. Saying goodbye to him would be hard enough. But walking into that church to face Joe's parents and his brother, Alec, seemed an impossible task. "My mother's been the Morgans' neighbor for thirty years, and even *she* feels awkward about coming."

Last night at the funeral home, Alec had even kept his closest friend—Colby's brother, Hunter—at arm's length, so he surely wouldn't welcome Mark or her today.

"I'm going. Wait here if you want." He tugged his arm free and opened the door, letting the cool air rush inside.

Colby sighed. She exited the car, squaring her shoulders and lifting her chin. Mark reached for her hand, which she grudgingly offered. Being dragged inside might be the only way she'd cross the threshold.

Alec and his family would resent the whole world today, and who could blame them? But she knew that deep down, they resented her husband most.

They'd barely stepped into the vestibule when Alec's unerring gaze fell on Mark. Normally, Alec smiled at her, but today his mouth remained fixed in a grim line, and his green eyes mirrored the mossy color of Lake Sandy on a cloudy day. Grief had carved lines into his handsome face, giving more depth to his boyish good looks. His chestnut hair fell lopsidedly across his forehead thanks to the cowlick he could never quite tame.

She wrestled free of Mark's grip when Alec began his approach. Words clogged her throat, making it tough to swallow, much less speak. She opened her arms to greet her old friend with a hug, but he brushed past her and walked straight up to Mark.

Alec stood at least two inches taller than her husband. His eyes, as intimidating as a wolf's, glared down his finely chiseled nose at Mark. "Leave before my father sees you."

His typically mellow voice held an edge today that scraped against her skin like rug burn.

"I've apologized to your family." Mark didn't flinch. "You have to forgive me, Alec. You know I loved Joe like a brother."

"Lucky for me *we're* not close." He then spared Colby a brief glance. "Make him go, Colby. He shouldn't be here."

When their gazes locked, she noticed a cold, yawning distance that had never before existed. The loss of warmth hit her deep in her chest, choking off what little breath she still had. "I'm sorry. We don't want to cause you more pain."

She reached for Mark's arm, but he shrugged her off. "I'll sit in the back of the church and slip out early, but I'm staying. Joe would want me here."

"Would he, really?" Alec gritted his teeth. "We wouldn't even *be* here if it weren't for you."

The flicker of heat in Mark's eyes warned he was about to do or say something awful. Before Colby could pull him away, he snarled, "Joe'd want me here over you. If it weren't for what *you* did, he might not have been so eager to go on that hike, or take that dare."

Pain—bitter, brutal anguish—arrested Alec's features. She had no idea what Mark had meant, but apparently Alec did. Colby reached out to comfort him but retreated when he snapped at Mark, "Get. Out. Now."

Other mourners had started to stare at the two men despite the fact that, until Alec's outburst, they'd kept their voices low. Colby heard whispers, saw shaking heads. "Mark, let's go."

She yanked his arm, forcing him to bend to her will just this once. He ripped free of her grip and stalked to the car. Before he opened its door, he punched the roof and shouted at the sky. By the time she took her seat, Mark's head was in his hands, his shoulders shaking. Sniffling, he repeatedly banged his forehead against the steering wheel while muttering, "I'm sorry. I'm sorry. I'm sorry."

Colby sat beside her husband, in the wake of his suffering, and cried.

She cried for all the years Joe would miss. She cried for the Morgans' unending pain. She cried for Alec's tortured history with his brother. And she cried for the empathy she could not feel for her husband.

For the last bit of love that seemed to have died right along with Joe.

Chapter One

Present Day

People liked to tease Colby that, if she were ever late, they'd assume she was either dead or arrested. She'd prided herself on her punctuality. Today, however, a quick glance at the car's clock warned that she'd be late for her appointment.

It couldn't be helped.

Her grip tightened on the steering wheel as she stopped at the entrance to the Queen of Heaven Cemetery. Its gates always triggered the same flashback—Mark taking flight off their ninth-floor balcony several weeks after Joe's funeral. Like a cascade of dominoes, next came the sour stomach, the pasty mouth, the sweaty palms. *Breathe.*

Mark's refusal to properly treat his bipolar disorder had doomed their marriage, but Colby had never wanted that ending for him or herself.

The echo of survivor's guilt—as unshakable as her shadow—often steered her into the graveyard. Today, the second anniversary of *Joe's* death intensified the summons. Inevitably, a mental fog descended, clouding her thoughts about the two important men in her life who now lay buried beneath earth and memories and broken dreams.

Although her last three visits to these graves hadn't ended with mascara-streaked cheeks, the jury was still out on today. Having only recently weaned herself off the medication that had been prescribed to manage her PTSD, this visit would be a test. She'd been feeling stronger, banking on new memories and dreams to mend her broken pieces.

Colby parked along the narrow road that separated two larger plots of land. To her right lay Mark. To her left, one hundred yards across the road, was Joe's headstone. A bouquet of fresh hydrangeas lay at its base. No surprise, considering the anniversary. Thankfully, she hadn't run into his family. But for her whirlwind courtship and impulsive elopement with Mark, the Morgans wouldn't be visiting Joe's grave—a fact no one could forget.

Cold fingers of dread crept up her neck when she thought of meeting with Alec later this morning. Their former friendship had been another casualty of these tragedies.

Joe had been her childhood playmate, Alec her protector. Opposing images of Alec cycled through her mind like a flip book: him patiently tutoring her in French (which she'd only taken because, when she'd heard him speak it, it had sounded more romantic than Spanish), then politely brushing her off at the grocery store a few months after the funerals. Knowing her face would always be a painful reminder of Joe's death, she'd given Alec the space he'd demanded without words.

He must be desperate to be willing to work with her now.

She shut off the engine but remained inside the car with the window cracked open. Leafy branches swayed in the breeze, sounding like the ghostly whispers Mark had often spoken of during manic phases. In those moments, he'd declared himself a prophet, which had frightened her, although no more than many other things he'd done or said during their marriage.

If she hadn't become benumbed to his brain's pattern of recovery from mania, she might've noticed that his depression following Joe's death had been more acute. Might've realized that taking a little time off from work to comfort him wouldn't be enough. Might not have missed the fact that he'd been lying about taking his meds and seeing his doctor.

But Mark had been a pretty good liar, and maybe she'd been too caught up in her own disillusionment and grief about Joe to notice. She'd been running on autopilot just to get through those days, reluctant to do or say anything to make the situation at home even worse. It wasn't until Mark had mumbled incoherent apologies and hurtled toward the balcony that she'd awakened from that haze.

By then it had been too late.

Mark had jumped to his death, much like Joe had in the fatal dare.

She closed her eyes now to block the image of Mark's broken body on the sidewalk below. Defiantly, the gruesome vision of bone, blood, and gray matter surfaced. She forced her eyelids open, fixing her gaze on the rustling leaves as if they could erase the memory engraved on her brain. The tightness in her chest eased slightly, although her eyes still stung.

Two deep breaths later, she offered up a prayer. If she had one fervent wish since her husband's death, it was that he finally found the peace that had eluded him in life. Assuming things went according to plan, she might also know peace soon.

She twisted the platinum wedding band she still wore out of respect—and guilt—while staring blankly at the light rain now dotting the windshield. Like tears, she thought. She started the car and let the automatic wipers clear them away before heading out of the cemetery, toward her new venture, A CertainTea.

Toward the future.

◆ ◆ ◆

Even the rain couldn't mar the sight of the newly renovated restaurant. The elegant, one-story glass-and-stone structure sat at the end of a private driveway, amid a wooded, two-acre parcel bordered on one side by Lake Sandy. A lush, manicured lawn sloped toward the hexagonal cedar gazebo at the water's edge, where visitors could enjoy a panorama of the four-hundred-acre lake and its shoreline, which was dotted by private homes, docks, and boats.

Colby could hardly wait to be surrounded by families celebrating engagements, birthdays, and anniversaries here. Celebrating life!

Convinced that hosting other people's happiest moments in this peaceful setting would draw her from her perpetual state of limbo, she'd persuaded her father to invest some of Cabot Tea Company's funds in this endeavor. Of course, that purse had strings. Technically, CTC owned A CertainTea. She'd manage it, but she'd report to her brother, Hunter.

She accepted that condition because CTC had assumed all the risk. It wasn't like her former legal career had prepared her to be a restaurateur. But if she could run multimillion-dollar real estate and banking deals, she could manage this place.

"I was about to call a bail bondsman," Hunter teased, standing in the open doorway. Her brother's wire-rimmed glasses framed his owlish eyes, which constantly assessed his surroundings. His wife, Sara, had helped him acquire the bit of polish he'd never cared about: taming his thick brown locks into a neatly cropped style, and dressing him in well-made clothes. "I can't stay long. Meeting with Dad and Jenna."

His nostrils flared while mentioning their stepmother, like always.

When Jenna married their dad twenty-six years ago, Hunter hadn't cared much. Unlike Colby, he'd worshipped their father and looked for every opportunity to spend time with him instead of with their mother. But when Hunter finally graduated from Berkeley and returned to take his rightful place in the family business, he and Jenna had started butting heads over everything from strategy to paper clips.

"Sorry." Colby kissed his cheek before ducking inside, where a small cadre of workmen were finishing punch list items, like installing switch plates and drawer pulls in the bar, and touching up baseboards. "What do you think?"

"Beautiful. Now we just need Alec to work his magic." Hunter grinned for the first time since her arrival, delighted to hire his lifelong friend.

"I know how much you want that, but I'm concerned." Colby lowered her voice in case Alec was in the kitchen.

"Why? We're lucky to get a chef of his caliber." Hunter crossed his arms. "Besides, he needs this second chance."

As if she needed that reminder.

Alec's former restaurant, Une Bouchée, had won the elite James Beard Award for Best New Restaurant. That coup had happened just before Joe's death. The following year, Alec lost his mojo and, within months thereafter, his restaurant.

The veiled accusation Mark had hurled at Alec at Joe's funeral sifted through her thoughts, making her question—not for the first time—whether it had exacerbated Alec's downward spiral. Then again, having lived with secrets and regrets of her own, she could hardly criticize his.

"Is he ready, though?"

After losing his life's work, Alec had gone off the grid, returning home only two months ago. Colby wanted to help him, but the part of her that Mark's illness had wrung dry now cowered from the idea of working with another broken spirit. Especially one whose presence forced her to think about everything she wanted to forget.

"If your chef hadn't bailed last minute, I wouldn't push. But why go through another round of interviews when we don't need to?" Hunter glanced at his watch. "Not long ago, Alec was arguably one of the best chefs in the country. He's worked in some of France's finest restaurants. No one's better qualified than him."

"Except I'm not chasing awards and acclaim. I don't want this place to be stuffy. I want it to be a casually elegant place for people to relax and have fun. To celebrate, not judge. Can Alec put his ego aside and take orders from me?"

"What you *should* want is a customer wait list and big profit margin. This little place is yours to manage, but you can learn a lot from Alec." He impishly pushed her shoulder with two fingers. "Maybe it's you who needs to check your ego."

Colby bristled. "I know 'this little place' is nothing compared with the empire you all run up the road, but it's everything to me. I'm not stupid. Alec has experience that I don't, but that doesn't mean we can work well together."

"Sorry I offended you." Hunter tipped his head, his gaze softening.

During the past two years, he'd voiced concern about the circles under her eyes, earned from months of nightmares. He'd noted the way she'd no longer watch gory movies, go out on any balcony, or keep in touch with Mark's remaining family. How, for the most part, her sense of humor had withered. Like everyone else, Hunter had attributed the changes to her witnessing Mark's suicide—the very worst day of her life, yet only a part of what haunted her.

Given Hunter's ignorance of the diagnosis Mark had insisted remain carefully hidden throughout their marriage, she couldn't complain about how Alec's presence ripped the lid off a past she'd been working so hard to bury.

"Don't overthink this," Hunter continued. "Alec wouldn't have accepted the offer if he couldn't work with you. You two always got along well before. This is the perfect solution."

"'Before' being the operative word. I'm not sure this *is* the best solution for either of us now." She hadn't seen Alec in more than a year and wondered if he, like his parents, still blamed her for bringing Mark into their lives. Would he treat her coolly, or was he so in need of this job that he'd bend over backward to put her at ease? Either way would be awkward unless they could rebuild their former friendship.

"Well, suck it up, buttercup, because this is what Dad and I want." He patted her shoulder. She'd hated that dumb saying since they were kids, but, in a weird way, Hunter's consistency reinforced the familial link that gave her life an anchor.

"I think I'm going to hate answering to you." She wrinkled her nose.

"I *know* you will." He grinned. "You want to get rid of me? Buy out CTC. Alec can expedite that."

Hunter had kept her safe at high school parties, taken swipes at Jenna whenever she'd made Colby feel less of a daughter to their dad than their half sister, Gentry, and supported her idea for A CertainTea. Remembering those things made his bossiness easier to tolerate.

For a moment, her muscles unwound. Then Alec walked in.

The restive energy pulsing off his body magnified his presence, making him appear ten feet tall instead of six. Maturity had continued to transform the nerdy teen in skinny jeans into even more of a stunner than when she'd last seen him. Rather disconcerting, actually. She needed another awkward thing between them like she needed a bad hair day.

"Hunter." Alec shook his hand, then clumsily hugged Colby hello. Little more than two years ago that would've been natural—smoothly done and barely noticed. Today, her body flushed with discomfort. "Thank you both for this opportunity."

To the casual bystander, Alec's clasped hands and slight smile might've looked sincere instead of tightly wound. Of course, life with Mark had skewed Colby's senses. Years of living defensively—scanning for the warning signs of mania, as if seeing it coming might somehow prevent its pandemonium—had made her a slightly paranoid observer.

She could hardly trust her judgment about anyone anymore, even an old friend like Alec. Perhaps Hunter was right and Alec didn't harbor hard feelings.

"Don't mention it. We're lucky to have you," Hunter assured his buddy. "Listen, I've got another meeting, so I'll leave Colby here to show you the kitchen. You two probably have a lot to discuss before we open."

"Four weeks, correct?" Alec's intense gaze startled her.

"Yes," Colby replied.

"No time to waste." He appeared to have stifled a skeptical sigh. Or maybe that was her paranoia again.

"Agreed." Hunter shook Alec's hand, then kissed Colby's head. "See you later."

She and Alec stood in the entry, watching Hunter leave as if he were a life raft wrenched from their hands.

Her brother's absence let the elephant otherwise known as Joe stampede into the room. He'd always be there between them, as would Mark. But given today's anniversary in particular, Joe loomed large. Should she say something? No. Better to say nothing than risk saying the wrong thing.

"Guess you're eager to see the kitchen?" Colby smiled, determined to tiptoe across the eggshells.

"Sure. Let's start there." As he followed her through the dining room, he asked, "Who planned it?"

"The architect." She halted, curious as to why this would matter.

He stopped short of walking into her. "Not the chef?"

"No. But the architect had designed other restaurants, so he knew what he was doing." She flashed a reassuring smile, although the quirk of tension in his face told her he doubted it. *Great.* Reclaiming her peace of mind when forced to work with—and rely on—another demanding personality would be challenging.

"We'll soon find out." Alec shoved his hands in his pants pockets. For an instant he resembled the old friend who'd done that quite frequently. The one she'd liked and trusted so well.

"Hopefully it meets your needs." Pushing open the door to reveal a gleaming, stainless-steel kitchen, Colby risked a glance at Alec, in time to note the first sign of his approval. To her eyes, the place looked as sterile and unwelcoming as an operating room. But Alec's expression matched that of a father who'd just caught his first glimpse of his newborn.

She watched him disappear into another world, one in which she ceased to exist. Lovingly, he ran his hand along a prep counter. He knelt down to inspect the various bowls, bins, and other utensils before standing and handling a sauté pan. Utterly rapt.

Having never quite found her life's true passion, Colby envied his. To her, A CertainTea offered a new beginning, but it didn't stir her soul.

Alec milled around the kitchen, occasionally stopping to turn one way or another, as if envisioning people working there, checking on the functionality of the space. With each step, his posture relaxed. The lines between his brows faded, and he let out a satisfied sigh, like that of a man who'd come home after a long journey.

His transformation unlocked a piece of her guarded heart. She almost said something, but then he wandered into the walk-in refrigerator and the moment was lost.

Maybe her qualms about working with a living, breathing reminder of the past had overshadowed the merits of her brother's decision. Reconnecting with Alec might not only be the best thing for the restaurant, it might also help restore a friendship. Given the way she'd retreated from the world in recent years, she could use a friend.

Alec stepped out of the refrigerator, smiling. Not the old smile she remembered—that slightly shy but sincere one. This smile, more of a grin, really, at least was genuine. The first genuinely happy expression she'd seen him wear in two years.

Of course, that thought reminded her of the date. Of the death. Of that damn elephant she didn't know how to tame.

"It's a five-star kitchen, Colby."

Validation from an award-winning chef. Not bad for a first try. She grinned. "Thank you. Have we missed anything?"

"Nothing material. I might've planned a slightly different layout for the lines, but this should work fine. I'll do an inventory with the kitchen staff on my own. No need to waste your time with that." His hands found their way back into his pockets, which made her grin expand. "What?"

"Nothing." God, it felt good to relax a little. To feel, even temporarily, like they were the friends they'd been before the tragedies. So what if he was pretending for the sake of keeping this job? The old "fake it till you make it" concept worked for her.

"Oh, it's something." He shrugged. "Sure you won't share? You used to tell me lots of things."

"That I did." Of course, that was *before*.

After high school, Alec had taken off for the Culinary Institute of America in New York, and from there, to Europe. By the time he'd returned to Oregon, she'd married Mark and embarked on a new legal career. She'd learned to keep secrets by that point.

Mark had demanded his diagnosis remain private so that people didn't whisper and wonder. Only Colby's mother had had any inkling of the truth. Amid Colby's swirling thoughts, she led Alec back to the dining hall. The next thing she knew, she'd tripped and landed splayed across the floor.

"Are you hurt?" Alec knelt beside her, one hand hovering above her shoulder, concern in his eyes.

Pushing up to a sitting position, she tucked her hair behind her ear and glanced at him from beneath her lashes. "Only my pride."

He didn't move except for the quirk of his lips.

"Laughing at me?" Colby asked, heat flooding her cheeks.

"No." He lost the battle against smiling. "But it's nice to be the graceful one for a change."

He'd always been a bit self-deprecating, and she *had* always been the more athletic one.

Suddenly the chaotic emotions of her morning converged, forcing an exhausted snicker. Quiet at first, until she broke into a full-blown fit of giggles. The more she tried stifling them, the worse they got. Partway through her outburst, Alec chuckled, too, and a hint of warmth crept into his eyes—his lovely, kind eyes.

Once her laughter died down, Alec motioned for her hand. "Up you go."

When she placed her hand in his, he grasped it firmly and tugged her upright. They held hands in silence as if unwilling to let go of the brief moment of levity, which rose above the clouds like a kite.

When she eased free from his grip, Alec widened his stance and crossed his arms, resuming their business discussion. "Did the former chef hire the staff?"

This she remembered about him—efficient, driven, guided by logic. He hadn't often been one to goof off. Not like her and Joe. Of course, the last time she'd goofed off was probably three or four years ago—a pathetic admission.

"For the most part. When would you like to start working with them?" Colby fidgeted under his scrutiny. That chestnut cowlick flopped over his forehead in a way that made her want to reach up to touch it. That inappropriate urge skittered through her body until it hit her stomach and fluttered.

"Immediately. We've a lot to accomplish." Alec glanced around the dining hall again, his eyes focused. She could tell he was picturing the place in action. "Did you plan a soft opening the week before we open to the public? Invite your family? Some friends and colleagues?"

"Yes." She and the former chef had planned one. "It seemed like a good idea."

He grinned at her as if she were a child just learning to read. "Trust me, it's necessary. I assume you've hired a qualified waitstaff?"

"Of course."

Alec's perfectionism could be an excellent, if sometimes annoying, trait. Yet the emphasis he'd placed on the word "qualified" sent up a red flag. He doubted her. Would he try to exploit her inexperience?

Hunter's focus on the bottom line ensured that he'd pressure Colby to compromise with Alec, whose culinary background influenced his tastes. Tastes that, unlike hers, could run toward the pretentious. She'd have to be vigilant to protect her vision and authority. "Mondays and Tuesdays are normally days off, but I'll have everyone come first thing tomorrow morning to meet you."

"We should discuss the menu first. Can we do that now?"

"Actually, I promised my mother I'd swing by at ten to discuss 'something urgent.'" An inward sigh filled her chest at the dubiousness of her mother's request.

"Afterward?" he asked.

"Sure. I'll text when I'm ready."

He pulled his phone from his pants pocket and grimaced. "Low batts."

"This early in the morning?" She shook her head, amazed. "Gaming addiction?"

"No." He returned the phone to his pocket. "I usually forget to charge it. Honestly, half the time I forget to take it with me. Not many people are tracking me down, anyway."

In fairness, she didn't get many texts, either. People tend to stop reaching out when you continually withdraw from them, which she did during her marriage in order to hide Mark's illness. Since his death, just getting through the workday had drained her energy, so socializing had been infrequent.

"I can wait. If you don't mind, I'd like to stay here and familiarize myself further with the facility and grounds." He glanced toward the lake.

"Of course I don't mind, Alec." It was the first time she'd said his name, which rolled softly off her tongue. He turned sharply toward her and stared, making her light-headed. When their gazes finally broke apart, she dropped hers to the floor, hoping staring at her feet might reset her balance. *What just happened?* Clearing her throat, she said, "I'll be back in forty-five minutes."

He nodded, watching her with an expression she'd almost describe as penitent. "I'll be waiting."

The moment called for something—a handshake, a quick hug—yet she faltered, doing neither.

As she turned to go, he touched her arm. "Colby, I promise to do everything I can to make this place thrive."

She looked at his hand, which lingered on her forearm, and felt her doubts subsiding. This was Alec, after all. Joe's death had opened a distance between them, but deep down he might still be the quiet guy who'd used her as a guinea pig in his earliest days of experimenting in the kitchen. The one who'd endured her and Joe's childhood antics without much complaint, unlike her own brother.

The look in his eyes persuaded her that they could bridge the gap between the past and present with a little effort. "I'm sure you will."

Alec waited until Colby strolled out the door before exhaling. *God, that had been difficult!* His feelings for her had always been complicated, even before his mistakes with Joe and Mark.

She'd been an open, enthusiastic kid—a bit of a tomboy, her light-brown ponytail bouncing behind her. Dirt-stained clothes had hung from her thin frame as she dangled from trees. She and Joe had followed Hunter and him everywhere, begging to join them in the tree house, or wherever else they'd bike off to.

His favorite trait, though, had been her big heart. He recalled when she'd been about ten and had cried after overhearing their mothers discussing Mrs. Cannon's breast cancer. Megan Cannon had only been thirty-six and had two young sons at the time. After drying her tears,

Colby had asked for Alec's help to create a unique pink lemonade she could sell on the street to raise money for the Cannons. The negligible income she'd earned paled in comparison with the awareness and goodwill she'd inspired. Other neighbors then sent the family food and cards during Megan's chemotherapy, and everyone rejoiced when she survived. To this day, pink lemonade reminded him of her.

Then puberty hit. Granted, it hit most girls earlier than Colby, which had caused her endless angst. Having viewed him like another brother, she'd griped to him about her boyish figure, mostly when she'd sat in his mom's kitchen watching him cook.

Of course, he'd never viewed her as a sister. Barely three years older than she was, he'd battled his growing attraction. Her ready smile and straight white teeth, the intelligence in her cat-shaped hazel eyes, and even the long, lithe line of the body she'd wished were more curvaceous had appealed to him. Not that she knew it.

He'd buried his affection behind the bright line of friendship. Well, except for that one rainy afternoon. That surprising stolen moment when, seeking escape from his father, he'd gone to the tree house to read and found her there crying.

"What's wrong?" Alec set his book on a milk crate before collapsing beside her onto the musty, quilt-covered mattress on the floor.

An intense surge of delight gripped him thanks to the rare opportunity to spend time alone with her. Raindrops tapped against the roof, awakening the earthy scent of the Oregon forest around them. They sat, shrouded amid the mismatched garage-sale tapestries he and Hunter had hung on the walls. It would almost be romantic if not for her tears.

"Danny broke up with me to date Janey Thomas and her double Ds." Another tear trickled from her eye.

"Danny Wilcox is an idiot who won't even know what to do with Janey's double Ds." Alec bumped shoulders with her, hoping to make her laugh. No such luck. "You're too good for him, Colby."

She shook her head. "If that were true, he wouldn't have dumped me, and other guys would be interested, too."

Alec wished he could confess his interest, but he wasn't her type. She'd always liked the jocks with attitude. Pretty much his opposite. The last thing he needed in his life was more rejection. Maybe one day, when she grew up, she'd appreciate a guy like him. But not now. And besides, Hunter would probably freak out.

"You're barely fifteen. Trust me, there will be other boyfriends." He refrained from slinging his arm around her in comfort because she might hear his pounding heart.

"Or not! Besides, all my friends have boyfriends now. They've already gone past second base. Who's going to want me when there's nothing underneath my shirt to excite anyone?" She tugged at the front of her shirt to emphasize her point, and grimaced. "I've barely had my first kiss, and Danny said I did that wrong, too." Her eyes filled with more tears.

"Proving my point about him being an idiot." Although not usually violent, Alec imagined the satisfaction of punching Danny Wilcox in the face.

"Maybe he's right. I mean, I don't really know anything about kissing." Colby wiped her tears. She turned then, and he recognized the light in her eyes that often preceded one of her crazier ideas. "Alec, could you . . . would you teach me?"

He went rigid. Did she ask him to kiss her? Suddenly the sound of his racing heart filled his ears, blocking out the rain overhead. "What?"

Smooth he was not.

"Teach me how to kiss." She blushed. "Sorry. If you don't want to, maybe I could ask Joe."

"No!" Alec wouldn't let Joe—who already had more than his fair share of everything—steal this opportunity, too. This might be wrong, but he couldn't resist the chance to kiss her, especially knowing he didn't risk rejection. "If you really want me to, I'll do it."

Had he feigned nonchalance well enough, or could she tell that his entire body might explode at any second? Please, God, let the tremors be only on the inside.

"Okay." A hopeful grin replaced her frown, and, in typical Colby fashion, she became rather curious and businesslike. "So what do I do first?"

"Stop talking," he chuckled.

She closed her mouth and leaned forward. Holy shit, he was going to kiss Colby Cabot. It would probably be the one and only time, so he had to make it perfect.

His gaze dipped to her mouth. He reached out to touch her cheek, dragging his thumb across her lower lip. Her breathing hitched. His fell shallow. Fighting the sense of urgency building inside, he forced himself to be tender. Not to overwhelm or scare her. He glanced into her eyes before closing his and brushing his lips against hers.

Featherlight, once, twice. Colby butted against him, clumsy and awkward, so he cupped her face and ran his tongue along the seam of her mouth until she opened it and let him in.

Fire fanned through him then as his excitement ratcheted up ten notches. Weaving his fingers through her long, silky hair, every part of his brain begged for more, more, more. His tongue plundered her pouty mouth over and over while the rest of his body exploded like a tree struck by lightning. Fortunately, Colby caught on quickly and responded.

As if in a dream, he laid her down on the mattress. He heard and felt their breaths mingling. A satisfied rumble ripped through his chest when her hands found their way into his hair. His heart, one used to disappointment, soared and stretched and jumped around in his chest with a strange, aching joy.

"Colby," he uttered without thought. But his voice seemed to yank them back to reality. Her body tensed beneath him.

Beneath him!

He opened his eyes and eased away from her. They stared at each other, half-dazed, chests heaving.

"Thanks," she finally muttered, cheeks flaming, as she straightened her clothes. "I'm sorry if I made you uncomfortable, or if, well, just thanks. I mean, I think I get it now. So, thanks."

Fortunately, her embarrassed stammering gave him time to hide his raging erection. Good God, had she felt it?

He tried to play it cool, but cool had never been his shtick. "Don't mention it." And then, because he didn't know what else to say, he asked, "Feeling better?"

Although she appeared somewhat disoriented, she managed to speak. "Yes. But let's not tell Hunter or Joe about this. That could get . . . awkward."

"Agreed." Alec would never tell a soul. He wouldn't let anyone's opinion ruin the most perfect few minutes of high school.

"I'd better go home." She froze, as if still undecided, then stood and headed to the door. "See ya later."

After giving a little wave, she disappeared down the ladder.

The recollection reminded Alec of how she'd once trusted him. It also reminded him of how she'd never seen him as a man, and probably still thought of him as a brother. Despite it all, those two or three illicit minutes were burned into his brain for all eternity.

Did it ever pass through her mind? Wishful thinking. He laughed at himself, because she'd married someone completely unlike him. An uninhibited, athletic guy like his brother, Joe.

Joe.

His phone rang, thankfully steering him away from the abyss of guilty, dark thoughts. Down to 2 percent battery. He answered, "Hi, Mom."

"I hope I'm not interrupting."

"No." He rubbed one hand over the back of his neck. "Colby and Hunter have gone. I'm alone now, checking out the space."

"I've heard it's quite lovely."

"It is. The Cabots spared no expense in the front or back of the house. It's got the potential to be a real destination spot." It started rising—that yearning to be among the best. To create a one-of-a-kind menu and environment that drew people from afar. He'd done it before. He would do it again. He had to.

"I'm cautiously optimistic, then, that this might work out." His mom's voice carried a hopeful note. "It's been lovely to have you home again."

She'd been the only person in his family who'd encouraged his passion. Certainly his father hadn't. "Derogatory" would be a gentle adjective to describe that man's opinions about Alec's career. Words like "girlie," "fruity," and "weird" were often slung around like hash on a diner grill. His dad's attitude had gradually infected Joe, too, who'd emulated their father's machismo and followed him into the police force.

As his once-beloved little brother grew to scorn him, Alec's sorrow had turned to bitterness, resulting in Alec's decision that day. That regrettable day before Joe's fateful hike.

Again, blackness gathered at the edges of Alec's mind, so he forced his thoughts back to his mother. "You can relax, Mom. I'm home to stay."

He was. He'd make this restaurant great. He'd give Colby what she needed, as a weak way of making amends for his inadvertent role in her husband's suicide. And he'd prove to his father that he could be every bit as tough as Joe. That his demanding career was something only someone with strength, discipline, and dedication could achieve.

Maybe then his dad might realize he still had one son he could love.

"Wonderful. So, can you come for dinner tomorrow?" she asked. When Alec hesitated, she added, "Your father's meeting his old partner, Craig, so I could use some company."

"Well, then, I suppose that depends on what you're making." He smiled, lapsing into their comfortable banter.

"Nothing fancy. How about some old-fashioned barbecued chicken and jalapeño corn bread?"

"Wouldn't miss it."

"Six o'clock?"

"See you then." He didn't even need to hit "Off" because the battery died. He placed the phone back in his pocket and turned toward the kitchen.

Only four weeks until this place opened. It would be tough, but he could make it happen, and make it brilliant.

Chapter Two

Colby slammed on the brakes to avoid flattening Stitch in her mom's driveway.

Her mom had always hated being alone, so it had surprised absolutely no one when that tabby cat arrived just as Colby went off to college. Although her mother never stopped complaining about the vet bills, Colby suspected she'd be devastated whenever Stitch died. If he didn't stay out of driveways, that might happen sooner than later.

The aging, gargantuan beast had grown stubborn in his old age, refusing to budge, even for cars. Shifting into park, Colby removed him from the driveway.

"Stitch, you're going to be a pancake if you don't learn to scoot." She deposited him on the porch of the small bungalow where she'd grown up. Quite a different neighborhood from where her half sister, Gentry, had been raised. Colby had never cared much for material things, but her mom liked to bring that disparity up . . . often.

"Mom?" From the so-called entry, Colby could see most of the cozy living room and dining room and a bit of the kitchen thanks to a renovation she'd underwritten several years ago for her mother. Almost everything had been replaced. Only the orange-and-brown patchwork afghan quilt her grandmother had made in the seventies and the "antique" secretary desk in the corner that had been handed down for two generations—its sole value being sentimental—remained as reminders of yesteryear. A quick scan proved the main area to be empty. She strode to her mom's bedroom and knocked on the door. "Mom?"

No answer.

Walking to the rear of the home, she opened the French doors to the tiered deck—also a recent addition, courtesy of her checkbook. "Mom?"

"Over here!" Her mother dug her trowel into the dirt beside her, stood, and brushed off her knees. Unlike Colby, she was petite, with womanly curves that had always attracted men. At sixty, age-appropriate wrinkles collected around her eyes, forehead, and neck, yet she still looked vivacious thanks to her energetic cobalt-blue irises. Her mom reminded her of a rabbit, actually—twitchy and ever alert. Gesturing to a newly established garden, she asked, "What do you think?"

Colby's heels sank into the damp ground as she crossed the yard. "Wow! When did you plant this?"

The plot itself looked to be at least fifteen feet long and ten feet wide. Neatly labeled mounded rows—lettuce, carrots, potatoes, long pole beans, and others—stretched from one side to the other.

"I've been working on this for two days." Pride shone in her eyes as she tucked her graying blonde hair behind her ear and kissed Colby's cheek. "If you stopped in more often, you'd know that, wouldn't you?"

Colby let the lighthearted dig slide without mentioning that she usually stopped by at least twice a week. Maintaining a sense of humor about these things helped keep her sane. And despite the parrying, she and her mom loved each other deeply. "It's very nice."

"Maybe you can use some of these fresh vegetables at your restaurant later this summer. Farm-to-table is all the rage, you know." An elfin smile popped into place. "My garden could be a footnote on your menu!"

"You never know." Colby grinned. Her mom's legendary history of starting projects without finishing them suggested it would lie fallow within the year. Cute, though, that she wanted to be part of Colby's new venture. "So tell me, why'd you call me over today?"

Her mother's hands flicked toward the garden in a gesture that basically said, "Duh."

"Your garden?" Colby repressed the sigh pushing against her lungs. "What's urgent about this?"

"How will I keep critters out if I don't enclose it?" Her hands rested on her hips, brows pulled together in sincere concern. "I need a fence right away, or all my work will be for nothing."

Oh, the melodrama. At thirty-one, Colby should have been used to her mother's special brand of crazy. Sometimes it could be fun—whimsical excursions and projects that could entertain and educate, like the spontaneous day trip south, to Florence, to go on a dune buggy tour. Other times, when things weren't going her mother's way, not so fun.

Colby now knew where this conversation was headed: money.

Since childhood, she'd listened to her mom note the differences between the clothes, cars, and jewels her father bestowed on Jenna versus anything he'd ever given Colby's mom. Although Colby had no influence over any of it, seeing her mother's hurt and envy filled her with guilt whenever her father was generous with her. Whether or not with intention, her mother could always exploit that guilt.

But ever since Joe's and Mark's deaths, Colby's patience with First World problems had grown thin. Her mother, however, was still one person she'd placate, because her mom was someone who'd loved her unconditionally.

"Well?" her mother asked.

"I agree. You need a fence."

"I saw a beautiful home-garden fence in a magazine. It had a two-foot-high stone base and a picket-style gate." Her mother smiled, erroneously sensing victory within her grasp. "Wouldn't that go perfectly with the stone accent on the house?"

"Sounds very pretty, Mom." And pricey, which was really the point. Not that her mom would admit it. And so the dance began. "However, that'd take a lot of time to build, so it wouldn't protect this crop. Why not start with something less permanent and easy to install? Then, *if* you still love gardening at the end of the summer, you could explore the stone-and-picket option for next year."

Her mother frowned. "It hurts my feelings when you undermine my enthusiasm."

"I'm not undermining you. I'll even take you to Home Depot and help you install a serviceable fence some night this week." She raised her hands at her sides. "Truthfully, a stone fence will be costly. You can't bring equipment back here without destroying that hedgerow, so masonry would have to be done by hand."

Her mother waved dismissively. "If Jenna even thought about gardening, your father would have a massive garden and fence constructed in their yard."

"Please, Mom. I can't answer for Dad." Her parents had now been divorced for almost three times as long as they'd been married. Not that *that* made a difference to her mother. She'd been hopelessly in love with and devoted to that man, and devastated when he'd left. Rather than mope, she'd donned an armor of righteous anger to shield her broken heart.

"I see. You're just like him and your brother now. Tired of me." Her mother's eyes glistened. "None of you ever appreciate or understand me. You all can't wait to get away from me."

Colby knew those tears to be genuine. Perhaps her mom's perceptions were distorted, but they were real to her. An important distinction Colby had come to understand after living with Mark's illness. Unlike then, she'd never again underestimate the depth of another person's sorrow.

She slung an arm around her mother's shoulder. "I appreciate you. But you know I'm gearing up to open the restaurant and don't have as much free time to drop in."

"Fine." Her mother huffed, squaring her shoulders. Colby stifled a smile. The woman really should've been an actress. "I ran into Julie Morgan the other day. Imagine my surprise to learn that you'd hired Alec. Once again, I'm the last to know anything."

"Hunter hired Alec, so Julie might've even known before I did, Mom."

"Humph. So now you know how it feels." Her mother gave a sharp nod.

Oh, for the love of God. These circular conversations made her dizzy. "Speaking of Alec, I need to go meet with him about the menu."

"He was always a bit of an odd duck, wasn't he?" Her mother glanced toward the Morgans' house.

Nowadays overgrown shrubs blocked the view of their backyard and obscured the path leading through the woods to the tree house. Many fond memories of Hunter, Joe, Alec, and herself lingered back there.

Perhaps Colby should camp out in the old fort, where life had been simple. Where she'd felt secure and certain that people were exactly what they appeared. When she'd been free to give her heart away without fear. A time and place when everything had been easy and anything seemed possible.

"Odd?" *No.* Alec was shy. Awkward, at times. But interesting and talented.

"Joe was more normal. More fun." Her mother touched her own cheek and shook her head.

Colby didn't like exalting one brother over the other. Joe was an extrovert to Alec's introvert. Joe had been athletic; Alec, intuitive. Both had been her friends.

"What's *normal*, anyway?" Surely no one in Colby's acquaintance fit neatly into that mold. "There's nothing wrong with Alec. The key is that he's always been an amazing cook, and that's all I care about right now."

Not entirely true, but her mother didn't need to know that Alec's return had thrown Colby mildly out of sorts.

"Remember those delicious fruit tarts he used to make? It was fun to be his test audience." Her mother smiled now, apparently thinking back to the days when Alec would deliver shoe boxes of food he'd prepared. Colby and her mother never met a sweet they didn't love, including Cherpumple and deep-fried candy bars. "Maybe he'll make me some, now that he's working for you."

Like clockwork, her mother swung the conversation back to herself and her wishes.

"Actually, you'll get a chance to ask him at the soft opening in about three weeks." Colby's stomach pinched as the words left her lips, because that made everything more real. In the beginning, this enterprise had been as wispy as a wish and a prayer. Suddenly it seemed fraught with obligations and responsibilities.

"I suppose your father and Jenna will be there." Her mother tugged at her shirtsleeve. "And Gentry."

"They *are* part of my family."

"Like I could forget. Jenna and Gentry always make sure I know I'm on the outer circle." She glanced down at her clothes and then up at Colby. "I'll need a new dress."

Colby wouldn't invest in the preposterous fence, but she would buy her mom something pretty to wear. It would be a nice thing to do, to assuage her mother's discomfort about seeing the "other" Cabots. "I'll take you shopping at Pioneer Place on Sunday. Sky's the limit. A whole new ensemble just for the party."

Her mother smiled and patted her cheek. "Thank you."

"You're welcome."

"I think I'll bring a date, too." She twirled a lock of hair in her finger, as if the gesture alone could transform her into an innocent young girl.

"Who?" The question escaped as more of a demand. Had her mother been seeing someone? It had been more than a year since the last "love" affair.

"I met a man last week at the dog park."

"You don't own a dog."

"He didn't know that. I pretended I was checking out the park to see if I wanted to bring my dog."

"Your imaginary dog?"

"I *could* own a dog. Maybe I'll get one." Her mom shrugged with a pout. "It *is* lonely around here."

Ignoring the bait, Colby rejoined, "That's why you have Stitch."

"He's a loner." Her mom flitted her hands in the air. "Like all of you."

Round and round. Colby smacked her hand to her forehead. "Let's get back to this man you met."

"Richard." An extra twinkle lit her mom's eyes. "He's very distinguished and has a poet's heart."

An image of a man with long, slicked-back silver hair, a trimmed goatee, and coal-black eyes sprang to life. Did *he* have a dog, or was he also a poser like her mom? "Really? A poet's heart?"

"Don't judge, Colby. He has a very sweet manner and zest for life." Her mother grasped Colby's hand and fingered her wedding band. "Come to think of it, maybe you should go to the dog park. There are lots of younger men there."

"You want me to pretend to have a dog, too? No, thanks. Besides, I'm not interested in all that." Her throat tightened unexpectedly, almost as if at the idea of romance. Her mom must've heard her voice catch, because she released Colby's ring finger. Her family thought she still wore the platinum band because Mark had been the one true love of her life. She'd once thought he was, too, until he wasn't. In truth, she wore it because, having failed to save Mark from himself, she owed it to him to keep some part of him alive.

In order to avoid another conversation about Mark and moving on, Colby added, "But please do bring Richard to the party. I'm filled with curiosity now. Should we squeeze in a trip to the pound this week? Are you thinking teacup poodle or golden Lab?"

"Now you're just making fun of me."

"Playfully teasing, Mom. There's a difference." She smiled and squeezed her mom's hand. "But honestly, I've really got to go."

Colby turned to go back through the house.

"What about my fence, Colby?" Her mom held her hands out to her sides. "If your father had been more generous, I wouldn't need to ask for your help. Are you sure you can't spare a little of the dividends you get from his business so I can build the stone wall? I thought you'd be proud of my new hobby."

Her father *had* been generous at the time of the divorce, although Cabot Tea Company had still been in its early years. Her mom had opted for a cash settlement and alimony over stock. Bad decision in hindsight, although no one—not even her dad—had predicted CTC would become one of the largest privately owned tea companies in the country.

"I'm always proud of how you try new things, but I need to conserve my extra income now so one day I can buy Dad out of the restaurant. Otherwise I'll be answering to Hunter forever." When her mother frowned, she added, "We'll go to Home Depot together. But at the moment, you might be wiser to fence in Stitch rather than those vegetables."

"Where is that wanderer, anyway?"

"I put him on the porch after I almost ran him over."

"Would you please take him inside? I need to finish up out here, even if the rabbits are going to eat everything before we get a fence installed." She fluffed the back of her hair again, like some old-fashioned TV housewife.

Miraculously, Colby didn't roll her eyes or mention the fact that perhaps her mom should've constructed the fence prior to planting. "I'll grab him, then I'm leaving."

Colby trotted through the house, but Stitch was no longer lazing on the porch. "Stitch?"

She meandered around the driveway, calling out his name before spotting him in the Morgans' front yard. As a kid, she'd probably spent as much time in the Morgan home as she had her own. Ever since Joe died, she hadn't crossed the invisible line that now existed between the two.

It seemed difficult to reconcile Mr. Morgan with the man who had once been so helpful to her mom after her dad left them—helping put up Christmas trees and string lights on the house, mowing the lawn until Hunter was old enough to take over. He'd always liked Colby when she'd been Joe's buddy. Now he couldn't stand the sight of her.

As if crossing hot coals, she dashed across their driveway to grab Stitch, who sat there staring at her with a bored expression on his furry face. She hoisted him up and tickled him under his chin. "I'd love to know what you're thinking, old boy."

That question reminded her of when she and Mark had been cat sitting while Mark had been manic. He'd spent two full days "talking" to Stitch, then relaying the cat's thoughts to Colby. He also hadn't been able to stop petting the poor animal, having been fascinated by the soft texture of his fur. She'd worried the cat would be bald by the time her mom returned.

Sighing, she forced the memory aside and started to cross back over the driveway, but Mr. Morgan pulled in. She froze, having only spoken to him twice since Joe died. Neither time had been particularly pleasant.

He rolled down the window, expression grim. No wonder he could effectively terrify criminals. "Tell your mom I won't be responsible for that furball's fate if she doesn't keep him out of my yard."

The window rolled back up before she could say a single word, and then Mr. Morgan pulled into his garage. Stung by the abrupt "greeting," Colby took Stitch home and then got in her car, thankful she hadn't peed her pants from fright. Clearly Alec's return hadn't diminished his dad's grief.

◆ ◆ ◆

Alec leaned against the gazebo railing and stared across the lake at the distant tip of Mount Hood. Lake Sandy, like most of the greater Portland area, was lushly populated with enormous lodgepole pines and other trees, swaddling the town in various shades of green.

The eco-friendly neighborhood, its retail outlets adorned with stuffed flower containers, surrounded the gorgeous lake. A paddle-boarder took advantage of the break in the weather, idly crossing the lake's dark, glassy surface. Hypnotic ripples fanned out in his wake. Peacefulness: a status Alec rarely sustained. Maybe someday.

For now, he'd simply enjoy the view.

Mougins, France, an ancient town fifteen miles from Cannes and populated with pine, olive, and cypress trees, had been a picturesque place to live for several years—at least, for those rare free hours he escaped the kitchen—but it had never awakened his senses like home.

Home. The word—the concept—didn't quite fit. Not yet. Too many ghosts whispering in his ear: his brother, his father, his conscience.

"Alec." Colby's voice called from behind.

He glanced at his watch. Forty-five minutes on the nose. He smiled before turning around to watch her stroll down the lawn. She wore a pencil skirt that skimmed her knees. Its silk-blend fabric—painted with navy-blue and gray watercolors—contained a splash of red to match her short-sleeve button-down shirt. Classic, like her. A sun ray broke through the clouds, glinting off the gold and red streaks in her light-brown hair, and she joined him in the shade of the gazebo.

"This is gorgeous." He gestured toward the lake, although she was just as pretty. His finely trained nose detected a new citrus scent in the air. Maybe her shampoo or perfume? He kept himself from being too obvious about catching another whiff.

"Hard to beat, right?" She stood beside him and glanced toward Mount Hood, unaware of the way every muscle in his body tightened from being so close. "The weather around here makes planning outdoor events iffy, but I hope some people will take advantage of the grounds."

Working with the Cabots had been a gamble. His mother tolerated the idea. His father hated it. But Hunter had been a true friend to Alec, in good times and bad. Colby had been . . . Colby. There, but not there. Friendly, but beyond his reach.

Now she would be within reach. Every day, right there in front of him. It would be a fantasy come true if not for Mark's note. That damn note he'd never shared with anyone.

"Getting the inside scoop on this property might be one of the best things to come from my old job," she rambled on, blessedly oblivious to the conflict in his head and heart.

"I thought you enjoyed that work." He leaned forward, redirecting his thoughts.

"I did at first. But lawyering is basically solving other people's problems. No one comes to us when they're happy. It can be draining." She shrugged with a soft smile. "I needed a change. Here I'll be working with people who are planning a wedding or celebrating another milestone. People who are already happy."

Not for the first time, he noted a difference in her. Her former spunky attitude had been subdued. Did it lie dormant, or was it as dead as Joe and Mark?

"Just beware. Customers can be draining, too. Particular, demanding." He leaned closer and murmured, "They don't call some Bridezillas for nothing."

She chuckled. "I'll keep that in mind."

Her laughter seemed to brighten the sky. Of course, she usually had that effect on him.

"How's Leslie?" Alec still remembered when Mrs. Cabot had insisted he call her by her first name. She'd always been a funny woman, so different from his more traditional mother.

"The same." Colby grimaced. "Always looking for something new to fill the void. A cat, a garden, a dog, a poet . . ."

"A poet?" Alec could only imagine what that meant.

"Don't ask." She shook her head and grinned. "But I almost feel sorry for a stranger named Richard."

Alec faced her. "Hunter used to call your mom the 'black hole of neediness.'"

"One he had no interest in trying to fill." She smirked.

"Unlike you." He'd spent years watching Colby leap through hoops and over fences trying to keep her mother happy. To keep everyone happy, actually, including him. She'd sat with him, chatting away in the kitchen. He knew those visits had mostly been about sampling his food, but he suspected she'd also thought he'd needed company. Colby had never liked seeing anyone be lonely.

She glanced up, chagrined. "We both know Hunter was always smarter than me."

"Not really. Just more focused, and less compassionate." For a second he allowed himself to pretend that the warmth he saw in her eyes was more than a melancholy memory of faded friendship. "I always thought your mom was fun."

"To think I thought you were smart, too." She playfully punched his arm, like the old days.

He laughed. The foreign feeling caught in his chest, and for the first time in forever, a thread of real hope weaved through him. "You know, you're a lot like your mom, or you used to be, anyway."

"In what way?" She sounded horrified.

"Are you really going to pretend you were never outlandish?" When she raised her brows in question, he continued. "Remember when you wanted to be a hair stylist and asked me to let you cut my hair after you'd destroyed all your old doll heads?"

"And you let me." She grinned, one brow raised. "You were brave."

Or stupidly infatuated, which maybe was the same thing. Having her fingers running over his scalp had been worth every penny he'd spent later to fix the bad haircut.

"Or before that, when you were desperate to see the Seattle Space Needle, but your mom refused to drive you, so you decided you could bike there . . . at night."

"Well, I did have that new ten-speed," she teased. "Meanwhile, you crushed my dream. After you told on me, my mom locked up my bike for weeks."

"I had to tell. If you and Joe had sneaked off like you'd threatened, it would've been a disaster."

The mere mention of Joe—whose life had ended in disaster, anyway—soaked up every hint of humor like a dry sponge.

"I just ran into your dad . . . sort of." Colby gripped the railing.

"Sort of?"

"Stitch was camped out in your yard. Your dad pulled into the driveway before I made my getaway. He paused long enough to warn me to keep Stitch off the property." She twisted her wedding band. "He still blames me for bringing Mark into Joe's life."

Alec knew that to be true and wouldn't lie—at least not about that much.

"Do you?" Her stiff demeanor informed him that she expected a yes. He'd suspected she believed that and had been dreading working with him, which made sense given that she had no idea why he'd retreated from her these past years.

"No." He didn't blame Colby. If anything, she suffered as much as anyone. She'd loved Joe, and she'd loved and lost her husband, too. The irony of it all was how much Alec blamed himself for the entire mess.

"Thank you."

"Saying goodbye to Joe wasn't easy for any of us. My dad can't seem to get over missing all the day-to-day things they'll never do. It's almost like he resents the future." Alec rested his hip against the railing. "Maybe you do, too, having lost Mark before you had kids."

Colby looked away, but not before he saw pain cross her eyes. He should've kept quiet. Now all he wanted to do was hold her, although that desire persisted regardless of a reason.

Mark. Like always, the name summoned the memory of the man's bold signature. Alec's stomach churned. He didn't remember every word of the three-page handwritten letter, which had skipped from thought to thought. All he did recall was the part he should've told someone.

"I can't eat. I can't keep living this way, Alec. You and your family have to forgive me, please."

Only words, he'd told himself back then, when he'd been too caught up in his own remorse to care about forgiving anyone else. Mark had always been prone to exaggeration. Moody. Sometimes entertaining, with his big ideas and energy, other times sullen and lethargic.

Alec had never for one second actually believed the guy was suicidal, so he'd tossed the note and ignored him. Said nothing. Warned no one. A week later, Mark dived off their balcony right in front of Colby.

The familiar pang of guilt wedged itself inside his chest now as he imagined her horror at that moment. Did it haunt her? Did she have nightmares?

She must. *He* did.

Maybe working together was too big of a gamble, after all.

"And what about you?" she asked. "Are your parents more clingy now?"

He snickered, God help him. "I think we both know my dad would rather it'd been me who took that dare."

Accustomed to his father's disdain, it barely even hurt to admit that aloud. Barely. He wished that he didn't care at all. That he didn't need to reunite his family. That the nonsensical, childlike part of him wouldn't still like his dad's approval. Approval he'd never win if his dad knew about his fight with Joe.

"I'm sorry you feel that way." Colby sighed. "I'm sorry for so much . . ."

She glanced at Mount Hood, seemingly lost in her own thoughts. Her preoccupation gave *his* bleak thoughts another chance to rise. For two years he'd stewed in his own guilt until his skin hurt as if torn open like a tomato dropped into boiling water.

Perhaps if he'd come clean back then—about Mark's plea, about his fight with Joe—he wouldn't have lost his way, his reputation, his restaurant. Colby might not have lost a husband and the future she'd been planning. She'd still be warm and carefree. His parents would still have both of their kids.

With no way to go back and fix those mistakes, he could only atone for them now. If he confessed, she might fire him, and then he'd never be able to help her reclaim the life she was meant to have.

Colby wanted a fresh start and second chance at happiness. She might still grieve the death of her husband, but Alec would make her dream for A CertainTea a reality.

Ironically, doing so might make her see him as something more than the shy geek who liked to play in the kitchen. Years of slaving under the supervision of egocentric perfectionists had taught him about command. He'd honed those skills in a relentless pursuit of perfection to prove to his dad and Joe that he wasn't a joke.

And then everything fell apart. Now he'd have to work twice as hard to reclaim his reputation and make his father see him as a "man's man" like Joe.

Colby might see him that way, too. He smiled then, even as he knew his were futile dreams. "Let's go inside and talk."

Once they were seated at a table, he led the conversation. "I'm planning to rotate the menu on a weekly basis, selecting seasonally appropriate options. Hunter said it'll be a dinner-only restaurant, open Wednesday through Sunday, excepting special bookings for weddings or other parties."

"That's the plan. Well, that and the Saturday-afternoon tea service."

Tea service?

"I'll come back to *that* in a second. First, you might consider making Sunday a brunch and closing early. Brunches can often draw a bigger crowd than dinner on Sundays. With Monday and Tuesday off, the early dismissal also extends the staff's 'weekend.' Given that during normal days, they'll be clocking twelve or more hours on their feet, that can be a much-appreciated break."

"I hadn't thought of brunch. I suppose that's worth considering." She retrieved a rough copy of a menu from her bag. "Here's the menu the former chef and I agreed upon, which I've sent off to the printer. Standard fare with weekly specials."

"That's uninspired and boring." The abrupt response landed between them like a hammer, making Colby flinch. Then pride flickered to life in her hazel eyes.

"Or *comforting.*" She leaned forward, elbows on the table. "Favorite dishes keep people coming back."

He shifted in his chair, stunned she'd condescend to *him* about the industry he'd lived and breathed his entire adult life. "What keeps them coming back is curiosity about what might come next. Consistent quality. Unique twists on old favorites. The freshest ingredients. Beautiful presentation."

She shook her head. "I don't want this to be a place only foodies can enjoy. People like me, which are *most* people, enjoy basic, recognizable options. A fussy menu will limit our reach."

Alec sensed his steely expression but couldn't relax. Not with something this critical at stake. After scanning the menu, he tossed it on the table. "Do you actually expect me to churn out the same meals night after night?"

"What's wrong with that?"

The fact she'd even asked sent him shooting out of his chair. *Merde!* Hunter told him he'd have control over the menu, not be relegated to run-of-the-mill *cook*.

"Everything." He began pacing. He needed this job, but he couldn't imagine being content preparing things as commonplace as chicken marsala year after year. "Ninety percent of restaurants fail in the first year. If you don't want to be a statistic, then listen to me. I'll make A CertainTea a destination—someplace that draws people from farther away than the neighboring suburbs. But to do that, we need to think bigger. To create a menu worth traveling to experience. You need to trust me, Colby." *Oh, the irony.*

"Maxine and I went through a lengthy analysis to come up with this menu." She tipped up her chin. "I've already paid to have leather-bound, embossed menus created."

"I don't know Maxine, but this overly extensive menu is going to cost you a lot in wasted inventory, not to mention making it harder for the cooks to be efficient in the kitchen. And don't get me started on the distraction of a gimmicky Saturday-afternoon tea service right before the busiest night of the week."

Colby folded the menu and stuffed it in her purse. She looked paler, despite the grim line of her mouth. "If this is going to work, you need to respect me. This is *my* place. *My* dream, not yours."

"Except that Hunter hired me, and, unlike you, I know this business. I've succeeded at the highest levels." He crossed his arms.

"Until you didn't."

It smarted. He wouldn't lie. He hated reminders of his failure almost as much as he hated seeing her so hard-nosed. To her credit, she looked as if she wished she could take that last remark back.

"If all you want is to mimic every country-club menu in the Portland area, why hire *me*?"

"*I* didn't."

He went still then. Torn between hating and admiring her honesty. Between feeling responsible for restoring her happiness and needing to reclaim his own. "I don't think I can settle, Colby."

"Settle?" Although her expression remained firm, he noted the pulse point of her neck throbbing.

He'd upset her. He should feel bad about it, but he couldn't let her win this argument. "I can't be the executive chef and not be free to control the menu. To create and experiment. That's the quintessential purpose of my job."

Colby finally stood. He thought he noticed her lip tremble, but then she decreed, quietly but firmly, "Then perhaps you should reconsider this position. I understand your feelings, but I can't work with you if you're going to belittle my opinions. Let me know by tomorrow afternoon. If you choose to stay, I'll assemble the team on Wednesday morning."

Before he could respond, she grabbed her purse off the back of her chair and marched out the door.

Chapter Three

Like some new kind of PTSD response from her turbulent marriage, Colby's bones had turned ice-cold when Alec snapped at her about the menu. She'd bolted so he wouldn't catch her shaking. Apparently she'd given up the Xanax too soon. Nausea gurgled in her stomach as she pulled into the parking lot at Cabot Tea Company.

Rolling over, giving in, keeping the peace. She'd done that for five years to keep her husband happy, only to have it blow up in her face. Lesson learned. Indulgent compassion and bending to the will of another had nearly destroyed her. Never again—especially not with respect to A CertainTea, the one bright spot at the end of the dark tunnel through which she'd been crawling.

If she didn't establish her role from the outset, she risked being trampled at every turn. Still, the memory of Alec's expression when she'd flung Une Bouchée's ruin in his face—yes, she almost threw up.

Cruelty had never been her go-to position before Mark. His refusal to properly treat his illness had warped their love into something unrecognizable. Risky behaviors with his health and their finances, philandering during his highly sexualized manic phases (followed always by profuse apologies), her own feelings of inadequacy and guilt in the face of the deterioration of the marriage—all of it had shoved her against a wall. Having failed to be a wife Mark valued enough to commit to therapy for, she'd built a fortress around her heart.

That barrier enabled her to be cruel when threatened. A lesson she sometimes regretted having mastered.

As she approached her father's office building, the perfumed air from the abundant rose bushes offered no balm. She breezed through CTC's lobby, flashing her badge to Jerry behind the security desk, and went straight to the elevator. When she reached her father's office, she stopped at his assistant's desk. "Hey, Cindy. Is my dad available?"

"He's in there with Jenna. Let me check."

While Cindy buzzed her father, Colby glanced down the hall toward Hunter's office. To say he'd be unhappy about the ultimatum she'd handed Alec would be a massive understatement.

"You can go in." Cindy smiled, unaware of the perspiration breaking out over Colby's scalp.

"Do me a favor, please. Find Hunter and ask him to join us." Colby drew a deep breath and headed into her father's office.

Even though he was the founder and CEO, his office remained rather Spartan, sort of like the man himself. Nothing ostentatious or unnecessary. A large desk, flanked by two comfortable navy leather chairs. A round conference table with six swivel chairs. A whiteboard and a SMART Board. Functional, if not conventionally handsome. The opposite of Jenna's smaller but beautiful office with its sumptuous Tibetan carpet and handcrafted desk.

Her dad had already stood to greet her with a kiss. He was tall and lean, like her, and his salt-and-pepper hair lent him a hint of sophistication. His eyes slanted upward slightly, also like hers, but with deeper laugh lines. "Hey, sweetheart. What brings you by?"

He gestured toward the table where Jenna, who nodded a greeting, remained seated. Jenna, the hardscrabble businesswoman, who'd started working here soon after college and captured her dad's heart.

At first blush, one might assume her statuesque figure and flaming-red hair had won him over. But Jenna was also driven and savvy. Over the years, she'd worked her way up to a senior executive marketing position, proving herself his equal in many ways.

Jenna was a better wife and employee than her mother, but then again, what did Colby know about being a mother? She'd wanted children but had refused to bring any into the chaotic world of her marriage. If Alec had known of that conscious decision, he wouldn't have been so sympathetic this morning about her childlessness.

Alec. The reason she now sat before the firing squad.

"Restaurant business." Colby laid her purse on the table.

"Trouble so soon?" Jenna asked. The woman had mastered the art of sounding sweet yet poking for weaknesses. Unfortunately, Colby's dad seemed blind to this habit.

"Let's wait for Hunter." Colby offered a tight smile.

"Want some water, or tea?" her father asked.

"No, thanks."

He sat beside her. "You look stressed."

"I guess I am."

He patted her hand. "Remember, business isn't like lawyering. You can't be so conservative. Take risks. Expect to fail now and then. That's how you learn and grow. The key is getting back up and in the fight."

If it hadn't been for the side-eye Jenna surreptitiously shot Colby, she might've actually relaxed a bit. Her father had an easy manner, which belied his business success.

As a child, Colby had resented him for leaving her, thanks to the steady diet of her mom's "That damn business was more important than this family" rants. Colby had blamed Jenna, too, especially when she and Gentry enjoyed the "whole family" life that Colby and Hunter had lost. All that had made it easy to keep her stepmom at arm's length.

But after learning firsthand how difficult marriage could be—how much could happen within a relationship that no one else knew—she'd softened her attitude toward her dad. Her newfound understanding had helped her forge a closer relationship with him, as proven by his offer to help her start over. "Thanks, Dad."

"Thanks for what?" Hunter entered the office without sparing Jenna more than a dismissive glance. Colby barely resisted the reflex of ducking for cover from the palpable animosity between those two.

Hunter took a seat beside her.

"For the pep talk," she answered.

"So tell us the crisis, because we've got other items on our agenda." Jenna set down her notepad.

Impatient as ever. Colby guessed that Jenna's attitude stemmed from the fact that she wished her husband didn't have another family—other children. Or maybe Colby was making more out of the simple gesture than necessary. Reading between the lines had become a reflex—an exhausting one that kept her mired in a state of constant defensiveness.

"Crisis?" Hunter clenched his pen, but he didn't snap at Jenna. Instead, he turned to Colby. "When I left you and Alec, things seemed fine."

"They were, at first. He loved the kitchen and the grounds." She glanced from Hunter to her father. "But then he trashed the menu. The one I've already budgeted for and paid to have printed. He's insistent on substituting his vision for mine, so I gave him an ultimatum. He might quit, which means I'll need to find another chef. Since you hired him, I thought I should tell you in person."

Hunter and her father exchanged a meaningful look, while Jenna doodled dollar signs on her notepad.

"When you came to me for help to get this idea off the ground, I agreed, partly because you've been struggling since Joe's and Mark's deaths. Between the hefty acquisition cost, renovation, insurance, advertising, and personnel expenses, we're in this for close to four million in order to make it everything you wanted." Her dad cast Jenna a quelling look to keep her quiet. "I knew you'd need time to learn this business. That you'd make mistakes. But setting aside the personal issues, dismissing a chef with Alec Morgan's credentials rather than finding a compromise seems both unprofessional and foolish."

Her dad had been generous, yet the majority of those expenditures were now fixed assets on CTC's balance sheet. If CTC sold the land and building, it would recoup 90 percent of what it had spent to date, maybe more. She hadn't blown through $4 million on a whim, and she wouldn't let him lord that over her as if she had.

"Alec says he won't *settle* for being a 'country club' cook. He hates my vision, but it's my restaurant. He's being inflexible." Deep down she admitted she hadn't tried to compromise, either. Instead she'd knee-jerk reacted to feeling bullied. Overreacted, actually.

Hunter shrugged. "Is the printing cost of the original menu really worth sacrificing the potential boon Alec could be? Why not learn from him? Use his experience to avoid rookie mistakes."

Colby noticed Jenna toss an incredulous look at Hunter, probably because she believed she knew more than he did about everything, yet he butted heads with her at every turn.

"You're not listening. I know he's a fabulous chef, and Une Bouchée was amazing. But it's not like the only restaurants that succeed are fancy French ones. My favorite place in town is the Gab-n-Eat diner. And look at Gunther's Pub, or Sesame Palace, or Taverna. They've all been around forever without architecturally challenging meals that no one can pronounce. Haute cuisine might impress those in the know, but normal people like me want decent portions of recognizable foods that taste great. I can't help it if Alec thinks A CertainTea's menu is 'beneath' him."

"It is." Her father crossed his arms. "I called my old friend—Rob Salvetti, up in Seattle—when I was deciding about whether CTC should invest in your idea. He freelances for *Saveur*, *Food & Wine*, and *Bon Appétit*. During our conversation, he mentioned that there's been a big increase in interest in haute cuisine because of all the cooking shows and stuff."

She'd expected Hunter to defend Alex, but not her dad.

"That might be true, but it's beside the point. I can find another qualified chef who's happy to cooperate with me and *my* vision." Colby's leg bounced beneath the table.

"Is that best for the bottom line?" Criticism colored Hunter's question.

"Hunter, Jenna, give us a minute." Her dad waved them out. "I'll catch up with you later."

Without delay, those two parted without a kind word between them.

Her father leaned forward. "What's really going on, because it's got to be more than a simple fight about a menu?"

That damn stinging behind her eyes started up, but she wouldn't cry while discussing business. Why was it that every time she patched up one gush of emotion, it just leaked out through a different crack? "Do you think I'm being stupid?"

"I think you're being rash. So I'm guessing you're taking a stand for reasons that go beyond your vision. Because, honestly, I can't imagine why Alec's loftier ambitions don't excite you."

Her gaze fell to her hands, which were clasped tightly in her lap. "I don't know if I can work with him."

"Because of Joe?" Her father touched her arm.

She nodded, then confessed something she didn't like admitting, not even to herself. "And Mark. I'd finally gone ten straight weeks without a nightmare. But anticipating seeing Alec today had me on edge all night. Now I'll be working with him—a constant reminder of both Joe and Mark. What if the nightmares start again?"

Her dad set his chin on his fist. "Did he say anything to upset you?"

"No." She privately acknowledged he'd been quite forgiving. That there had been moments when she'd even thought it could work. When she'd imagined it would help them both. But she'd been wrong about so many things before that she didn't know which feelings to trust. It seemed safer to push Alec away. "This restaurant is supposed to be my fresh start. Seeing Alec brings the past all back. And on top of that, he wants me to roll over and let him make all the decisions."

She'd let Mark make most decisions, and that had been disastrous for them both.

"Not all the decisions. Just the menu, which seems like something he's extremely qualified to do." Her father had one of those rich voices, like a late-night DJ. Deep and silky. Soothing. Amazingly effective at calming and persuading her whenever she let her guard down.

"That's not the point."

"It's precisely the point. You've got to put the past behind you, honey. No one but you can do that, though." He glanced at her ring finger. "Don't let ghosts interfere with your objectivity, in business and otherwise."

He sat back, arms crossed. She recognized the signs that the kid gloves were being removed.

"Apparently I can't separate from people and emotions as easily as you." The knife's edge in her voice caused him to frown. She shouldn't have gone there. Not when he'd been trying to help.

Again, her eyes stung as unruly emotions fought for release. Would the legacy of her marriage to Mark *forever* be the feeling that someone was trying to force her head under water?

"You want more autonomy? Pledge your personal shares of CTC against the investment we made. Hunter and I will ease up then, because you'll be shouldering most of the risk. Maybe if you have everything to lose, you won't be so quick to turn away good advice when it's offered."

Her CTC shares were her safety net, and he knew it. She wanted to be angry that he'd called her bluff, but that would be childish and wrong, and she'd already been childish enough for one morning. How many times had she heard him say "Shit or get off the pot" in her life? A million? Two million?

Now he'd boxed her in, just like Mark had always done. If she refused, she revealed her weakness, and he and Hunter would continue to make the decisions.

Outside the office, she could hear people walking and talking, going about the day as if everything in her world weren't tipping on its axis. Her father sat in silence, except for the tapping of his forefinger on the table, while she considered the ramifications of her choices. Although she was mired in self-doubt, a tiny voice deep in her heart whispered, "You can do it."

Colby stood and picked up her purse. "Let's separate the restaurant legally. Have your lawyers draw up a partnership agreement where CTC keeps a ninety-nine percent stake as a limited partner, but I'll be the general partner with a one percent interest. In exchange, I'll surrender the *income* from my shares if the restaurant loses money. You'll have limited liability and rights to distributions until I can afford to buy you out, and I'll be free to make decisions as I see fit without needing to kowtow to Hunter."

Thank God lawyering taught her how to negotiate. Failure at A CertainTea would be a material financial hit, but not bankruptcy. She could live with that. Her mother, on the other hand, might have a breakdown when she learned that her private bank could run dry for several years.

Her father nodded, and she noted a gleam of respect in his eyes. "So what are you going to do about Alec?"

"I'll let you know once I decide."

◆ ◆ ◆

Alec unpacked the basket of fresh produce and edible and other flowers he'd cobbled together from the farmers' market. His body buzzed with creative energy and determination.

Colby had agreed to meet him at his apartment tonight to talk. Of course, he knew talking about food was never as effective as showing and tasting. So he'd dedicate the next several hours until her arrival to preparing a meal—an experience—to convince her that they could find a compromise.

Tonight would be the first time he officially invited to his apartment the woman for whom he'd always felt a tortured kind of affection. His heart knocked around inside his chest thanks to his decision to base the entire meal around flowers.

Unprofessional? Yes. But he'd do it, anyway. The romantic in him couldn't *not* do it for her. And maybe setting an intimate mood would remind her that she was safe with him. Might coax her into dropping her guard and remembering who she really was at heart—a girl who'd patiently stopped and answered all of crabby old Mrs. Miller's questions whenever she'd come out to her mailbox rather than run away like the other kids. *Not* a woman who threw someone's failures in his face, although he'd take that from her because he'd earned it, even if she never knew why.

After snipping the bottoms off the pink and yellow tulips he'd bought, he arranged them in a square vase. She'd always liked tulips. And hydrangeas. And peonies. Pink peonies. Pink like her lips . . .

He shook his head. With only a few hours at hand, he needed to start cooking. Table setting and daydreaming would have to wait.

As an executive chef, he rarely got to cook at work. He'd almost envied his chefs de partie at times. Tonight, however, he'd indulge his love for food and aesthetics without interruption or pressure. Or a never-ending line of dinner orders from the front of the house.

Methodically, he began pulling out cutting boards, bowls, and platters. He smiled, recalling when he'd first been taught the importance of mise en place. Everything, *everything*, would be set out and organized before beginning—cookware, utensils, recipes, ingredients, and prep.

A quick glance at the clock made him work faster. Thankfully, he'd been experimenting with a new sorbet yesterday. Colby and her mother had always had a sweet tooth.

This meal marked the first time he'd ever cooked specifically for her. Sure, she'd sampled his experiments in the past, but those had been recipes he'd made for himself. He supposed this, too, was for him in some ways. To keep his job and persuade her to alter her vision. But still . . .

Gingerly, he unpacked his knife roll. His best friends, sadly. Razor sharp. Perfectly worn handles. The most prized: the Messermeister Meridian Elité chef's knife he'd received as a parting gift when he left France. He set his hands on the counter and drew in a cleansing breath. Some people worshipped at the church altar. He did so in the kitchen.

At work he could never listen to music, but at home he could crank it up. He scrolled through his phone to find Nirvana's "Come as You Are" and hit "Play." A tune that turned back the clock, almost as if he thought he could finally go after what he'd always wanted.

Alec folded the napkins to resemble water lilies and then set them on the table between spotless, gleaming silverware. He lit the tapered candles and placed the flower vase in the center of the table. Little details made a difference, even if Colby didn't yet realize it.

After a moment he remembered she'd never much liked the grunge-music scene, so he opted for Jason Mraz. He swiveled, checking to make sure everything was set. His pulse throbbed in anticipation.

An olivewood platter with charcuterie and cheese, grainy mustard, and Johnny-jump-ups sat waiting on the kitchen bar next to a basket of homemade multigrain crostini. He had chilled prosecco on hand, and—

Knock, knock, knock.

His stomach clenched. Another quick glance made him wish he were living in something nicer than a cheap rental apartment.

Knock, knock.

He opened the door. "Sorry. Come in."

Unlike him, she hadn't changed her outfit for the occasion. Of course not. To her, this was nothing more than a quick business meeting. One in which she likely planned to hold him to her ultimatum.

"Thank you." She kept her gaze locked on his as she stepped inside. "I won't keep you long, I just—" She paused, having peripherally noticed the ambience. Her eyes widened. "What's all this? Do you have a date tonight?"

"No." He fought the flush rising up his neck. "This is for you."

"For me?" She wandered to the table and fingered one of the napkins, brows pinched in the cutest show of confusion. "I thought we were going to talk about our disagreement."

"We are . . . in a manner of speaking." He went to the kitchen, tossed a hibiscus bud in a champagne flute, and filled it with prosecco and a dash of St-Germain elderflower liqueur. "Have a drink and try some cheese."

She hesitated before taking the glass from him. "Ham?"

He tsk-tsked. "Jamón ibérico, from Spain."

Her sardonic stare reminded him that she didn't appreciate the distinction.

"Yes, Colby. Ham. Very special ham."

"So special it needs flowers, apparently." She grinned, fingering the Johnny-jump-ups on the platter.

"Those are edible. Minty. Good with the goat cheese." He made her a crostino with cheese, meat, and the flower. "Try it."

He then spread some mustard on another piece of toast, covered it with "ham," and popped it in his mouth. The combination of salt and spice with the hint of garlic-seasoned olive oil on the toast sprang to life in his mouth.

"This ham is delicious." Colby said.

"I'm glad you approve. We should include a proper charcuterie-and-cheese selection on our menu. And as you can see, it's not fussy, although it makes an impression."

She raised a brow. Without addressing his remark, she glanced around. Her gaze stopped on the half-finished 3-D puzzle of Notre-Dame Cathedral residing on his coffee table. "Three-D now?"

He'd loved jigsaw puzzles—every kind of puzzle, really—for as long as he could remember. He wondered if *she* remembered sending him a personalized jigsaw puzzle she'd had made from a photograph of Une Bouchée as a congratulatory gift when he'd earned the James Beard Award. "Keeps me out of trouble."

"Oh, yes. You were always such a radical," she joked. Following another assessing look around, she asked, "How long have you been living here?"

"Almost two months."

"No photos anywhere? Nothing on the walls." She tilted her head. "Unsure of whether or not you'd be staying?"

He gulped down his prosecco. He was going to need more of it to get through the evening. "Yes."

"Why?"

How to answer that complicated question? "Lots of ghosts."

Probably not the reply to toss offhandedly at a woman whose husband had killed himself. Dammit, she made him nervous, and he'd always been stupid whenever he'd been nervous.

Colby peered into her glass at the flower surrounded by golden bubbles. "What changed your mind?"

Alec leaned against the counter. "My mother, and Hunter. When I took off after losing everything, it broke my mom's heart all over. I came back for her but didn't have the money to start another restaurant. My former colleagues had lost faith in me, so my options were limited. Then Hunter called. I took it as a sign."

He watched her while she carefully constructed another crostino. She closed her eyes when she bit into it, then finished it off with a sip of her drink. After swallowing, she opened her eyes. "So you plan to use A CertainTea to prove everyone wrong. To reclaim what you lost."

Alec didn't want to discuss his motives, especially the more personal ones. None of them undermined his earnest belief that following his lead would be her best shot at making A CertainTea a wildly popular restaurant.

"That doesn't mean our goals conflict." Alec gestured toward the table, sidestepping her question. He couldn't tell her that handing her *her* dream was one of his goals, because that would raise questions he didn't want to answer. "Take a seat and I'll join you in a minute."

While she seated herself, Alec ladled white gazpacho into two bowls. After drizzling them with his secret emerald-green oil and adding sliced almonds, he garnished each bowl with lavender blossoms. He looked toward the dining table, where Colby sat, looking perfectly at home. Oddly, it seemed to him the most natural thing in the world to have her there. To cook for her. To serve her. To just look upon her made him happier than he'd been in years.

He carried the bowls to the table and set one in front of her. "Voilà."

"It's gorgeous, but it's . . . green." She sniffed twice, trying to discern the soup base.

Green. Such a boring, meaningless word. The pale soup—veering toward white—would be better described as pistachio. It glowed, evoking a sense of renewal. Something he suspected they both were seeking, if for different reasons. "White gazpacho."

An approving grin appeared. "And these flowers are edible, too?"

"Lavender. Yes."

He watched her face as she sampled her first spoonful, and waited. Waited for the delighted, surprised look that would light her eyes. When it came, his chest expanded with victory.

"Yum!" She smacked her lips together.

Yum, indeed. He snickered. "Not the praise I'm used to, but it'll do."

"Well, I'm no Michelin Guide critic. Yum is as good as it gets." She laughed then and raised her glass. "The tulips are a nice touch, Alec. I'm sensing a theme here with all the flowers."

"Bonus points for keen observation, Ms. Cabot-Baxter." If Alec weren't acutely aware of everything about Colby, he might've missed the brief moment of tension in her shoulders when he'd mentioned her married name. "Finish up, there's more to come."

"My mom will be so jealous." Colby spooned another mouthful. "Just today she was reminiscing about the fruit tarts you used to bring her."

"I'll bring her a little takeout box when I see my mother tomorrow night."

"She'd love that." Colby's grateful smile melted him, like always.

"Perhaps I can help you fill that so-called black hole of neediness, since your brother won't." He wouldn't ask why Colby didn't prod Hunter for more help. She'd always been the caretaker in that family. He suspected it had been some time since anyone had taken care of her. A role he'd happily adopt through placating her mom.

"A chef and a caretaker?" Her brows rose, and then she chuckled. "Careful not to bite off more than you can chew."

"Is that a lame attempt at a culinary joke?" He sipped his drink.

"Stop talking and let me enjoy this green soup." She put her finger to her lips to shush him.

He envied that finger. "Take your time while I finish making the next course."

Alec worked quickly, infusing the salmon confit with a brown butter hollandaise, garnished with young asparagus and beetroot, along with some daylilies. "I hope you like salmon."

"Who doesn't?" She craned her neck to peek at the plate in his hand.

"Exactly." He set the plate down, and she let out a sigh.

"That's really pretty. I feel like I should be taking pictures and posting them on Instagram."

"Well, they'd certainly be more enticing than a dull-brown photo of chicken marsala." He cleared his throat.

Colby fell silent for a moment or two while eating. "This must've taken you all afternoon."

Alec shrugged. It had been his pleasure, in more ways than one. Of course, sitting across from her tonight had been the best part of all. He could almost pretend it was a date. Almost.

"You've always been so passionate about food I suppose it didn't surprise me today when you snapped about the menu."

He wiped his mouth. "I'm sorry I lost my temper."

"Apology accepted. And *I'm* sorry I insulted you." Colby cut more salmon, her voice soft yet strong. "But Alec, I won't be manipulated and bullied in my own restaurant."

"I understand." Did that mean that, even after all this, she wasn't persuaded to give him control of the menu? Would he be forced to walk away? Because he knew he couldn't make a career of overseeing grilled fillet, baked potatoes "with all the fixins," and steamed vegetables. "Before you make any final decisions, how about *la pièce de résistance*. I haven't forgotten about your sweet tooth."

She smiled. "You're playing me well. Fitting together all the pieces like another kind of puzzle."

He collected their plates without confessing. Despite years of accumulated observation and fascination, she'd likely be the one puzzle he'd never be able to solve. "Excuse me."

When he returned, she clapped her hands. "Ooh, pretty. What is it?"

"Pink-lemonade lavender thyme sorbet, with mint and violet garnish."

Feminine, complex, and beautiful, just like Colby. A tiny nod to that tenderhearted person who wasn't afraid to show compassion to her neighbors, because *he* remembered her even if *she* didn't.

She didn't even wait for him to sit before she tasted it. "Oh! This is delish."

"Yum?" he teased.

She shook her head, savoring another bite of sorbet in her mouth. "Double yum."

"I'm deeply humbled." He spread his hand across his chest and bowed his head.

"I doubt it." She smirked.

She licked her spoon, glazing her lips with sorbet. Despite everything standing between them—past and present—he wanted to kiss her. Sweet, citrusy, sticky kisses. He almost groaned at the thought.

While he fantasized about her mouth, she'd obviously turned her thoughts back to business.

"Alec, in all seriousness, can you compromise? Can you work to make my dream happen without replacing it with your own?" She sat back, hand on her stomach, looking both sated and contemplative.

He paused, thinking about what he could and couldn't do. "That depends."

She raised her brows. "Go on."

"Did you enjoy this meal?"

"You know I did."

He leaned forward, strung tight with the need to be understood. "If you didn't know me, and if this was your one and only experience with food from my kitchen, would you return again to see what else I might create?"

"Yes." She looked at him now, her gaze softening. "Yes, I'd come back."

Perhaps that second glass of prosecco played with his head, but it almost sounded like something more than the simple answer he'd requested. Might she come back here, to eat with *him*?

Candlelight glinted off her wedding band, reminding him of the truth. He pushed his foolish wish aside and pressed her in order to secure her cooperation. "If I'd grilled a decent steak, would you have had as much fun experiencing the meal?"

"No." Two little lines appeared between her brows. Her thinking face. He resisted the urge to press his lips to her forehead and kiss away those lines.

"That's my point, Colby. I'm not trying to usurp your dream. Just let me make A CertainTea an experience your customers will remember. One they'll share with friends and on Facebook or whatever. We can create buzz with the right menu." He waved his hand over the table. "Simple foods served exquisitely."

She stared at him as if trying to judge his sincerity. "Okay, let's try to make this work. Come tomorrow with some ideas to discuss. We can meet at nine, and I'll make sure the other staff arrives by ten o'clock."

"Thank you." Saying less would be the right strategy. He'd just won a major battle.

"Thank *you*." She rested her chin in her hand. "That was the best meal I've had in ages."

"Does it rate a triple yum?" Suddenly Alec felt fifty pounds lighter.

She laughed. "Well, I can't stroke your ego too much. Besides, you don't want to peak too soon, right?"

"No." He'd always preferred the slow build to a fast burn.

"Let me help you clean up, then I'll get out of your hair." She took their bowls into the kitchen. He followed with their glasses, wishing she'd decide to stay longer.

"Hunter says you still live in the city."

"Yes." A pained look flared, making him regret his thoughtless comment. "I moved to a different neighborhood, closer to my old office.

Now it's not so convenient, though. I should probably think about selling it and coming back this way."

He began rinsing dishes and loading the dishwasher. "I suppose it's more fun, though, being in the center of Portland. More to do."

"I'm busy enough getting up to speed on this new career. Securing permits, designing the space, hiring the staff, creating employee manuals, learning the laws about food handling, and, well, just everything." She wiped down some of the empty counters, then rinsed and wrung the dishrag. "No time for anything else, really."

Again, he noted tension in her shoulders and face. Clearly she hadn't yet moved on with her personal life. He hated the image that came to him then, of her sitting in her condo, surrounded by objects but no people. No laughter. Colby used to laugh easily.

"The work hours of this industry make it tough, but don't neglect your personal life."

She playfully slapped his shoulder. "I don't need another mother. One is more than enough."

Ah, yes. She'd always view him like a family member. He raised his hands. "Fair enough."

"I should go." She went to get her purse.

"Hang on." Alec strode to the table and plucked the tulips from the vase. After soaking some paper towels in cold water, he then wrapped them around the base of the stems and secured them with a rubber band. "Take these."

Her mouth opened, just a little. Just enough to tell him that he'd surprised her . . . in a good way. If he didn't know better, he'd swear his feet had left the ground.

"Thanks, Alec. For the flowers, the meal." She smiled at him. "For proving me wrong. That's not something I normally enjoy. I'd better watch out for you."

"Perhaps you ought to."

She laughed, completely unaware of how serious he was. He wanted her, but he couldn't have her. My God, he could've saved her husband's life if he'd only mentioned the damn note to her or anyone in her family. If he would've forgiven Mark.

If she knew the truth, she'd hate him.

"What's wrong? You look sick." When she touched his arm, he flinched.

"Nothing. Sorry. My mind wandered." He opened the door, now desperate for her to leave. "Drive safely."

Chapter Four

"I can't stay too long because Mom's waiting for me." Colby sat on the world's least comfortable, ultramodern barstool at the marble island in her father's massive kitchen. As with most things, Jenna favored the style of the wood-and-nickel stool over other considerations such as comfort. Colby sipped the Earl Grey iced tea her father had handed her and set aside her mental to-do list for the moment.

"How'd things go with Alec last night?" He sat beside her, his long frame dwarfing the stool.

The memory of Alec's intent expression as he sweetly bundled up that bouquet of tulips warmed her chest. That meal *had* been more memorable than chicken marsala—elegant without being fussy. The music, flowers, candles, and presentation had made her feel pampered and relaxed, which was precisely what she wanted A CertainTea to do for its guests.

Of course, her dad only cared about the bottom line.

"We came to an agreement about making changes." Alec had also offered to reimburse her for having to reprint new menus. An offer she'd declined because, honestly, Alec needed a fresh start as much as she did.

"Good." Her dad smiled, his brown eyes lit with a bit of humor. "I'm glad you compromised. Your brother's been concerned about Alec. And I knew you were smart enough not to ignore his feedback."

Although somewhat manipulative in his tactics, Alec had proved his point, and they'd had a productive discussion that morning with the staff about next steps. She assumed his high-handed way of establishing authority with the cooks stemmed from the fact that he hadn't been involved in hiring any of them. If he didn't settle down once they all got to know one another, she'd be playing mediator every day—the opposite of what she wanted. Of course, her dad played mediator every day at work.

"How can you stand being in the middle of Jenna and Hunter all the time?" If she had to work with those two every day, she'd be pulling out her hair. "Isn't it exhausting?"

"Sure." He nodded. "Then again, you know something about that from being in the middle of your mom and me for so long."

"Not every day, though." Even she heard the whoosh of relief in her voice.

Her father laughed. "I'll take dealing with Jenna and Hunter every day to dealing with your mom *any* day."

"Be nice, Dad." Colby understood her parents' inherent incompatibility, but she wouldn't let him pick on her mom. "If it weren't for her early love of green tea's health benefits back in the eighties, you might never have started CTC."

"Sorry." He patted her hand without acknowledging the truth of her remark. "I'll give Leslie this much—you and Hunter turned out great, and I can't take much credit for that."

"Thanks, Dad." Colby couldn't mask the surprised grin prompted by his confession. Truthfully, the quiet admission of his absentee-father status was the closest he'd ever come to an apology. "I'd pass along the compliment, but she'd probably faint from shock."

"Actually, this topic leads to why I asked you here. I need help with Gentry." His smile evaporated as deep grooves lined his forehead. "She needs . . . ah, hell, I don't know what she needs, but some direction would be nice. Honestly, she's more like *your* mom than you are."

At twenty-five, Gentry hadn't yet accomplished much more than provoking her parents. Having been raised by a series of nannies, she'd predictably gone through a healthy dose of teenage rebellion, the inky evidence of which still decorated her left wrist and ankle. After dropping out of college for a while "to travel," she'd tried photography. When that didn't take, their father had coaxed her back to college. Still a few credits shy of graduating, Gentry was no closer to setting any serious goals.

"Maybe Mom and Gentry don't always have their feet on the ground, but in some ways I think they get more out of the journey than we do." When her father shot her a cockeyed stare, she added, "I talked to Gentry a few days ago. She's found work as a live mannequin and has started dating a new guy."

"The hot dog guy, for chrissakes." He drummed his fingers on the counter.

"Hot dog guy?"

"She told us he was an entrepreneur," he snorted. "Turns out he's a hot dog vendor in the city."

Colby smothered a grin at her sister's way of goading her parents. "To be fair, she didn't lie."

Her father rolled his eyes, then he glanced at the floor, frowning. "Nothing in her life has any permanence."

The concern in his voice cut through any humor Colby might've found in the situation. Like her dad, she worried about her sister's untethered way of drifting through life. Enjoying the journey had its merits, but so did security and purpose.

"So what can I do? I won't spy. Besides, Gentry doesn't exactly listen to my advice any more than yours and Jenna's."

"Would you consider hiring her to work at the restaurant?" He raised his hands in surrender. "I know we're in the process of restructuring our roles, so I'm not forcing you to do this. But I'm asking you to think about your sister."

Colby froze. She loved Gentry but didn't exactly relish the idea of babysitting *another* difficult person every day. Her marriage had proved that job to be futile and painful. "Did she ask you to talk to me?"

"No. As far as I can tell, she's perfectly content to be aimless." He shook his head. "I'd like you to pretend it's your idea. Make her feel like you need her. Like you want her to work with you."

A CertainTea was supposed to be Colby's "happy place," not a job where she'd be a mediator, counselor, and pseudo mother to people like Alec and Gentry. Colby rubbed her hand over her face. "She may be aimless, but she's not stupid. She'll see you engineering this from a mile away."

Colby knew Alec wouldn't want to train Gentry in the kitchen, nor could she picture her sister carrying heavy trays or waiting on customers. Colby had hired a hostess, which left office support as the sole option. Now that she'd put her personal assets at risk, she didn't need anyone around who would make her job harder.

"Is that a no?" Her dad sighed with resignation.

He looked exhausted—maybe even a little sweaty—sitting there rubbing his knee like it ached. And he *had* invested in her dream. The least she could do for him was help manage his stress.

"I'll ask. Just don't be shocked if she's not interested." Colby glanced at the clock. "I've got to go. Is she around?"

"No, she's shopping with Jenna."

"They do have *that* in common." Censure colored her voice.

She respected Jenna's accomplishments, but the woman's picture was probably listed in Merriam-Webster's dictionary under the term "acquisitive." In the twenty-six years since marrying Colby's father, she'd redecorated their McMansion four times and remodeled the kitchen twice. Her shoe closet was bigger than most people's dining rooms, and her jewelry collection rivaled Harry Winston's Beverly Hills store. In particular, Colby thought the kitchen remodels monumentally wasteful because Jenna's cooking skills consisted of reheating whatever leftovers remained from wherever they'd eaten the night before—if that.

"It's what girls do." Her dad sighed.

"Not all girls." Colby stood, wishing that hadn't slipped out. He'd been open with her, after all. And Jenna worked exhaustively for the money to buy her precious things. "Sorry, that was mean. I'm just feeling a lot of pressure lately, and now I'm late for Mom."

"Well, I won't keep you." He rose from the stool. "Thanks for helping. I hope you can get through to Gentry."

Colby rose up on her toes and kissed her father goodbye. "I'll do my best."

"You always do." He waved her off.

◆ ◆ ◆

Colby fastened a bit of wire-welded fencing to a corner post in the garden. She gulped down half the bottle of water she'd brought out to the yard and gazed at the horizon. The sun hovered just above the trees now, painting a golden-peach wash across the sky.

Skies like this had been one of the few things that Mark had been able to appreciate when depressed. She withdrew from the memory of him lying in bed silently gazing out the window at such sunsets, and wondered if the guilty reflex of comparing the present to her past would ever end. Unfortunately, it seemed Alec's return had set her back a step or two from that goal.

Setting the bottle down, she assessed her progress. Two sides completed, two to go. "Mom, if we want to finish tonight, I need more help."

"My fingers are sore from handling that wire." Her mom gently pressed her fingertips together twice.

Colby suppressed the urge to roll her eyes. She'd split two nails tonight, but unlike her mom, she wouldn't complain. The instant gratification and sense of accomplishment from doing handiwork were worth it.

"How about wearing the gardening gloves?" Colby unrolled more fencing from the spool by kicking it across the grass. "At least come help cut this section, please."

"Don't get snippy. If you would've let me hire someone to do the work, we could both be inside having a glass of wine like normal people." Her mother came over with wire cutters.

"I'm pretty certain you'll still squeeze in that glass of wine." Colby shot her mom an amused look. "Come on, we're almost finished."

"Don't rush me. I'm going as fast as I can. My arthritis hurts, you know."

Colby's chuckle emerged as more of a brief snort. Her mom didn't have arthritis. She *did* have a habit of throwing out references to old-people problems as a way of reminding Colby that she needed help.

"When we're done, you should stay for a while. There's an interesting documentary I taped on this whole thing with legalizing marijuana." Her mom tapped a finger to her cheek. "Wine is one thing, but these . . . potheads . . . I don't know if this is a good decision for Oregon."

"Potheads?" Colby smiled. "I think the term is 'stoners,' and I wonder if your poet warrior is one, like Yeats."

"Richard is not a pothead!"

"How would you know?"

"He's not!" Her mom drew her brows downward. "I'd know."

"Oh? You mean like he *knows* about your dog?" Colby scoffed. She, too, had let infatuation trick her into thinking she *knew* Mark much too soon. "Have you admitted yet that you don't have a dog?"

"Of course." Her mom then grimaced. "Although he may be under the impression that I recently lost one."

"Oh, Mom! That's a terrible lie."

"It's a white lie." She flipped her hands upward. "Who does it hurt?"

Colby shook her head. "Now I'm going to have to pretend, too. What's our dearly departed dog's name?"

"Snickers—a brown, gold, and cream-colored collie." She smiled, proud of her inventive fib. In a twisted way, Colby almost admired her mother's fluid relationship with reality. It would be much easier to ignore bad memories if she could continually reinvent herself and rewrite the past.

"Don't cry to me when the truth comes out and Richard can't believe another word you say." She couldn't blame her mom for wanting a relationship. Most people did. *If* Colby ever took that leap again—no, even that thought tightened her stomach.

"According to you, he'll be too high to remember, anyway." She sniffed, and then, in a classic maneuver, steered the conversation away from her flaws to someone else's. "I'm just glad I don't have to worry about you or your brother wasting your time and money in those pot stores. Your sister, on the other hand. She'll probably camp out there."

"Mom!" Colby set her hands on her hips. "Don't start in on Gentry."

Gentry may have been in need of guidance, but she was basically good-hearted, if still a bit juvenile and self-centered. And honestly, Colby's mother had made a habit of trying just about everything once. If she hadn't tried pot yet, it was only a matter of time before she wandered into a legal dispensary. Perhaps even with her new poet friend.

"Sorry." Her mother had the grace to blush.

"Hello!" Alec's voice beckoned from the side of the house, surprising them both as he rounded the corner carrying a small box. "I saw your car in the driveway, but no one answered the doorbell."

He'd made good on his promise from last night. She hadn't been able to count on Mark to follow through with something as important as his therapy, let alone little things like this. Alec nodded at Colby, and a swell of gratitude and temptation cracked that fortress around her heart. How long had it been since anyone had done her a small kindness without expecting something in return?

"Alec." Her mom wiped her hands on her jeans and started toward him with open arms. "My, my! Such a handsome young man. Come give me a hug."

He did look handsome. Dark jeans, a crisp white shirt, his floppy bangs playfully dangling above his eyes. The late-afternoon sun bathed him in a movie star–quality glow. Colby gave herself a mental smackdown for that dippy reverie.

"Not so young, Leslie. But thanks." Alec gave in to her embrace. "You look wonderful, too."

"Thank you, dear." Her mom smoothed her hair, preening. "What brings you by?"

"I'm having dinner with my mom, so I thought I'd drop off a few extra pear croustades." He smiled broadly before winking at Colby. "I remembered how much you always liked them."

Colby's reluctant heart skipped another beat in response to his thoughtfulness and soft spot for her mom. Then again, maybe he just wanted to secure his job. The sad fact that she couldn't trust his intentions skimmed plaster over those cracks Alec had just opened.

Her mother's hands waved excitedly before she took the box and opened it. "Oh, thank you! This calls for coffee."

Coffee, of course. Never tea. Her mother *never* drank tea anymore.

"Shouldn't we finish this fence first? The rabbits, remember?" Colby guzzled her last bit of water, belatedly realizing that she must look frightful in her grubby jeans, gray T-shirt, and sweaty ponytail.

"Let's finish tomorrow. Give my fingers a chance to recover." Her mom wiggled the fingers of her one free hand.

"Looks like quite a project. I didn't know you gardened, Leslie." Alec's gaze wandered from the garden to Colby's mom. "I'm impressed."

"You come grab fresh ingredients whenever you need them." Her mother cast a proud grin his way and touched his shoulder like a practiced flirt. Colby itched with discomfort at her mom's behavior, given that her own sexual impulses had gone into hibernation until yesterday. "Can you stay for coffee?"

"Thanks, but no. My mom's waiting on me."

"Another time, then." Her mom patted Alec's cheek. "We have to catch up, especially now that you'll be working with Colby. I still can't believe it. After all those years you practiced your cooking on us, and now you two are running a restaurant."

"I'm grateful for the opportunity to do what I love." A wistful expression passed over his face. "And who could ask for a better boss?"

"We'll see if you're still saying that in a month," Colby teased, grateful that he acknowledged that she was, in fact, his boss, not his partner. Although, in a parallel universe, she could imagine a partnership with him being satisfying.

Alec's heart had taken a lot of beatings thanks to his dad's antagonism, but apparently his rib cage had absorbed the blows without puncturing the resilient little muscle. Alec might not be considered a tough man by other people's standards, but those folks weren't using the right measure.

"I need to run, but it's nice to see you again." Alec shoved his now-empty hands in his pockets, like always. His nervous tell.

"Say hello to your mom from me." Her mom turned uncharacteristically serious. "She's over the moon to have you back home."

A hush settled over the yard as Joe's ghost floated among them, right where they'd all played so often. She could almost hear the giggles and shrieks coming back to life as nostalgia grabbed hold. Now her mother, Alec, and she stood there waiting for something, or some words, that never came.

"See you tomorrow." Alec nodded at Colby and then disappeared around the corner.

"Let's eat these fresh tarts now." Her mom waved her over. "Alec looks much better than I remember. Such a gangly teen, and then so gaunt after Joe died. Guess I never paid enough attention to that one."

Neither did I, Colby absently thought, glancing over her shoulder toward the Morgans' house.

◆ ◆ ◆

"That was excellent, Mom." Alec loaded his dish into the dishwasher. "Nice and tender."

"I learned from the best," she said, teasing him.

He smiled and slung his arm over her shoulder. Her brown hair had grayed substantially, but her green eyes still sparkled with gold, like his. He also shared her Eastern European square jaw and high cheekbones, her long neck, and her introverted personality.

If Joe had been his father's favorite, then Alec had been his mother's. Thank God, because he'd needed someone on his side. Someone who'd encouraged his passion rather than disparaged it. His desire for his family to heal was complicated by his dad's disposition, but Alec could swallow his pride—act more like Joe to make his father happier—if it'd save his family. He owed that much to his mom, anyway.

"My best student." He crossed his arms. "And my best teacher."

She sighed. "You look happy. Things must be going well with Colby."

Colby. Even muddied and sweaty from working in her mother's garden, she'd looked sweeter than his croustades.

Her grateful expression tonight had made him feel better than when he'd won his James Beard Award. As far as amends went, his tiny gesture with her mom wasn't much. It would take hundreds of those efforts, but eventually the cumulative effect would make Colby's life better.

Sadly, nothing could make up for everything his silence had stolen from her.

"So far, so good." He sat at the kitchen table where he'd grown up, and stretched out his legs. He'd left here at eighteen, still such a boy. Life since then had hardened him into a man. "Leslie asked me to say hello, by the way."

"I rarely run into her, now that all you kids are grown and out of the house." His mom folded the dishrag over the sink and stared blankly out the kitchen window. Like earlier this evening, Joe's specter danced in the shadows.

Being in this house had been tough for Alec ever since his brother died. Photographs and memorabilia were scattered everywhere. The oldest ones showcased two close brothers with their arms slung over each other's shoulders, or Joe sitting on his shoulders. But as they'd grown up, they were more often photographed sitting across from each other—always separated by some invisible force field—the pictures reflecting a new reality. *Those* photos taunted him, reminding him of how much time they'd wasted on one-upmanship.

"A lot has changed since then," his mom continued. She turned, her expression contemplative. "I'm grateful you're staying in town, but it's awkward to feel indebted to the Cabots. Are you okay with it?"

"I'm fine." Colby reminded him of Joe and Mark, but not in the way his mother presumed. She had no idea of the guilt Alec carried around like a pack mule.

Her aging eyes took on a cloudy, faraway look, something he noticed with more frequency since Joe died. His brother's death had been a tragedy, but for his mom, Alec's leaving had dealt another blow. She'd been stuck here with no one to turn to for comfort, because her husband sure couldn't offer any. Anger and bitterness had made that man's already-insensitive nature as impenetrable as a coat of armor.

"Do you still have a crush on Colby?" Her gaze refocused on him.

"What?" Alec sat up straighter, his body warming.

"You heard me. She might've palled around here with Joe most of the time, but you'd watched her every move whenever she came by. She was also the only one you didn't yell at for sneaking licks of batter when you were experimenting."

Alec scratched his neck. "We've been friends for a long time."

"You're avoiding the question, which tells me you still like her."

"Likes who?" His dad's voice shocked them both. When had he sneaked into the house? And how the hell did he manage it?

At six feet two inches and with 220 pounds of firm muscle for a man of his age, Alec's dad wasn't normally light-footed. His chestnut hair—the only trait they shared—had its fair share of gray highlights. Deep grooves in his forehead and bracketing his mouth always gave his father a grim appearance. Of course, the lack of good humor and affection didn't help, either.

"No one," Alec said at the same time his mother said, "Colby."

His father barely acknowledged Alec as he passed by on his way to the refrigerator. He retrieved a beer and popped the tab. "I can't believe you can work for Colby, let alone *like* her. If it weren't for her and that son of a bitch she married—"

"Frank," his mom said, "you always liked Colby."

"That was *before*. Things changed . . ." Alec's dad waved her off. "You'll accept anything that keeps him in town, but don't expect me to."

"Dad, how was happy hour?" Alec diverted his father's attention to prevent his parents from arguing. "Mom said you went out with Craig."

"He's thinking of moving to Los Angeles to be near his daughter. She just had a baby, and Craig's wife wants to be closer to their grandkid." His dad shook his head, apparently unable to comprehend his old partner on the force embracing family or change or life. He'd given up on all that when Joe died.

"I'm jealous." His mother then smiled at Alec. "I can't wait to be a grandmother one day."

Oh, brother.

His father rolled his eyes. "Well, this one's not going to meet any women if he's always in this kitchen with you."

And there it was. The "mommy's boy" put-down he'd heard for much of his life. Maybe he should take comfort in the fact that some things never changed. Not even the way his dad grinned after those remarks, as if this kind of teasing was funny.

"It could take a while, Mom." Alec recovered from the swipe. "My hours make it tough. Working nights, weekends, and holidays. Not exactly a profession for a family-oriented man."

Then again, Colby would be sharing those hours. It made them uniquely compatible in that one aspect. Too bad his conscience wouldn't let him pursue her while keeping his secret about Mark. He had no choice if he hoped to do everything he'd come home to do, even if his secret ate away at him bit by bit each day.

"Excuses are like assholes; everybody has one. Work isn't the problem. The truth is that you'd have to break out of your shell to go after a woman. Not exactly your strong suit, is it?" His dad chugged from his beer can, crushed it, and tossed it in the trash.

Alec could recount all the ways he'd toughened up. Could mention he wasn't that same shy teen his dad never took the time to know. But his dad wouldn't believe him, so the argument would only put his mother in the middle. Alec clamped down on his temper, knowing that if he wanted a relationship with a woman, he could have one, no matter what his dad thought.

Plenty of women had found Alec and his success very attractive, a lesson Joe had unfortunately learned the hard way the night before his fatal hike.

Alec mentally recoiled from that memory when, for the first time that evening, his father looked him squarely in the eye. All traces of humor, twisted or otherwise, were gone. "But that's fine with me, 'cause I don't want any Cabot babies in this house."

Time for another change of subject, because he wasn't about to argue with his dad about his nonexistent relationship with Colby. "Want a croustade?"

"A croustade?" His dad shook his head derisively and laughed. "A *croustade*."

Still, he took one before stalking into the family room and turning the TV volume up to full blare.

Alec unclenched his fists, which had been balled up on his thighs.

"Don't pay attention to him." His mother patted his shoulder.

How often had Alec heard that advice . . .

"It's time for me to go." Alec rose. "I guess Dad won't want to come to the soft opening in a couple of weeks, but will you? Maybe bring a friend or two?"

She pressed her lips together, brows raised. He'd put her on the spot, but he wanted her support when he officially returned to the local restaurant scene.

"Sure, honey." She patted his arm. "I can't wait to hear everyone rave about your food."

"Thanks, Mom." He kissed her cheek. "I'll see you soon."

Instead of going directly to his car, he wandered through the darkening backyard, grateful for the warm breeze. Whacking through the overgrown arborvitae, he found the path that led to the aging octagonal tree house, centered on the tree trunk, about eight feet above the ground. Although long neglected, it still appeared to be in decent shape thanks to Mr. Cabot's and his father's solid clapboard construction job. He smiled, remembering being seven and thinking this fort was the coolest place on earth.

Alec tested the ladder rungs before climbing inside. He used the flashlight on his phone to peek around the space that held his boyhood hopes and dreams.

Animals had chewed through the old quilts and mattress, but an abandoned tapestry still hung on one wall. Plastic milk crates, emptied of their old treasures, littered the floor. The clear PVC curtains they'd hung in the windows to keep rain out were missing a few panels. Colby would be horrified. She'd always kept it clean, mostly because that had been the price Hunter demanded if she wanted to hang out with them.

Closing his eyes, Alec inhaled through his nose, taking in the familiar scents that opened the floodgates to many memories. The good ones. The years when Joe had wanted to be part of Alec's life.

"Why can't I stay?" Joe whined.

"Because you're too young."

"I'm in middle school now." Joe straightened his spine, as if trying to compete with Alec's height.

"Barely. Besides, Hunter and I have our own plans." Alec tossed his sleeping bag on the mattress. "I'll sleep out here with you some other night, Joe."

Joe's frown softened. "Promise?"

"Promise." Alec tossed Joe a peanut-butter-and-fudge brownie, which Joe shoved into his mouth in almost one bite.

"One more?" he managed to say between chews.

"Only if you go home now."

"Okay." Joe held out his hand, and then, with a little sigh, turned to leave. At the top of the ladder, he said, "Next weekend is my turn, right?"

"Sure." Alec sighed, anticipating a sleepless night in the tree house with Joe and his thousand questions. "Now go home."

Naturally, Alec had taken his brother's love for granted. He'd shooed him away as often as he'd given in. What he'd give now for a second chance. To turn back time and clear the air rather than let his wounded pride drive him to twist the knife.

Clearing his throat, Alec climbed back down the ladder, guilt cinched around him like a straitjacket. On his way back along the path, he heard faint music and other noises coming from Leslie Cabot's. Veering to his right, he pushed through the shrubs leading to her yard.

In the distant glow of the back-porch lights, he saw Colby finishing her mother's garden fence.

"Need help?"

"Oh!" She jumped. "Jeez, you scared me. What were you doing back there?"

"Checking out the tree house."

Her face lit, and with her high ponytail, she looked almost as young as when they'd actually hung out back there. "Really? I haven't been in ages."

"We've been replaced by a family of squirrels."

She laughed, lifting his mood. He'd always loved the sound of her laughter and the twinkle in those tipped-up eyes. "I hope they've enjoyed our little haven as much as we did."

She blushed then, and he wondered if she might be remembering that old kiss. Probably not. It had only counted for one or two minutes among the thousands they'd spent there. Insignificant to her, anyway.

Her flush faded as her expression turned melancholy, and he suspected she thought of Joe.

"Too bad adults don't have tree houses, too," he said.

"Maybe I should've named my restaurant The *Tea* House," she teased.

"A place for grown-up dreams." They stared at each other, her face filling with approval, and he suspected she, too, missed the comfort that place of lost innocence had provided. Alec reached for the fencing. "Let me help."

Colby paused before handing him the wire cutters. "You know, I'd worried things between us would be awkward, but you've gone out of your way to make it easy. Now it sort of feels like old times with us."

If reminding her of old times made her smile like that, he'd find a million other ways to be the friend she remembered fondly.

Chapter Five

"Sorry I'm late." Gentry waltzed into A CertainTea and lobbed her brown leather Miu Miu satchel on the table where Colby had been impatiently waiting.

At five feet ten inches tall, Gentry commanded attention. Factor in her auburn hair and green eyes, and no one could deny her sister's striking, if not beautiful, appearance. Her quirky fashion sense—today in a heavily patterned, short layered skirt and an intricate mesh top—only enhanced her eye-catching looks. The outfit looked like something she'd cobbled together from a secondhand store, but it probably bore a Gaultier label.

Gentry glanced around the space she hadn't once visited during the renovation. "Looks nice. Love the gray floors and all the taupe and cream accents. The wood beams and live plants are a nice touch. Classy yet Zen."

"Thanks. I'm shooting for hip yet pretty enough to be a wedding venue." Colby particularly loved the floor-to-ceiling retractable glass doors that offered guests beautiful views of the lake.

"You nailed it." Gentry collapsed into one of the leather-covered chairs. "So why'd you call me here?"

Colby held her breath. *Here goes nothing.* "I need your help."

"*My* help?" Gentry's disbelieving smirk pricked at Colby's conscience. "With what? Dad?"

"No, not with Dad. With all of this." She gestured around the restaurant.

Gentry sat forward, her long legs lazily sprawled to the sides, and rested her chin on her fist, causing the dozen bangles on her arm to jangle. "How can *I* help?"

How indeed?

"I'm overwhelmed by everything on my plate. You know I hate social media, so I thought maybe you might take the lead on keeping the website and media pages fresh and appealing. Between your photography background and your online presence, it seems like a good fit."

Gentry's pretty eyes narrowed. "Did Dad put you up to this? Is this his way of keeping me busy so I don't have time to hang out with Jake?"

Colby could lie, but she suspected Gentry would know it. Maybe if people started treating her sister like a responsible grown-up, she'd start acting like one. "Okay, yes. Dad asked me to consider it, but he didn't force me. After thinking about it, I realized you could help. You'd do a better job than I would with using apps to drive business our way."

Gentry sat back, lips pursed. "What about my classes?"

"We could work around those. A lot of the work could be done on your own time. I'd only need you here a few half days each week to help me with other things in the office."

"Why are you really doing this?" Gentry cocked her head, clearly untrusting.

"I just told you; I could use help. And it would be nice to work with my sister—someone who has my back—instead of an employee who doesn't care if I succeed or fail." That part was true, even if Colby had exaggerated the rest. "It'll be a nice way for us to reconnect, too. I know I haven't been the best sister these past few years."

Gentry's expression softened. "It's okay. You've been grieving."

"I still could've been better." Colby hated that Gentry gave her a free pass. If anything, hadn't Mark's suicide reinforced the dangers of *not* paying attention to the people you loved? "So, will you help me?"

Her sister flashed the quick, eager grin Colby remembered from the days when Gentry had desperately tagged along behind her and her teenage friends. "Okay."

"Good." Colby slid a report across the table. "Read this market demographics report and think about how we might best reach our target audience. Take a stab at crafting some press releases, and we'll meet back here in a few days to discuss your ideas. Initially I'll retain oversight just to make sure we're on the same page in terms of the brand image, but once I'm comfortable, you can run the show."

Gentry wrinkled her nose. "Reports are so boring."

"But necessary. Preparation is key, okay? Promise this won't sit on your dresser until ten minutes before we next meet."

"I thought you trusted me to have your back." Gentry's smile faded.

"I do. But don't pretend you're not easily distracted, especially by guys. Speaking of that, what's the deal with Jake?"

"What did Dad say?" Gentry's green eyes sizzled despite the cool, clipped tone of her voice.

"He's eager to see you settled with something, and someone, stable."

"It's a little late for my mom and him to start being parents, don't you think?" Gentry stuffed the report in her bag. Before Colby could reply, her sister declared, "Jake's great. He's sexy, fun, independent, and he doesn't treat me like an afterthought."

Alec arrived before Colby could further explore Gentry's motives.

"Good morning," he said, gaze falling on Colby.

Such a handsome face. The stray thought rattled Colby. Thankfully, he hadn't noticed because he'd become distracted by her sister.

"Gentry." His eyes widened. "It's been a while. I can't believe how you've changed."

Colby's body tensed when her sister gave him an appreciative once-over.

"So have you." Gentry's saucy smile returned. She stood and hugged Alec, subtly thrusting her ample cleavage forward, as if he might somehow miss it on his own. "The idea of working here just got a whole lot more interesting."

"You'll be working here?" Alec's brows rose.

"You didn't get my text?" Colby asked.

He grimaced and shook his head.

"Alec, charge and carry your phone!" Colby heaved a sigh.

"I'll do better." He turned back to Gentry. "Will you be waitressing?"

Colby knew Alec well enough to recognize the concern in his expression.

"Hell, no. Would this manicure survive carrying all those trays around?" Gentry held up a hand and wiggled her bejeweled fingers. At least she was honest.

"In the kitchen?" Alec spoke with the level of caution required to navigate a minefield.

"Ha! You do remember who my mother is, right? The only thing I can do back there is reheat leftovers." Gentry proudly embraced her spoiled life. Then again, she didn't know anything different. The shopping, the frequent dining out, the weekly mani-pedi—all of that was her norm.

"Gentry's going to help me in the office and with our social media." Colby exchanged a knowing glance with Alec.

"Ah. Sounds like a plan." He nodded, clearly relieved not to have to train her. "I'll leave you two to talk. I'll be testing new menu items with the staff today."

"Good luck." Gentry flirtatiously touched his arm before he made off to the kitchen. Once he was out of sight, she shot a wide-eyed gaze Colby's way. "He looks good."

"I think he's finally coping with Joe's death and losing Une Bouchée." Colby hoped so, anyhow.

"No, I mean he looks *good*." The purr in Gentry's voice grated on Colby's nerves. "Hot!"

"What about Jake?"

Gentry shrugged. "Dad always says it's important to keep your options open."

"Alec is off-limits." Her staccato delivery caught Gentry off guard. In truth, it caught Colby off guard, too. "We can't have coworkers getting together. That's bad for business. Got it?"

Her sister raised her hands in surrender. "Okay. But you'd better have an all-male staff if you expect that rule to be followed."

"I've hired mature, career-oriented waiters, and the two women cooks on staff are married."

"Phfft." Gentry rolled her eyes. "As if that ever stopped anyone."

"When did you become so jaded?"

"Not jaded. Realistic. Look around. Your parents divorced. Mine work more than they have any fun. *You* may have had a good marriage until everything with Mark and Joe happened, but not everyone is that lucky."

Good marriage. Lucky. The front she and Mark had put up in order to hide his diagnosis. Neither term applied, though, no matter how great of a snow job she'd pulled off.

She'd tried to make it true. Given every part of her heart and soul to her marriage. Patiently cleaned up after he'd do things like spray down the entire condo with fire extinguishers in order to "reveal" the ghosts he believed haunted him. Clung to the shining moments of Mark's generous spirit and surprising bursts of romance. Voraciously read about his illness and tried to implement different coping strategies, hoping he would be like many other bipolar sufferers and learn to manage his illness and his life.

But in the murky places of her heart, she'd blamed Mark for not committing to treatment. Worse, she'd blamed herself for being unable to motivate him to stick with therapy and medication like other spouses in her shoes could.

In that light, loneliness seemed safer than entrusting her future happiness to any man.

Colby swatted the depressing memories away like flies even as they deepened her concern for her sister. "Promise me you won't rush into anything."

"What part of keeping my options open suggests that I'm rushing into anything?" Gentry grabbed her purse. "I've got to run. I'll read this report and come up with a plan. Maybe I'll swing by the day after next and get some photos. I think it's supposed to be sunny."

"Thanks, Gentry." Colby stood and offered her sister a hug. "This will be good for both of us."

"Unless we end up like my mom and Hunter." Gentry snickered. "Just kidding. See you later!"

She flounced off, her little skirt swishing around her thighs, loose curls flowing down her back. Colby sat and drew a deep breath to quiet the fear that hiring her sister might be the best *and* worst decision of her week.

◆ ◆ ◆

"Are you fucking kidding me?" Alec barked at the sous chef, Chris, his voice reverberating off the metal surfaces in the kitchen. "I don't know whether to laugh or cry!"

"Why?" Chris shot him a vexed look.

Alec pointed at the meunière sauce smeared on the outer lining of the dish. "Does that look spotless to you? Do you think any customer wants to pay thirty-eight dollars for a dish and have it served looking so sloppy?" He whirled around on the chef de entremetier. "And do these first courses look consistent? Don't answer. I will. They don't. This one, too much sauce. This one, wilted chiffonade. That one isn't properly seared!"

"You didn't even taste them." Chris flipped his palms heavenward, defending his subordinate.

"I don't need to, because I wouldn't let any of these items leave this kitchen. *Look* at them!"

"No one but you would notice the chiffonade," Chris challenged.

Pressure built up behind Alec's eyes. "What did you say?"

"Most people toss that aside." Chris shrank back a step or two.

Clearly, none of these cooks had trained under the masters in Europe. They hadn't worked eighteen-hour shifts on their feet for twenty grand a year and slept on hostel floors just for the chance to learn from the best.

"How do you think a restaurant earns a James Beard Award, or, if Michelin ever expands its US review territories to include the Northwest, a star? By being lazy? By ignoring the little details? No. No!" Alec's palm slammed against the metal counter. He needed each of them to adopt his perspective if he had any chance of making Colby's restaurant the best, or of winning awards and proving to his dad and the world that his talent wasn't a fluke or a joke. "Every single plate that leaves this kitchen must, *must*, meet the standard I set. It will be perfect. It will be clean. It will be consistent. No one knows which customer out there is a critic. You can't afford not to be perfect every single time."

Chris dimly stared back at Alec, as if Alec were a madman. "Okay."

"Okay? *Putain!*" Alec turned toward the rest of the cook staff, voice tight and rough. "Do none of you have the passion required to be the best? To produce the finest meals in the area? Because if you don't aim for perfection, then I don't want you in this kitchen."

"Alec?" Colby's voice cut through the room.

He whipped his neck around. "Yes?"

She offered a conciliatory smile to his staff. "Could I please see you out here for a minute?"

Alec noticed Chris's smug satisfaction. Whether intentional or not, Colby had undermined Alec at a critical moment. He forced a lid over his temper. "Of course."

He followed her into the dining room, counting to three in his head while she straightened her pencil skirt. For chrissakes, did she think he had time for a lecture? He didn't need to be micromanaged in his own kitchen. Her restaurant, *his* kitchen, dammit.

"What's going on?" she asked. "I heard you yelling from out here."

"The staff isn't up to par, Colby, and I only have a couple of weeks to train them."

"Training? It sounded like screaming to me."

Alec inhaled slowly, reminding himself that Colby disliked conflict and had never once worked in any kitchen. She had no idea of the difficulty, the coordination, the trust and teamwork that needed to be pulled off, hour after endless hour. He resented the way she now looked at him with distaste. Her husband had been a loudmouth, so why Alec's behavior bothered her, he couldn't quite say. "I need them to do exactly as I say. *Exactly.* If they don't learn to work like clockwork, you'll have increased costs beginning with wasted inventory and ending with higher workers' comp claims because of injuries. That means I can't have you undercut my authority."

"Surely there's a more respectful way to earn their respect and cooperation." She folded her arms. "I told you, I want this restaurant to be a happy place for everyone."

"This is a restaurant, not a spiritual retreat. *Surely* you understand the difference." When his remark caused her to scowl, he blew out a breath. "Sorry. But if you want to ensure that your guests have an exquisite experience from the moment they enter to the moment they leave, let me worry about the kitchen staff's 'feelings.'"

"I don't want to work in a war zone, Alec." She folded her arms across her chest.

"Now who's exaggerating?"

She looked him up and down. "When did you become an arrogant jerk?"

"When did you become a fragile flower?" He reeled in his emotions, reminding himself she was his boss, not his employee. "I can't believe you're offended by *me* after spending so many years with Joe and Mark."

Her mouth fell open. "Don't change the subject. I'm trying to avoid a spate of harassment suits."

"Harassment?" He practically choked on the word. "I'm setting the standard by which they must perform. It's your restaurant, but it's *my* reputation on the line, Colby. No one cares who *owns* the restaurant. The executive chef gets all the credit or all the blame. So don't tell me to relax—or how to do my job—when you've never worked in a kitchen."

"I asked you before not to belittle me." Her voice had grown deadly quiet.

He raised his hands overhead. "Since when is stating facts belittling?"

"Since you keep dismissing my concerns as if I have no brain. I might not have kitchen experience, but I know poor management when I see it. I'm telling you right now, I won't tolerate constant turnover. Maybe you had to endure shitty 'training' as a young chef, but I bet you didn't like it much. Be a better man and find a better way." Before he could respond, she twirled on her heel and stalked off, leaving him stewing in his own stomach acid.

Seemed she now made a habit of quick exits after laying down the law, so to speak.

Be a better man and find a better way.

Those words echoed in his mind as he made his way back into the kitchen. No doubt the staff had overheard their discussion.

For most of his life, he'd been considered weak. Quiet, thoughtful, a little shy. The kitchen had been the one—the only—place where he'd reigned supreme. Where he'd had complete confidence and control. If she expected him to go back to being that Alec everyone else pushed around or ignored, she'd better think again.

She didn't appreciate his style? Too bad. It had worked for generations of chefs, and had made Une Bouchée an award-winning establishment. His dad would respect it. "No holds barred" had been that man's motto for as long as Alec could remember. No one had criticized Joe for taking it to heart, so Alec wouldn't worry about Colby's current perception. Securing his dad's respect, reclaiming his reputation, making her restaurant the best. That had to be the priority.

She'd forgive him once A CertainTea was featured in *Bon Appétit*.

"So, tell me. Who isn't willing to meet my standards?" *Find a better way.* What Colby didn't know was that there was no better way. "It won't be easy, but a year from now, you'll be proud of what we'll accomplish together. You'll learn more than you've ever learned before, too, but it won't come without some pain and suffering."

They all stared at him in silence. Some looked barely older than twenty-one. Good God, had he ever been that young?

"Shall I take your silence as meaning you're on board? That each of you understands that every single detail matters?"

"Yes, Chef" came the reply in unison.

"Good. Let's try again, from the beginning." Alec called out a number of orders from the menu in another attempt to create a real-time test. "The soft opening is only two and a half weeks away. Let's be ready."

Yet despite his private pep talk, Colby's words disrupted his concentration. *Be a better man and find a better way.*

Chapter Six

While in her office, Colby set down her pen and listened for another outburst from the kitchen. He'd fooled her these past several days, masking an egomaniacal temper with a soft voice and delicious pastries. More proof of her poor judgment when it came to people and, more specifically, men.

Her phone alarm beeped, reminding her of her appointment with her former colleague Todd Martin. He'd agreed to bring the final estate paperwork here. Todd had been a true friend during her tenure at the law firm. Given that he'd started in family law before switching to estates and trusts, he'd also been the one person she'd confided in when she'd been considering divorcing Mark.

She'd made those inquiries just prior to Joe's accident. Even now a sense of disloyalty pervaded. It hadn't been easy to admit that she'd no longer loved Mark the way a wife should love her husband. She disliked herself immensely for it, and yet he wouldn't commit to a protocol, and she hadn't been able to envision another forty or more years on that uncertain path.

She hadn't *wanted* to hurt him. Or abandon him. Or do anything to make his already-difficult life any harder or more isolated. To this day, Mark's defeated expression when he'd discovered her change of heart gripped her throat like an angry pair of hands.

"Colby?" Todd knocked on her office doorjamb, jerking her from the painful memory.

A little on the short and stocky side, Todd reminded her of a teddy bear, with his boyish, dimpled face and light-brown curls. A teddy bear with tortoiseshell glasses, a pink-and-blue bow tie, and an encyclopedic memory.

"I didn't hear you come in." She walked around her desk to give him a friendly hug. "Thanks for coming all the way out here."

"No thanks needed. I love any excuse to get out of the office." He sat in an empty chair and placed a manila envelope on her desk. "The place looks great, by the way. All this *and* you jumped off the billable-hour train."

"I don't miss that!" she chuckled. "But I do miss the people."

"We miss you, too." His warm smile helped her set aside disturbing comparisons of Alec and Mark. "Your replacement is competent, but she isn't a team player."

"Sorry." Colby grimaced.

"No, you're not." He pursed his face comically while shaking his head.

"I swear I am!" She grinned. Then her gaze landed on the large envelope, and she let loose a quick sigh. "So this is it."

"The last of the paperwork for Mark's estate." Todd's voice turned sober, and his cheerful gaze softened. "I'll witness everything and finalize the filings."

"Sometimes it's still so unreal." She stared at the envelope, toying with her wedding band. "How can these papers be all that's left of someone who, at his best, was so energetic and charming?"

"It's not all that's left. You have your memories. I know there were issues in your marriage, but there'd also been a lot of love. Hold on to the good memories, and let the rest go."

Like a slide show, she remembered their first date, when Mark had serenaded her with his guitar. How she'd lain in his arms for hours kissing and talking. Their wedding, when he'd gotten teary during their vows. His terrible home science experiments, the enormous bookcase he'd built and painted her favorite color (lilac), his love for Monty Python movies, the way he always sought Hunter's and her father's approval.

But she couldn't hold back the other memories. The sexts from other women. The annoying impulsiveness, like when she'd come home during a "creative" burst of mania to find he'd purchased a dozen expensive instruments he didn't play because he suddenly planned to compose the world's greatest symphony. The anger and exasperation and depression he'd display, no matter how much it frightened her.

His illness had steamrolled straight through the center of their lives and her heart, destroying all the promise of their love.

Love. For all the love Mark had professed for her, it had never been enough to convince him to stick with therapy when he'd crave the highs of mania. And at the end of the day, it hadn't been enough to give him the will to live. It hadn't even been enough to keep him from taking his life right in front of her.

Her eyes watered. "Easier said than done."

"I know." Todd shifted in his chair.

"Sorry." She dabbed at her eyes, wishing she didn't still lapse into pointless musings about the past. "I'll sign these and let you get back to your day."

Colby thumbed through the tabbed pages and signed where indicated, then handed everything over to Todd. He double-checked them before closing the folder and then heaved a short sigh.

Leaning forward, he said, "This place is a solid fresh start, but you also need a little fun in your life. Come out with me one night before this place opens up."

She shook her head. "I'm not a good wingman anymore, Todd. I'll just cramp your style."

Two red stains colored his cheeks as he cleared his throat. "No, not as a wingman. Let me take you out. Dinner. A movie. Whatever you want."

"Oh." She froze, blindsided. She'd never thought of Todd as anything other than a friend. Had she missed seeing his interest in her? Probably. Apparently, she missed seeing most everything when it came to men. "Like a real date, or a friend date?"

He shrugged. "Maybe a little of both?"

Her pulse hammered at the base of her throat while she stalled. A date. A date with *Todd*? She tried to picture it but couldn't. She hadn't been attracted to a man other than Mark in years. Well, except for Alec recently, which was obviously the height of stupidity. "I'm sorry, Todd. I'm not interested in dating anyone yet."

Honestly, she might never be ready. The flutters of attraction Alec inspired terrified her more than anything else. Panic didn't seem like a good ingredient for a relationship.

"Okay." Disappointment marbled his benign expression. "If you change your mind, just say so."

"I will." Would she? She didn't know—impossible to think during an out-of-body experience. The small office closed around them, yet Todd sat there looking comfortable and familiar. Unruffled. Calm.

Maybe a date with Todd was *exactly* what she needed. She'd known him for six years. He'd been consistent, levelheaded, and kind. The opposite of Mark in some important ways. And apparently the opposite of Alec, too. If she didn't want a spinster's life, maybe someone like Todd was the answer. Genuine—if friendly—affection couldn't hurt her like passion.

"You're still coming to the soft opening in about two weeks, right? Maybe I should invite some of the gang, too."

"A little reunion."

"If you all enjoy it, you could lobby to hold the firm's annual holi-day dinner here in December." She remembered being a first-year associate at that dinner years ago.

"I love you in a dark suit." She laughed as Mark twirled her around the dance floor to the band's rendition of "I Could Write a Book." All around them, her colleagues were dining and drinking in the ballroom decorated with twinkling light-strewn garland.

"I love you . . . period." He pulled her close, bussing a quick kiss on her lips. "Next year will be so much better, I swear. I don't want to lose you, Colby."

They'd been frightened by his behavior and diagnosis, but with treat-ment, he'd been doing better. "You'll never lose me. We're in this together, and together we can conquer anything."

He'd been so dashing and happy. It had made it easy to pretend they weren't hiding the truth from the world or from themselves.

"Impressing a roomful of lawyers and rich clients could be very good for business." Todd winked before stuffing the paperwork back in his briefcase, and she was glad to see that her putting him off hadn't made things between them awkward.

"Let me walk you out." She followed him into the dining room, where they ran into Alec, who'd just blown through the kitchen doors like the Tasmanian Devil. *Now what?*

He stabbed one hand through his hair before he saw them. "Sorry."

Colby's body heated from a mix of irritation and embarrassment as she watched Alec open and close his fists.

She turned her face away from Todd. Shooting Alec a warning with a look, she then spoke through a forced smile and clenched teeth. "Alec, this is my former colleague Todd Martin. He'll be here for the soft opening."

Alec stepped toward them and shook Todd's hand. "Nice to meet you."

Funny how she used to consider Alec a little geeky, but next to Todd he appeared vital and intense. Determined. And, despite better judgment—or rather, because of her *lack* of judgment—sexy.

"This is our executive chef, Alec Morgan." Colby's phony smile faltered thanks to her screwed-up thoughts.

"Alec." Todd returned the firm handshake with a pleasant grin. A puppy compared with Alec's pit bull presence. He pushed his glasses farther up the bridge of his nose. "I'm looking forward to being your guinea pig."

Alec rocked back slightly on his heels and nodded. "I'll aim to make it memorable."

"For Colby's sake, I hope you succeed." Todd brushed his hand along her shoulder but didn't let it linger. Still, Colby noticed Alec's gaze home in on Todd's gesture.

"Todd is on his way out, so we'll leave you to whatever it is you rushed out here to do." Colby nodded and led Todd away from Alec, who stood there blinking.

As they approached the door, Todd said, "Think about dinner, okay? Anytime, anyplace. I'll even do Thai."

"You hate Thai."

"But you like it." He grasped her hand and squeezed it. "At the very least, we'd have a pleasant night out, Colby. How long has it been since you've had one of those?"

Very recently. With Alec. The night she'd been bracing for a fight but instead had been treated to a delicious meal. Not that she, his boss, should entertain thoughts in his direction. His family would never look at her without thinking of Joe's death. Most important, she shouldn't invite another man into her personal life who could change so suddenly and violently, no matter how oddly mesmerizing he looked when brimming with emotion.

If she were to date again, she'd have to choose someone with less baggage. Was that so much to ask? "Let me think about it."

Deep down she knew a fresh start meant more than a new career. It meant taking chances again. Calculated chances. Todd might not rock her world, but he wouldn't blow it up, either. They were true friends with similar interests, and that was as good of a foundation as any for a relationship.

She waved goodbye and then turned to find Alec still standing in the dining room, staring at her. "What's wrong?"

"Nothing." His quiet tone drew her in. It was as if he'd bottled up all that vitality with a heavy-duty cork. Unnerving, really, the way he could turn it off and on so fast.

"If nothing's wrong, why'd you blow back out here looking like you wanted to kill someone?"

"It's nothing I can't handle."

"Then why are you looking at me with that tight face?" What kinds of screwed-up moods were coursing through him, and when had this become part of his personality? Mark's illness hadn't surfaced until his midtwenties. Had Alec also changed dramatically after college, and she'd just never been around him enough to notice?

"Now?" He didn't blink. "I suppose I'm just surprised."

"By what?" She stood, rooted to the ground, wondering why he looked almost dejected.

"By the fact you'd go out with *him*." His jaw ticked before his gaze skittered away from hers.

What did that mean, and why did it feel like the temperature in the room increased by ten degrees? "Why does that surprise you?"

"Because he's nothing like Mark," he replied without any hesitation.

Exactly, she thought, and then swallowed the lump of guilt in her throat from years spent living in the gray area between truth and lies. She stepped closer to Alec—the invisible energy from his body gripping her like a magnetic pull.

"You never liked Mark. And, anyway, just the other night you told me to get back out there." Her pulse drummed rapidly thanks to this uncomfortable conversation. Did she care what Alec thought, or whether the idea of Todd and her bothered him? "Has something changed?"

Alec rubbed the back of his neck before shoving his hands in his pockets. "No. I want you to be happy."

As if love secured happiness. Not in her experience—nor her mom's, for that matter. Maybe Gentry had a point about love and marriage, after all.

In any case, she detected melancholy in Alec's voice, although she didn't doubt his sincerity. Her thoughts skipped back to the puzzle on his coffee table. She pictured him sitting alone night after night, working on that instead of being with people. She'd always assumed he'd preferred his solitude, but now she wondered. Could he, like her, be using it as a shield against disappointment and hurt? Had his experiences, like hers, made him wary?

Is that why he bullied the staff?

"I think we should end each day with a staff meeting where we offer some kind of positive feedback." She braced for his reaction.

"What?" He was looking at her as if her skin had changed color.

"You heard me, Alec."

"You're serious?"

"Deadly. Maybe if you're forced to acknowledge the things that are going well every day, you won't be so quick to blow your top."

"Why on earth would I pander to my staff, especially with so little time until the opening?"

"You just said you wanted me to be happy. This will make me happy."

He stared at her, his jaw clenching as time stretched between them. "Fine."

Before she spoke again, he wandered toward the kitchen.

"Alec?"

"We've both got a lot of work to do." This time *he* forced a smile. "Let's stay focused on that for now."

He held her gaze intently for another moment and then disappeared behind the kitchen doors, leaving her in the middle of the dining room. She spun toward her office, straightening her skirt before returning to her desk.

Resting her fingers on the pulse at the base of her neck, she willed her thoughts and heart to settle. The restaurant—not a man—would be her salvation. She knew this to be true. Yet Alec's soulful gaze tempted her beyond reason.

◆ ◆ ◆

"Whoa, that's a big pour!" Colby held up her hand to her sister-in-law, Sara, with whom she'd immediately bonded the first time Hunter had brought her home from college to meet the family.

"Don't worry, I'm having more, too." Sara poured herself an equally large glass of sauvignon blanc. She'd been drinking all through dinner, which meant she still hadn't gotten pregnant. Twenty-seven months in a row with no luck and one failed round of IVF. No wonder she wanted more booze.

Colby had stopped asking about their pregnancy status back in April. Now all she could do was pray for her brother and sister-in-law. Parenting required a kind of bravery Colby didn't yet have, but she'd love a niece or nephew.

"Besides," Sara continued, her startlingly sky-blue eyes filled with mischief, "you need it. You've been jumpy tonight, and it's *not* because Hunter called you here to sign those new partnership documents."

"I'm not jumpy." Colby sipped the chilled wine, aware that she had, in fact, been jumpy, especially when forced to watch Gentry's coquettish behavior toward Alec. Trust Sara's uncanny ability to sniff out sexual tension like a foraging bear. Colby had admitted her ill-advised attraction to herself, but she could resist it in favor of smart choices. If only Hunter hadn't invited those two to dinner. "But I *am* a little anxious. Taking on all that risk just to avoid answering to Hunter is a big leap," she teased.

"I don't blame you," Sara commiserated. "He can be a dictator."

"One you adore." Colby envied her brother's solid marriage. If she could be guaranteed their kind of steady love and respect, maybe she'd risk another try.

"Most of the time, anyway." Sara quickly unwound and readjusted the loose knot of sandy-blonde hair piled on top of her head. Her generous, wide mouth turned upward in a knowing smile. That Julia Roberts smile might be Sara's best feature. "But you don't fool me. Alec has you worked up."

Sara grinned like she'd just thrown a bull's-eye, but Colby refused to cop to that suspicion. "Don't be ridiculous."

"Oh, come on. In all the years I've known you both, I've never seen you so *aware* of him before." Sara backhanded Colby's arm. "Don't worry, they can't hear us from the patio while Gentry's yakking."

Colby didn't need that reminder. Gentry, in her skimpy, cleavage-bearing black romper and high-heeled sandals. As if her laughing, devil-may-care sister needed any help making herself more appealing than other mere mortals.

Oh, dammit. Colby would *not* allow herself to feel jealous of her sister. Or possessive of Alec. She must be unhinged, because nothing else explained why she didn't run in the opposite direction after witnessing his Jekyll and Hyde transformations several times this past week.

"I'm not aware of him, for Pete's sake." Of course, she *was* aware that he'd brought her mom some chocolate éclairs two nights ago, and Colby hadn't even encouraged that visit. Moreover, he'd stayed and chatted for a half hour, which had thrilled her mom. How could Colby *not* be grateful? She'd also caught him consoling Margo, the entremetier, after she'd had an argument with her husband. Glimpses of Alec's finer points let her gloss over his bad behavior, until she reminded herself of where that kind of thinking had gotten her in the past. "Dinner was great, but you're brave to cook for Alec."

"I've cooked for him dozens of times. He doesn't scare me." Sara's expression grew pensive. "In fact, I feel sorry for him. He's still grieving, even if he won't talk about it with me or Hunter."

"Considering the fact that he and Joe weren't that close as adults, I'm surprised it's hit him *so* hard for this long."

Alec had turned the other cheek against Joe's snarky remarks for years. She'd admired his maturity and assumed Joe would grow up and stop after high school. Then Alec was in Europe, and when he returned, he was so busy with his restaurant she barely saw him. At that point, she'd written most of Joe's sarcasm off as jealousy, because no one could dispute Alec's success.

"That's probably exactly why it's so hard." Sara's gaze turned distant as she smoothed her hand along the farm table she and Hunter had purchased at some antique shop a few years ago. "He'll never get the chance to resolve anything with Joe."

Colby knew how that kind of remorse poisoned the soul. If Mark hadn't known that she'd been considering leaving him, maybe he wouldn't have completely given up on life. That particular "what if" always formed a thick lump in her throat.

She'd never know the answer, and she'd never be able to make it right. Her inadvertent role in his suicide taught her that she could never predict the ripple effect of *any* choice, which made *every* choice seem more dangerous.

Another thing she now knew—something had hardened Alec. Part of her wanted to know what that was, but another part dreaded the truth. Past experiences had etched her consciousness with fear. Fear of never trusting whether the next man she might love would also be someone so different from whom she believed him to be. Fear of making another mistake and living another lie.

"Alec's changed," Colby blurted.

"You make it sound ominous. He's still Alec, just a little sadder."

Clearly Sara had never heard him working in the kitchen.

"There's an edge to him now. An instability." Surely Sara and Hunter had noticed.

"No one is more stable than Alec. He just needs to find his footing again and move forward." Sara glanced at Colby's left hand, which Colby then withdrew from the table. "Come to think of it, you two could help each other. You're both a little stuck."

"I'm getting unstuck, thank you very much." Colby gulped her wine and eyed the bottle to make sure there'd be more. She'd need it if Sara planned to keep needling her about Alec.

"With work, maybe. But don't you get lonely?"

"I don't really think about it." She wouldn't confess that the thought of dating was more terrifying than being caught naked in a crowd.

Because Mark and Colby had avoided family and friends whenever he'd swing to either extreme, Sara and Hunter had little idea of her marital ups and downs. Or of how difficult it had been to keep his secrets, even when she'd understood his concern. Mark hadn't feared much, but that stigma had scared the shit out of him. He'd been convinced it would hurt his career opportunities by making his boss and peers doubt and fear him. And he'd already been somewhat of an outsider in her family, so she hadn't wanted to widen that gap.

"I'm not suggesting you can ever replace Mark." Sara squeezed Colby's hand, apparently sensing her surge of sadness. "But you should consider your future and the family you may want."

"Not everyone's like you, Sara. Maybe some of us aren't meant to be wives and mothers." *I failed miserably.*

Sara frowned. "Maybe not, but *you* are."

"She is what?" Gentry asked, having waltzed into the kitchen carrying some dirty dishes, which she set in the sink.

"Meant to fall in love again and have a family." Sara smiled.

Gentry rolled those green eyes. "Why get married when you can date around?"

"You're only twenty-five. We'll see how you feel in another five years." Sara laughed. "Or if you meet Mr. Right."

"Mr. Right Now is just fine with me." Gentry grabbed the bottle of wine and poured herself a fresh glass. "Not that you'd understand that. Jeez, you picked Hunter. Who could be more predictable than him? Clearly you and I don't want the same things."

Her tone had been light, but Colby noted a defensive sparkle in Sara's eyes.

"We should be so lucky as Hunter and Sara." Colby raised her glass like a toast. "They're perfectly matched."

Sara's gaze wandered away for a moment. Before Colby could ask why, Sara said, "Let's go back outside with the guys."

"Actually, I'm going to grab my laptop from my car to show Colby the photos I took for the website. Hunter will probably want to see, too, even if he no longer gets a vote." She flashed an impish grin and dashed outside.

"She's so frank." Sara wrinkled her nose. "One of these days her lack of discretion will be her undoing."

"I know she drives Hunter crazy." Colby sighed. Her type A brother couldn't comprehend Gentry's laissez-faire attitude, or the way Dad and Jenna pampered her. Neither could Colby, but it didn't irk her the way it got under Hunter's skin.

"Only because your dad tolerates so much from Gentry that he never let you and your brother get away with." Sara pressed her index finger to her lips, ending the conversation just before they passed through the French doors to the slate patio.

Hunter's Craftsman-style house, which clung to a wooded hillside, had a partial view of Lake Sandy. A vigorous fire burned in the copper fire pit, infusing the night air with heat and a smoky aroma. Summer evenings like this were the stuff of movies, not real life.

Colby slid onto one of the empty Adirondack chairs. Given Sara's heightened observations, she made herself look at Alec and smile as if it were old times. Hopefully, the fact that she'd pressed her hand against her stomach to settle its cartwheels went unnoticed.

Gentry returned with her laptop and her camera bag. "Come see."

Despite Gentry's pretense of indifference, a spark of pride lit her eyes. *Ah, good.* Colby might've failed to save Mark, but she wouldn't fail her sister. No more taking tomorrows for granted when it came to her family.

Gentry flipped open the laptop and began scrolling through her photos. She'd taken some artistic shots of the interior: wood and glass, tables and chairs, the modern chandeliers, and some of Alec's dishes. The exterior shots were a bit more generic but did the job, showing the garden beds, gazebo, and lake views.

"These are wonderful." Colby patted Gentry's back.

"What's missing are photos of you and Alec. I think we need those for the 'About Us' page. Let's do that now, before the sun sets." Gentry reached for Alec's hand. "You first, handsome."

Sara's eyes bugged with surprise. Hunter scowled, and Alec froze in the face of the bald flirtation. Then his lips quirked and he rose. "Lead the way."

Gentry led Alec to the corner of the patio and positioned him to take advantage of the soft evening light. Colby's focus on whatever Hunter and Sara were discussing faltered because she was eavesdropping on Gentry and Alec. Epic fail there. Only Gentry's playful laughter pierced the melodic murmur of Alec's deep voice.

"Colby, your turn," Gentry finally called. Before Alec could escape, she grabbed his arm. "Actually, let's get some with you two together."

Colby glanced at Alec. The setting sun glinted in his eyes, making the gold in his olive-colored irises sparkle. He shrugged before stuffing his hands into his pants pockets. Those gray pants that fit him so well, their flat front calling attention to his trim waist and narrow hips.

Horrified by her observation, she yanked her gaze back up to his face only to catch him cocking one brow. *Shoot.* Busted like a kid with a mouthful of cookies.

Her entire body flushed, but she managed to walk toward him and Gentry with confidence. She stood beside Alec and smiled for the camera, hoping her photos didn't turn out like those awful middle school ones where she'd tried to hide her braces.

"Side by side doesn't look right. Stand in front of Alec, like a prom picture," Gentry ordered.

In her peripheral vision, Colby noticed Sara watching them with her head tipped, her wineglass at her lips.

Colby stepped in front of Alec. She could feel the heat of his body in the space between them. That, plus the faint bergamot scent of his cologne, made her dizzy. The hairs on her neck and arms prickled with awareness when his breath brushed softly against her hair. Had he just touched her waist, or was that wishful thinking? Honestly, this mad infatuation couldn't continue. *Hyde. Hyde. Hyde,* she reminded herself, determined not to make another impulsive mistake like she had with Mark.

Gentry shot Colby an annoyed look. "It would help if you'd smile instead of giving me that deer-in-the-headlights look."

"Sorry," Colby mumbled, wishing she could rein in her thoughts. She noted Sara smothering a giggle.

"Should I tell a joke?" Alec was clearly fishing for a way to break the tension.

"She asked me to smile. If I recall, your jokes were never very funny." Colby remembered his childish jokes, and how he'd often ended them with a silly "bah dum bum."

"Did you know that atheism is a non-*prophet* organization?" He paused. "Bah dum—"

"Stop it." Colby elbowed his ribs, grinning.

"You're smiling now, though, right?" he murmured.

She was indeed.

"You two look good together." Gentry snapped several photos, then turned off her camera. "Maybe you ought to rethink that stupid rule, Colby."

Colby's heart stopped. Truly.

"What rule?" Sara asked.

"No *luuuv* between coworkers." Gentry winked at Alec. "Maybe *I* ought to rethink this job."

"Maybe," Alec joked, playing along with her flirtation. Or maybe he wasn't playing. Maybe he liked the attention. Colby felt a frown form.

"Good rule." Hunter nodded at Colby.

"Shocking that you agree with her." Gentry zipped up the camera case and then sank onto a chair. She crossed those long legs, letting the one with the Taurus ankle tattoo casually swing. "Sultry" would be the right word to describe Gentry's poses. No doubt most were done for effect, although this one might have been accidental. Colby buried a pathetic sigh, having never been sultry a day in her life.

"You never told me that," Alec announced, tipping his head to the left. His quizzical gaze effectively snapped Colby from her depressing self-assessment. "When did you decide it?"

"The second I told her I thought you looked hot." Gentry swallowed some wine, shameless as ever. Smiling, even.

Colby checked the ground for the pools of blood that she actually felt draining from her body. My God, her sister had no boundaries. She risked a glance at Alec, who sported the same expression she'd seen him wearing whenever embroiled in solving a difficult puzzle.

"Okay, stop." Hunter waved his hand. "I know you love to shock people for attention, but let's not be ridiculous, Gentry. Besides, you're making Alec uncomfortable."

"Are you uncomfortable, Alec?" Gentry asked, lips playfully pursed.

Everything about her teased and provoked. It must be exciting to be a woman like that . . . to draw notice and attention like nectar does bees.

"Not really," he chuckled. Yes, he *was* enjoying Gentry's games.

Great. Another frown seized Colby's forehead.

"Don't panic, Hunter. Gentry lives on her phone, while Alec's is always missing or dead." Sara snorted. "They'll never be able to make plans."

"There are *other* ways to communicate." Alec wiggled his brows.

"Alec." Hunter shot his friend a warning look. It seemed he didn't like the idea of his friend flirting with his baby sister. *Good. An ally.*

"Oh, come on." Alec waved his hand. "We all know Gentry's joking."

Gentry shrugged. "Like I told Sara, I'm just out for some fun. And speaking of, I've got to roll. Jake asked me to hang with him tonight at the cart."

"Wait a sec." Hunter leaned forward. "You're going to spend the night standing on a city street corner?"

"We'll be in front of the Tunnel."

"I didn't know that club was still open," Sara remarked.

"It is. Jake's hoping to do great business once everyone pours out of its doors looking for a late-night snack. He says I'll help attract the guys, so he's going to give me a share of the night's take."

"Just what I wanted to hear. My sister being pimped out in the city by her boyfriend for money." Hunter shook his head. "You'd better not let Dad find out."

"God forbid people find out his daughter sold hot dogs. We wouldn't want his pride to take a hit." Gentry's bubbly demeanor had swiftly shifted to irritation.

"Just be safe," Colby pleaded.

Gentry turned, apparently surprised by the sincerity. "I will."

Alec watched Colby and Gentry, wishing he could have overheard the conversation that triggered Colby's workplace ban on relationships.

"Catch you later." Gentry gathered her things and left, her barely there outfit lifting in the breeze with each step she took.

Alec liked that Colby always wore tasteful but feminine skirts that didn't risk a crotch shot, and dresses that didn't reveal her bra straps. Her sophistication made her stand out compared with the Gentrys of the world.

Gentry was a handful. He wasn't interested in a handful. He wanted compassionate. Calm. Steady. Smart. He wanted Colby. Her new rule was just one more thing on the list of reasons why he could never have her, and that just sucked.

Alec stared at the fire, only half-aware of the conversation going on around him. His thoughts jumped and crackled like the mesmerizing flames. He shouldn't allow schoolboy yearnings to distract him from his priorities. A CertainTea's soft opening had to be as perfect as possible in such a short time frame. His dad might be ignorant enough to write off one James Beard Award as a fluke. But if Alec could make A CertainTea earn one, too, perhaps his father would finally look at him like he'd always looked at Joe—with pride.

"Alec?" Sara asked.

"Hmm?" *Dammit.* He had no idea what she'd asked.

"Where'd you go?" Hunter asked.

"Nowhere important." He swigged his beer, but not before he caught Colby staring at him as if she didn't believe him. As if she cared. Of course, she cast her gaze the other way when she realized he'd noticed her watching him. Ever since she'd caught him scolding the staff, she'd acted funny around him. To say he found that shocking would be an understatement. As far as he knew, she'd never shied away from assertive men before.

"Colby, your workplace rule is genius," Hunter said. "Not only because Gentry could cause all kinds of trouble, but remember Colette, Alec? That didn't work out so well for you in Mougins."

"Stop." Alec waved him off to shut him up, but not before his thoughts veered to Colette, the sexy brunette with the fullest lips he'd ever seen.

"That's some grin." Colby cocked a brow.

"She was some girl!" Hunter joked. "And that was some visit."

"I didn't get the appeal." Sara shrugged. "I mean, she was attractive but kind of bitchy. Anti-American, which didn't make much sense given that she seemed so into you."

"She admired my *potentiel incroyable*." Alec winked. Of course, at twenty-six, broke, and not often the object of a hot woman's attention, he couldn't have cared less about her bitchy personality. She had worked his hours and pulled him away for quickies on their breaks whenever possible.

"I remember seeing Sara's photos from that trip. Colette looked . . . confident," Colby ventured. "So what happened?"

"I came home."

"No, I mean, what's Hunter referring to that made the trip, and her, so memorable?" She stared at him, waiting.

Oh, that. "I was first commis to the poissonnier, whom she also flirted with. When he found us together, he made my life even more of a living hell for months." He nodded toward Hunter and Sara. "These two were there when he caught Colette and me getting *friendly*."

"Exactly why you shouldn't shit where you eat." Hunter swigged his beer and fended off a light punch from Sara.

"Hunter, that's gross." She frowned.

"Sorry, babe." Hunter leaned over and kissed his wife with the kind of carefree intimacy Alec had never really known. "So, how's it going with the restaurant?"

"Busy," Colby said. "Actually, I've been doing some reading on restaurant promos to generate ideas to support a strong opening. I'm thinking about trying a 'Hump Day Happy Hour' on Wednesdays to draw customers."

Alec coughed up his drink. "A CertainTea isn't Hooters."

Her cheeks colored. "We have a beautiful bar. Why not use it to our advantage?"

"The *food* will draw people in." Alec rubbed his hand over his chest to loosen the band of stress constricting his lungs. *Hump Day Happy Hour?*

"People like to be social, Alec, especially over cheap drinks."

Alec leaned forward, hoping his voice sounded calmer than he felt. "I choke out praise to the staff every day for your sake, but listen to me on this. 'Hump Day Happy Hour' is *not* the tone to set. If you insist on using alcohol to create interest, at least go upscale and do wine pairings."

"I agree with Alec," Hunter interjected.

Thank God!

"Shocking." Colby rolled her eyes at her brother. "Luckily, I just signed those papers tonight, so you don't get a vote."

"Not officially, but I hope you still consider my opinion." Hunter cocked a brow in challenge.

Alec didn't want Colby to assert herself on this issue just to prove she didn't have to answer to the men in her life.

"Colby, you won't need gimmicks at A CertainTea." He kept his voice calm despite the panic rising as he imagined loudmouths at the bar while *his* customers were trying to enjoy Kingfish–Osetra Caviar Tartare with Smoked Crème Fraîche Emulsion. "Please, save the happy-hour plan as a fallback if the restaurant falters, which it won't."

Everyone was quiet for a moment while Colby stared at a spot in the distance.

"I should head home." Colby stood suddenly and straightened her dress.

Hunter rose to give her a quick hug. "Don't be mad. We're only trying to be helpful."

"I know," she conceded and then hugged Sara goodbye. "Dinner was delicious, thanks."

"I'll go, too." Alec bolted from his chair without knowing exactly why, or what, he hoped to gain by following Colby to her car. He only knew he had to do it.

"Oh?" Sara's brows rose.

"You two will enjoy the rest of your night better without a third wheel." Alec gave her a quick peck on the cheek.

"You got that right." Hunter grinned, tugging Sara against his side.

A flood of envy rippled through Alec. He'd had women—even hot ones like Colette—but he'd never experienced love. Except for the unrequited kind, he thought dimly. "Good night."

He and Colby silently strolled through the house and to the driveway until they reached her car. As much as he had to convince her to drop this happy-hour nonsense, he was just as interested in what prompted that no-dating rule.

"I don't like being lectured about what to do in *my* restaurant, Alec." She sounded tired.

"I'm sorry, but I'm passionate about this." He'd promised his goals wouldn't conflict with hers, but this was too important. "You told me you want your customers to relax and be happy. How relaxed and happy will they be with a buzzed, disruptive crowd guzzling cheap drinks at the bar?"

"How *limiting* is it if the only people who come are foodie snobs?"

She had it all wrong, but he didn't say that. "Restaurateurs generally like people who appreciate quality food. And locally sourced, organic, artisanal cuisine is hot now."

"I agreed to let you handle the menu, but A CertainTea isn't Une Bouchée 2.0."

"Why not mimic a place that won Best New Restaurant the year I opened it?" *My God, did that even need to be asked?*

"It was excellent, but it isn't what I'd planned. I want A CertainTea to have broad appeal and be a venue for parties and weddings and whatnot for *ordinary* people. Believe it or not, ordinary people like me don't give a fig about amuse-bouches."

Alec's focus snagged on the sexy pout her lips formed when pronouncing the "sh" end sound of "bouches," so it took him an extra second to reply. "If your primary goal was to be involved in planning parties, then maybe you should've started an event-planning service instead of a restaurant."

She glared at him, making him regret that last quip. Now she might institute the happy hours out of spite.

"Have a good night, Alec." Colby fished her keys out of her purse.

He'd already stepped in it, so he might as well ask the other question that had been bugging him for the past twenty minutes. "Did you make that no-dating rule because you don't think I'm good enough for Gentry?"

Her eyes widened. "Of course not."

"Honestly?"

"I promise." She hugged her purse. "Why would you think that?"

"I know your whole family thinks Gentry needs some direction, so I would've thought her interest in me would be welcomed, given that I'm older and certainly more stable than her current boyfriend."

Colby nibbled at the corner of her lower lip. "Are you interested in Gentry?"

"No." *Only you.* It seemed impossible that she couldn't feel the depth of his longing.

She huffed. "Then why are we even talking about this?"

"Because I get the feeling you don't trust me anymore. With few exceptions, you're edgy around me lately."

She sighed. "I think we both know why."

"I don't."

"Well . . ." Her voice trailed off before she finished her thought.

"Well, what?" His demand made her flinch. Carefree Colby no longer existed. Now all she did was jump and recoil, or lash out defensively. All changes caused by her witnessing Mark's suicide. If possible, he loathed himself even more for the way he dismissed Mark's note. Two men dead, one woman splintered, all unwittingly because of him.

"Your temper . . . it's not like the friend I remember. You were never so ruthless." She looked at him now, her luminescent eyes seeking reassurance that the old Alec still existed.

That stopped him. He *was* harder. And given his secrets, he couldn't reassure her. She *shouldn't* trust him. Why the hell was he pressuring her when he couldn't be honest? Did he *want* to lose his job? His one path to some kind of redemption?

"You're right. I have changed, and you should keep your distance." He turned before she could grab hold of his arm. Without glancing back, he waved over his shoulder. "Drive safely."

Chapter Seven

"Welcome to A CertainTea." Colby shook hands with Melissa Westcott, an ambitious young reporter from Portland's largest newspaper to whom Gentry had reached out as part of her PR strategy. "I'm thrilled you're writing a feature piece on us."

"Alec Morgan's return to the Portland restaurant scene is exciting news in the 'Lifestyles' space." After introducing Colby to the photographer, Phillip, Melissa scanned the room with an alert gaze. She looked to be slightly older than Gentry. Although not as striking as Colby's sister, Melissa shared a similar cavalier air and disregard for punctuality. The arrogance of people who valued their own time more than that of others annoyed Colby. "Is Chef Morgan here?"

Alec's claim that the executive chef gets all the credit or blame was proving to be true. Not that *that* fact justified his periodic outbursts, which seemed to have increased since she mentioned her happy-hour idea the other night. If Ms. Westcott interviewed the staff, Lord knew what they might reveal.

"He's in the kitchen at the moment." For days now, Colby had mulled over his recent warning about keeping her distance. Naturally, it had only made her *more* curious. Her weakening resolve would frighten her if she had spare time to think about it. "Should we get started first and then call him in?"

"I'd prefer you to be together." Melissa smiled and then mumbled something to the cameraman about taking some photos of the venue.

Colby could either bemoan the fact that, as usual, her desires ranked beneath everyone else's agenda or exploit the reporter's enthusiasm for Alec's local celebrity. Intellect was always better—and less dicey—than emotion.

"Let me grab him." Colby excused herself and scurried to the kitchen, where she found Alec criticizing one of the line chefs. Now wasn't the time to address the untenable friction that had become commonplace in the kitchen. Privately, she conceded that the daily staff pep talks might actually be making things more awkward, not less. "Alec, the reporter is here."

He swiveled, his mossy eyes darkened by impatience. "Good."

After dictating a few orders to his sous chef, he crossed to her. While they walked toward the door, Colby muttered, "Please wipe the scowl off your face and smile."

"I'm not scowling." His scowl intensified.

"You are!" She waited for his expression to change.

"Colby, I'm not an idiot. This is my first opportunity to publicly announce my return, so I'm not going to scowl at the reporter." Alec fixed the most ingratiating smile on his face and gestured toward the door.

His ability to shift from one emotion to another unnerved her, but she opened the door and crossed the dining room beside him.

He held out his hand to the reporter. "I'm Alec Morgan."

"Alec, I'm Melissa Westcott." When Melissa smiled, Colby noted the way she licked her lips. "I've been eager to speak with you both."

Both? Hardly. Melissa had barely spared Colby a glance.

"Thank you. We're equally eager to discuss the restaurant." Colby took a seat beside Alec, while Melissa sat across from him. Colby noticed that she'd unbuttoned her blouse a notch, although Alec didn't seem to be interested in Melissa's cleavage, even as the flirt leaned forward to set the phone down between them.

"Gentry briefly mentioned some of the history between your two families." Melissa looked innocent, but Colby sensed danger the way a dog could sense an oncoming storm.

Only someone as boundaryless as Gentry would arm this stranger with personal details. When Alec stiffened beside Colby, she recalled Sara's remarks from the other night about his grieving, and her nurture reflex kicked in.

"History has nothing to do with our plans for A CertainTea." Colby smiled, steering Melissa away from the topic of the tragedies and Une Bouchée so the woman couldn't poke at Alec's wounds. "We prefer to look forward rather than rehash the past."

"Doesn't everybody?" Melissa chuckled. "But this history gives an intensely personal angle to the piece, which makes it more engaging. So, Alec, you were the executive chef and owner of the former Une Bouchée."

"Yes." Alec's controlled tone surprised Colby, although his smile had thinned. "Did you dine there?"

"Never that lucky, but I'm aware it earned the James Beard Award for Best New Restaurant."

"It did." Alec's face remained impressively impassive.

"I understand that around the same time, your brother fell victim to the lure of cliff jumping at Punch Bowl Falls." Melissa's blunt delivery stunned Colby into silence. She watched Melissa study Alec to gauge his reaction.

He offered almost none. Only the slightest clench of his jaw signaled any discomfort. When no one spoke, he casually asked, "Is there a question?"

Colby wanted to slap him a high-five, but she kept a leash on her emotions. She needed this promotional opportunity, but she detested selling out to such a heartless witch.

Melissa intertwined her fingers. "Care to elaborate on how that accident played into the closing of your former restaurant?"

"Not particularly," he said.

"I'm offering you a chance to explain what happened, and tell us why this new venture won't fail." Melissa tapped her pen on the table. "This is a golden opportunity to invite your fans back."

"My former patrons' foremost interest would be getting a sneak peek at the menu." He smiled, but his shoulders remained rigid. "My brother's death isn't relevant to our plans."

"On the contrary." Melissa feigned compassion. "Readers will be hooked by your journey. Without that, this is just another new restaurant in town. So, please, tell me something about why you left and what brought you back. And why choose this suburban venue rather than something in the city?"

Alec's gaze wandered up over Melissa's shoulder. Colby sensed he might explode or bolt from his chair, so she surreptitiously clasped his hand, which he'd balled up on his thigh. She heard his breath catch, but then his fingers relaxed enough to close around hers. His hands—scarred from knives and burns—made Alec's touch another newly callused thing about him.

"Melissa, let me answer that," Colby interjected, trying not to wince from Alec's tight grip. "As Gentry must've mentioned, Alec and I were childhood friends. When he returned to town, it seemed a natural fit to have him help me get this place off the ground."

Melissa speared Alec with another stare but then shifted her attention to Colby. "Okay, let's talk about you and your well-known family. You used to be a lawyer, and your family is in the tea business. What made you decide to open a restaurant?"

"I needed a change. Lawyering can be exhausting—always solving other people's problems. I wanted to bring a little joy into the world. I envision this beautiful location as the site for many happy memories for families celebrating all kinds of accomplishments and milestones." Colby noticed Alec's grip loosening.

She could've eased her hand away, but she didn't. Initially she'd reached out to comfort him. Now his touch soothed her, producing a pleasant hum in her chest. That should worry her, but at the moment, it didn't.

"That's sweet. Of course, you, too, suffered a loss not long after Alec. My sympathies." Melissa briefly bowed her head in a phony show of empathy. "Did your husband's suicide play a role in your career change?"

Melissa's question had struck like a pickax. The broken, bloody image of Mark's body on the sidewalk surfaced, making Colby's mouth turn pasty. Every light bulb in the restaurant buzzed in her ears as she fought to suppress the image.

"I'm sorry." Melissa's expression, however, didn't look the least bit sorry. "I should've been more tactful."

If there had been flatware on the table, Colby might've picked up a spoon and hurled it at the woman's head.

Alec's thumb stroked the top of her hand as he leaned forward. "Melissa, I'll discuss Une Bouchée if you agree not to mention Mark in the article."

"Alec—" His parents would hate reading about Joe, but Alec cut off Colby's response with a quick hand squeeze. He intended to rescue her, and he'd never looked more attractive to her than he did then.

"Fine. And again, I apologize for my blunt delivery." Melissa's lame apology would be filed in Colby's "too little, too late" drawer. "So, Alec, tell me about what happened at Une Bouchée and how you ended up here."

Alec glanced down, steadying himself with a deep inhalation. "Prior to my brother's accident, our relationship had become . . . contentious. I'd assumed we'd eventually clear the air, but when he died, so did that opportunity. The wasted time and petty arguments gnawed at and distracted me. Made me question my priorities. On top of that, I was dealing with my parents' grief. That all drained my creativity."

Colby watched Alec, wondering how forthcoming he'd be, and if she might learn the truth behind Mark's accusation that day at Joe's funeral.

Alec tapped a few fingers on the tabletop. "Anyone who's worked in a kitchen—long hours, dangerous work, a need for precision—knows that there's no room for distraction. My preoccupation cost me my restaurant and reputation. I left town to escape the memories, but returned for my parents. Fortunately, Colby's giving me a chance to redeem myself by helping her build a first-class establishment."

He'd woven a believable tale, but Colby suspected he'd kept something to himself. Like her, he had no one he trusted enough to unburden his guilty conscience. What if they could learn to trust each other? The wish flared like a twinkling firework and then turned to smoke just as quickly.

"You must be very grateful for Alec, considering your lack of experience." Melissa turned her attention back to Colby. "What convinced you that you could make this major career jump?"

Colby cleared her throat, swallowing a confession of sheer desperation.

Alec interjected, "Colby's a sharp, savvy, successful woman. She's certainly smart enough to run a restaurant. I've no doubt that, with or without me, she'd make this place a success."

"Thank you," Colby managed. Given the numerous disagreements they'd been having about the restaurant, she knew he'd exaggerated his opinion, but she wanted to kiss him for it, anyway. *That* thought did nothing to ease the tension that had tightened all the muscles in her shoulders and back.

Melissa tipped her head and gestured between them. "You two seem close. Any relevant *personal* history here?"

"Just friends since childhood." Colby smiled as if their hands weren't still clasped together beneath the table.

"But never a couple?" Melissa's expression revealed her personal interest in the answer.

"No," Alec replied, his hand releasing Colby's. The loss of warmth traveled all the way to her heart.

"No crush on your older brother's friend?" Melissa teased Colby.

Colby tensed because she could neither deny nor entertain the idea.

"How about we finally discuss the menu?" Alec suggested.

While he and Melissa discussed food, Colby's thoughts strayed. Alec confused her. One minute a dictator, trouncing people in the kitchen, the next a gentleman and friend. Yet always holding something back. Exactly the kind of dissembling she knew she should avoid. Yet here she was again, finding herself drawn to someone complicated and passionate. The same words she'd called Mark in the beginning, before the depths of his troubles were known.

"Sounds divine. Women must line up for a dinner invitation from you." Melissa's flirtatious tone irked Colby. "Let's get Phillip to snap a few pictures of you two, and then we'll be on our way."

Like the other night when Gentry had been snapping pictures, this photographer arranged Colby and Alec in a series of poses that had their bodies brush against each other. Colby's skin flushed from Alec's touch. Under other circumstances, it might've been enjoyable. But today her thoughts ran in circles—Joe, Alec, Mark—right until the moment Melissa and Phillip walked out the door.

Breathing out the anxiety she'd pent up during the interview, Colby barely made eye contact with Alec. "Thank you for making time for that. We should both get back to work."

Without looking at him, she went to her office and closed the door. She'd barely escaped having Mark's and her history end up in the paper for everyone to judge. Laying her hands on the desktop, she leaned forward and drew deep breaths, determined not to open her drawer and pop a pill. Determined to be stronger.

Stronger—ha! Instead of coming across as the eager new proprietor of the Portland area's newest restaurant, Colby had frozen at the mention of Mark, proving she still hadn't put to rest the history that now buckled her knees.

"Colby." Alec rested a hand on her shoulder.

She hadn't heard him come in. Squeezing her eyes closed, she kept her back to him.

"Are you okay?"

"Of course." Colby blinked back her tears before facing him. "I'm sorry you had to talk about Joe because I shut down. But thank you for keeping Mark out of the article."

A tremor whipped through her, which Alec subdued with a hug. "Don't apologize. You did nothing wrong."

"I did nothing right, either." She allowed herself to relax in his embrace. At another time in her life it might've led to something else. That thought led to a shameful confession. "I'm sick of feeling weak and confused . . . and lost. I'm afraid, Alec. What if this sorry version of myself is the best I can be now?"

He squeezed her, his voice thick with feeling. "There's nothing sorry about *any* version of you. You're resilient and generous and kind. Someday you'll be able to look back without being overwhelmed. Until then, lean on me. I'll start by making you laugh a little every day."

"That's not your job." She sniffled against his shirt, listening to the soothing rhythm of his steady heartbeat. An unbidden memory surfaced of another time when she'd been crying and he'd comforted her. He'd kissed her, actually. Her first real kiss. The one she'd forced him to give her, back when she'd been bold and heedless of consequences. Too bad she wasn't that bold anymore.

Her grip slackened, so he eased away and studied her face—a favorite pastime. "You're flushed. Maybe you should sit."

"I'm fine." She looked embarrassed by the show of vulnerability. Yet this was how he liked her best—bravely facing life instead of hiding from it. "Let's just hope she doesn't write a hatchet job."

"That's the only reason I cooperated." Seeing Colby stricken by the mention of Mark's suicide had intensified his guilty conscience. Redemption would come only after he made this place a phenomenon and replaced that wary look on her face with her old smile.

"Let's talk about something else." Colby smoothed her hair and rounded her desk, putting distance between them. "Is the kitchen ready for the test run this weekend?"

"Almost, but we'll need every bit of the extra time after the soft opening to prep for the grand opening." He crossed his arms in front of his chest, a poor substitute for having her body pressed against it.

"Should I be worried?" Her delicate brows knit together.

"Still working on attitudes about consistency and perfection." He tempered his concerns because he didn't want to give her a reason to revisit his aggressive menu and last-minute changes.

Quietly, she said, "Maybe attitudes would improve if you were less tyrannical."

This again? He refused to discuss it. The problem was that the daily coddling she'd forced was undermining his authority and making the staff feel like they were performing better than they were. That just increased his stress.

Eventually she accepted his silence and moved on to the next topic. "I'm working on the seating. I've stuck Hunter with my mom, which won't thrill him but is better than seating him with Jenna. Also, I can't put my mom too close to Jenna and my dad." She looked up from the paper she'd been studying, wearing a serious expression. "I'm sorry *your* dad won't be coming. I know it's because of me."

"Even if you weren't involved, he probably wouldn't come. My career doesn't exactly make him proud." Alec shoved his hands in his pockets because he didn't know what else to do with them.

"You're a celebrated chef. How could he not be proud?"

He smiled at the perplexed look on her beautiful face. The depth of emotion in her voice might as well have been a kiss for how it ignited his heart.

"I'm not a cop like him and Joe, or a first responder, soldier, or pro athlete. Those are pretty much the only jobs he admires." Alec shrugged and then joked, "Maybe he'd have accepted me as a doctor or a billionaire tech geek."

"Well, I love that you followed your passion, come what may. That makes you very brave and committed." She smiled—a gentle, compassionate smile meant just for him. One he'd tuck away in his memory to revisit again.

"Thanks." He wished she were still snuggled against his chest. What if he tossed her papers off the desk, set her on top of it, and kissed her? The mere thought sent a potent shiver through him, so he gave himself a mental headshake. "Guess I'll get back to the kitchen."

"We have lots of work to help us forget about Melissa." A tired grin spread across her face.

Burying pain behind a mountain of work hadn't done the trick for him in the past, and he doubted it would help Colby now. She needed more than this restaurant if she wanted to rebuild a normal, happy life. He'd love to be the guy to get her to remove Mark's wedding band, but he couldn't without coming clean. Her earlier reaction to talking about Mark quieted the doubts he'd had about whether confessing might do more harm than good. Besides, he couldn't help her or his family if he got fired.

"You should go out with that lawyer." *Hell.* That'd come out without thinking it through.

"What?" She set down her pencil.

Alec gestured around the room. "This isn't enough, Colby. Not if you really want to reclaim your life. You need more than work."

She sat back, staring at him. "I could say the same to you—he who spends his nights in the company of puzzles."

He'd finished the recent one, actually. Not that she'd be impressed by that particular boast. "And you'd be right."

"Yet I don't see you dating."

Because I want you. "We're talking about you."

"*You're* talking about me. And I'm not interested. Even if I were, it wouldn't be with Todd. He's a good man, but we've been friends for too long. I doubt I could ever see him as more than that." She pressed her lips together and looked away.

Alec's heart slowed. In fact, his body suddenly seemed ten times heavier and wilting. Against all odds, somewhere in the back of his mind, he'd apparently clung to a childlike wish that someday, in some way, she might choose him.

But he'd been her friend even longer than Todd, so she'd likely also relegate him to that sexless zone. He should count himself lucky that he'd never be forced to tell her about Mark's letter. He didn't feel lucky, though. He felt deprived of the one thing that might eclipse a family reconciliation.

That must be why his next thought slipped past his lips. "Maybe a man who's been your friend for a long time is the perfect man for you."

He willed himself not to look away while she weighed her words in heavy silence. His heart pounded out each second until her reply.

In a voice as soft as a summer breeze, she uttered, "I don't know much, but I do know that there's no such thing as a perfect man."

Everything in him rebelled against the door she'd just closed. "That sounds almost like a challenge."

She hesitated, her eyes filling with questions he hoped she wouldn't ask. Apparently, she thought better of them, too, and simply ended the discussion by saying, "One I know I'd win."

Chapter Eight

"The hostess said you wanted to see me?" Alec stood in the door to her office looking formidable in his freshly pressed chef's coat. Shoulders back, spine arched, tautly strung like a crossbow. Faint circles beneath his eyes revealed the eighteen-hour workdays he'd been clocking all week in a feverish quest to make the soft opening perfect. "Doors open in less than an hour, so I don't have much time."

Colby had battled the butterflies of excited anticipation all afternoon. The renewed flutter in her stomach, however, had nothing to do with the soft opening and everything to do with the man in front of her. The bewildering man who'd reawakened feelings she'd rather lie dormant.

Earlier this week she'd said there was no such thing as a perfect man, and she still believed it. But Alec had worked tirelessly to help make her dream a reality, and that actually made him pretty close to perfect.

"Our hostess is named Becca, and I only need a minute of your time." She opened her desk drawer and withdrew the gift-wrapped package she hoped he'd appreciate.

Alec's chin jerked back. "What's that?"

Colby circled her desk and handed him the token gift. "Something to mark the occasion."

Her mouth watered when she caught a slight whiff of shallots and thyme. Edible Alec. If only he weren't so volatile and she so brittle. If he weren't her employee. Or the old *friend* whose family still blamed her for their son's death. In no universe did this risky attraction make sense. Yet it had blossomed steadily despite every attempt to weed it out.

"Thank you." Alec's fingertips turned white where they gripped the box. After staring at the gift as if it were an alien, he cleared his throat and teased, "This box looks too big to be a phone charger. Should I open it now?"

"Sure." She smiled, forcing aside her wistful musings.

Alec unwrapped the package with the same careful attention he gave the most intricate dish. His eyes widened when he saw the silver-framed photograph Gentry had taken of them at Hunter's the other week.

"I thought it might make your apartment feel more homey." As soon as the words left her mouth, she felt shy and presumptuous—as if she somehow represented home.

Alec's straight brows pinched together while he fingered the image. "I didn't get you anything."

"I didn't expect it, Alec. This idea just came to me when Gentry sent me all the photos." Colby shrugged.

"I love it." The corners of his eyes crinkled above his gentle grin. Then he surprised her by reaching for her. Colby's heart turned over, unsure of whether or not she wanted him to kiss her. It then sank when he pressed his lips to her forehead instead of her mouth. He lingered there a moment—a tender point of contact she savored—before backing up. "I'm sorry I'm not as thoughtful as you."

Sensing the need for a joke, she teased him, saying, "I set a high bar, so don't beat yourself up."

He chuckled. "Is it okay if I leave this in here until the end of the night?"

"Of course. Speaking of the night, how do you feel?"

"Eager." He lifted his chin, but the harsh lines of his face only proved him to be tense.

"Me, too, but you seem anxious."

"Determined." Any momentary softness he'd revealed had fled as he turned his thoughts back to business. "You need to pay attention to what people are eating, what they're pushing aside. Listen to what they say to each other, *not* what they say to you."

"Got it."

"I know your family and friends will be a distraction, but stay attuned to the rhythm of the room. Make sure the waitstaff is attentive to every detail. Otherwise, we'll be going into the grand opening with weak information."

"Yes, sergeant."

"It's important, Colby." He pinched the bridge of his nose. "This requires perfection from everyone, including you. It may only be a dress rehearsal, but it's still our first impression. Everyone who comes tonight will leave here and talk to their friends."

"I understand, but everyone coming tonight wants us to succeed. They'll be forgiving of little errors." Colby wished his emphasis on awards wouldn't eclipse his perspective.

"That doesn't mean we can slack off." The force of his voice caused her to step back. He must've noticed her reaction, because he attempted a joke. "This is where *you* could say something encouraging like 'Everything you make is perfect, Alec, so I don't expect any complaints.'"

"And inflate your oversize ego?" She poked his shoulder.

He captured her hand and squeezed gently before letting go. "I'd better get back to the kitchen."

"Yes, do that." She shooed him off before his nervous energy sapped her stamina.

He set the photo on her desk, momentarily lapsing back to being her friend instead of her chef. "I'll treasure this."

His expression then grew fiercely determined before he left her office. Silently, she sent up a prayer for the kitchen staff. Sitting against the edge of her desk, she then lifted the frame. She'd ended up with dozens of pictures of Alec throughout the years, in some combination with Mark, Joe, or Hunter.

She and Alec hadn't spent time alone since high school, although she'd been in his company with Hunter on occasion since he'd returned from France.

Now she wondered about him. What made him such a perfectionist? What did he want, aside from professional recognition? Mundane questions rattled around her head, too. What did he read? Did he have a favorite movie? Aside from Colette, had he ever been in love?

Not that answers to her questions would reveal more about him than his actions did.

Mark's emotions had come in tidal waves. Easy to spot, larger than life, chaotically crashing around him. Alec's were more like a geyser, hidden away with his secret thoughts beneath a deceptive surface until the boiling point caused them to surge upward. Different from Mark, yet equally disquieting. Enough so that she should resist temptation and ignore the whisper in her heart.

Setting the photo down, she straightened her skirt and went to the reception desk to speak with Becca about the seating chart.

Gentry breezed through the door with a man Colby assumed was Jake, the infamous "hot dog guy." An emerald-green off-the-shoulder minidress hugged Gentry's curves. Her spiky rhinestone shoes made her an even height with her date, whose faded blue jeans sagged on his hips. His collarless black shirt did little to upgrade his attire. He wore a leather-and-silver chain bracelet on one arm, a silver ring on the opposite hand, and a thick, small hoop earring in one ear.

Colby couldn't tell whether he'd forgotten to shower, or if this particular disheveled look was intentional. He definitely could use a shave. The black stubble was too long to be considered sexy, yet far too sparse to be a proper beard. Beneath it all, Colby acknowledged the appeal of his strong, sharp features and coal-black eyes.

"I sacrificed making a grand entrance to come early and help." Gentry smiled and kissed Colby's cheek. "This is Jake."

Colby shook Jake's hand. "Nice to meet you, Jake. Welcome to A CertainTea."

"Thanks." No "you, too" or other remark. His blank expression offered no hint of personality. Of course, an empty look probably came in handy at times. Maybe he'd give her a lesson. She'd about given up on the idea he'd say more when he added, "Tight digs."

When Gentry shot her a cockeyed look, it clicked. Jake's "dude 'tude" and appearance would piss off their dad.

"We're serving drinks in the bar until everyone has arrived," Colby said.

"Cool." Jake grabbed Gentry's hand to go, but she jerked free.

"Go ahead, I'll catch up."

He ambled over to the bar and ordered himself a beer.

"What do you think?" Gentry asked in a way that told Colby she expected pushback.

Only someone so young and pampered would waste time on games. Games Colby had no interest in playing. Her gaze slid over to Jake, whose raven locks glinted underneath the lights at the bar. Poor guy had no idea her sister might be using him to send a message to her family. Then again, as Hunter had pointed out the other week, Jake was probably using Gentry, too. "I'd kill for his hair."

Gentry giggled. "It is pretty awesome."

Colby couldn't remember ever acting as *young* as her sister. "Go be with your date. You're off the clock tonight."

"Have you checked our Facebook and Instagram pages?" Gentry stalled. "They're getting nice engagement. I'll post pictures tonight, too. How are reservations for the opening shaping up?"

"They're coming in." Colby smiled because Gentry had become invested in this job, after all. She'd have to give her sister a little more responsibility to keep her motivated. "You're doing a great job."

"Don't sound so shocked." Gentry crossed her arms. "When the newspaper interview comes out on Sunday, you should get lots of interest."

Colby recoiled from the memory of Melissa's shifty eyes. "That reporter was extremely insensitive about Joe and Mark. Honestly, I don't think any of that should've been part of the discussion."

"Sorry, but giving a personal angle helped pique her interest in doing a story. Voyeurism sells. Look at the Kardashians." Gentry patted Colby's shoulder. "It worked. Now we're getting free publicity in a major paper."

"At a personal cost to Alec and me. I'm not interested in being like a Kardashian." Colby practically shivered at the comparison. "Next time, let's not do that."

"Okay." Gentry shrugged, dismissive of the wounds she'd probed.

Colby realized her pampered sister had no clue about that kind of pain.

"Guess I'll go hang with Jake."

Colby did a last-minute sweep of the dining room, spoke with the waitstaff captain, tended to the floral arrangements and, when no one was looking, shook her hands out to dispel her nerves.

"There's my baby!" Her mom's voice rang out from the hostess station, where she stood proudly wearing the bias-cut black silk dress Colby had bought her for the occasion. Chunky turquoise jewelry added a bit of flair to the ensemble and set off her eyes.

Beside her stood a barrel-chested blond man who bore no resemblance to how Colby had imagined Richard. His cherubic face looked younger than her mom's. Like Jake, he sported an earring, but *his* shirt had a collar, and he wore a linen blazer.

"Mom, thanks for coming." Colby kissed her hello.

"I wouldn't miss it." She beamed. "Dear, *this* is Richard."

His warm, topaz eyes sparkled. Quite dashing for a man of his age. Perhaps her mom meant to prove something to Colby's dad and Jenna by bringing him. Colby then chastised herself for suspecting everyone had hidden agendas. Maybe her mom and Richard actually liked each other, despite having met under false pretenses.

"Welcome, Richard. It's nice to finally meet you." Colby shook his hand. "I hope you enjoy the evening."

"How could I not when I have such wonderful company?" He squeezed her mother's shoulder, earning her wide smile. Then he looked at Colby. "You two look like sisters. She's very proud of you, you know."

"Thank you." Colby looked like her father, but she appreciated Richard's attempt to flatter her mom's youthful mien.

"Isn't he a darling man? I'm getting smarter, aren't I?" Her mom beamed. "Speaking of your father, seems that he's late."

"You're early," Colby replied.

"*I'm* eager to support you and Alec." Her mother's face lit. "Did he tell you about our little rendezvous last night?"

"No." Alec and her mother had *another* rendezvous?

"Stitch had sneaked off on a walkabout. Alec found him half a mile from my house around ten. When he brought him to me, he visited for a while. So interesting to hear all about that commune. I think I might like to try that one day."

Commune? Is that where he'd vanished to last year? "Why'd he tell you about that?"

Colby didn't like that her mom knew something about Alec that she didn't. And she really didn't like how much *that* bothered her.

"I asked him where he'd been, and then I had so many questions. He went on and on about the small community in Virginia. Even passed on some gardening tips. Wait until next year!" Her mother smiled and thrust her thumb toward Richard. "Between this one and Alec, life's been a whole lot more interesting lately."

Richard said something to her mother, but Colby's attention had turned toward Alec. *Perhaps I can help you fill that so-called black hole of neediness,* he'd said. Two baked goods and one cat delivery later, Colby had realized something wonderful about him. He did kind things for the sake of doing them, without showboating. In that way, they had something in common.

"Will your brother be sitting with Richard and me?" Her mother interrupted her thoughts with that unnecessary question. As if Colby would ever seat Hunter with Jenna when any other option existed.

"Yes, I put him and Sara with you. Why don't you go to the bar and have a cocktail?"

Her mom noted Gentry and Jake in the bar area and adjusted her dress. "I see your sister has a new man. She runs through them like paper towels."

"Leslie, let's let your daughter get back to work." Richard winked at Colby, who smiled appreciatively at his attempt to distract her mother from more nitpicking. "What would you like to drink?"

"A fancy champagne cocktail, please." She squeezed Colby's hand. "See you later."

Within thirty minutes almost everyone had arrived, including Mrs. Morgan with three friends in tow. Colby hadn't seen her up close in a while. She looked about the same as Colby remembered, but her eyes weren't quite as merry. Hair styled in a neat bob. Dressed in an ecru A-line dress with cap sleeves. Reserved, like Alec. Of course, Colby had seen beneath Alec's reserve.

"Mrs. Morgan, welcome." Colby didn't know whether to hug her or just offer her hand, so she ended up in an awkward kind of half embrace. "You must be so proud tonight."

"I am." With a prim smile, she introduced her friends. After a few pleasantries, she said, "Alec didn't exaggerate. This is a *beautiful* restaurant."

"Thanks. We're so lucky to have Alec in the kitchen. He's like a fine wine, getting better with age."

"I agree." Mrs. Morgan smiled, and her eyes finally shone with some of their old merriment.

"I'm so glad you came." Truthfully, Colby was grateful not to be confronted by Mr. Morgan's glare tonight, until she stopped to consider Alec's feelings. Being ignored by his father must sting, no matter how much he pretended it didn't. Did that buried disappointment drive him? Was it what fed his temper? That possibility planted a thorny ache in her chest. "My mother's in the bar if you'd like to say hello."

If Mrs. Morgan didn't want to, she faked it pretty well. "Who's the gentleman friend?"

"Richard." Colby considered mentioning the Snickers lie, but why inflame her mother's already ridiculous reputation? There shouldn't be any reason for Snickers to come up tonight. Let sleeping dogs lie. Colby chuckled to herself at that thought. "Enjoy the night."

Colby's father and Jenna had arrived while she'd been speaking with Alec's mom. Her dad leveled a cool look at Jake over the rim of his champagne glass. *Shoot.* Seating Gentry with him might've been a mistake.

Meanwhile, Hunter had been only marginally happier to sit with their mom and Richard. He'd scoffed when Colby had "reminded" him not to forget about their dearly departed dog. Sara, thankfully, smiled and promised to make him put down his phone and converse. A reprimand Alec would never require, she thought with a grin.

Todd breezed through the door with Jacqui, Craig, and John, some of Colby's former colleagues, carrying a bouquet of pink and white roses. He kissed her cheek. "Congratulations."

"These are beautiful. Thank you." Thoughtful, sweet, candid, steady. Apparently, these traits alone were not enough to make her heart patter. "Thank you all for coming."

"We wouldn't miss it." Todd smiled. Tonight's bow tie featured a turquoise background littered with tiny snails. She'd hand him this much: he wore it well.

"Becca will seat you, and I'll catch up with you a little later." She left the group with the hostess and went to put the flowers in water. Most women loved roses. Colby favored less formal flowers, like the tulips Alec had given her a few weeks ago.

She returned to the dining area to observe the waitstaff as each took dinner orders and delivered starter plates with items like Poached Marrons on a Crab Pillow with Truffle Emulsion, and Warm Artichoke Panaché with Vegetable Risotto with Lemon Emulsion. Watching them in action—moving in unison in intricate patterns—made her think of an old-fashioned quadrille. So far, no missteps. Her attention, however, lapsed when her father cornered her on his way back from the restroom.

"Things are going well, honey. I'm proud of you."

"Thanks. I'm cautiously optimistic."

"I know it hasn't been easy for you with Alec." He gently rubbed her back, blessedly unaware of the complicated ways Alec affected Colby. "I see Julie Morgan came without Frank."

"I assume he didn't want to see me."

"It's not your fault." Her father kissed her temple.

"I know, but he's still grieving over Joe. He needs someone to blame, and I'm the only one left. I only wish Alec got some support from his father."

"You can't fix everything for everyone. Focus on your own goals." She must've frowned again, because he waved a hand. "Let's change the subject. How's Gentry working out? Is she pulling her weight or just wasting time like she is with this Jake?"

"She's helping." Colby glanced over her dad's shoulder to watch the floor. "Really, Dad. She is. Go easy on Jake. I think she's using him to get to you and Jenna."

"Why the hell does she want to needle me? I give her everything." He scowled. "She should kiss my damn feet."

"If she lacks perspective, maybe her life's been too easy. Don't be mad at *her* for that." Colby struggled to see beyond her dad's tall frame.

"It's not like you and Hunter had rough lives," he griped.

"No, but our family broke apart. And we didn't grow up in the McMansion with the pool and endless shopping sprees and a car at sixteen and . . ." Something in her periphery caught her attention. "Can we talk about this later, please? I need to pay attention to what's going on."

"Of course." He patted her shoulder and returned to his table.

While she milled around the tables to observe and eavesdrop, Todd grabbed her hand.

"Sit with us." He gestured toward the open chair at their table.

"I can't. I'm sorry."

"Come on . . . a few minutes." His earnest grin, and the fact her friends had come out of their way for her, broke her down.

She glanced at them all, noting the remnants of Pan-Roasted Lobster with Stuffed Zucchini Flower and Tangy Persian Lime Sauce on Todd's plate. Her mouth watered because she'd enjoyed taste testing that one yesterday. "How's everything so far?"

"The food's almost as good as that view." Todd pointed through the open glass doors to where the sun was setting over the lake. "We're all a little jealous you get to spend your days looking at that lake."

"I'd miss the energy of the city." Jacqui sipped her wine. "But this is a great little getaway."

"Come whenever you need to escape Warren Blackstone," Colby joked, thinking about the firm's curmudgeonly managing partner.

"You'd better expect me on a regular basis," Todd rejoined with laughter. His wistful glance, however, suggested he'd intended the double meaning of his words. Colby hoped their friendship didn't suffer because she didn't return his interest.

By the time she excused herself from her friends, most of the other tables had been cleared of the first course. Too late for her to determine whether the other guests had devoured their meals, like her friends had, or simply moved food around their plates.

She did, however, discern the fluidity in the way the waitstaff continued working the room. Gentry now wandered around, snapping candid photos. Guests were chatting and laughing. The upbeat energy took root somewhere in her chest and revved her.

That fizzy lightness lasted until her mother charged toward her—expression panicked—like a steaming locomotive about to hit broken railroad ties. "Colby, did you remember to tell Hunter about Snickers?"

"Yes, and I told Sara as well." *Good grief.* This? Now?

"Richard mentioned him, and Hunter forgot to play along. He tried to cover his mistake, but I'm not sure Richard buys it."

Colby glanced at Hunter, who speared her with bug eyes. Thankfully, Sara kept Richard distracted with bubbly conversation.

"I told you not to lie," Colby murmured, "Just come clean tonight."

"Then he'll never trust me." Her mom toyed with her necklace.

"Exactly why you shouldn't lie in the first place."

"Don't lecture" came her harsh whisper. "I need your help."

"I'm kind of busy, Mom. The main course is about to be served. Here's my best advice: get back there before Hunter does more damage."

Her mother's eyes widened before she dashed back to her table.

As the main courses began to arrive, Colby decided to check on Alec. She popped into the kitchen and froze. Cooks frantically assembled each dish. Alec barked out orders and, alongside Chris, inspected and wiped every plate before it left the kitchen. Flames shot up from the stove, clatter erupted from the dishwashing station, waiters whirred past. Heat, noise, chaos.

The heart of the restaurant, and Alec made it beat like that of an Olympic athlete.

Another satisfied jolt stole through her. This was hers—or it would be once she paid off CTC's investment. With Alec at the helm, they couldn't fail. As if hearing her thoughts, he looked up.

"What?" Alec spared her the briefest glance before fixing his attention on the next plate set in front of him.

"I . . . I just came to check in."

His brows knit together as he adjusted something on the dish. "We're fine, but I need to focus."

"Sorry." She backed out of the kitchen in time to hear Jake's voice rise above the din of conversation.

"At least people know what they're eating when they buy my hot dogs." Jake poked his fork at the pork croquette on his plate. It occurred to Colby that Jake would be the type to show up for a happy-hour deal, but not necessarily stay to eat. Maybe Alec had been right about her idea.

Colby hustled to their table in time to hear Jenna's cool reply. "Eating with silverware must be a real change of pace."

Jake shot up—his chair screeching against the wood floor—drawing everyone's attention. "Bunch of snobs, praising bullshit food that people pretend to like, but everyone goes home hungry."

Colby glanced over her shoulder and saw Mrs. Morgan's cheeks turn red. Another black mark against the Cabot family in the Morgans' book.

"Please sit down," Colby implored. "If there's a problem, may we discuss it privately?"

"No problem. I'm outta here." Jake tossed his napkin on the chair and squinted at Gentry. "You comin'?"

"You're making a scene." Gentry kept calm, but Colby wanted to strangle the jerk.

"That's on them." Jake pointed at her dad and Jenna, then stormed toward the front door.

"See what you did?" Gentry sighed, almost as if she enjoyed the fiasco.

"Let him go." Jenna sipped her wine. "He's beneath you."

"You *are* a snob," Gentry sniped. Offering Colby an apologetic look before taking off after Jake, she said, "Sorry."

Painfully aware of the eyes watching them, Colby fixed a calm grin in place. Not that she wanted to regress to a life of brave faces, but the skill she'd acquired during her marriage did come in handy in a crisis.

"Sorry, honey," her dad muttered as she turned away to salvage the scene that had distracted everyone.

That's when she noticed a victorious light in her mother's eyes. Rarely did Jenna fail at anything, so Colby's mom delighted in being present when she did. Despite her mom's gloating, Colby loved Gentry and her dad and couldn't shake the sinking feeling that her sister's current path would lead somewhere terrible. After living through Joe's and Mark's deaths, she would've thought her family might stop taking one another for granted.

Tonight they'd pulled her attention from watching for people's reactions to dinner. Had Jake's response been the anomaly?

Focus. Dessert. Dessert was next. For the first time in forever, she thought she might prefer a stiff drink to the Grilled Pistachio and Chocolate Mille-Feuille she knew would be coming.

Determined not to get distracted again, Colby meandered around the tables and paid attention, as Alec had asked. By the time the dessert dishes were being cleared, Colby's back and feet ached. If *she* was this wiped out, how could Alec keep upright?

His methods weren't her favorite, but he'd pulled it off. With the exception of Jake's tantrum, the night had been amazing. Alec had brought her one step closer to success. He might not seek the spotlight tonight, but he deserved it.

Crossing to the back of the house, she found him watching the plates as they came into the kitchen on the bus trays.

"Come take a bow." She smiled because he looked like a marathoner who'd just crossed the finish line.

Following a brief hesitation, he nodded. When they entered the dining room, Hunter stood and clapped, which led to a round of applause from the rest of the guests.

He blushed and winked at his mom before bowing his head. Seeing him flushed yet proud might've been Colby's favorite part of the night.

"Thank you for being our test crowd." He walked to the center of the dining room, smiling. "My goal is for the service and meals to rival this beautiful space, so please be sure to pass along any complaints. Your feedback will be appreciated. Have a good night and a safe drive home." He waved briefly and, turning slightly to her, murmured, "Let's talk once everyone's gone?"

"Okay."

He promptly returned to the kitchen.

Colby ignored her throbbing feet and made one last round to each table to offer her personal thanks as well.

On his way out, Todd quietly asked, "Have you given any more thought to Thai?"

Although flattered, she wished he'd stop asking. She couldn't make herself feel more for her friend than she did, despite him being capable of offering the open, respectful relationship she needed after dealing with Mark. "I'm sorry. I adore you and our friendship. I'm just not looking for more. But I'd love to grab lunch soon."

Todd's disappointed sigh preceded a nod. "Anytime."

She kissed his cheek and sent him home, certain she'd made the right decision.

After the final guests had left and the waitstaff and kitchen help were nearly finished cleaning up, Colby ducked into her office to shut things down. She removed her shoes and rubbed her throbbing feet. She moaned just as Alec walked in holding two glasses of champagne.

He set one beside her, unbuttoned his chef coat, and slumped into a chair. "I dismissed the staff. Long—but good—night. Cheers."

The unbuttoned collar gave her a perfect view of his throat working to swallow the champagne. He had an elegant, strong neck. Everything about him seemed so deliciously masculine lately. Instead of the infatuation filling her with hope, it made her sad. What if, after all this time, the one person she might be able to fall for was the *least* suitable person of all?

"I'm shocked you can keep your eyes open, especially after last night's late-night cat rescue and coffee klatch."

Another rosy blush colored his cheeks. "I've always liked your mom."

"Someday *I'd* like to hear about the commune. Of course, whatever you told her has convinced her that those are her people, so maybe I'll see it for myself when forced to visit." Colby sipped her champagne, shoved her feet back into her shoes, and sat against the edge of her desk. "So, are you satisfied with the cooks?"

"I'm never satisfied. But we can build on this." He leaned forward then, elbows on his knees, eyes alert. "Tell me what went wrong in the front of the house."

Oh God. He'd performed his role to perfection, while she'd basically failed to do the one thing he'd asked. She braced for one of his spectacular temper tantrums.

"For the most part, people seemed pleased with everything." She smiled, hoping he wouldn't push.

"I noticed one untouched pork croquette. And the Grey Mullet with Pickled Mushrooms didn't look like a favorite." He frowned. "Did I miss anything?"

"The pork dish was Gentry's boyfriend, who never tried it because he stormed off after he and Jenna got into an argument."

"Oh, well, that's good." Alec smiled.

"Good?"

"If he tasted it and didn't like it, that would concern me. But if he didn't even eat it, then I'm going to stick with it. The others who ordered it cleaned their plates." He nodded. "What else?"

Here goes nothing. "I got sidetracked by a variety of family quarrels." She chewed her lip. "I'm sorry. I know you were counting on me for better information."

He stared at her, his face impassive except for a tic of his jaw. She waited, nerves sparking painfully beneath her skin like they had anytime she suspected Mark might erupt.

Alec slouched deeper in his chair and stroked its arms. "It's okay."

It was?

"Are you going easy on me because I'm your boss?" She crossed her arms.

"I knew it'd be hard for you to focus when family and friends were vying for your attention. You'll get better."

She'd expected him to bellow—had imagined his brow furrowing and his face turning as crimson as the lava that spewed out whenever he thought his reputation was at stake.

Instead, he swigged the last bit of champagne, set down his glass, and stood. When he reached beside her to the photo she'd given him earlier, his nearness made her body temperature spike. She reminded herself this was only Alec, but somewhere along the way, *Alec* had come to mean much more than she'd ever anticipated.

"Besides, I'd never scream at you, Colby. If anything, I've been trying to make you laugh more." He grinned. "Have the videos helped?"

"Nightly YouTube links to babies sucking on lemons and 'Bat Dad' *are* a step up from your grade-school jokes," she conceded, trying to suppress a broadening smile.

"My favorite was the little boy running from his shadow." His expression turned more contemplative as he held up the framed picture she'd given him. "You've always wanted to comfort others and see them happy. I just want that same thing for *you*."

"Oh?" Part of her wanted to back up so he wouldn't see the way her heart was pounding in her throat. But even if she wanted to, she couldn't. The desk was at her butt. He looked at her with such intensity she couldn't tear her gaze away. The sizzle of his attention traveled through her limbs and to her core. She hadn't experienced this full-body buzz in ages.

She froze, waiting. Waiting for what, she couldn't say. Every time she thought she had him figured out, he surprised her. Now she almost wished he'd flown into a rage so she'd remember why she shouldn't look at him this way. Why this desire consuming her was unwelcome and dangerous.

He cocked his head, as if sensing her interest. How could he not when her body throbbed with it?

Alec didn't move. Like her, he seemed to be waiting—that or toying with her. Had Alec Morgan become a master of seduction when she wasn't looking? The anticipation of his touch stoked her hunger, even as she believed inviting it could well be a huge mistake.

Slowly he set the picture back on the desk and inched a little closer.

His hip now leaned against the edge of the desk so that their shoulders nearly touched. He didn't even need to make contact for her insides to quiver, and yet her eyes remained locked on his.

Spellbound. Deliciously, dangerously magnetized.

"The only real question now is whether or not *you're* happy." He nudged even closer. "Was the evening everything you hoped for?"

"It was."

It had been. The night had passed in a flurry of conversation, twinkling candles, beautiful views, and even prettier plates. The tinkling sounds of china and crystal had sounded as lovely as any quartet she'd ever heard. And most important, everyone but her dad and Jenna had left smiling. It was exactly the environment she'd envisioned, and she owed its success largely to her perplexing chef.

"I'm glad." He fingered the fresh roses on her desk and frowned, softly muttering, "You prefer tulips."

"I do." *How did he know?*

"From your dad?"

She shook her head. "Todd."

"Ah. He's persistent . . . and thoughtful." Alec dropped his chin, his gaze now on the floor, but really someplace distant.

She took advantage of the opportunity to study his strong profile. The sensual shape of his lips. The sharp line of his jaw. If she had a soft heart, she believed his to be softer, no matter how loudly he might yell. Even now, she knew he restrained himself for her sake. "Alec."

It came out as a whisper, lying between them, unplanned. Gentle. A question. A sense of wonder at the surprising, powerful curiosity surging beneath her skin.

He snapped his gaze back to her, and, without thought, she craned her head toward his. Her hand landed on his chest, where it felt perfectly at home. "I'm not interested in Todd."

His breath caught, or was that hers? Their lips were a hair's breadth apart now, heated breath mingling. His heart beat against her palm, while hers knocked urgently against her ribs. She didn't have time to analyze more because he cradled her jaw and kissed her.

Warm yet tentative, like he didn't quite believe she wanted it. She did, so she gathered the open collar of his jacket in her fists. Her simple gesture had been enough of a signal. In an instant, hesitation fled, replaced by a firestorm of heat, of deep kisses, of fingers raking through her hair. Strong, confident sweeps of his tongue scattered any lingering doubts. Goose bumps fanned over her scalp, chased by tingles that drove through her limbs and pooled in her core.

He tasted like champagne and something earthy. The aroma of fresh herbs and spice wafted around them. Her body trembled until his arms closed around her with assuredness and strength, tugging her snugly against his chest, where she felt a vibrating hum.

She dug her fingers into his hair, holding tightly for fear of falling over if she let go. Alec's hands swept down her back as he settled himself between her legs, dragging her hips to meet his. Right to where she could feel exactly how much he wanted her. A whimper stuck in her throat as tiny prickles skittered along her nerve endings.

His rough hands were on her thighs, inching her skirt up. He shuddered, then his mouth found the little spot behind her ear, which made her body respond in kind. The glorious sensation swept through her ferociously, making her tingly and restless.

Her legs—her whole body—went limp from the onslaught of pleasure and surprise. Of lust. Of desire she hadn't felt for anyone for years. To want and be wanted. To give and to take. To meld an emotional connection that had spanned decades with a shiny, unexpected physical one. Only this man could satisfy that need. The reawakening of this part of her soul caught in her chest.

Alec growled her name and unzipped the back of her dress, his hands and mouth more commanding, more demanding. He pulled at her dress to expose her shoulder, which he then kissed and nibbled.

Her body welcomed his hot assault after two years of celibacy. Longer, even, because her sex life with Mark had tapered off significantly before Joe's accident.

Mark. Joe. A tsunami of unwelcome emotions quickly laced her pleasure, the ring on her finger suddenly warm and heavy. Things with Mark had started off hot, too. She'd thought him the answer to all her dreams, until life with him became a nightmare. What if Alec was another mirage like Mark? Alec wasn't uncomplicated. He had layers of difficult history and a father who hated her.

Irrational panic took root when she couldn't shake the cautionary whispers. If anything, the whispers got louder, causing her eyes to sting. When an errant teardrop trickled over Alec's thumb, he pulled away.

She mutely kept her clutch on his clothing, their labored breathing the only sound in the office.

"You're crying." His eyes reflected shame and concern. "I'm sorry. God, Colby. I thought . . . I must be stupid-tired." Without hesitation, he yanked her dress back into place and zipped it up.

"Alec," she said, but he jerked back as if burned on the stove, forcing her to release his jacket.

He shook his head. "Blame it on the champagne."

"Alec, don't apologize. *I'm* sorry." She hugged herself. "It's not your fault."

Alec could barely breathe, making it difficult to focus.

Weeks of seeing her every day had churned his desire. Like a drug, it made him hallucinate invitation in her eyes. His reckless heart had abandoned caution and now lay lifeless in his chest. "It's been an emotional night. I should've known better. And I broke your rule."

"Screw the rule. I wanted you to kiss me. It's been so long since I even had that thought, let alone acted on it. It was perfect until I got overwhelmed. Seems I'm not ready for anything more personal than friendship, no matter how much I thought—wished, even—I was."

Her cheeks were pink, and he knew that degree of honesty probably wiped out her last bit of energy. He could hardly believe his ears. She'd wanted him to kiss her. She wanted him. Colby Cabot-Baxter liked him.

But it didn't matter.

She remained painfully outside his reach. By her own admission, she wasn't over Mark yet. Unlike other young widows, Colby not only mourned the loss, but she had to cope with the horrible memory of watching his suicide. That tragedy Alec might've prevented if only he'd have said something . . . to anyone.

Shame rushed in. Guilt. Anger at himself for thinking for one second he deserved a happy ending with her when her marriage only ended because of him.

"Let's pretend it never happened." He forced a light grin, hoping to dispel all awkwardness. "Like the other time."

He wanted to scoop those last words back until he noticed Colby smile. "So you *do* remember that embarrassing day. I really forced you into an awkward position. Maybe I am more like my mom than I think."

Alec could admit that he'd been her more-than-willing victim, but then she'd know that he'd pined for her all these years. No reason to make working together and being friends even more difficult. Neither of them needed a more difficult relationship in their lives. "It wasn't so terrible."

"Faint praise."

"Now whose ego needs stroking?"

She grinned. "I'm glad we can tease each other about this, Alec. I wouldn't want to hurt you or make things more awkward. I've been counting on this place to help me, but I didn't count on this." She gestured between them. "Our friendship has been an unexpected but wonderful bonus."

"I'm glad, considering it didn't start off on the best footing."

"Which is why I'd hate myself for doing anything to damage it."

"You haven't." If he stood there talking about it any longer, *he* might do or say something stupid. Time to regroup. He took the photograph she'd given him. "Thanks, again, for this. How about you let me walk you to your car?"

"Okay." She grabbed her purse and shut off the lights.

Together they meandered through the darkened dining room in silence. Moonlight filtered through the plate-glass doors, casting blue-black light around them that enabled everything that had transpired between them to lurk in the shadows.

When they reached her car, he pecked her on the forehead. She hugged him, squeezing his waist for an extra second or two. "Thanks, Alec."

"Drive safely."

She looked up, and he could tell she had something to say but chose not to. Now he'd forever wonder what that was.

He repressed the "fuck it all" urge to kiss her again. To mimic guys like his brother and Mark, who'd felt entitled to take what they wanted and seized any opening to do so. But he'd never been like them. When it came to relationships, Alec always waited—for acknowledgment, respect, and love.

"Good night." Colby slipped into the driver's seat and started the car.

"See you later." He stood back and watched her pull away, down the long driveway that led through the woods back to the main road.

She liked him, finally. He'd been infatuated with her for years. He wanted to surround her with his affection so she'd never feel alone. Todd had brought roses, but Todd didn't *know* her. Alec could do better. He *would* do better. Flowers. Videos. Visits with Leslie. Hell, he'd continue praising his staff every day to make her happy, no matter how detrimental he considered that practice.

Spinning around, he caught a view of the moonbeam on the lake. It looked like the kind of thing one should make a wish upon, so he did. Of course, few of his wishes had ever come true, but he never gave up hope.

Chapter Nine

"You had no right to slur your brother." Alec's father slammed the newspaper onto the kitchen table, causing his mother to flinch.

Seeing his mom recoil made every muscle in Alec's body tighten. She deserved better. For her sake, Alec strove to make peace with his father.

"I'm sorry, Dad. I didn't mean to upset you or smear Joe's memory." Alec rubbed his forehead. Melissa's article about his return and A CertainTea had garnered a slew of new reservations for the upcoming grand opening but set him back a step from his personal goals with his family. "I was talking about my perspective. *My* regrets."

"Well, add this interview to *that* growing list," he scoffed. "This and working for Colby, for chrissakes."

Working for Colby might be a mistake, but not because of Joe. Alec had relived their recent kiss every ten minutes in the days since it happened. Of course, they'd both pretended to set it aside and move on, but he suspected she hadn't found that any easier to do than he had. There were feelings there that wanted to be explored.

Too bad timing and truth stood between them. That and Alec's father, who'd be doubly enraged to learn Alec wanted to get closer to Colby.

"Frank, settle down." Alec's mother took her glass to the sink and stared out the window, shoulders rounded. She'd always daydreamed in that spot, although Alec suspected she'd had more waking nightmares than daydreams these past two years. With her back to them, she said, "Stop yelling at Alec."

"Don't defend him. Not on this." His dad pointed at the discarded newspaper even though she wasn't looking. "There's no excuse for making Joe look bad when he's not here to tell his side."

She whirled around, her finger jabbing the air. "Don't *you* keep pushing our son away! You act like you're the only one who lost something when Joe died. Like you have the right to control how we all deal with making peace with it." Her voice cracked. "Let me tell you something, Frank. You don't get to deny Alec the right to talk about his grief. And you don't get to rain on his chance to reclaim his old life, either."

When a sob broke through that final statement, she rushed out of the kitchen. In the distance, Alec heard her bedroom door close. He stared at the space she'd vacated, shocked. The pain in her voice had punched his chest harder than any blow his dad's barbs could land.

"See what you've done now?" His father glared at him, paying no attention to his wife's warning.

Alec could explode from anger. Lord knew he had plenty in reserve. But he wanted a family that functioned, even if it would never be whole again. He couldn't fix what had broken between his brother and him, but as long as his parents were alive, he had a chance to fix *this*. He just didn't know how. Maybe if he acted more like Joe, his father would respect him more.

What would Joe do?

Joe would fight back.

"I'm sorry I upset you, but I didn't vilify Joe. I just explained what happened with Une Bouchée. I've got a shot at recovering from that, and I'm taking it. Mom's right about one other thing. You aren't the only one who grieves Joe's death." Alec stood and evenly met his father's furious gaze. Wiping any trace of bitterness from his voice, he said, "We all know he was your favorite. But why keep pushing Mom and me away? Don't *we* mean anything to you?"

"Now the melodrama." His father gruffly waved his hand. "You should've pranced around the stage instead of becoming a chef."

"You spit that out like what I do is pathetic." The blatant prejudice practically begged Alec's temper to join the party. "I'm *outstanding* in my field. And, by the way, my job requires as much stamina and discipline as yours, maybe more. You might know that if you ever bothered to take any interest in what I do."

"Don't be ridiculous." His father's derisive laugh scalded like a steam burn. "You cook, Alec. You don't save lives. You don't face danger."

"Now who's being ridiculous?" Alec scoffed. "You and Joe faced the 'mean streets' of Lake Sandy—shoplifting, petty theft, vandalism. Not exactly Detroit or Baltimore."

"We weren't making pastries!" His father's stupefied expression might have been funny under other circumstances.

Despite his father's reddened cheeks, Alec remained calm. In fact, they almost egged him on. With a casual shrug, he quipped, "No, just eating them in the patrol car."

"What?" Outrage turned his dad's face aubergine.

"You heard me." Alec forced himself to stand tall. "People worldwide revere chefs like Roger Vergé and Alain Ducasse, yet you disdain them and me. Maybe you're just too ignorant to appreciate us."

"You think you're some hotshot because you lived in Europe. Like the fact you speak French makes you better than me and your brother." His dad snorted. "Don't you ever call me ignorant!"

Apparently, his dad's glass house couldn't withstand a single pebble. Alec's insult had shattered another attempt at reason. Maybe one day they'd manage a civil disagreement. Just not today. "Fine. Forget it."

Alec marched out of the kitchen without looking back, even after he heard a chair crash against something. The multitude of household items held together with superglue or duct tape revealed the inventive ways his father had taken out his frustrations throughout the years. Since it had never escalated to physical abuse, Alec accepted it as his dad's way of letting off steam. In the wake of Joe's death, though, that temper had grown less predictable.

When Alec's mom emerged from her room to investigate the racket, he grabbed her hand and tugged her from the house. "Come for a drive while he cools down."

She followed him to his car in silence. He shooed Stitch out of the driveway and then drove his mother toward the new gelato shop by the park at the south end of the lake. The sun drew nearer to the horizon now, bathing the sky in striking shades of rose and lilac—a peaceful tableau at complete odds with the chaos on the ground.

Neither he nor his mom spoke for a while. He couldn't have said much, anyway, thanks to his mental cartwheels. Who'd believe that any family lucky enough to call this picturesque town home could be living under such a cloud of despair? As he whizzed along the south shore, he wondered what ugly secrets other people in this neighborhood hid behind their quaint homes and gardens.

Absently, he also wondered if Joe could see him now. Had Joe had any regrets? Would he have been pissed at Alec for the article and the fight with their dad? Truth was, Alec wasn't exactly proud of arguing with his father, but he wasn't exactly sorry, either.

"I'm sorry." His mother squeezed his hand once they took seats on the park bench overlooking the lake.

"Why are *you* sorry?"

"I should've been a better mother to my sons and not allowed the gap between you to fester." She scraped the plastic spoon at her gelato without much interest in eating it.

"That had nothing to do with you."

"I'm your mother, Alec. It's my job to teach my children right from wrong. To knit a tight family." Her forehead wrinkled with regret. "I failed."

"You didn't fail." He looked across the lake. "You just drew the short end of the stick when it came to all the men in your life."

She brushed his bangs from his forehead like she used to do when he was young. "Not with you, sweetheart."

She only believed that because she didn't know all his secrets. He slouched lower on the park bench and licked his cone. The explosion of flavor temporarily distracted him, although *his* pistachio gelato was better.

"Your father's a hypocrite." She set her melting dessert aside. "He always resented how his father belittled him, yet he's done the exact same thing to you."

"Grandpa wasn't gruff." In fact, Alec's vague memories carried a definite hint of warmth. "He used to read to me and play Legos."

"He was stoic. An engineer with a sharp head for math. But your father never worked to his potential in school, which bothered *his* dad to no end. Grandpa scorned your dad's choices and career as much as your father does yours. Frank never forgave him for that."

Alec now had a long-missing piece in the puzzle of his existence—a reason for his father's dislike that went beyond Alec's failings. Not only must Alec's academic bent have reminded his dad of his own father, but Alec had also won Grandpa's affection when his dad could not. That had to have stung, and might explain why Alec's "ignorance" insult had been so potent.

"I could. Forgive Dad, I mean. Or, I would, anyway, if he'd meet me halfway. We're already such a small family; we need to stick together."

"Maybe, if Joe hadn't died . . ." His mother squeezed his hand. "I can't live with the gloom much longer. I ache, too, but there are still beautiful adventures ahead if we embrace them, like travel, and grandchildren."

Her wish for a grandchild floated like a leaf in the breeze, landing silently between them. His mother would be a loving, patient grandmother. If he could hand her that gift now, he would. Instead, he sat there, holding her hand, hoping he could be enough for her.

Together they watched a few young kids and moms packing up their things after a day at the public beach.

"I remember bringing you two down here when you were little." His mother's eyes watered as she traveled back in time. "You'd work so diligently, building structures out of this muddy sand, and no matter how many times Joe messed them up when trying to help, you never once got mad. You were so patient with him."

Alec's last bite of gelato barely slid past the lump in his throat. His memories of those summer outings were mostly sad because of how things had changed over the years. None of his patience had amounted to much with Joe at the end of the day.

Would his parents' marriage be another casualty of Alec's lie and Joe's stupid jump? So far, he hadn't done jack shit to improve his family situation. He hadn't the faintest idea of his next move, either.

Moments like this made him second-guess everything. Rebuilding his reputation would be meaningless in the face of his family's deterioration. But with Colby . . . the prospect of her affection kept him from throwing in the towel. Of course, even that would be based on a lie.

"I'm glad you stuck with our tradition today. You could use some sun." Sara elbowed Colby and smiled, then tugged her into yet another jewelry booth.

Every July except the one last summer, they'd attended the annual Sunday Sidewalk Sale in the Pearl. Thousands of people poured into the neighborhood as local shops and restaurants set up tents or tables filled with discounted items. In nearby Jamison Square—a square-block-size urban park bordered by a tree-lined, wood-slatted sidewalk—kids squealed while playing in the expansive water fountain and dancing to the dulcet tones of a local folk band. Idyllic, if it weren't for her memories.

Last year she couldn't make herself return to her and Mark's old neighborhood. Today she forced it, although she'd avoided looking any farther north. Still, recollections kept bursting through her subconscious like pinpricks. These streets held history she couldn't quite face without feeling a little faint and sweaty.

"Sorry I couldn't make it earlier." Colby eyed a bunch of purses hanging in front of one tent, forcing her mind to focus on the here and now. "Brunch didn't shut down until three."

They'd packed a full house today. Early success had given her a heady feeling. Almost as heady as finding a dainty crystal bud vase on her desk with a single pink tulip this morning. Alec hadn't said anything, but she knew he'd done it. A bold move. One that had flustered her into silence. Now she felt silly for not thanking him.

"It's fine. I shouldn't shop too long anyhow." Sara fingered earrings hanging on a jewelry tree, refraining from coddling Colby or pressing her to talk. She didn't intrude into other people's personal affairs, instead offering unwavering support in a gentle, silent way. "The restaurant had an excellent first weekend, right?"

"Totally booked, and next week and weekend are booked solid, too. That article sparked a lot of interest." A proud grin spread. Together, she and Alec just might make A CertainTea *the* place to eat. He'd said others had lost faith in him, but she couldn't believe no other restaurant owner wanted him. No. He'd chosen her over others, and, selfishly, she was glad.

"Too bad it also sparked problems for Alec and his dad." Sara sighed, her gaze continuing to scan the accessories on display.

"It did?" Colby's grin faded. Alec hadn't mentioned that when he'd been sending her funny videos and surprising her with her favorite flowers. Maybe it wasn't her business, but the fact he'd hidden it from her niggled. It also reminded her of how much easier Alec's life would be if he worked for someone—anyone—else.

"Alec mentioned it to Hunter during one of their cycling work-outs this past week." Sara then raised a silver-and-moonstone necklace for closer inspection before Colby could probe for more information. "They say moonstone helps with fertility. What do you think?"

Sara held the necklace against her breastbone and cocked her head. If moonstone worked, Colby would empty her wallets and drape Sara in the gemstones. Unfortunately, she doubted they'd help more than the failed fertility treatments. "It's very pretty."

"Can't hurt." Sara's wan smile tugged at Colby's heart. At the same time, she admired the way Sara and Hunter faced life and loss together.

While Sara paid for the item, Colby's thoughts returned to Alec and his father. Alec had thrown himself on Melissa's sword to keep Colby from having to discuss Mark. If Mr. Morgan gave Alec an ultimatum, would Alec leave A CertainTea and her? She wouldn't want him to become estranged from his family for her, but she also wouldn't want him to leave. What *did* she want?

The memory of their recent kiss rushed back, washing through her, warm and frothy. It did that on a regular basis, like ocean waves rhythmically pounding the shore. But she'd sensed sharks in that surf and yanked herself out.

"Where'd you go?" Sara clutched the little white bag in hand, her brows slightly pinched in concern.

"Nowhere. Just a lot on my mind." Colby guessed that Sara thought she was thinking about Mark, who'd ended his life mere blocks away. The only other time she'd come back to the Pearl, she'd consciously avoided looking toward Lovejoy Street. When she and Mark had first moved here, they'd been so in love, they'd believed their street name to be a good omen instead of the perverse joke it became.

"I thought you asked Gentry to join us." Sara hooked arms with Colby as they meandered to the next booth, effectively steering her away from the memory.

"She's working here with Jake today, so keep an eye out for the hot dog cart." Colby chuckled. "That's driving my dad over the edge."

"Isn't that her goal? Ooh, Bonnet!" Sara's attention snagged on that store's sale tent, so she dragged Colby inside. "I love these hats. Especially this red-and-gray Lady Mary." Sara placed the cute hat on her head and framed her face with her hands. "See?"

She removed it and then lifted a lovely straw hat with a wide black ribbon and plopped it onto Colby's head. "You're definitely a Gigi. So classic."

Colby swiveled her head to glance in the mirror, then froze. It was a sweet hat, but Mark had always loved her in hats. She expected him to be on her mind today, given that she'd come back to their old stomping grounds, but wished the endless barrage of memories would finally end. Then, now, now, then—love, anger, sorrow, regret, resentment, guilt, horror. Movement reflected in the mirror—of Sara snatching the Lady Mary back from the rack and taking it to the cashier—broke Colby's runaway train of thought.

While Sara rang up another purchase, Colby returned the Gigi to its shelf and watched the crowd in the street. It parted slightly as people milled around, at which point she caught a glimpse of Gentry.

Her sister's super-short turquoise-and-black-sequined Betsey Johnson dress with turquoise-and-black leopard-print boots made Gentry's red hair the least loud thing about her today.

Colby spied on her sister, who bent down to talk to two young girls whose mom was paying Jake for some hot dogs and enormous cookies. After the family strolled away, Jake mumbled something, to which Gentry dismissively waved a hand. Jake shot her a quizzical look, then she giggled as she whispered something in his ear. His hand slid over her hip, and he bit her earlobe.

While witnessing the little intimacy, Colby momentarily envied her sister's ability to live in the moment—a skill she hadn't yet reclaimed. More than that, she missed being looked at the way Jake looked at Gentry—with fascination and attraction, like he couldn't wait to get her alone.

Alec had gazed at Colby that way last weekend when he'd kissed her. She'd spent all week pretending it meant nothing yet fantasizing about how far that passion might have gone had she let it. Imagining the heat of his body against hers. The sound of him moaning her name. The taste of his skin. Those musings gathered in her abdomen and squeezed, making her ache with longing. Making her wonder if his baggage might be worth the heavy lifting.

"Are you cold?" Sara asked when Colby shivered.

"No."

"Mark?" Sara asked gently.

"No. I found my sister." Colby pointed across the road, only the slightest bit guilty for dissembling. "Let's go say hi."

Sara stopped short. "What's she wearing in the middle of the day?"

"Something that's sure to get attention." Colby couldn't help but smile.

"There isn't enough attention in the world to make her happy." Sara grimaced.

"Hunter and I need to spend more time with her." Colby sighed. "We might be too late, though."

Sara shook her head. "It's never too late for love."

Colby hoped so. On so many levels, she wanted that to be true.

"Hey, Sis." She hugged Gentry then smiled at Jake. Even though he'd criticized her restaurant's food, she'd take the high road for Gentry's sake. "Let me have one of these famed hot dogs. Just mustard and ketchup, though. No relish or onion."

"Sure." Jake went to work. No friendly smile. No apology for the scene he caused in her restaurant. No "Thank you." Nothing. Jake didn't appear particularly complicated or encumbered by baggage. Another reason to toss that particular yardstick.

Jake handed Colby a hot dog in exchange for four bucks.

"Looks great, thanks." In fact, it tasted better than she'd expected, too. Natural casing gave it that snappy texture she liked. Not that he seemed to care one way or the other about her opinion.

"Can you take a break and walk with us for a while?" Sara asked Gentry.

"Nah." Gentry wrinkled her nose. "It pisses me off to see all this stuff on sale after I paid full price."

"You could try waiting for things to go on sale," Colby teased.

"I'm a trendsetter, Sis. Not a follower." Gentry playfully swept her hand down her body as if to say "Voilà!" Then she ruefully shook her head at Colby's simple belted black-and-white gingham dress.

Gentry's disapproving eye didn't change the fact that Colby was most comfortable in simple, understated dresses.

"What'd you buy, Sara?" Gentry craned her head toward the bags like a heat-seeking missile.

"A hat and a moonstone necklace." Sara shook her bags. "But, actually, I've got to be off already. Hunter and I have plans."

"Vague." Colby cocked her head, but Sara stayed mum. Colby guessed they'd planned a "date" of some sort. Her brother worked tremendously long hours, but today was Sunday. Those two made love and marriage look easy. She wished they could teach her, but deep down, she knew she'd have to learn for herself.

"What will *you* do now?" Sara asked Colby.

"Hit up Powell's on my way home. I want to pick up *100 Days of Happiness*."

"Sounds like something we could all use. Pass it over to me when you're done." Sara kissed her cheek. "Sorry we didn't get to spend much time together today."

"No apologies, please. My new work schedule is killing what little social life I had." Colby shrugged.

"Maybe you should lift that stupid ban and hook up with Alec." Gentry's oh-so-casual tone didn't fool Colby. Her sister never said anything without some agenda. It only surprised her that Gentry now seemed to be pushing Colby toward Alec instead of nabbing him for herself.

Sara's hot gaze homed in on Colby, too.

"You don't actually expect a response, do you?" Colby asked them, brushing the suggestion aside as if she hadn't been obsessing about it since she and Alec had kissed.

Sara and Gentry exchanged a quick glance, then Sara said, "No time to argue about this now, so I'll see you both later."

"Give our brother a kiss." Colby and Gentry waved goodbye to Sara, then Colby turned to her sister. "Any news for me on the social media front?"

"It's all good. I told you that article would help, and we've received a lot of great comments from people who dined over the weekend. We've got a dozen five-star reviews on Yelp so far, too."

"Excellent." She should tell Gentry about the family backlash Alec endured because of the article as a reminder not to be so careless, but Alec hadn't shared it with her, so she stayed quiet. "Thank you for keeping on top of that."

"No probs." Gentry shifted her weight from one high-heeled boot to the other. Trendsetting looked painful. Selling hot dogs also looked painful—or, rather, painfully boring.

Jake's impassive expression made Colby want to grab Gentry and head for the hills. "Come with me to Powell's. We can grab a drink after."

"Can't. I promised Jake I'd hang." Gentry shrugged. "I know everyone in our family thinks I'm a flake, but I'm not."

"I don't think you're a flake."

Gentry glanced away for a second. "Well, anyway, it's more fun people-watching than going to a bookstore." Gentry made a show of shuddering, as if books were akin to the tedium of ice fishing. On second thought, maybe for Gentry, reading was tedious, considering that it required hours of concentration unrelated to selfies.

"Fine. I'll see you Wednesday morning at the restaurant." Colby flashed a smile at Jake. "Enjoy the day. Hope it's lucrative."

He nodded and gave her a thumbs-up. *Oh, boy.* He'd better be excellent in bed to make up for his dull personality. Not that one really made up for the other. Obviously, Colby had sex on the brain. Something that hadn't taken up much space there until recently.

She turned her back on her old neighborhood and strolled toward Powell's, wishing it were that easy to turn away from her bad memories.

Minutes later, the massive brick bookstore beckoned like an old friend. Entering the venerable labyrinth could be overwhelming to a newcomer. Cement floors covered sixty-eight thousand square feet of space, crowded with endless rows of wooden bookcases containing roughly one million books. Its multiple rooms had color-coded names, like the Coffee Room, where the romance novels were shelved, or the Rose Room for children's and YA books. Fortunately, Colby had spent enough hours here throughout the years to know her way around without the map.

She found her book and proceeded to the café to grab some tea. To her surprise, she spotted Alec at a table, his attention absorbed by a crossword puzzle.

Seeing him here temporarily disoriented her, as if her constant overthinking things had conjured him.

"Alec, what're you doing here?" She lived only minutes away, in Eliot Tower, but Alec had driven over from Lake Sandy.

His wide eyes proved him equally stunned to see her.

"Killing time until I check out the competition at Beast." He closed his puzzle book and smiled. He'd worked such long hours this week, she didn't know how he managed to stay upright let alone think through a crossword puzzle.

"Sneaky." She nodded with approval.

"Naomi's an excellent chef, and I like to be challenged."

"I know this about you." She fidgeted with her book.

"Innovation and attention to detail make all the difference."

Details that went beyond his professional pursuits, like her favorite flowers. Colby smiled, feeling oddly shy. "I meant to thank you for the vase and tulip earlier."

"You're welcome." He held her gaze.

This was only the third time they'd spent time together outside the restaurant since dinner at Hunter's. The first since the recent kiss. That kiss. She caught herself staring at his mouth. Which quirked. *Shoot.* Busted.

"What'd you pick?" He peeked at the cover, letting her off the hook. "Hmm. Self-help?"

"No. Fiction. An Italian author wrote a story about a man with an inoperable tumor who's given one hundred days to live, so he makes a plan to win back his ex and accomplish a bunch of stuff so he can die happy." It may have sounded morbid to some, although to her the description carried a hopeful note.

"A bucket list on steroids?"

She laughed. "I suppose you could frame it that way."

They both hesitated, unsure of what to do or say next.

"Where were you before you came here?" he asked.

"At the sidewalk sale with Sara."

"By Jamison Square?" He raised his brows, looking worried yet impressed. "And where are you off to next?"

"Home." To her empty condo. To sit alone and read and while away the time until she could go to sleep . . . by herself. And yet, here was Alec. Also alone. Also burying himself in a book to avoid reality, or his father, or both.

Seeing him here with his puzzle book took her back to high school. To the Alec who'd often been alone, whether in his kitchen or the tree house. Who'd almost always been there for her when she'd needed him. Maybe fate brought him here to remind her of that. Before she thought better of it, she asked, "Would you like to come over for a drink or something?"

His eyes went wide and cautious. "Right now?"

"Yes." A restless feeling rose inside, making her excited and flustered at the same time. What the hell was she thinking? "Well, after I pay for my book."

"Okay. Sure." He stood so abruptly that his chair scraped against the cement floor. Offering the others nearby a sheepish grimace, he then followed her to the counter.

Minutes later they were ducking and weaving through the crowded sidewalks, trying to avoid the steady stream of cyclists and homeless along the one-mile walk to her condo. Alec spent the journey sharing his take on the weekend's receipts, customer feedback, and so on.

Colby couldn't concentrate on business, though. Not when his cargo pants, soft chambray shirt, and uncharacteristically free expression looked even more appealing than him in his crisp white chef's coat.

For a blissful moment, she wanted to simply be one of two single adults enjoying a breezy Sunday afternoon with a frisson of attraction sparkling between them. A pair that onlookers might even mistake for a couple. A happy couple.

Lately, the voice that wanted Alec as more than her friend had been drowning out the one advising caution. Who was she to judge Alec's baggage when she had a cartful of her own?

Perhaps Alec was another chance to force herself out of a comfortably numb existence, like today when she'd survived going back to the Pearl. If she couldn't make herself trust Alec—someone she'd known most of her life—who *could* she trust?

"Pretty building." Alec squinted up at the gleaming glass structure. "Do you have a nice view?"

"No. Second-floor unit." She'd never again live on a high floor with a balcony. A little shiver danced down her spine, but she made herself look into Alec's eyes before that final image of Mark could fully materialize. It worked, but the sudden intimacy inside the elevator nearly suffocated her when the doors closed.

Alec shoved his hands in his pockets. That old habit comforted her, actually.

Once inside her apartment, she went to the refrigerator, pulled out an open bottle of sauvignon blanc, and poured two glasses. A quick flick of the remote turned on some mellow music to calm her nerves.

From the kitchen, she watched Alec meander around the living room, studying her photos and gazing out the plate-glass windows. His hand grazed the soft chenille sofa and fingered the bronze sculpture on the sofa table.

She'd decorated A CertainTea much like her own home. Grays, creams, woods, with occasional charcoal. A perfect model unit, yet lacking in the essentials that made a house a home. Not even the pop of lavender pillows and artwork had made a difference. Alec, on the other hand, might.

She crossed to him. With a slightly shaky hand, she handed him a wineglass, blurting, "I want to talk about the kiss."

Alec's wineglass halted in midair. "I thought we already did."

Colby gestured toward the sofa. When he sank into its deep cushions, Colby settled beside him. Although they weren't touching, his heat and energy warmed her.

"I've been thinking." She gulped some wine for courage, then set her glass on the reclaimed-wood coffee table. "I overreacted. I've done that a lot since . . . Mark. I haven't quite found my balance."

"You're still grieving your marriage." His brows drew together, lending him a guilt-ridden appearance. She didn't want him to feel guilty about kissing her. In fact, she wanted him to do it again. He stared at her wedding ring. "You witnessed something no one should see. And to lose someone you love that way . . ."

Colby almost confessed the truth about her troubled marriage and the guilt that clung to her like the freshman fifteen. But Mark had never wanted anyone to know. She couldn't betray his memory now.

"I'm trying to move on. A CertainTea is a good start. But as much as I love the happy diners and sampling all of the amazing things you prepare, it hasn't helped me here." She gestured around her home and then settled a hand over her heart. "Or here."

"You can't force it, Colby." He set down his glass and scrubbed his face. "A kiss shouldn't make you cry."

She edged closer. "I think it'd been so long since I'd experienced any kind of lust. It shocked me, especially because it was you."

When he looked away, she realized how that might have sounded. She reached for his hand. "I only meant that we've been friends for so long. It was a little weird, right? I mean, we've got this whole platonic history. Surely part of you still thinks of me as the little brat who always chased after you and Hunter. Who bullied you into haircuts, tutoring, and kissing lessons." She smiled, her mind sifting through a hundred moments from their youth.

"It's weird, but not for those reasons." Alec released her hand, stood, and went to the window. Not the response she'd expected. Maybe her indecisiveness all week had pushed him away. "We can't leave the past behind until we talk about Mark and Joe."

"Please don't make me dissect my marriage and everything that led to Mark's jump. It's too painful." The familiar lump wedged in her throat, making it hard to swallow. She closed her eyes for a second to will it away. "Talking about it changes nothing. I'll simply say that not everything is how you or others may think it was. All I need—all I *want* now—is to close that door." She studied Alec's profile. His jaw clenched while he thought. "Just tell me, are you interested in helping me move forward?"

His thoughts boiled over like a poorly tended stockpot. She didn't know she was handing him his deepest desire, or that the truth stood between them like an invisible fence poised to deliver a painful shock. "My interest is obvious, isn't it? But we have to discuss the past. There's something I haven't told you."

"I know." She looked down then, so she didn't see the blood drain from his face when his heart stopped.

"You know?" He'd never considered that perhaps Mark had told her about the letter. He couldn't speak, standing in a sort of frightened fascination about what she'd say next.

"I remember Joe's funeral, when Mark accused you of having something to do with Joe's mood on the hike. You two had a fight, right?"

Alec imagined he looked like a carp, the way his mouth opened and closed at least twice before he formed a response. "That's true, but—"

"But nothing. Brothers fight." She waved her hand as if one airy stroke could erase all those years and battles. "Whatever happened didn't push Joe off that cliff."

He sucked in a breath, his thoughts veering from Mark to his brother, an equally shameful and unpleasant deliberation. "Maybe not literally, but the night before that hike, I not only wanted to hurt him, I *reveled* in it."

Colby shifted on the sofa. Her cat-shaped eyes wide yet gentle, waiting. Apparently curious to know more about the ugliness living inside him.

He'd come this far; he might as well finish the story. "Remember Beth?"

"Hard to forget." Disdain colored her words. "I put her in the same class as Gentry's current guy, Jake. Neither is particularly kind or caring."

"I don't know Jake, but you're right about Beth."

She tipped her head in question. "Did you share that opinion with Joe?"

"No." Her thermostat mustn't have been working right, because the room temperature spiked. Alec paced as the memory replayed, as vivid and 3-D as the night it happened. "She showed up drunk at my place that night. Said she and Joe had been fighting. Begged me to let her in to talk. I made a pot of coffee and offered platitudes about how Joe cared about her and she should go work things out with him. Then she excused herself for a minute."

He remembered her stumbling in her heels and feeling her way along the wall back toward his bathroom. "Honestly, I thought she went to throw up, but then she came back stripped down to her underwear. Started touching me, telling me how much she admired my success. How I was the 'impressive' brother. I was trying to get out of the situation when Joe pounded on my door. Apparently, he'd tracked her down using some mobile app. He walked in before she put her clothes back on, then jumped to a bunch of conclusions."

Alec hadn't stopped turning in circles. His thoughts were so steeped in the memory of Joe's reaction to finding Beth there half-naked, that when Alec did finally look up, he was shocked *not* to see Joe standing in front of him, fist balled, face red and sweaty.

"I can see why *Beth* should feel bad," Colby began, "but you didn't do anything wrong."

With shame on his mind, he met Colby's gaze. "I did. Joe started in on me, called Beth a loser and so on. After years of tolerating all the put-downs—of taking the high road, even when he didn't deserve it—I snapped. I let him believe that I'd been with Beth. I was an ass, but in the heat of the moment, I thought I'd earned the right to hurt him . . . or he'd earned it, however you want to look at it. I woke up planning to tell the truth, but he'd taken off with Mark up to the falls, and then it was too late."

Wilting onto the sofa, he buried his face in his hands. He'd hoped to feel better after making that confession, but right now he couldn't settle his stomach.

Colby bumped her knee against his. "Not your finest moment, but not unforgivable, either. Maybe you were an ass, but not an unforgivable one. Your fight didn't make Joe take Mark's dare."

"I think it did." He remembered the wounded pride on his brother's face. "The idea that his girlfriend cheated on him with *me*, a guy he considered so beneath him, shattered his ego. I'm sure he hiked to the falls full of piss and vinegar. Mark's dare gave him a chance to reclaim his manhood. If he hadn't been reeling from shock, he probably wouldn't have been so rash."

"Don't jump to conclusions. What-ifs will drive you crazy. Joe's ego is on him, not you. Trust me. I'm sorry your last conversation with Joe went so horribly, but you loved him your whole life, and he knew that. We *both* need to let go of whatever we wish we'd done differently." She blinked, as if she'd revealed too much. "Alec, our history is complicated. I get that. But I can't keep hiding from life, either. It feels like I'm on the brink of something new and exciting. Maybe we'll find our way forward together, but *not* if we keep looking back."

"It's not about looking back, it's about confronting mistakes. We have to talk about Mark's suicide."

"Why? Why make me talk about that when I work so hard every day *not* to remember? It took eighteen months to sleep through the night without nightmares." Her eyes glistened as her expression tightened. "I still can't always shut out that final image of him when it wants to surface. But I'm tired of everything in my life being defined by what happened with Mark. All I want is to stop thinking about him. Please, Alec. Please don't keep bringing him up."

She tugged the wedding band off her finger and tossed it on the coffee table. They both stared at it while she wiped a tear from her cheek.

Shaken by her breakdown, he paused. Ignoring the past wasn't healthy, but maybe it wasn't his choice to make. She'd handed him an out. One that enabled him to stick to his original plan to do anything he could to secure her happiness. If that required him to keep his mouth shut about Mark, at least he'd be loving her the way she asked to be loved.

"Okay."

Even teary she looked beautiful. "Thank you."

Now what? Neither of them knew the first thing about taking steps forward. They sat together in awkward silence until she interlaced her fingers with his—her hand soft and warm in his large, scarred one. Only then did the impact of the situation fully register. He was holding hands with Colby, talking about the future. Their future.

His heart beat out her name like a favorite song. He wanted to make love to her more than almost anything. But the ring she'd thrown on the table like some eerie gauntlet warned him to exercise patience. Her pushing herself to be ready wasn't the same as her actually being ready.

His thoughts strayed, searching for some kind of redemption for his secret. A few minutes passed before he said, "I have an idea."

"Oh?" She shot him a flirtatious look. Honestly, he couldn't get used to that. He stared at her, savoring the fact that she *liked* him.

Collecting himself, he said, "Let's do something to honor Joe and Mark."

She straightened, eyes alert. "Like what?"

"Maybe host a fund-raiser at A CertainTea in their names to raise money for some cause?" He shrugged, assuming the idea would appeal to her.

"I love that idea." Her perfect little nose flared. "We could start a memorial fund."

"A fund is even better." He pulled her against his side, offering his shoulder as a pillow. Alec's father would hate having Mark's name tied to Joe's. Truthfully, Alec didn't love the idea, either, but he owed it to Mark, and to Colby. "We'll have to think of a good cause. Do you still make gift baskets and deliver them to the children's hospital?"

"Sometimes, but we should think bigger."

"Whatever you want." He'd made a promise to see her happy, and he would. He'd worry about his dad's reaction to all of this later.

Chapter Ten

Colby's muscles loosened as if she'd just stretched and sighed. Her body fitted against Alec's as perfectly as one of his beloved puzzle pieces.

Although she'd spent the better part of her week daydreaming about more kisses, simply resting in the crook of his arm seemed enough for now. No pressure. No expectations. She stayed there, listening to Alec's heart beating, letting her mind wander aimlessly, like a butterfly, fluttering from thought to thought.

One thought: he smelled like her favorite fabric softener—eminently snuggly. Another: the late-afternoon light made her cream-colored furniture look peach. A third equally random thought: despite the hot dog she'd chowed down earlier, she was hungry. That one broke through the silence. "I'm starving."

He muttered a curse, his body tensing to stand. "My dinner reservation at Beast."

Colby tightened her grip around his waist. "Can you cancel?"

He paused before resting his cheek on her head. "Yeah."

A little smile formed. She wanted him to stay even though she didn't know where the night might lead. In truth, it didn't need to lead anywhere else. His comforting presence was more than enough.

"Want me to whip up something to eat?" he asked.

"I doubt I've got much to work with."

"You forget who you're talking to." He tapped her shoulder so she'd let him up, which she did with great reluctance.

With long, assured strides, he crossed the room to her refrigerator. She watched his confidence fade as he took inventory of its contents. If memory served, there should be jelly, butter, some mango chunks, broccoli, half-and-half, and maybe some slices of Muenster cheese. Maybe. Oh, and seltzer. Grapefruit-flavored seltzer.

Without a word, he closed the door, wearing a faintly dazed expression. He then rummaged through her cupboards, where he likely spied a lot of tea, a half-empty bag of Cheetos, a few slices of bread, and some random oils and spices.

He turned, his face aghast, head shaking in dismay.

"This is the most pathetic kitchen pantry I've ever seen. *Ever*, Colby." For Alec, food had always been a serious business. "Don't you eat here?"

"Sometimes. But this month I've been filling up on everything you've been testing, or eating with my mom. I haven't been to the store in a while."

"I'll say."

Colby shrugged. "Let's order pizza."

"No." He scowled. "I won't be defeated."

"Alec, there's nothing here."

His eyes lit at the challenge. "Refill your wine. I'll have something ready in twenty minutes."

"You don't have to prove anything to me." She sat forward, recognizing a man on a mission.

"I have to prove it to myself." He smiled, shrugging.

From her distant spot on the sofa, she watched an amazing flurry of activity. One pan sizzled with seasoned oil, another with butter. A third roiled with boiling water. At one point, he worked at the counter, giving her a clear view of his face. The image transported her back in time to his mom's kitchen, where she'd often found him working with his mouth slightly open and his tongue pressed against his top row of teeth—a picture of concentration. The fact that hadn't changed made her smile.

Her curiosity piqued when he grabbed the bag of Cheetos.

He looked up as she craned her neck. "No peeking!"

Minutes later, he gestured toward the kitchen barstools. Unlike Jenna's torturous seats, Colby's stools had soft suede cushions.

Once she sat down, he said, "Normally I wouldn't put these particular dishes together as a meal, but as you know, there weren't many options."

Following the disclaimer, he placed a grilled-cheese-and-jelly sandwich in front of her, followed by a bowl of sliced mango with some sprinkled spices. Finally, he revealed a platter of broccoli with crumbled Cheetos.

"That's pretty funny, Alec," she chuckled.

He forked a broccoli crown and held it out. "Try it."

To her surprise, a complexity of flavors exploded as she crunched down on the veggie. Red pepper flakes and garlic? Some Parmesan, perhaps? And, of course, a dusting of crunchy Cheetos. "You truly are a master."

He bowed like a Broadway actor and then speared a crown for himself.

"Watching you now reminded me of hanging out in your mom's kitchen. I loved watching you cook. If only I'd become a great cook just from watching." She grimaced. "Fail on that score."

"Why didn't you ask me to teach you?" He took another bite of broccoli.

"It was more fun to watch. Plus, if you were teaching me, I wouldn't have been able to talk your ear off. It seemed like a fair trade: you were my unpaid counselor and I was your food tester. Speaking of which, what's on the mango?" She tentatively tested one, treating her senses to a little heat and tang.

"Chili powder and a squeeze of lime, though that lime looked a bit suspicious."

"It tastes amazing!" Then she pushed at the sandwich. "But grilled cheese and *jelly*?"

"*That* I know you'll enjoy. Sweet and savory always mix well." To prove his point, he took a bite from the corner of the sandwich, tugging it a little to reveal the perfect stretch of melted Muenster.

"Show-off."

She'd pretty much thrown her plans to date a baggage-free guy out the window, yet all she could do was smile. Then she remembered Sara's remark about Alec's fight with his dad. It occurred to her then that this meal shouldn't have surprised her. Alec's ability to make something out of nothing had been learned from a young age thanks to what little affection he got from his father.

"You never mentioned your family's reaction to the newspaper article." She speared another broccoli crown.

He turned away, suddenly very interested in washing the pans. "They're fine."

"Alec." She set down her fork, waiting for him to turn around.

When he finally did, he settled his hip against the sink and crossed his arms.

"That's a crock." She rested her chin in her hands. "Your dad hates us working together, so there's no way he's okay with that article. Please don't bottle up your feelings. Whatever this might become, it won't stand a chance if we can't share things with each other."

Colby had already tried the "under the carpet" approach with Mark. She didn't know much about healthy relationships, but she knew one shouldn't start the way her marriage ended. Keeping a lid on the past was fine, but they had to be able to openly discuss the present.

His posture deflated like a balloon with a slow leak as he walked around the bar and sank onto the stool beside her. "We argued. Nothing new for me."

"I hate being a source of *more* conflict." She took another bite of her sandwich, but, truthfully, her appetite had waned.

For weeks she'd been resisting inviting his complicated problems into her life without considering how she made *his* life harder. "Will getting more involved with me cost you your relationship with your dad?"

"What relationship?" Alec hoped the glib remark would end the conversation. There were better ways Colby could raise his blood pressure than bringing up his dad.

"Be serious."

"I can handle my dad." He wanted to shut this conversation down before she had second thoughts, although he couldn't deny his own concerns about how he'd manage a relationship with her while still working on one with his dad.

"What about Hunter? This might interfere with your friendship."

Alec didn't welcome her concern. He wanted her to be freed *because* of him, not *in spite* of him.

He grabbed her hand. "Trust me to sort out my relationships. There's no rush, anyway. We'll wait until you're sure about what you want."

"You're pretty patient." She grinned.

"You have no idea." He'd wait forever for the chance to give her back the wings Mark's suicide had clipped.

On the radio, the soft tune of dueling guitars floated through the room.

"I love this song." Colby smiled and took another bite of her sandwich, licking a bit of jelly from the corner of her mouth.

"I've never heard it," he said absently, wishing he could lick that jelly from her lips.

"'Bloom' by the Paper Kites."

The melody bubbled along like a brook in the springtime, carrying his heart along with it.

Colby's face lit as she slid off her stool and tugged his arm. "Let's dance."

The sun had nearly ducked below the horizon, casting the apartment in shadows except for the light coming from the stove hood. Colby rested her head against his chest and followed his lead, neither of them talking.

Every aspect of the moment captivated him. The rosemary-and-mint scent of her hair, the weight of her head on his chest, the feel of her cotton dress beneath his palm, the sway of her hips, the sound of their feet shuffling against the wood floor, the lilac-and-gray light shrouding them in a peaceful haze, the sound of her breath, the feel of her thin hand in his.

He raised her hand and pressed his lips to her wrist. She might not feel strong enough to confront the past, but he believed that compassionate, brave girl she'd been still existed, even if pain had locked her away deep inside. Colby would believe it, too, once he stitched together her torn pieces tight enough that she no longer noticed the seams.

"I haven't danced in years." She raised her head, her gaze soft.

"Maybe instead of reading about some fictional character's hundred happy days, we should tick through our own bucket lists together."

"That's sweet." She grinned but didn't appear eager for adventure.

"I'm serious. What's on your list?"

After a moment, she said, "My top three would be a trip to Holland during its tulip festival, a hot-air-balloon ride, and to meet Adam Levine."

"Adam Levine?" he chuckled.

"No judging. What about you?"

"I've never given it any thought."

"Off the top of your head, what have you always wanted to do?"

Make love with you. "Earn a Michelin star—or two, or three—someday. Cycle through French wine country. Fish in Alaska."

"I can't help much with that first one."

"Michelin doesn't cover the Northwest US at this point, but maybe in the future. In the meantime, I want to win another James Beard Award, and you've given me a place to start trying." He set aside concerns about the way she kept wanting to tweak his menu for "broader appeal." This wasn't the time for that discussion with "the boss." Instead, he teased, "Of course, the other two might be a little difficult to squeeze in on Mondays and Tuesdays, and I can't have the boss catch me slacking off."

"She's a taskmaster. Her and that dumb rule against coworkers dating." Colby wrinkled her nose.

"Sexual harassment suits *are* messy." He kissed her temple, then twirled her around. "But if I play my cards right, I could end up owning the joint."

"First she'd have to sexually harass you."

"I can't wait!" He'd never spoken truer words in his life.

Her eyelids lowered slightly. "Maybe you won't have to."

The heated words shot through him. She slid her hands up his chest. Her fingertips brushed along his neck to the line of his jaw, then back down and over his shoulder blades. His body grew hot and hard wherever she touched him.

He traced the curves of her hip, her spine, the back of her neck. Her lips parted slightly, but her gaze followed her own hands as they swept down his torso, then snuck around his waist and over his ass.

Colby's featherlight touch was the most erotic of explorations, despite his being fully clothed. He willed time to stop and let himself savor the moment building between them. The thrum in his chest and elsewhere awakened every part of his body, inside and out, imprinting her touch on his soul. They swayed to the music, and everything around him receded into a fog as he lightly rested his hands on her hips.

"Alec." The whisper drifted around him, making him dizzy.

He didn't know how to respond to the onslaught of emotion, because what *did* one do when his dreams came true?

Eyes closed, he kissed her forehead, her nose, her eyelid, her jaw—which made her shiver—then finally her mouth. She tasted like jelly and cheese and a hint of the pepper flakes, but mostly she tasted like Colby. *Colby, Colby, Colby.* His heart brimmed over with rich sweetness, thick and decadent like molten caramel.

Her arms wound around his neck, holding him close. So close it seemed as if their hearts might knock into each other.

He wouldn't open his eyes for fear that this dream would disappear. Need tightened his entire body with the groundswell of desire and hunger that had built up for years.

Colby eased away and took his hand. "Let's take this someplace more comfortable."

No tears. Today she shed no tears. Still, jumping into bed could be the wrong move. High heat, while seductive, could be tricky. Like trying to sear steak in butter, the results would likely be smoky and bitter.

"Wait."

Her brows rose.

"Let's slow down. I think you—we—need time."

She smiled. "Haven't we waited long enough?"

If you only knew.

He gathered her close so she wouldn't misread his intentions. "There's a lot at stake. Our friendship. Our working relationship. Let's not rush into something and risk one of us ending up hurt."

Of course, chances were that person would be him, not her. He'd be her rebound lover, and then she'd wake up and remember that he'd never been the man of her dreams.

Her hand touched his cheek before he realized that his gaze had wandered.

"Why do you look sad?" She brushed his bangs away from his eyes.

"I'm not sad." He masked his self-doubt with a bad joke. "I'm concentrating. It takes a lot of restraint to keep from throwing you over my shoulder and racing to the bedroom."

"Then let go."

"If this has any chance of being meaningful, we should treat it with reverence."

"Reverence," she almost whispered, her face registering esteem. Esteem, however, wasn't near enough regard to satisfy him.

"Yes, reverence. Starting with a kiss." He walked her backward toward the wall. "A perfect kiss."

He pressed her against the wall, then brought her hands up over her head, lightly fastening them there with his one hand.

"What's a perfect kiss?" The pulse point of her neck visibly throbbed.

With his free hand, he swept a bit of her hair away from her face and tucked it behind her ear. He stared into her eyes the entire time, even as his thumb stroked her cheek and then brushed along her lips.

"A perfect kiss begins with me touching your mouth." His gaze temporarily dipped to the cupid's bow of her lips before returning to her eyes, emboldened by the desire he saw reflected.

Before she replied, he closed his mouth over hers and nipped at her lip, then traced its seam with his tongue. He sucked her lower lip and then sank his tongue into her mouth. Probing once, twice, and a third time until he heard her breathing grow heavier.

"A perfect kiss," he murmured against her cheek while kissing her jaw and neck, "will brand your heart with my desire." He released her hands and cradled her face, looking in her eyes. "It will restore you and make you forget every kiss that came before." He kissed her again, this time with more urgency. Then, almost like a prayer, he whispered, "It will make you dizzy until the answer to every question is my name."

Her body shivered as she fell under the spell of his perfect kiss. He almost regretted his talent for restraint, now that being one with her seemed essential.

"So we're agreed." He kissed her again because, when her lips were so close, he couldn't resist.

"Not at all." She unbuttoned his shirt, then smoothed her hands along his chest. "Show me what else you can do so perfectly."

This time when she yanked on his arm and led him to her room, he followed.

He barely registered the surroundings because the only thing he could see was her beautiful, silky hair in his hands. Her flushed cheeks and swollen lips. The curve of her shoulders, breasts, and hips as she stepped out of her dress as it fell to the floor.

Her hot skin, so smooth and taut beneath his fingertips, warmed his hands. Lust surged when she pressed her lips to his chest, then made way for more tender yearning.

Closing his eyes, he unleashed the umpteen years of passion he'd hidden away in fear of rejection or scorn. *Ma moitié*. He didn't say the words aloud, but love—red, rich, and complete—consumed his heart and soul.

Heat flared in anticipation of seeing her naked and sweaty and staring at him. Of hearing her call out his name and feeling her mouth on his eager body. Of losing himself in her, utterly and completely.

Seconds turned into minutes turned into hours of tangled arms and legs, of beating hearts and panting breaths, of murmured ecstasy, until they drifted into blissful sleep as one.

Chapter Eleven

Disoriented by dawn's first rays, Colby wished she'd remembered to close the blinds. She pressed her fingers to her slightly tender lips. Lips ravaged by hundreds of perfect kisses. Limbs heavy from hours of lovemaking.

Most guys had made short work of foreplay. Alec, however, had never been like most guys.

After a lifetime of watching him pay particular attention to every detail, be it a puzzle or a recipe or any project he'd ever attempted, it didn't surprise her to discover he was also that kind of lover. The memory of his touch unleashed a rush of warmth that coiled in her tummy, making her smile. Words that rarely entered her vocabulary anymore—"sweet, emotional, moving"—came to mind.

She watched him sleeping on his stomach, arms and legs akimbo, and studied his graceful cheekbones, shiny hair, curve of his shoulders, outline of triceps. At once familiar and yet so fascinatingly new.

Only inches separated them in her bed. It had been nearly two years since she'd shared this space with anyone.

Mark had been a belly sleeper, too. When they'd first met and made love, he'd also enthralled Colby even as her instinct warned her to slow down. She should've listened to that instinct instead of being impulsive—of getting swept up in emotion and lust. But she'd been young and had rushed into marriage with all the assuredness and hopefulness of any inexperienced young woman. Now the ashes of that marriage still gathered in the alcoves of her mind, no matter how often she tried sweeping them away.

And yet, without much hesitation, she'd given in to impulse again last night. Alec's perfect kisses had swept her away, just as he'd promised. Now what? Could she and Alec share something like Hunter and Sara had, or were the obstacles and history too overwhelming? Doubts began circling the bed, making her chest tight. The urge to push away—to run as far and fast as she could—gripped her with astonishing force.

She slid out of bed and, after quietly slipping on some clothes, went to the living room and paced. She'd forgotten how awkward "the morning after" could be with a man who wasn't one's husband, not to mention one who'd been a friend, an adversary, a pseudo brother . . .

Oh, good God. *Alec Morgan* was naked in her bed. How could that seem right and wrong at the same time?

Sun rays streamed through the plate glass, glinting off her wedding band and stopping her heart. She lifted the ring, now warm and familiar in her palm. It didn't belong on her ring finger after last night.

She tested the band on her right hand, which felt odd. Odd but necessary. Unwelcome, irrational feelings of betrayal of both Mark and Alec tangled her thoughts and emotions into a thick knot. Food might help. She grabbed her keys and headed for a convenience store to buy eggs and milk. At the very least, cooking would give her something to do until Alec woke up.

Along the three-block walk, she passed by a homeless man sleeping in a corner near a garage. Many of the homeless clustered closer to the highways, where the mayor allowed them to pitch tents at night. The population seemed to be expanding lately, with more scattered throughout the city, especially near the parks.

That man's fate—alone, penniless, and covered by a thin, dingy blanket—could've easily been Mark's, too. He'd burned through his accounts during manic phases, spending ungodly sums on crazy things like plane tickets for a spiritual trip to Tibet and cases of sixty-dollar bottles of organic elderflower lemonade from Europe. Once he gambled away nearly his entire savings in Vegas. Had it not been for her job and her CTC stock, he could've easily ended up huddled in some corner of the city.

Mark's family lived in New Hampshire and had kept in touch sporadically at best. Without her, Mark would've been lost long before they'd learned he went missing.

Not that she'd ultimately been able to save him. That thought always twisted her stomach. She knew, deep down, she'd never fully shirk the weight of her share of responsibility for what happened to her marriage and to her husband. To her. Did other people walk around hiding that level of guilt and pain?

She glanced over her shoulder, wondering if the stranger had any family. If he, too, was mentally ill.

On her way home from the convenience store, she set a small bag with bread, peanut butter, and apple juice near the still-slumbering homeless man. He stirred but didn't waken. Slightly afraid, she scooted away, wishing she were braver. Wishing she could do more. Then she remembered Alec's wonderful idea. A smile formed, not only because she knew just what she wanted to do, but also because it reminded her of Alec's best trait: his kind heart.

When she returned, Alec was already dressed and ready to go. His gaze landed on the bag in her right hand and then homed in on the ring. "I didn't know where you went. I thought . . . Are you upset?"

She recognized that "bracing for pain" expression he'd always donned whenever his father entered the room. He must've thought she'd run away this morning, which she sort of had. Now he expected to be hurt.

The thought of adding to the vein of rejection that ran through Alec like a wormhole wrung her heart.

"You were sleeping so soundly, I didn't want to wake you." She gave him a quick kiss, willing her lingering doubts into submission as she raised the bag up. "Not even you could whip up breakfast without a quick restocking. This time, I'll cook."

He stared at her an extra second, assessing and hopeful. She pushed down the knowledge that she'd already started repeating the bad patterns from her marriage of hiding her doubts to spare his feelings.

"Trying to prove that you actually *did* learn to cook from watching me in high school?" His grin lit a match in her chest, loosening the tightness.

"Something like that." Although she felt as vulnerable as he looked, she could do this, dammit. She wanted to do this with Alec. "Tea or coffee?"

"Neither, thanks." He sank onto a kitchen stool. "What do you have planned today?"

"During my walk, I got an idea. What if we use the fund we discussed to help the homeless?"

"I'd assumed we'd support an environmental cause, given Mark's and Joe's passion for the wilderness." Alec rubbed his chin. "Why the homeless?"

"It's a real problem in the city. I also think many suffer from mental illness. Without the support they need, they end up alone and lost. I think Mark—" She shook her head and prayed Alec didn't catch her slip of tongue. "I think Mark and Joe would support that. The environment is important, but people matter more."

"Okay, then." Alec's warm smile wrapped around her heart. "The homeless."

"Thank you." She cracked eggs into a bowl. "We could visit the Burnside Shelter this morning and find out what they need—food, beds, clothing."

"I can't today. I skipped my morning cycling with Hunter, but I can't blow off my mom, too. I promised I'd drive to the coast with her to visit my gram."

She whisked the eggs, wondering if Alec was keeping Hunter's reaction from her. "Hunter must be pissed about being blown off."

"I texted him an apology in case he waited around."

The wire whisk landed against the edge of the bowl with a clank. "You have your phone?"

"I know. Shocking!" He pulled it from his pocket, smiling, then set it on her counter.

"How'd he react to this?" She gestured between them, forcing the issue.

"I didn't mention it. You were gone. I thought you'd had regrets." He glanced at her ring again, a stoic mask covering his emotions. "Do you, Colby?"

She'd sworn she wouldn't start a new relationship with dishonesty, yet she couldn't hurt him. Especially when her doubts didn't rise to the level of regret. She might fear the part of her heart vibrating with happiness and hope, but she didn't want to shut it off, either. Her hesitation must've telegraphed uncertainty, causing his crestfallen expression.

"It's okay, you know." He stood. "I should get out of your way this morning. On Wednesday you can let me know what the rescue shelter says, and we'll work on that project together."

Her throat tightened, but the voice in her head shouted *"Don't go!"*

"Wait." She turned off the stove and dashed around the breakfast bar, placing her hands on his chest. "I don't regret last night, Alec. I don't."

"I hear a 'but' in there . . ." He didn't embrace her. "Last night you said you wanted to put Mark behind you, but today you're wearing his ring again."

"I know. I can't explain it because I don't understand it. My feelings about Mark are complicated. I need to take baby steps." She tugged at his shirt. "You said you'd be patient."

He nodded. "I will be."

"Thank you." She wound her arms around his waist, resting her head on his shoulder. Once he hugged her, she breathed again. This part felt so right she couldn't let her chickenshit heart steal her chance at happiness with this man and his perfect kisses. "Let's talk to Hunter together, unless that makes you uncomfortable."

"You're ready to go public?"

"I don't want to hide my life from my family." In this way her relationship with Alec would differ from her marriage. "I'll probably visit my mom this afternoon. Maybe we can swing by Hunter's in the evening?"

"I'll be back by then, so I'll pick you up at your mom's." Alec grinned. "I wonder what Leslie will think."

"*Leslie* will be thrilled—and sure to expect an endless supply of pastries and visits," she snickered. "Now maybe *you're* having second thoughts."

He cupped her face, his expression sober and intense. "Never."

Unexpectedly, relief whooshed through her. "Even if *your* parents freak out."

"Stop focusing on my parents."

"Your dad really dislikes me." Colby eased out of his arms, even though it was chilly outside of his embrace. "This could be explosive."

He squeezed her hands. "He won't hurt you."

"What if he hurts *you*?"

"After last night, nothing he does can touch me." He sounded light-hearted, but she suspected he'd done that for her protection.

Baggage. They both had enough to fill a 747. But she had no doubt Alec had her interests at heart. If ever there were a man she could trust to be whom he appeared to be, it should be him.

Alec kissed her—a warm, slow kiss. A kiss that eased her worries and rekindled the desire she'd been keeping at bay. She ran her hands over his hips and then fiddled with his pants button. He moaned and kissed her deeper, but then pulled back.

"If my mom wasn't expecting me soon, I'd keep you in bed all day." Following one final, too-quick kiss, he said, "See you later."

After he left she noticed the hum of the fridge, the tick of the vintage wall clock. The sounds of the lonely life she'd grown accustomed to before Alec reminded her of what she'd been missing.

◆ ◆ ◆

"I'm not surprised." Alec's mother stared at the pine trees aligning the road along the drive home from visiting Gram. "You always liked Colby."

Given Colby's circumspection, he'd considered keeping their relationship quiet awhile longer. But that would be another secret, and he could barely shoulder the crippling weight of the others.

"She's always been special—the way she puts others' feelings first." Alec recollected the earliest signs of that trait and realized her protective stance toward his staff should never have surprised him. "The empathy she's had for others. How she quietly goes about making sure people know they matter. She makes me feel like *I* matter."

"You matter to *me*." His mom looked affronted.

"That's different. Plus, look at how she's survived everything with Mark and Joe. She's not bitter and broken. She's taking risks with a new career, with me. How can someone not admire her?" He needed his mom to accept Colby because he knew his father would not. "You used to like her, Mom."

"She's lovely, but it's complicated. Your father . . ." More silence preceded a sigh.

"My coming home hasn't made things better."

"It has for me." She patted his thigh. "I love spending time together, honey."

Alec aimed for optimism. "Maybe he'll surprise us, especially when he hears about the memorial fund. Doing something in Joe's name should please him."

From the corner of his eye, he noticed his mother's grimace. "He'll hate having it share Mark's name."

"Mark didn't push Joe off that cliff." Alec took his misgivings out on his hair, raking his hand through it for the fifth or sixth time in the past forty-five minutes. "At some point, don't we have to accept that fact?"

"It's brutal, Alec. Losing a child . . . you want someone to blame—someone other than your child." Her voice wobbled, making him regret causing her to defend her feelings. "It's not logical, but grief rarely is."

"I'm sorry, Mom. But blaming Colby is as tenuous as blaming yourselves for moving next door to the Cabots."

"I've had that thought, too." She blew out a sigh. "The 'if onlies' are numbing."

Numbing? That'd be a nice change from the way his "if onlies" ate at his conscience like acid. He didn't have the courage to confess his fight with Joe, but maybe sharing his role in Mark's suicide would convince his mom that forgiveness mattered for everyone's sake.

"I need to tell you something else." His rough voice startled her.

"What, honey?"

"A week before Mark killed himself, he'd sent me a suicidal apology note. I didn't take the threat seriously, so I didn't respond or warn Colby." His chest grew heavy while thinking back on Colby's teary plea last night. "If I'd have said something, Colby wouldn't have witnessed that violent death and become a widow. She might even be a mother by now."

His mom absorbed his confession in silence for several seconds. "Does Colby know?"

"No."

"Why not?"

"Take your pick: shock, horror, shame. I was still reeling from Joe's funeral and could barely concentrate at work." He shook his head. "When Hunter told me what happened, I didn't see the point of a too-late apology. As time passed, Hunter said she was healing, so it seemed unfair to dredge it up just to ease my conscience."

When Alec saw his mother's skeptical expression, he said, "I know, Mom. That's part of why I left town, and also one reason I came back. I'd planned to make it up to her. To make sure she found some happiness again. The job gave me that chance. Then yesterday, when things got personal, I tried to confess, but she begged me not to make her talk about the past."

His mother rubbed her temple, as she was prone to do when thinking. "Mark could be so dramatic; I understand why you didn't take his threat seriously." She clucked to herself. "If Colby doesn't want to discuss the past, why tell *me* this?"

"So you understand why the memorial fund should be in both names." When she appeared confused by his logic, he added, "If our family blames Mark for Joe's death, then I'm at least as culpable in Mark's."

His mom's face twitched, but she didn't say anything. He turned onto Lakeshore Drive, although the familiar streets of Lake Sandy— quaint storefronts with overflowing flower boxes—offered no comfort.

When they passed Leslie Cabot's house, his heart skipped at the sight of Colby's car. Despite everything that could go wrong, a smile formed at the thought of Leslie's reaction. His smile deflated when he parked in his parents' driveway. "I'll wait to talk to Dad until you aren't around."

She stared out the window, biting her thumbnail. "No. If I'm in the room, he might restrain himself."

"I can handle him."

"You shouldn't have to." She touched his cheek before opening her door. "I don't care how old you are, you're still my baby."

"I don't need you as a buffer, Mom."

"I didn't fight hard enough for you in the past, so I won't let you stop me from trying now. Besides, this is a *family* matter." Her determined stare warned him she wouldn't back down.

He surrendered in order to preserve his energy for taking on his dad. The ground beneath him seemed uneven as he walked with her into the house. Perhaps he shouldn't charge in and blow up a powder keg to be with Colby, especially when her feelings weren't yet dependable.

"You're back." His father looked up from the television, expression neutral, as if the other week's insults hadn't occurred. He'd always been that way. Screaming and cursing one day, then acting as if everything was fine the next. "What's for dinner?"

"Grilled chicken salad." His mom set her purse on the entry table, looking battle weary.

"Rather have a burger or ribs." His dad grinned before tossing back a fistful of peanuts.

"*I'd* rather keep your cholesterol down." His mom smiled pleasantly and took a seat on the sofa, moving the can of nuts to the end table out of his reach. "Alec, will you be staying for dinner?"

"No, I've got plans." He stood stiffly, wishing he could find some way to connect with his dad instead of picking this battle.

Alec gathered his courage, remembering his mom's story about Grandpa and trying to convince himself that his father's bitterness toward him sprang from envy, not antipathy. Of course, as soon as his dad learned about Colby, it could turn into both. Things might get worse before they got better, but surely his father would eventually accept her.

His father's gaze flicked to him. "I was a cop, remember? Despite what you think, I did more than eat donuts on the job. You two just spent the whole day together, so I'm pretty sure your mom already knows about your plans. If this is an opening to tell me something unpleasant, just out with it already."

Rather than soft-pedal, Alec channeled Joe and jumped right in. "I have a date. With Colby."

His father stared at him. Nothing moved. Not a brow, a nostril, a hair on the man's head. He didn't even blink for what seemed like an hour. The pained shock on his face caused an ache in Alec's chest.

When his dad finally spoke, his voice sounded hoarse. "You have no sense of family loyalty."

Alec's heart caved in on itself. Years of turning the other cheek for the good of the family had gone unappreciated by his dad. By Joe. "That's not true."

"That girl—" Disdain colored his dad's tone.

"'That girl' has a name," Alec interrupted. "That girl gave me a job. *That* girl, our lifelong neighbor, grieves for *her* friend Joe." Alec crossed his arms, anticipating the need for additional protection. "In fact, Colby and I are starting a memorial fund in Joe's and Mark's names to raise money for the homeless. We're planning a fund-raiser at the restaurant. This could be an opportunity for our two families to heal."

"Like hell you'll link your brother's name with the man who killed him." His father sprang out of his recliner. "What's wrong with you?"

Fortunately, Alec stood far enough outside his father's range to avoid being showered with spittle. He didn't flinch, although he wondered whether his dad might actually strike him. Alec had anticipated blowback, but not the level of animosity he saw in his father's eyes. For the first time he realized he might never find a way to hold on to both his family and Colby. He glanced at his mother and knew, if handed an ultimatum, he'd be forced to sacrifice his own happiness. Quietly, he said, "Mark didn't kill Joe."

"He sure as hell did." His dad lunged forward, now inches away, face tight with fury.

"Frank," came his mother's stern warning. Alec wished she'd leave. It'd be easier to deal with his dad if he didn't have to worry about her feelings. But she'd made her choice, and he had to see this through.

"Mark didn't push Joe, Dad." Alec stood tall.

"Daring Joe to jump was like handing a gun to a criminal and expecting him not to shoot. As far as I'm concerned, Mark Baxter should've been charged with negligent homicide."

"You know the law better than that. Besides, Mark suffered for what he did. So much so, he jumped off his balcony in front of his wife. He paid a steep price for making that dare. Does Colby have to keep paying, too? And me? Mom?" Alec gestured toward her, the one person he believed his dad did still love. "When can all the suffering end?"

"Why should anyone else's suffering end?" His father's grief-stricken face collapsed, his voice as close to a sob as Alec had ever heard. "Mine sure as shit hasn't, and it never will."

The pain radiating through the room stilled everyone, as if one wrong move would trigger a cataclysmic explosion. Alec didn't know which scared him more, seeing his dad's anger or witnessing his vulnerability. Hesitantly, he reached out to comfort, but his father shrugged him off.

Another rejection nicked at his heart. That muscle had more scars than both his hands and forearms put together.

"Dad." His own eyes stung. "Colby lost her friend and then, less than three months later, her husband. Maybe if our family had stopped blaming Mark, he wouldn't have jumped."

"You think I give a shit about Mark Baxter?" his dad shouted. "As far as I'm concerned, he got what he deserved."

"Did Colby?" Alex shot back, desperate to make headway so he wouldn't have to choose sides. "If you can't muster any sympathy for her, can you at least stop treating her like the enemy?"

His father shook his head. "You want to work for her, lay her, start a foundation with her, go be my guest. But don't expect me to like it. And don't make her out to be the victim. Joe was the victim." He circled his hand around the room. "*We're* the victims."

"Frank, enough!" Alec's mom stood, but his father waved her off and stormed out of the house. They heard him zoom down the driveway before he peeled off to God-knows-where.

"That went well." Alec made a face at his mother.

"Nothing got broken. It could've been worse."

"You think he'll come around?" Alec needed her to tell him yes, even if she was lying.

"I don't know."

Chapter Twelve

"I can't believe it," Colby's mom uttered for the third or fourth time since learning about Alec.

Stitch wandered into the living room and made himself comfortable on that old afghan, staring at Colby like an inquisitor who knew exactly what she was thinking.

"You think it's a mistake?" She looked away from the wise old cat to her mom, although why her mother's opinion on love meant anything remained a puzzle.

"Do *you* think so?" Her mother sipped her seltzer, legs curled beneath her like a young girl. The deep cushions of the corduroy sofa nearly swallowed her petite frame.

"More like a gamble." An all-or-nothing kind of bet.

Her mom patted Colby's knee for encouragement. "It's time to get back on the horse, whatever happens. Besides, Alec is very handsome."

"*Handsome* is irrelevant."

Her mom cocked a brow and snorted.

"Fine, his looks are a bonus. But that's not what got to me. Alec *knows* me and cares about my happiness. He's patient. He's obsessed with making my restaurant a success. And the way he looks at me . . ."

She paused, body flushing from that perfect kiss. It *had* branded her. "I just wish I knew how it will turn out."

"The unknown is half the fun." Her mom shrugged. "Speaking of unknowns, how'd Hunter react?"

Colby leaned forward, knowing her next words would please her mom immeasurably. "You're the first to know."

Her mother's mouth fell open. "Really?"

"Yep."

"I'm the first?" She set down the drink, a delighted smile distorting her cheeks.

"Yes, Mom. The very first." Colby chuckled at this simple side of her mom. Needy? Sure. But also easily enthused.

"I'm so proud that you confided in *me* first. Before Sara, even! It absolutely makes my day." Then her mother's expression became one of self-pity. "Almost erases my depression about Richard."

Uh-oh.

Depression? The word still called forth visceral memories, making Colby's pulse flutter until she reminded herself that her mom tossed it around every time she felt anything less than bliss. "I thought you really liked him."

"I do!" She dismissively waved a hand, her frown solidifying into feigned resolve. "I did, anyway."

No one performed self-possessed nonchalance like her mother. Colby couldn't decide whether to admire it or be wary.

In any case, the news rocked her. Richard and her mom's relationship had encouraged her to consider dating. He'd seemed so sweet; her mom had been so happy. Wrong again? Not exactly news that boosted Colby's confidence about her instincts. "What happened?"

"He broke it off." Suspiciously pink cheeks hinted at a story.

Colby crossed her arms. "Why?"

Rather than look at Colby, her mom stared at the throw-pillow fringe she was tugging. "Snickers."

"The imaginary dog?"

"Yes." She wrinkled her nose.

Softening her tone, Colby asked, "He busted you?"

Her mom nodded.

"How?"

"I was careless." She shook her head in a self-pitying manner. "I invited him here for dinner last night. I even cooked."

Colby stifled a chuckle. "Are you sure the dinner isn't why he ran?"

"I used to cook all the time," her mother defended. "Maybe not like Alec, but I *can* cook."

"I'm teasing, Mom." Colby squeezed her hand. "Back to Snickers."

"We were enjoying a perfect evening out on the deck, actually. Stargazing to Kenny Garrett's *Triology*." A dreamy expression signaled that her mom had traveled back to that moment, but then her smile drooped. "When we came inside, I took some things into the kitchen and left him milling around here. I returned to find him studying the photos of you, your brother . . . Stitch. He quizzed me about why Snickers wasn't in any."

"Oh, no." Colby covered her mouth with her hands. She shouldn't giggle, but this sounded like a cheesy sitcom episode.

"I was so flustered. I mean, I hadn't thought about that, you know." She stared into space while gulping more soda. "I had two choices. Keep fibbing or fess up."

"So you confessed."

"I did." She sighed and sat back, now stretching out her legs. "I'd hoped he might chuckle about the lengths I went to in order to spend time with him."

"He didn't see the humor?"

"No! He was 'deeply troubled' by my lie, and by how I made Hunter lie. Said he couldn't be with someone so dubious." Shaking her head, she added, "I mean, really. *Dubious.*"

"I'm sorry, Mom." Breakups. Another kind of special hell relationships often bring. In fact, Colby might be sitting on this couch crying over Alec someday.

"He acted like I lied about another man or something." Her mother snorted. "Honestly, he *over*reacted."

Perhaps he had, but Colby couldn't completely dismiss his uneasiness. "Some people think if you're willing to lie about something frivolous, then you'll definitely lie when the stakes are high."

Alec had lied to Joe to cause pain and then kept it a secret for years. Might he also lie to or keep secrets from her? After a marriage riddled with half-truths, that idea held no appeal.

"Don't pretend you've never fibbed." Her mother rolled her eyes. "Everyone tells white lies. Most people tell real lies once in a while, too."

"Maybe." In truth, Colby hadn't been completely honest with anyone in years. Where exactly was the line between protecting one's privacy and lying? And would she and Alec agree on that line? "But you can't be shocked when a lie causes you to lose someone's respect, either."

"Let's not discuss this anymore." Her electric-blue eyes dimmed.

Fine with Colby. What business did she have telling anyone what to do, anyway? What mattered was that her mother was hurting because her boyfriend broke up with her. That sucked at any age. "Give him a day or two. Then call or send a note."

"No." Her mom huffed, bravado rebuilding. "I can't be with someone who expects perfection. Who wants me to wear the right clothes, say all the right things, and all that."

"Did he criticize your *clothes*?"

"Of course not." Her mother's eyes widened, indignant. "I have fabulous taste!"

"I'm confused." Colby resisted slapping her forehead.

"It's a slippery slope. If a man won't accept a little mistake about this, then he'll never forgive a mistake about that or the other. These things always start the same: they *love* you for being unique and spontaneous until they lull you into feeling secure. Then come the criticisms and the 'Don't do that' and 'Why can't you do this?' demands. You twist into a pretzel to please them, and they end up leaving, anyway."

She'd stealthily broadened the conversation to encompass Colby's dad—the filter through which all men were now viewed. Colby supposed every woman's—every person's—former relationships affected how one viewed love. Hers certainly had.

"But that won't happen with Alec, honey." Her mom's eyes regained a little of their twinkle. "He always seemed more sensitive than other men."

Colby didn't remind her mother how, just a few weeks ago, she'd considered Alec an odd duck. *Now*, thanks to his pastry and cat-saving runs—and apparently his looks—he'd swayed her mother's opinion. "That's true."

"Your brother trusts him, and Hunter doesn't suffer fools. All things considered, this is a good step for you. It's about time you took a chance on something again."

"Leaving my job to run a restaurant wasn't a big enough risk?"

"Heavens, no!" Her mother brushed that off with a quick wave of her hand. "You have the option to go back to lawyering if this doesn't work. Failure won't hit you here." Her mother pointed at her chest. "Before you got married, you'd fling yourself into everything with your whole heart. That changed, even *before* Mark's death. You never confided in me, so I couldn't help. Maybe you thought I didn't know much about marriage, given my own failure."

"That's not it, Mom. Mark and I . . . well, we thought we could fix things on our own. In retrospect, that was a terrible mistake."

"Don't blame yourself for what he did." Her mom stared at her, as if those energetic blue eyes could chase away the guilt. "Focus on what you have now. Be happy, sweet girl."

The doorbell interrupted them. Colby placed her hand over her stomach. As encouraging as her mother had been, she doubted Alec received that same reception from his parents.

"That's probably Alec now." When her mom's face lit up, Colby added, "Don't expect pastries or a visit. We're going to Hunter's."

An unladylike snort escaped. "I'd pay to see Hunter's face when you tell him, but Sara will be supportive."

Her mother dashed ahead, beating Colby to the door. Alec flashed a warm smile at her mom, and Colby hated the fact that she wondered what he was hiding behind that mask, and whether he'd be honest about his parents' reaction to their news.

"I couldn't be more tickled." She patted his check. "Partners in every sense of the word. We should have a glass of wine."

"Not now, Mom. I told you we have plans."

"If Hunter gives you grief, don't listen to one word he says." Her mother rubbed Alec's arm like she was preparing an athlete for competition.

"Hunter and Sara have been together for more than a decade. If there's anyone we should listen to, it's probably him," Colby exclaimed.

"He got lucky. Only Sara could deal with his single-mindedness and stay happy." Her mom shrugged. "Doesn't mean *he* knows anything."

"He knows how to pick the right person," Colby grumbled.

Colby's mom flashed a flirtatious smile at Alec before looking at Colby. "Honey, I think you're on the right track now, too."

"See why I like her so much?" Alec hugged her mom again, his broadening grin lighting the entry.

Colby clasped his hand. "Let's get you out of here before she does something to embarrass us both."

"Good night, Leslie." Alec quickly kissed her cheek before Colby dragged him from the house.

"Is it safe to say your parents didn't react like my mom?" she asked once seated in his car.

"*No one* reacts like Leslie." He checked the rearview mirror while backing out, conveniently avoiding eye contact. "Some people will need time to adjust."

If two years hadn't helped them forgive her, more time didn't seem like the answer.

Almost as if in afterthought, he uttered, "If only I were more like Joe . . ."

"God, no, Alec." Her sharp reply startled him. Softening, she said, "Don't be like Joe."

The car slowed as Alec's bewilderment took hold. "I thought you loved Joe."

"I did, but he wasn't a better man than you. Not in any way."

Alec shifted uncomfortably as he turned onto Hunter's street, looking completely unconvinced.

"I mean it. You are a kinder, wiser man than your brother ever was. Even as kids, that much was obvious." She leaned across the console and kissed his cheek.

Alec remained quiet. That had always been his way. He thought; Joe acted. She supposed years of being unfavorably compared with Joe wouldn't be undone by her single declaration. But she'd prove to Alec that he no longer needed to compete with his brother.

When they arrived at Hunter's, Sara greeted them at the door. "Alec, my friend Susan had dinner at A CertainTea this weekend and is telling everyone it's *the best* food around. She's not easy to please, either."

"Good word of mouth is priceless." Alec pecked her on the cheek. "Next time she comes, I'll try to stop by her table and meet her."

"She'd love that. She likes to feel important." Sara hugged him and then Colby.

They followed Sara back to the kitchen, where she'd already opened a wine bottle and set out four glasses. Unlike Colby's sleek kitchen and empty pantry, Sara and Hunter's kitchen screamed "home." Colorful plates were displayed on a baker's rack. Fresh flowers filled a vase on the island. A checkered dish towel was carelessly draped over the edge of the sink. Colby envisioned a future where kids' artwork might be displayed on the stainless-steel refrigerator, too. For the first time, she suddenly wanted a *home* of her own.

"It's a nice night. Maybe we'll sit outside." Sara poured herself a glass. "Let me get Hunter. He's in his office, as usual." She rolled her eyes with the remark, which had been delivered with an uncharacteristic edge, and sauntered off in search of her husband.

"You okay?" Alec asked Colby, having accurately read the surprise on her face.

"I wonder if we've come at a bad time?" she answered, but the conversation ended when they heard footsteps approaching.

Hunter trailed Sara as they entered the kitchen.

"Hey, loser," Hunter joked with Alec. "You missed a gorgeous morning. Squeezed in twelve miles. Why'd you bail?"

Hunter waved off the glass of wine Sara offered, so Colby guzzled it, earning herself a quizzical grin from her sister-in-law.

"I was in Portland." Alec also declined wine.

"At six thirty?" Hunter crossed his arms. "Produce market?"

"No. I went up yesterday evening to check out the competition and bumped into Colby. We ended up talking late into the night."

Sara glanced from Alec to Colby, her gaze dropping to the point of contact where Alec's hand rested lightly against the small of Colby's back. Sara grinned, but Hunter remained clueless.

"So you crashed up there," Hunter said, reaching inside the fridge for a beer. "Want one?"

"No, thanks." Alec's composure helped Colby tap into some courage.

"He didn't just crash up there." Colby cleared her throat. "We came to a decision."

Hunter cracked open the bottle and took a swig. "Don't tell me you're fighting about the menu again. People love Alec's food. Letting him take the lead there is the right call, Colby."

She held his gaze, unwilling to discuss her desire to add a few comfort foods to the menu to satisfy people with her palate. "That's not what we were discussing."

"What, then? Not that happy-hour idea again, Sis?" Hunter's brows pinched like they always did when he went on a fact-finding mission. "Did Gentry mess something up?"

"No, none of that." Poor Gentry—everyone always assumed the worst.

"Inventory? Accounting? What?" He cocked his head. "How can I help?"

"Stop talking, for starters." Colby rested her hands on the island. "This isn't about the business."

If Colby could've whipped out her phone and snapped a photo of Hunter's perplexed expression to share with her mom without being rude, she would've. Rarely was he this confused. Sara, on the other hand, appeared to see what was coming and decided he needed a little help.

"Honey, take a seat." Sara slid a barstool out for him.

"Why do I feel like I'm about to be punked?" Hunter glanced at Alec and took a bigger swig of beer.

"Your sister and I have decided to see each other outside of work," Alec said.

Hunter choked on his drink. "What?"

"We're dating, idiot." Colby rolled her eyes.

Hunter's lemon-faced expression telegraphed his thoughts loud and clear. "Dating?" He looked at Sara as if somehow she'd right the ship, which had clearly tilted beneath him. He attempted a smile, grasping for something that made sense. "Is this a joke?"

"No." Colby sympathized with her brother's shock.

"You two are dating?" Hunter repeated dumbly, his brows lowering. "Why?"

"Hunter!" Sara slapped his arm.

"I just mean it's not a great idea. They work together." He frowned and turned on Colby. "You're breaking your own policy. It's not too smart, Sis."

Before Colby could respond, Sara interrupted. "Everything doesn't revolve around business. At least not for most people."

"Here we go again." Hunter heaved a massive sigh.

"Yes, here we go again." Sara raised a hand overhead. "Why can't you set aside work for five minutes and think about your sister and your friend?"

"I *am* thinking about them. Colby's finances are tied up in the restaurant. Alec's career is, too." Hunter shrugged, hands held out in question. "If this relationship doesn't pan out and they can't work together, they're both screwed."

"You're hopeless." Sara shook her head, then grabbed Colby's hand. "I think it's awesome. You've both been through so much, and I think you're perfect for each other."

"Oh, yeah. Kumbaya!" Hunter rolled his eyes. "You're all being a little naive. Alec, seriously, my sister?" Then his face contorted, as if certain activities involved in dating just registered. "What *are* you doing with my sister?"

"Nothing that makes her unhappy." Alec remained calm, although he looked weary.

"Don't want to hear it." Hunter waved his hands in front of his face. "Don't even want to think about it, actually. Way to start off my week. Like I don't have enough to worry about with CTC and Jenna's stupid ideas, now I've got to worry about our investment in A CertainTea, and whether or not one of you will hurt the other?"

"Maybe you could stop thinking about yourself for a second, unless you like emulating Jenna." Colby wrapped her arm around Alec's waist. "How about we start over and you choose to be supportive?"

"Don't hold your breath," Sara muttered. "It's practically impossible for him to drag his head away from CTC for more than five minutes."

"Everyone back off," Hunter huffed. "It's a bit much to absorb in three seconds. Even without the business issues at stake, Alec and Colby dating is a little weird. I need time to adjust."

"Grow up, Hunter." Sara stood there looking like Khaleesi gearing up for battle.

The energy in the room shifted.

"Please, don't argue," Colby interjected. "Hunter, I get it. It's a shock. It's caught us by surprise, too. But the time we've spent together these past several weeks changed things. We aren't kids anymore, but the fact we've all been friends forever is exactly what makes me trust Alec and think we could be happy. I'd hope you'd want that for us."

"I do." Hunter hung his head for a second and then stood tall. "Of course I do."

"Our friendship is important to me, but I'm not here for permission," Alec stated. "We just didn't want to sneak around behind your back."

"Thanks." Hunter shifted his weight to his other leg and shot Sara a sidelong glance. She didn't smile or poke fun at him or do any of the things she normally did to make him feel better.

"We should go. Obviously, you were busy when we showed up." Colby hugged Hunter. "I'll touch base with Sara tomorrow and find some other time when we can all go out."

"Sure." Hunter crossed his arms. "But tell me this. Will you announce this at work or keep it on the down low? There are a lot of implications to consider before you jump into this in front of your employees."

Sara groaned and then gave Colby and Alec a quick kiss. "Call me tomorrow, and we'll look at the calendar."

She spun on her heel and stalked out of the kitchen, her heavy footsteps echoing as she jogged up the stairs. Hunter stared over his shoulder to where she'd gone. "Not what I needed tonight."

He tossed his empty bottle in the recycling bin, where it shattered. Colby hoped that wasn't some kind of omen, for her brother or her.

"Thanks for telling me. I didn't mean to be a dick about it." Hunter bro-hugged Alec. "But don't hurt my sister."

"I won't," Alec promised, and she believed him.

Hunter gave Colby a heartier hug. "We'll talk later."

"Woo-hoo." She smirked, but she knew he felt bad, and now he'd have his hands full with Sara. They'd work it out, though. Theirs was the kind of love that always found a way to survive. Maybe, just maybe, Colby would also find that this time around.

Chapter Thirteen

Alec welcomed the breeze on his face once Hunter closed the door behind them. Box checked, but those twenty minutes were the least comfortable he'd spent in that kitchen, ever.

"That was weird." Colby twisted in the passenger seat beside him as he backed out of the driveway.

Alec didn't respond. Hunter had been Hunter, raising valid concerns and having trouble dealing with something he couldn't control. Nothing weird about that.

"I've never seen Sara so fired up." Colby stared out the window. "Do you think she's started hormone treatments again?"

Alec shrugged. Apparently living with his father's outbursts had desensitized him to anger. Right now, though, worrying about his parents' marriage took precedence over Sara and Hunter. It was one thing for Alec to fight with his dad over Colby. Quite another if his father perceived his own wife as betraying him.

"You're quiet," Colby said when he didn't respond.

"It's been a busy twenty-four hours." He glanced at her, thinking about what other fallout they might face. "Hunter raised a good point about the staff."

Alec would rather keep quiet, at least for a while. She'd already weakened his authority with the praise she insisted he dole out. Once the staff got wind of their relationship, his authority would be more diluted.

She bit her lip while thinking. "When people try to hide personal relationships at work, it usually backfires. Secretiveness adds another layer of stress and makes the couple more gossip-worthy." Her voice wavered a bit. "Let's be open. But we shouldn't flaunt it, either."

He disagreed. Privacy and secretiveness weren't the same thing. Privacy would allow them to explore the relationship in peace. But he'd promised to be patient and to make her happiness his priority, so what could he say?

"You're the boss." He had to remember that, because lately the restaurant had started to feel like theirs instead of hers. The lines were blurring, and blending their personal and professional relationship would make them even fuzzier, validating Hunter's concerns. He needed to keep the peace there, because that job was the key to reclaiming his reputation. And his reputation might help him earn his father's respect.

"Maybe I'm the boss there, but not here. If you disagree with me, be honest."

The gravity of her tone snagged his attention. Had Mark made her feel like she couldn't speak up? Did it matter? Because in this particular case, there was no way to separate the girlfriend from the boss. If he disagreed with his girlfriend, he'd be asking his boss to change her decision about how to handle her staff.

"It's your restaurant. If you want to announce it, that's fine."

She raised her brows. "It won't undermine you?"

"Do you *want* me to talk you out of it?" He glanced at her, gauging her.

"No. I think it's important to be open, with others and each other."

Okay, then. He'd suck it up and deal with the staff's snickering. As far as being open with her, nothing he was keeping to himself had anything to do with his feelings for her, so he saw no purpose in burdening her with his bullshit. "Then why are we still discussing it?"

She leaned on the center console and stared at him. "You seem edgy."

Yeah, well, she'd be edgy, too, if she'd seen his father's pain tonight, or witnessed him storming off.

"It's been a long day." He pulled up to her mother's house, torn between wanting her to come over and needing to check on his mother. "I've got a splitting headache. Do you mind if we call it a night?"

She frowned. "Are you sure you're not upset about Hunter?"

"I promise I'm not upset about Hunter." Gratefully, he could answer that much with 100 percent honesty. "Will you go back to the city?"

"I think I'll swing by my dad's first. I might as well share our news with the whole family at once, plus it'll give me a chance to talk to Gentry about Jake."

Gentry seemed like a woman who could handle herself without Colby's interference. "Did something happen?"

"Not yet, but I'd rather prevent a disaster than wait until it's too late."

Of course she would. She'd always hated seeing anyone hurt. Someone like Colby should've been spared having to suffer the disaster he could've prevented. "Okay. I'll talk to you later."

"I'll call you on my drive home." Colby leaned across the seat and kissed him. It'd take weeks for him to get used to that.

"Sorry to bail. I'll see you in the morning." He cupped her face and kissed her deeper, determined to convince her that he was worth her esteem. "Bye."

"Feel better." She smiled before exiting the car and climbing into her own. He watched her drive off before going next door to his parents'.

The porch lights were off even though it was getting darker. Tension coiled in his gut as he approached the front door. He knocked before entering. "Mom?"

He wandered from room to room, finding no one. Uneasiness stole through him, but nothing appeared to be broken—at least nothing inanimate.

◆ ◆ ◆

Colby found her sister lounging in the hot tub with a Moscow mule in one hand and the stereo remote in the other. A pulsing beat and high-pitched vocals blared from the speakers.

"Can you turn that down?" Colby edged a corner of the lounge chair closer to the hot tub.

Gentry lowered the volume. Nodding toward the icy pitcher on the table, she asked, "Want a drink?"

"No, thanks."

"Your loss." Gentry's free hand tapped out the beat on the slate around the hot tub. She'd piled her auburn hair on top of her head and fastened it with some bejeweled hair sticks.

When Colby had been twenty-five, she hadn't had time for Monday-night hot-tub cocktails. She'd already graduated from law school, been approaching her first wedding anniversary, and just received Mark's bipolar I diagnosis. It hadn't been all roses, but she'd had purpose and meaning in her life, and she'd still believed that the love she and Mark felt for each other would be enough.

Hardship had forced personal growth. And no matter how broken Colby might still feel, she'd learned that she was a survivor. But Gentry? She'd never been tested, and Colby wondered how her sister would fare when confronted by real hardship.

"What brings you by?" Gentry's toes broke through the water. "Dad's not home."

"I came to see you."

Gentry raised a brow. "Something wrong?"

Her sister's defensive reflexes exhausted Colby, although in this case they were justified. "Must you always jump to negative conclusions?"

"So you came to hang out?" Gentry's sardonic delivery called Colby out.

"Not exactly," she admitted. "I wanted to talk, that's all."

"I sense a lecture." Gentry sank deeper into the water, steam rising up to curl her hair. "I don't need another person telling me that my life is on the fast track to nowhere."

"That's not why I came." Not exactly, anyway.

"If this is about my 'loser' boyfriend, don't start. If you need to report back to Dad that you talked to me, go ahead. I'll pretend I'm thinking seriously about what you said." Gentry leaned her head back and closed her eyes, dismissing Colby.

Perhaps a few confessions of her own might help Colby sneak past Gentry's armor. "Alec and I have decided to date."

Gentry shot up, water sluicing everywhere, brilliant green eyes wide and sparkling with mischief. She raised her copper mug in the air before taking a gulp and said, "To Colby Cabot-Baxter breaking a rule."

"Ha-ha," Colby smirked, although her sister's silliness could be infectious at times.

"I knew you liked him the second you snapped at me for saying he was hot." Gentry broke into a shit-eating grin before drinking more of her cocktail. "You've always sucked at hiding things."

"That's not true." The words escaped before she'd thought better of them.

"Oh, please. Your face is an open book." Gentry set the empty cup down and wiggled her eyebrows. "Easier to read than comic strips."

The dismissive tone grated.

"Gentry, trust me." Colby leaned forward, holding her sister's smug gaze. "I've hidden a lot from people."

Gentry swam across the hot tub and rested her chin on her hands along the edge near Colby's feet. "Cheat on a high school paper? Double-bill a client once? Shoplift a candy bar?"

"No!" Colby laughed. "I said I keep secrets, not commit crimes."

"Well, spit it out. You can't make that claim without offering proof." Gentry flicked some water at Colby's legs, causing Colby to scoot back.

Bonding would require her to be vulnerable. To take another leap she'd been resisting. If she could save her sister heartache down the road, it'd be worth it. And if she wanted to be convincing, she might as well drop a bombshell. "I had a troubled marriage. Now I'm not sure I know how to have a healthy relationship."

Gentry's face sobered. She pushed away from the wall and latched on to the other side of the hot tub, putting distance between them. Apparently, her sister was equally uncomfortable with intimacy. "Troubled?"

"Yes."

"You and Mark were always affectionate." Gentry's distrustful gaze narrowed. "He bragged about you all the time."

"In front of others, yes. But in private, we had problems. Big ones. I even consulted a divorce attorney."

Colby could practically see the cogs spinning in Gentry's head. "Because of the stupid dare with Joe?"

"No, because Mark . . ."

Gentry waited. "Mark what?"

Colby glanced at her wedding band, still unused to its new home on her right hand.

"Cheated." A true, if incomplete, explanation. One that allowed the conversation to continue without sharing Mark's diagnosis and inviting dozens more questions. "He made me wary, and lonely."

Gentry grew very quiet and then sank beneath the water. When she came back up for air, she asked, "Did you ever tell anyone else?"

"Never."

"Why not?"

Good question, Colby thought. "I didn't want the family to turn on him in case we worked it out."

"What's to work out?" Gentry's derision smacked Colby upside the head. "I'd *never* put up with someone cheating on me."

Colby's first instinct was to get angry at her sister's insensitive comment. But Colby would've thought the same thing before her marriage to Mark. Youthful ideals are easy to believe until you're faced with tough choices involving love, disappointment, and commitment. "You'd be surprised what you might forgive under a given set of circumstances."

"Were you fighting about divorce when he . . . you know." She mimicked a dive, which shocked Colby into holding her breath for a second.

"No!" *Breathe.*

The haunting look Mark had given her over his shoulder just before he took flight surfaced, but Colby shook her head before the rest of the memory formed.

She fell speechless, having not expected this turn of conversation. The tight band of pain cinching her chest would be worth it if this discussion helped Gentry to be more thoughtful about her relationships. Now she'd have to navigate from Mark to Jake without Gentry clamming up.

"Joe's death—the dare—drove Mark into a serious depression. The fact I was thinking of leaving him probably amplified his hopelessness. He acted so suddenly—no note—so I'll never know for sure what he was thinking." A flickering image of his forlorn gaze resurfaced. "It haunts me. It always will."

"That sucks." Gentry looked down at the water bubbling around her body, lost in her own thoughts. "No wonder you checked out around here for a while. So why tell me this now?"

"Because you're my sister. We can't get back all the years our mothers didn't foster our relationship in the past, but we can start now. Talk about things sisters discuss, like boyfriends." Colby intentionally lightened her tone now, getting to the heart of the matter. "Like Alec and Jake. Tell me about Jake."

"What's to tell?" Gentry shrugged one shoulder. "You've met him. He's sexy and I'm having fun, like I told you before."

"So he's fun?" Colby leaned forward. "In what way? I haven't heard him say much."

"He's better at using his mouth for other things," Gentry snickered, taking obvious pleasure in shocking Colby.

"I'm serious." No wonder their dad was exasperated.

"So am I!" Gentry laughed. "What's the big deal?"

"I guess I worry that he might be using you to drum up business and to buy him stuff."

"That's okay, 'cause I'm using him for sex." The casual remark rolled off her tongue as easily as "please" and "thank you."

"Gentry!"

"Listen, I appreciate the sisterly-love thing you're going for here, but you really don't need to worry about someone taking advantage of *me*." Under her breath, she added, "I'm not you."

As if anyone would confuse them. "That sounds like an insult."

"It's not . . . but you *did* rush into a marriage with a guy you'd only known a few months, which I'd never do. And you have to admit you've let people like your mom manipulate you a lot. I'm not interested in smoothing things over and avoiding conflict. I look out for myself 'cause no one else does."

Colby gestured around the mansion and pool area, galled. "Says the girl who's living in this place free and clear."

Gentry's emerald eyes looked fathomless and pitying. "Did your money and pretty condo make Mark look out for you?"

Another shrill pop song frayed Colby's nerves while she collected her thoughts. She stared at her sister—who sat amid the steam still billowing into the sky—unable to respond.

"No?" Gentry gloated in the face of Colby's silence. "Didn't think so."

Colby wanted to knock that chip off Gentry's shoulder more than she needed to defend herself, so she kept calm. "Why are you attacking me?"

"Because you're judging me."

"No, I'm not. I'm *worried* about you."

"Then stop projecting your baggage onto me. Trust me, I respect myself too much to be taken for a ride I'm not willing to go on."

"You think I don't respect myself?" Colby's thoughts raced.

"Your words." Gentry shrugged.

"I see. So because I tried to honor the commitment I made to a man I once loved deeply, I'm weak and insecure?" Colby wanted to scream, but that would give her sister the satisfaction of having baited her into a fight.

"All I'm saying is that I don't need anyone's approval, okay? So chill! I'm not planning a future with Jake. I like living in the moment and being independent. You might give it a try if you don't want Alec to get bored and cheat on you, too."

Her sister's cruel remark tipped Colby off the edge. Gentry had opened the door to some harsh reality, so now Colby would force her through it. "You pretend well, I'll give you that, but you're full of crap, Gentry."

"How would you know? Like you said, it's not like we've ever been super close."

That retort sounded depressingly like Jenna.

"You don't exactly make it easy. And since you're so eager to judge and insult me, here's a little truth for you. We both know you're dating Jake to piss Dad off. And if you were actually as independent as you claim, you'd be living on your own instead of here with your parents, for whom you have such contempt. But that's the rub, isn't it? You're stuck here because you're intimidated. It's easier to mock all of us than to risk failing at something, or risk getting close to someone. So go ahead and say I'm easily manipulated if it makes you feel better, but at least I went out and did something with my life. And maybe I failed at marriage, but at least I took a chance. As for Alec getting bored, he prefers grown-ups to children, as proven by the way he politely rejected all your flirtations." Colby stood, fists on her hips. "How's that for smoothing things over?"

"Nice." Gentry got out of the hot tub and dried off. She lifted the pitcher off the table. "Let's see how long it takes before you feel guilty for unloading how you really feel about me."

She started to leave, then glanced over her shoulder. "By the way, I quit. You're just too intimidating for me to handle." She snorted and scurried up the steps into the house, leaving Colby with nothing but some truly bad music.

Colby waited for the guilt to bunch up in her gut, just as Gentry had predicted. When it didn't form any kind of knot, she stared up at heaven. If Mark was watching her now, what would he think about who the person she'd become? Would he feel sorry about how he'd hurt and changed her?

Then again, Gentry had to learn not to start something she couldn't finish. No matter how weak others might think Colby for her willingness to compromise and forgive, she knew it took more strength to do that than to run away. She'd lost sight of that these past couple of years, though. Maybe she'd just needed this reminder.

Chapter Fourteen

"Whoa, what's the rush?" Colby's dad caught her before she made it out of the house.

He seemed to be huffing, like he'd raced up a flight of stairs. Colby was just about to ask if he felt okay, when Jenna piped up.

"What are you doing here?" She smiled in that empty manner she managed around Colby, while putting their restaurant leftovers in the refrigerator.

"Visiting Gentry."

"Where is she?" Her father glanced around.

"Probably in the shower. She was in the hot tub when I arrived." Colby forced herself to stop fidgeting with her purse strap. So she'd had a fight with her sister. Big deal. Sisters fought all the time. She paused, replaying that last thought—the one she'd used to justify Joe's ragging on Alec. A dynamic she didn't want to copy.

"How's the marketing thing working out?" He leaned against the counter, one foot crossed over the other, his face filled with hope. Hope Colby would have to dash.

"She just quit."

Jenna shot Colby's dad a worried look. "Why? She told me she'd created a lot of buzz. She liked the PR work."

Colby had suspected Gentry had been enjoying the job despite her cavalier act. "We got into an argument. She didn't like what I had to say, so she quit."

"What did you say?" Jenna's fists balled on her hips while Colby quickly summarized the tail end of their conversation.

"Why would you say those things?" Jenna ground out. "Do you get off on making her feel small?"

"You know we're trying to keep her motivated." Her father's disappointment nipped at Colby's conscience. "I was counting on your help."

"I *did* help, Dad. I hired her. I came here tonight to spend time with her, and then she insulted me—more than once." Colby's raised her chin. "Am I supposed to roll over just to keep her happy? You've tiptoed around her crappy attitude for years, and where's it gotten you? I didn't treat her any differently than I'd treat Hunter or Sara under the same circumstances."

"I'd better check on her." Jenna tossed a cold glare her way, but Colby couldn't care less about Jenna. There, another truth.

"What's gotten into you tonight?" Her dad crossed his arms.

"Oh, I don't know. Maybe the fact that your wife's making me the bad guy after I confided in Gentry and she threw it in my face?" She paused, realizing that she'd armed Gentry with information no one else had. Serious misstep—especially considering Gentry's lack of discretion even when she wasn't out for revenge. "Don't expect me to take whatever she dishes out just because you spoiled her."

"If I spoiled her, it was to compensate for all the time I didn't spend with her while I was busy building the business."

Colby sighed and shook her head. *Really?* "You didn't spend time with Hunter and me, either, you know."

"You had your mother, who was able to stay at home with you because of her generous alimony, by the way. Gentry didn't even have Jenna."

By Jenna's choice. Given that Jenna's nurturing skills were nonexistent, however, it might not have been the worst choice she could've made. Of course, Colby didn't get *that* honest with her dad. "Seems to me that you all need to have some serious discussions then, because Gentry's bitter, and you two continuing to kowtow to her isn't working."

"We'll see how easy you think it is once you have kids." He closed his eyes and rubbed his forehead, and for the first time he looked every minute of his sixty-five years.

"I never said it was easy," she replied, although the idea of motherhood briefly bewitched her. While with Mark, she'd given up the idea of having kids. Now, that possibility didn't seem so hopeless. Maybe, with the right man, in the right relationship, she'd want to be a mother. "In other news, Alec and I have decided to see each other outside of work."

"Alec Morgan?" Her father's brows rose to his hairline.

"Yes." Colby braced to defend her decision, like she had with Hunter an hour ago.

Instead of issuing warnings, her dad grew thoughtful. "I can see that working out, actually."

"Really?"

"Sure. You have a lot in common." He shrugged. "You're also working together to build a business. It's very seductive, that part."

"So you don't think it's a mistake to mix our personal and professional lives?"

He gestured toward the door that Jenna had recently exited through. "Obviously not. It worked out well for me."

Colby hadn't considered that. Her dad and Jenna had made a formidable team and stayed married for decades. Maybe Hunter was wrong about something for a change.

That thought instantly lightened her heart. "Thanks, Dad."

"Sure. Now let's get back to your sister." He shifted his weight to his other leg. "Are you going to hold her to this resignation?"

She should. Gentry needed to learn about consequences. On the other hand, Colby didn't want her family to become like Mark's, with siblings scattered about, barely involved, never knowing the intimacies of one another's lives, or sharing the joys and sorrows. She also didn't want to mimic Joe and Alec, who'd lost years of time they'd never recover. "Give me a few hours to cool off. I'll call her later."

"Thanks, honey." He went to the refrigerator and pulled out a pitcher of tea. "Want a drink?"

"No." She noticed him perspiring a bit. Knowing how Mark often ignored *his* malady, she had no faith when it came to men and doctors. "Dad, how are you feeling? Lately you've been tired and achy."

"I'm fine."

"You were huffing earlier, and now you're sweating despite the air conditioning."

"Stop worrying about your old man. I've got a wife on my back. I don't need you climbing up there, too."

"Why do men always think they're invincible?"

"I can take care of myself. You go enjoy Alec. I'm happy to see you finally moving on. This is a good step, honey." He kissed the top of her head and released her.

"Thanks." She glanced at the clock above the oven and realized it wasn't too late. "See you later."

Shortly thereafter, she pulled up to Alec's apartment, hoping he wouldn't mind a surprise visit. Colby's entire being was wound to the point of splitting apart thanks to her argument with Gentry. Her sister had been right about one thing: Colby did prefer to avoid conflict. But ever since life with Mark had beaten her down, she couldn't quite regulate her emotions.

Now she hoped Alec's headache was gone, so his perfect kiss and nimble fingers would make her feel better. When he opened the door, she practically leaped on him.

"What happened?" he managed between her kisses.

"Later," she murmured.

She wanted to feel him moving over, under, and inside her body. To have his gaze bore into hers with the heat and intensity he'd shown last night.

Somehow they stumbled through the apartment to his room, where they made short work of their clothing and fell onto his bed. A feverish lust spread through her body as she explored the defined muscles of his abdomen and chest. Felt the gruff hair on his legs and arms brush against her skin. Welcomed his hot mouth on her neck, breasts, and stomach. Unlike last night, this was adrenaline-fueled, white-hot sex.

Minutes bled together, fused by warm, wet kisses. By panting breath, fingernail scratches, leave-nothing-on-the-table lovemaking.

Afterward, they lay together in his bed, quietly caressing each other as their breathing settled. It still surprised her to find herself in the afterglow of making love with Alec. He had a smattering of freckles on his shoulder, and a tiny indent at the tip of his nose. All these things to explore that she'd never quite noticed before. How had she missed seeing what had been right in front of her for so long?

The photograph she'd given him stared at her from the nightstand. "You keep that in here?"

"Yes." He tightened his hold on her. "I see you before I fall asleep and as soon as I wake up."

"Suck-up," she teased, kissing him. The lone photo did little to make his generic apartment a home. Clearly she had work to do. "What happened to all those photos of your puzzles that you used to tack on your wall at your mom's house?"

"They're in a box in the closet."

More evidence that he was that same sweet guy she knew before. "Do you still take one every time you finish a new one?"

A touch of crimson colored his cheeks. "Yes."

"I bet you could wallpaper this whole room with them." She brushed his cowlick aside. "Fess up, how many?"

Without hesitation, he said, "One thousand four hundred and ninety-eight."

She laughed, unable to imagine it. "When do you find the time?"

"Most were done in middle and high school, and then right after I closed Une Bouchée." He closed his eyes for a second and sighed. "Puzzles help me unwind. When I focus on one thing, problems fade away."

"Like meditation."

"I suppose." He settled one arm behind his head. "Speaking of which, you seem more relaxed now. What revved you up earlier?"

"Gentry accused me of being a pushover, so I laid into her." She felt him wince before she saw it. "What?"

"You laid into her?" His gaze turned distant, as if he might be thinking of Joe. That, coupled with his disappointed tone, soured her stomach.

"Yes. To defend myself," she countered.

He kissed her temple, softly saying, "You used to stand up for yourself without insulting people and storming off."

She couldn't escape his reference to the way she'd chewed him out and run off when they'd argued about the menu and his management style. Apparently, her capacity for compassion had been buried under the weight of Mark's death and the impotence she'd had in her marriage. She frowned, wishing she could hide from Alec's observation.

"Hey, look at me." He tipped up her chin. "I'm not saying you can't argue. Just remember combat isn't your only option. That said, you never have to hide or hold back with me."

Her eyes stung a little, although she blinked back tears before he saw them. He'd never understand how deeply those words affected her after years isolated from everything and everyone but Mark. Maybe she hadn't yet struck the right balance, but with Alec's help, she would. Once she was certain her voice wouldn't waver, she teased, "Careful what you ask for."

He rolled her onto her back and pinned her to the bed with the luxurious weight and heat of his body. He grinned in the way only Alec could—a glint of humor in an otherwise sober face, his eyes brimming with emotion. "I'll make sure you only have glowing things to say to and about me."

No relationship would ever be a fairy tale, but right now he was very much her hero. "I forgot to tell you, my father totally supports a workplace romance. In fact, he thinks we can be just like Jenna and him."

"Determined to achieve as much as they have?"

"Maybe. And while we're on that topic, I've been thinking about the menu." She winced when his arms tensed. "I know you need creative control, but I still think we can add one or two basic items."

"Why bastardize the menu?" He stared at the headboard and breathed slowly rather than look at her.

"Because not everyone's a foodie. If we expand the menu, we could capture groups that otherwise wouldn't come because one or two people don't like fussy food."

"There's nothing wrong with my food, Colby." He rolled off her body, propping himself up on his elbow. She immediately missed his warmth. "My 'fussy' food wins awards."

"I know that's important to you, but not everyone likes haute cuisine." She stroked his cheek. "Do this and I promise: no happy hours."

She could tell he was holding back but decided not to push.

"Let's table this for another time." He trailed his finger down her arm. "I can't make career decisions when you're naked."

"Well, perhaps you're not so single-minded that you can't make time for things like this, after all." Her thoughts hovered around the vision of an imaginary young family, but then retreated. Way too soon. She turned on her side and traced her fingertips over his shoulder and along his chest, her insides tightening with a rising need.

"There's always time for this." He kissed her again, this time a little roughly. When he flattened her with his weight again, his erection, hot and hard, rubbed against her thigh.

He nuzzled her neck, and then his tongue trailed down to her breast.

"Alec," she whispered, threading her fingers through his hair, urging him on.

Then the doorbell rang, stilling them both.

"Who's that?" she asked.

"I don't know." He hesitated. "They'll go away."

He kissed her again, but then the knocking began. "Alec, are you in there?"

He popped up, his face now stricken. "It's my mom."

Colby reached out to him. "Alec, what's wrong?"

"I don't know." Without another word, he bolted out of bed, pulled on his sweats, and left the room.

Colby slid out from under the covers. Lifting her discarded dress off the floor, she wondered whether she should stay hidden or join the conversation. His mother's voice carried through the open bedroom door.

"Let's go get his car from the bar before he wakes up," she said.

"How'd he get home?" Alec asked.

"Craig drove him in his car and carried him into the house." His mother's sad tone seeped into Colby's chest, where it turned to ice.

"He's that drunk?" A blend of disgust and worry rang out.

"Passed out. Now, please, let's hurry."

Colby heard Mrs. Morgan's light footsteps on the tile entry, but then Alec said, "Mom, wait. I'm not alone."

Colby's pulse skipped. Did he want her to come out of his room? What would she say to Mrs. Morgan when it seemed a fair bet she was the reason Mr. Morgan got so drunk?

"Oh?" Following a brief pause, his mom said, "Oh! Oh, I'm sorry. I didn't mean to interrupt, but I don't have anyone else to turn to without embarrassing your father."

"It's okay. Just give me a minute."

Alec whitewashing his dad's reaction to their relationship painted an unwanted similarity between Mark's and his ability to lead a double life. Worse, a tug-of-war between her and his family might distract him from his professional goals, like Joe's death had done before. Could Alec be happy without more awards, or would he become depressed by the failure to recapture that glory? How would that disappointment affect them?

When Alec came into the room, she remained seated on his bed, rattled by her thoughts.

He grabbed a shirt and some shoes. "I assume you heard?"

She nodded. "I wish you would've told me how your dad reacted earlier."

"You pretty much guessed it, anyway." He shrugged, as if his sugar-coating conflict wasn't a problem. "Do you want to wait here?"

"Your mom needs you now." Colby couldn't help him with this family problem tonight, nor was it the time to discuss it. Instead, she'd focus on their mutual goals for A CertainTea and the memorial fund, with a few hours of research and planning. "I don't want you to feel rushed, so I'll go home."

He hung his head. "Okay."

"I'm sorry we got interrupted." When she hugged him, his rigidity proved a level of tension he was trying to brush off.

"Me, too." He clasped her hand and tugged her out of the room. Summoning her courage, she followed him, hand in hand, to see his mother.

"Hi, Mrs. Morgan." Colby reached for her purse, which she'd dropped by the front door earlier.

"I'm sorry to disturb you, Colby." The woman pressed her hand to her heated cheek.

"It's fine. Really. I have a list of things to research tonight for the fund." That and the criteria for James Beard Awards.

When Mrs. Morgan's gaze skittered away, Colby regretted mentioning the fund. Itching to leave, she gave Alec a quick kiss. "Call me later."

On her way past Mrs. Morgan, she touched her arm. She wanted to apologize for Mark, for Joe, for being an ongoing source of irritation, and for selfishly taking up with Alec while knowing all the above. In the end, she merely said "I'm sorry" before rushing out the door.

Alec watched Colby retreat, knowing this incident did nothing to strengthen their relationship. Even passed out, his father managed to chip away at Alec's happiness.

He went into the kitchen to grab a box of coconut water and some blueberries. When his mother questioned him, he grumbled, "For his hangover."

She flinched, then held out the car keys. "I *am* sorry I interrupted your night."

The last thing he wanted was to make his *mother* feel worse than she already did. He needed to be the son she deserved.

"*Always* come to me." He hugged her before taking his father's keys. "Let's go get Dad's car."

Twenty minutes later, Alec pulled his father's car into his parents' driveway. Inside the house, they discovered him still asleep on the sofa. His neck was bent at an awkward angle against one arm of the couch, and his legs dangled over the other. Alec mustered little compassion for him—certainly not enough to move him to a bed. The man deserved to pay *some* price for his obnoxious behavior.

"Go home, honey." His mom set her purse down. "You look tired."

"I'll wait until he wakes up."

"It's not necessary. He'll be groggy and disoriented, not aggressive." She sighed. "I know you worry that he'll hurt me, but he won't. He never hurts me."

"There's always a first time." If his father ever laid a hand on his mom, he'd finally learn that Alec was not a wimp.

Defeated, she scrubbed her hands over her face and followed Alec into the kitchen. He emptied the coconut water, blueberries, and ice into a blender, then grabbed a banana and whipped up a smoothie, secretly hoping the blender whir would wake his dad. It didn't, so he covered the drink and stuck it in the refrigerator while his mother retrieved a box of chamomile tea.

"Want a cup?"

"No, thanks." He took the box and nudged her toward a kitchen chair. "I'll fix it for you."

She sat in silence, trapped in her own thoughts, staring into space. The woman had already lost one son and now confronted a crumbling marriage. Both events could be traced, one way or another, back to Alec, which sucked the fight out of him.

"Do you want me to give up Colby to pacify Dad?" he finally asked, giving voice to the concern that had been running through his mind for the past forty-five minutes.

"I wouldn't ask that. I want you to be happy."

"Thanks, but we both know Dad expects it. Things here are bad enough without me making things worse for you."

She didn't respond because she didn't like to lie.

He added sugar and cream to her tea, wishing it were that easy to make her life as sweet and mellow. He set the cup down and, sitting across from her, drummed his fingers on the table. "What *can* I do to make that man happy?"

With a blank stare fixed on her face, she shook her head. "No one can make him happy. He has to find his own way there."

"I think seeing me makes having lost Joe worse for him." Accepting that stark truth was no easy thing. The too-tender scars of rejection ran deep, no matter how tough Alec talked. "It might be easier on him if I stayed away."

"Don't leave me, Alec. Having you around is the only thing keeping me from falling apart." A weak smile contradicted her watery eyes. "Everyone said that time would heal us, but it isn't working out that way."

"If the fund is going to cause more problems, I'll take Joe out of it."

"No. The fund is a lovely idea. Mark and Joe were good friends. If you can gather their friends and others together to help people in crisis, then that's the *right* thing to do. I don't want our family dysfunction to keep either of us from doing what's right. In fact, maybe I can help plan the fund-raiser. I used to be good at that back when you boys were younger."

Alec smiled, remembering how involved she'd been in every organization, from the school, to Boy Scouts, to the Portland Art Museum. "You like putting the squeeze on donors, don't you?"

That earned him a genuine smile, erasing ten years from her face. "My year as Parent-Teacher Council president raised more funds than in any year prior."

Alec enjoyed that childhood memory. Her committee had raised enough money to stock the school computer lab with new Apple computers. He still remembered the pride he'd felt when other kids were dazzled by the extravagant equipment.

"Can you work with Colby?" His workdays were so long, he wouldn't be as available during the planning phase.

"Yes." She shoved her half-empty cup aside. "Colby loved Joe. Between him and Mark, she's lost as much as we have. It's time we all help each other heal."

"Thanks, Mom." Alec glanced toward the living room, where his father's snoring tore through the room like a buzz saw. "How will Dad react to you helping us?"

"I'll handle him."

The steely resolve in her voice didn't ease his concern. "That doesn't really answer my question."

"He may break things in this house, but after all the domestic-abuse calls he's handled in his career, he'd never make himself the culprit."

An arrest *would* humiliate him in front of his brotherhood, Alec conceded. His dad clung to his reputation almost as tightly as he did to Joe's memory. But would the threat of shame be enough to keep him from snapping under the pressure of unmitigated, raw grief?

Snoring continued rumbling in the other room.

"Sounds like he's out for the night." Alec stretched to fend off exhaustion. He'd barely slept in the past twenty-four hours. All he really wanted now was Colby, but she'd gone home.

A thirty-minute drive.

Decision made, he stood. "Add more ice to the smoothie when he wakes up, and make him drink it. Coconut water has lots of electrolytes."

"He doesn't deserve you, you know." She clasped his hand. "Most sons in your shoes would've written him off by now."

Her proud smile made him cringe. His dad was far from perfect, but so was he. His mom didn't need to know about Joe and Beth as long as, eventually, his good deeds made up for his lies.

Chapter Fifteen

"I didn't expect to see you tonight." Colby answered the door wearing pink cotton pajamas with white piping. Not sexy by most standards, but Alec was so grateful for a peek at the intimate details of her life that her pajamas turned him on. "Did you text?"

"My phone's at home." He held up his hands when she frowned. "In my defense, I ran out of my house in a hurry. Then I just wanted to get to you. Is it okay that I showed up uninvited?"

"Of course." She kissed him once he entered her condo. "How's your dad?"

"Sleeping it off, as far as I know."

Her brows pinched together. "If this project will cause more conflict for your family, maybe we should hold off."

"No. It's the right thing to do." His mother's words echoed in his head. "My mom wants to help. My dad will have to accept it at some point. We just need to stay the course." He gathered her into his arms to reassure her and himself. "Stay strong."

She melted into his embrace. A week ago, he would've thought this kind of moment impossible. If he wouldn't look stupid, he'd pinch himself now to prove it wasn't a fantasy.

"I don't always feel strong." Her voice resonated against his chest, warm and rich.

He forced her to meet his gaze. "You're one of the strongest people I know."

"The way I snapped at Gentry tonight proves I'm not even strong enough to take a little heat."

"That doesn't make you weak. It makes you human." He kissed her forehead. "We've both stumbled a bit on our own, but together we'll be stronger. I promise."

"You sound certain." Faint wrinkles fanned out from the corners of her cat eyes when she smiled.

"I am," he lied. That fib didn't make him feel bad, though. Anything that helped her believe in herself again couldn't be wrong.

"Okay, then." She eased away and led him to the sofa, where her laptop sat open on the coffee table. "I've given more thought to the environmental causes you wanted to consider. If we start a broad non-profit foundation, we can accept grant applications from diverse causes and then divvy up our money as we see fit. What do you think?"

"I like that idea." This kind of drive and enthusiasm was exactly like the "old Colby" she believed to be gone. He hadn't helped his family heal, but he was helping Colby.

"Good. If I didn't say so before, I want you to know how much I love this idea. And I love that *you* thought of it. I know you have regrets about Joe, but I also know how much he and your family mean to you. Eventually your dad will see that."

Because this was another step along the path to redemption, he accepted the compliment.

"I'm psyched your mom wants to help." Colby slung her legs across his lap. "Since tomorrow's Tuesday, I asked my mom and Sara to meet me at the restaurant at one o'clock for an informal meeting. Can your mom come, too?"

"I'll ask." He tugged her closer to his chest. "I'm surprised you included Leslie. I thought you wanted a break from her."

Colby scrunched her nose. "She needs something to focus on now that Richard's out of the picture."

"What happened to Richard?"

"He learned the truth about Snickers."

"How?"

As Alec listened to Colby explain the breakup, her sympathy for Richard's logic made him a little queasy. Her mother's white lie paled in comparison with *his* omission.

"Richard overreacted," Alec insisted.

"Maybe, but trust is a fragile thing." Her gaze wandered off with her stray thoughts.

"The Snickers lie didn't hurt anyone," he argued. "Not all lies are wrong. Some are told to protect people. Truth isn't always absolute."

"You sound like my mom."

"I always liked Leslie," he teased, dropping this conversation to avoid a direct question he didn't want to answer.

"That alone makes you a keeper. Not many men would go out of their way for her just to satisfy me."

"I'd do just about anything for you." He cupped her jaw and brushed her cheek with his thumb. "Besides, your mom's lived alone a long time. Can't blame her for being a little needy."

"I guess not." She kissed him. "You've always been sweet to me, even when I was young and dumb."

"You were never dumb."

"Well, you know, oblivious and in my own world."

"You mean you were a teenage girl?" He feigned shock.

She chuckled. "A million years ago."

Not to him. He remembered her that way as if it were yesterday. Lying out in her backyard, listening to the radio. Passing him in the high school hallway with her gang of popular girls—flicking him a quick, sunny hello. Buying him DVDs of shows set in France for his eighteenth birthday, a gift Joe had mocked.

"Ignore Joe, Alec. He's just jealous because you're going to end up work-ing at some fabulous French restaurant and meeting all kinds of pretty French girls," Colby said.

"That last thing is the only part that sounds good." Joe tossed Chocolat *on the counter, shaking his head.*

"Big surprise." Colby snorted and then smiled at Alec. "I'm proud of you. When you're famous, I hope you'll still cook for me once in a while. If I get to study abroad, maybe I'll visit."

She'd never studied abroad or visited, but he'd cherished the confi-dence she'd shown in him that day.

"I've made a lot of mistakes since then," she said as an afterthought.

"Me, too." He closed his eyes and cuddled her against his chest. "But every bad decision brought us here, so let's not judge them. Maybe learning from them is enough."

"I like that idea." She kissed him again and then got a funny look in her eye. "I'd hoped A CertainTea would make me happy, and it has, but not for the reasons I expected. Even if the restaurant operates in relative obscurity, it won't matter, because it brought us together."

Gratifying sentiment aside, he *did* care about acclaim. "We don't have to settle for one or the other. We can have it all."

For the briefest second, he saw a flash of some emotion—anxiety? disappointment?—cross her face. Rather than give voice to it, she hugged him. "Should we finish what we'd started before your mom interrupted?"

"Absolutely." He started to unbutton her pajamas but stopped when her phone rang. Late-night calls usually meant bad news. "Do you want to check?"

"In case it's Gentry." She lifted the phone then set it down.

"Not Gentry?"

"Todd. I'd left him a message asking if he'd be a board member." She must've felt him stiffen. "What's wrong?"

"I thought this was *our* foundation."

"It is. But we need a board, and it's important to have at least one outsider involved so people won't be suspicious when donating."

"There are lots of smart lawyers. Why him?" He couldn't help himself.

"Todd's smart, diligent, and civic-minded. He'll assign first-years to do pro bono work if we need it. It also helps him to have board memberships on his résumé. Plus, I trust him." Again with the emphasis on trust, which Alec couldn't offer absolutely. "We always worked well together."

He eased her off his lap and stood, needing to move around. "Because he likes you, Colby."

"And I like him." She watched him, wide-eyed.

"Don't be obtuse. He *likes* you. He asked you out, brings you flowers, and I'm sure is still hopeful that you'll change your mind."

"He buys the wrong flowers and never sends me funny videos." When he didn't laugh at her joke, she asked, "Are you jealous?"

"No." Another lie. "But I'm not stupid, either. No guy wants his girlfriend working closely with another man who wants her for himself."

"Don't you trust me?" Now she looked hurt.

"I don't trust *him*."

"He's just a friend."

"So was I." Alec's hands fell to his sides. "I just wish you'd talked to me *before* you asked him."

"It honestly never occurred to me that you'd care." She came over and rubbed his biceps. "I'll rescind the offer. I'll say you'd already asked someone else."

He was being petty and childish. Colby wasn't likely to admire his insecurity any more than his own father would. "No. It's fine. You're right. I'm overreacting."

"I'm really sorry I didn't think to ask you first." Colby began unbuttoning Alec's shirt and kissing his chest. "Let me make it up to you."

Anytime she touched him, the twin pulls of desire and gratitude caused him to lose focus. Why was he arguing when he could be making love?

"If you insist." He knew one way to make sure she wouldn't be tempted to look in any other man's direction.

Lifting her off her feet, he carried her to her room, where he did some of his best wooing.

◆ ◆ ◆

"You summoned." Gentry tossed her purse on Colby's desk and adjusted her strapless minidress, causing the multitude of gold necklaces she wore to jangle. "You do remember I quit, right?"

"Thanks for coming." Colby gestured toward a chair and moved the bud vase aside before Gentry could break it with her purse. "Let's talk."

"Oh, joy." Gentry plopped onto a chair and stretched out her hand, offering Colby the floor.

"First—and this is not me smoothing things over to avoid conflict— I'm sorry about lashing out. You're my sister and I love you, even when we don't agree. I want us to be closer, which is why I asked you to work with me in the first place."

Gentry shook her head. "Dad asked you to hire me. It wasn't your idea."

"Dad suggested it; it was *my* choice. I thought it was working out well, too. So, do you really want to quit, or did you just say that in the heat of the moment?"

Gentry chewed on the inside of her cheek, averting her gaze. Despite her expensive jewelry and couture wardrobe, she looked terribly young. Young and lost.

"I'd like you to stick around, but I won't beg." Colby added, thinking it might prompt a response.

"Fine. I'll come back." Gentry then tapped her fingernails on the chair. "And I'm sorry I insulted you, too. I didn't mean to make you feel bad about being too nice."

Colby let the "too nice" remark slide. Things with Alec had left her optimistic, which went a long way toward making her feel magnanimous.

"Great. Next, Alec and I are starting a charitable foundation in Mark's and Joe's names. Would you be interested in helping? I've asked Sara, my mother, and Mrs. Morgan to meet today to start planning our first fund-raiser. We could use some help spreading the word."

"Hold on." Gentry edged to the front of her seat, expression tight with frustration. "Yesterday you said your marriage sucked. Now you're telling me you're going to canonize the cheater?"

"Gentry, I shared that with you in confidence, so I hope you won't throw it in my face or tell others. And I didn't say my marriage sucked. I said it was troubled. We had challenges, and I was unhappy toward the end. But my marriage began with love, and it ended, in part, because I gave up on Mark. I'm starting this foundation to heal, and to help the Morgan family heal."

Her sister sat back in the chair, shaking her head. "I don't understand you, Colby. Honestly, I don't."

"I could say the same to you. You're young, beautiful, and you've been given every advantage, yet you hold on to grudges and anger." Colby wanted to reach across the desk and shake her. "Don't you get tired?"

Gentry lowered her gaze. "Maybe. Sometimes."

Finally! A small step toward honesty. Colby would take it and run. "Perhaps working with this foundation can help you, too."

"Don't hold your breath." Gentry slouched.

"So you don't want to be involved?"

"I'll help. Just don't expect miracles, that's all." She sat up and clapped her hands together, clearly ready to change the subject. "In other news, I heard through the grapevine that the Trib's restaurant critic will be here the last Saturday of this month."

Colby stilled, wishing there were no such things as restaurant critics, James Beard Awards, and Michelin Guides. Reading about how so many master chefs' lives were destroyed because of an unhealthy obsession with those accolades had increased her concern for Alec's mental state. Didn't he realize that he was more than a chef? He was a son, a friend, a lover—all of which were more meaningful than anonymous critics' ratings. "Do you know that for sure?"

"No. It's a rumor, but a fairly reliable one, I think."

"The timing's not great."

"Why not?"

"We're telling the staff about our relationship tomorrow. I'd rather not have that coincide with Alec becoming more demanding, which will happen if he's focused on that information." She tapped her pencil on the desk and thought.

"Why do you have to tell the staff about your sex life? It isn't anyone's business."

"It's not just sex," Colby corrected. "And this affects them. They might not feel comfortable coming to me with complaints if they think I'm biased. I need to reassure them."

"Have they come to you yet?" Gentry pulled a face.

"No, but I think it's because I hold daily meetings where Alec and I offer positive feedback to counterbalance his criticism."

Gentry chuckled. "See? Too nice."

"Smart, actually. I want people to be happy here. I *don't* want high turnover or employee lawsuits. Raising Alec's anxiety based on a rumor could be a mistake with a potentially wide ripple effect. Get me confirmation, then I'll tell."

"I'll never get that. It's unethical."

Colby considered the pressure Alec was already under with his dad, and thought about the staff. "Alec says he treats each dish as if it were being served to a reviewer, anyhow. No need to spread rumors and have him fixate on a date that might not be real. It could also backfire if the staff thinks they have that much time to prepare and the critic shows up sooner." Colby felt 90 percent sure this was the right decision. "Let's get back to the foundation. Everyone will be here in ten minutes. Can you stay?"

"Did you leave my mom out on purpose?" Gentry smiled, taking too much delight in the perceived slight.

"Your mom has a full-time job. I didn't ask her, Dad, or Hunter for help."

"You have a full-time job, too."

"It's my foundation. Mine and Alec's." Keeping Alec involved with the foundation would remind him of the world outside his kitchen. She tuned out the fact that such maneuvering was eerily similar to how she'd managed Mark's moods. "Actually, it was his idea."

"How cuuuuute," Gentry teased. "You work together here. Now you have a foundation. And you get to have sex with the hot chef. Tell me, which is the best part?"

"Stop." Warmth flooded Colby's cheeks.

"Oh, come on. Tell me something juicy. I bet he's even hotter naked. He's got a cute butt, and those scars on his hands are sexy. Jake doesn't get scars from the cart. Well, except one steam burn on his forearm."

Colby barely heard the stuff about Jake because her thoughts had latched onto her first comment. "Quit looking at Alec's butt!"

"Just sayin'." Her sister shrugged.

As if conjured by Gentry's curiosity, Alec entered the room. Gentry leaned back in her chair and made a show of eyeing Alec's butt. He glanced at her and then at his butt. "Did I sit in something?"

"Nope." Gentry grinned. "Just proving a point to my sister."

"Do I want to know?" he asked Colby, and she shook her head. He smiled at Gentry, then turned back to Colby. "My mom's here. I'll go throw together a snack for the table. I assume your mom and Sara will arrive soon."

"They'd better if they don't want to get on her bad side." Gentry hooked a thumb at Colby.

"That's never made a difference to you," Colby rejoined.

"I like to live dangerously," Gentry snickered before leaning back to ogle Alec's butt again.

With that, Alec beat a hasty exit. "See you out there."

He disappeared and Gentry grinned. "This'll be fun."

Fun—her sister's only goal in life. "Gentry, can I give you a word of sisterly advice?"

"Like I can stop you."

"Spend less time teasing me and complaining about your parents, and more time figuring out who you want to be when you grow up." Colby watched for any glimpse of the candor with which they'd begun today's conversation, but that moment had been an anomaly.

"Who says I want to grow up? You all make it look tedious." Gentry shot to her feet, necklaces clinking. "I'll meet you out there after a stop at the ladies' room." With that, she strutted from the office, dismissing Colby and her advice.

Colby drew a deep breath, steeling herself to work with Mrs. Morgan and her mom. Thank God, Sara would be there. Of course, last night Sara had been rather worked up, too. Why did it seem like everyone else was falling apart just as Colby's life seemed to be coming together?

In the dining room, Mrs. Morgan was checking her phone.

"Good morning." Colby crossed to join her at the table. "Thank you so much for helping. We can really use your experience."

"I'm happy to be involved, for both of my sons."

Talking about Joe jarred Colby, especially because she and Mrs. Morgan hadn't done so since he died. Now wasn't the time for Joe stories, though maybe one day they might laugh and cry about him together.

"Your support means a lot to Alec." Colby smiled. "This is his brainchild."

"He told me." Mrs. Morgan had never been effusive, Colby reminded herself. The woman sat now with a polite smile, obviously as apprehensive as Colby. "Have you decided on a name?"

"No. I was thinking we'd keep it simple. Perhaps the Morgan-Baxter Foundation?" She'd intentionally put Joe's name first.

Mrs. Morgan nodded but didn't appear enthused. "Didn't those two refer to themselves as the mavericks?"

A crystal-clear memory of Joe and Mark emerged. Young, handsome faces burnished by the sun. Broad smiles and laughter while they stuffed backpacks in her living room. They'd been drinking beer and planning their first weekend-long mountain-bike excursion. Joe had wanted to attack the more extreme trails of Black Rock Mountain, while Mark had voted for the scenic beauty of McKenzie River Trail. *"We can't be mavericks if we're sightseeing like pussies!" Joe barked.* Mark had caved, and they went to Black Rock. Ever after, they'd referred to themselves as the mavericks.

"Colby?" Mrs. Morgan asked, reaching across the table to jar Colby back to the present.

She blinked, her eyes stinging. "Sorry."

Mrs. Morgan, sage as ever, simply said, "I understand."

Of course she did. The woman probably suffered through bittersweet memories every single day.

"The Maverick Foundation." Colby tested the name aloud. That name meant Mr. Morgan wouldn't have to see his surname mingled with Mark's. "Actually, I like that a lot. Let's see what Alec thinks."

At that moment, her mom and Sara entered the restaurant, their faces registering surprise when they noticed Julie Morgan.

"Julie! How lovely to see you here." Colby's mom gave Julie a vigorous hug. "Won't this be wonderful—working together like the old days?"

Mrs. Morgan must've been doing a mental eye roll because Colby's mom's volunteerism had been undertaken like many other things in her life. She began with a bang, but then petered out as her interest waned.

"Yes, I've always enjoyed raising money for a good cause." She turned to Colby just as Alec arrived with a tray of crudités. "What's the foundation's mission?"

Alec sat down and answered. "We'll review proposals from local nonprofits each year and then distribute the funds accordingly. That way we can help a lot of different causes instead of selecting one. Of course, we'll make a donation to the Burnside Shelter this year."

"Reviewing proposals will require more work." Sara pulled out a chair for Gentry, who finally joined the group.

"Hey, all." Gentry returned from the ladies' room and sank onto the chair. "What'd I miss?"

Colby's mother straightened, adopting a pompous air. "Alec was just telling us that the foundation will be taking proposals from local nonprofits each year and then deciding where to donate its money."

Gentry barely acknowledged Colby's mom with a nod before she turned to Sara. "What's the foundation's name?"

Colby's mother's cheeks flushed from the snub, but she lifted her chin.

"I don't know," Sara replied.

"Mrs. Morgan suggested the Maverick Foundation." Colby held her breath, wondering what Alec thought, even as the others murmured approval.

Alec's gaze drifted through the glass doors to the lake beyond. Had he been hit with a flashback, or did that name sting because he'd never once been invited to any of the maverick adventures? "Good name, Mom."

Colby released the breath she'd been holding when mother and son exchanged fond glances.

"This group will be the executive team, and Alec, my former colleague Todd, and I will make up the board. Sara's agreed to handle our finances, and Gentry will cover PR." She then looked at her mom and Mrs. Morgan. "And I'd hoped you two would focus on silent-auction donations."

"Whatever you need, honey. You and Alec already have so much on your plates with this gorgeous place." Her mom gestured around proudly, as if she'd had something to do with it. "Of course, maybe your sister should be involved with the silent auction. I'm sure all the local retailers know her by name."

Zing!

Gentry's gaze narrowed over a feline smile, showing a twisted kind of respect for the subtle barb.

"Mom," Colby warned.

"What?" She shrugged, all sincerity and innocence. "She'll have an easier time than I will convincing people to donate things, because they'll care about keeping her business."

Her mom's logic aside, Colby didn't need power plays.

"Leslie's right, Sis. I have more pull in town than her despite her having lived here almost three times as long." Gentry smiled sweetly, even as she thrust the sword. Her mom absorbed the blow with grace. "At a minimum, I should be able to get something expensive from Bend the Trend, Periwinkle's, and Cheeky Chic. Dad can probably hit up Harrington Jewelers."

"Great, thanks." Colby shot a quick glance at Alec, whose grin proved he found it all a bit amusing.

Thankfully, Mrs. Morgan wasn't interested in Mickey Mouse games and brought them back to business. "I assume we'll host the fund-raiser here?"

"Yes." Colby turned to Alec, grateful to end her mom and Gentry's pissing contest. "I'd like to do it before Feast Portland so we can capitalize on the momentum of the grand opening and go into the food festival with twice the buzz."

Colby watched everyone's eyes widen.

"That's not much time," Mrs. Morgan ventured. "I'm not sure what we can pull together in five weeks."

"Well, we have the venue. I'll donate the cost of the food and service on a Tuesday night so it doesn't interfere with normal operations, and Alec will come up with a special dinner menu that night. The big thing will be invitations, PR, and silent-auction donations." Colby shrugged. It didn't sound impossible to her. If anything, the challenge seemed exciting. After two years of living in limbo, she welcomed the buzz of being busy with two new enterprises.

Mrs. Morgan replied, "Most donors will ask for program advertising, but programs take time to design and print. Papers have lead times for ads . . ."

"Is it impossible?" Alec asked.

"No, but far from ideal." Mrs. Morgan clasped her hands on the table.

"I have a friend who's in graphic arts. She can turn around programs quickly," Gentry said.

"Let's set modest goals and keep this first effort small," Colby suggested. "We can learn from our mistakes and then plan something more lavish next year."

Gentry asked, "Am I allowed to use Mark's and Joe's story in order to drum up more interest, or is that a no-go?"

"Mention that the foundation is being started in Joe's and Mark's honor, but don't plaster their names everywhere. I don't want to upset Mr. Morgan further." Colby didn't make direct eye contact with Mrs. Morgan, though she could see her peripherally.

When Julie's gaze dropped to her lap, Colby's mother reached over and squeezed the woman's forearm.

Sara interjected, "Let's come up with a mission statement, and then make a logistics plan to pull the event together."

The next thirty minutes consisted of Colby and Mrs. Morgan talking while everyone else took notes. With marching orders in hand, everyone began making polite goodbyes.

"Sara, do you have a minute?" Colby asked.

"Sure, but I'm driving your mom."

Colby dragged Sara to her office and closed the door, leaving Alec to entertain her mom, who'd easily keep her occupied for at least ten minutes. "You seemed upset last night. Is everything okay?"

"I'm fine," she quipped with uncommon impatience.

"I don't mean to pry," Colby began gently, "but have you started hormone therapy again?"

"No." Sara sighed. "Not yet. We have an appointment today, and then we'll decide."

Colby squeezed Sara's shoulder. "What's the doctor say?"

"The same thing he always says." Sara sat against Colby's desk, her face a study in melancholy. "But this is it for me. I can't go through a third round. If this fails, maybe it's not meant to be."

"Motherhood?"

The faraway look in Sara's eyes suggested something more. "Never mind."

A chill rippled through Colby. "I hated seeing you and Hunter argue. Stress doesn't help the situation."

"I know." Sara stood to go. "Look, Colby, thanks for your concern, but I'd rather not talk about it now."

It was unlike Sara to be abrupt. Her demeanor made Colby uneasy, even if she couldn't put her finger on precisely why. "I'm sorry."

"Don't be." Sara flashed a shallow grin. "Let's get back before your mom gets antsy."

Colby set aside her concern for now. "Or before she takes another swipe at Gentry."

"Quite a group you've assembled." Sara raised her brows, then said teasingly, "Were you drunk when you chose us?"

"Just stupidly optimistic," Colby chuckled.

They wandered back into the dining room to find only her mother and Alec remaining.

"Let's all grab lunch," her mom suggested.

"Mom, it's two thirty. Didn't you eat before you came?"

She waved dismissively. "Coffee and dessert, then."

"I've got a to-do list as long as my arm, and now so do you," Colby said.

"Come, let's leave these two alone." Sara tugged at her mother-in-law's arm.

"Leslie, hang on. I have something for you." Alec jogged back to the kitchen and returned with a to-go box. "Enjoy."

Her mom opened the lid to reveal four gorgeous miniature glossy cakes topped with fresh strawberry slices and some kind of coulis. "What are they?"

"Chocolate mango cheesecakes." Alec smiled. "Our pastry chef's been experimenting."

"You're a prince!" Her mother beamed.

"None for me?" Sara teased.

"You don't like sweets," Alec replied.

"I know." She winked at Alec and dragged Colby's mom out the door. "Come on, Leslie, let's go."

"You holding up okay?" Alec slung his arm over Colby's shoulder once they were alone.

"Better than okay." She twirled to snuggle against his chest.

He kissed the top of her head. "The Maverick Foundation."

"That pleased your mom. Maybe it will make your dad happy, too."

"Don't count on it." He grimaced. "Do you really want to stay here and work?"

She craned her neck and kissed him. "Maybe we could work from your place after a little break?"

"Good plan." He smiled, looking unbearably handsome standing in the soft light streaming through the glass doors.

An exhilarating rush of gratitude swept through her, pulling her past the tragic memories, past her brother's warnings and Alec's father's reaction, out to where she stood, alone, vulnerable, and falling in love with one of her oldest friends. And for the first time in years, she didn't feel like hiding.

"Follow me." She clasped his hand and prayed her leap of faith wouldn't end in heartache.

Chapter Sixteen

"Thanks for meeting me for lunch." Hunter kissed Colby's cheek and sat across from her at Gab-n-Eat, their favorite greasy spoon. Nothing ever changed here: not the ripped vinyl seat cushions, chipped Formica tabletops, or funky mix of sausage, onion, and bacon aromas.

Of course, Hunter looked out of place—in his crisp bespoke shirt and Patek Philippe watch—but both she and he had laid claim to this booth eons ago, when they would sneak in to compensate for their mother's bland cooking.

"I never pass on a chance to clog my arteries." She sipped the diet soda she'd ordered before Hunter arrived, and wondered if Alec would ever cross this diner's threshold. She smothered a smile as she imagined his horrified response to the gargantuan portions. "So what's up? You rarely have time to meet me midweek."

"Two things." He clasped his hands together on the table, officious as always. "First, I'm sorry for reacting so badly to your news last week. I love you and Alec. You just caught me off guard. I still think you've created a tricky situation for yourselves at the restaurant, but from a purely personal perspective, I hope it works out."

"Thanks." Colby couldn't resist teasing. "Now tell the truth. Did Sara put you up to that apology?"

"No." He didn't crack a smile. Too bad, because his stony face could really benefit from a few more smiles. Maybe *she* should start sending *him* funny videos. "Sara's got only one focus these days, and that's a whole other issue. One I don't have patience for now that Jenna's talking Dad into selling the company."

"What?" Colby leaned forward, stunned. So stunned, she temporarily lost interest in Sara. "Why would Dad ever consider selling CTC?"

"Jenna's heard a rumor that Pure Foods might be interested in buying CTC." Hunter shook his head. "Honestly, I laughed at first, never imagining Dad might consider selling. But Jenna's got his ear, and even if Pure Foods doesn't make a play, she seems to want to go hunting for a buyer."

The waitress, Donna, interrupted them. Her grease-stained apron looked almost as ragged as she did. They ordered their usual bacon cheeseburgers with a side of onion rings. "Have you spoken to Dad?"

"Not yet. That's probably a good thing, though, 'cause I'm pissed as hell. I've given the last eleven years of my life to that place, believing I'd be running it all in the future. It's our damn legacy. Now Jenna's pushing him to sell out? How many more purses, cars, and kitchens does that witch need?"

"Hunter, lower your voice." She glanced over her shoulder to see if any of Jenna's friends were present. A dumb reflex, because Jenna's friends wouldn't eat here.

"I'm serious, Colby. If we sell CTC, you'll be sitting pretty, with enough money to buy out of the restaurant and go on as you wish. But that business is *my* future. My kids' future." He paused then, as if the significance of those words had slapped him on the cheek. Colby's heart ached in response to his and Sara's baby blues. Hunter shook his head to reclaim his train of thought. "I'm not saying Jenna hasn't been a part of CTC's growth, but what the hell? Dad always promised me we would run it together. It would be *ours*."

Now Sara's mood the other night made more sense. Hunter had probably been a bear lately, not that she blamed him. Her father *had* promised him that future. She'd heard it over and over from the age of ten. Hunter had also forgone Wall Street job offers, relying on that promise.

No wonder he was freaking out. All this stress over a rumor, proving the wisdom of her decision to withhold Gentry's gossip about the reviewer from Alec.

She grabbed her brother's hands and squeezed them reassuringly. "Dad can't unilaterally sell it. We all own shares."

"He's the tiebreaker." Hunter pulled his hands away and raked one through his hair. "Thanks to Dad's estate planner, you, Gentry, Jenna, and I all own a majority of the stock in equal shares, but Dad retains that swing vote."

"Don't be so sure that Gentry will vote with Jenna. There's a lot of animosity there." Even as she said it, she regretted it. While she had no love lost for Jenna, she didn't want Gentry to become a pawn in Hunter's chess match.

"Oh, come on. Gentry would love a big fat check." Hunter rolled his eyes. "She's not interested in working there or taking pride in its growth. Trust me, she'll sell out in a heartbeat."

"I've seen another side to her lately. Underneath all that attitude she's yearning for a place in this family. If you go to her and honestly tell her what you've told me, she might not cash out. Then we can block a sale."

"So I can count on you to stand with me if it comes to that?" The intensity of his gaze could be so unnerving she'd hate to be on the opposing side.

"Of course. I know how important this is to you. I don't want to work there, but maybe someday my future kids would want to." She managed to smile, even as the very notion of *her* future kids sort of rocked her. "You can count on me."

"Even if it means going up against Dad?" He cocked his head, assessing her ability to stomach conflict so keenly it might as well have been a strip search.

"Yes." She'd never *not* back Hunter, the one and only member of her family who'd never abandoned, manipulated, or disappointed her. They might not always see eye to eye, but he always had her back.

"Thanks." Hunter sighed and stretched deeper into the booth, loosening his collar before sucking down some ginger ale. "So how's this foundation going? I couldn't believe you involved Mom."

"It's only been ten days, but so far, so good." Colby knocked on the wood frame of the booth. "Mom and Mrs. Morgan have already received auction donations from several local retailers. Gentry's on top of outreach. Alec planned a nice menu. Sara has everything set up on QuickBooks. And I'm sending out the invitations."

"Mom and Gentry." Hunter shook his head. "I can't imagine either of them carrying their weight."

"I don't know about Mom, because Mrs. Morgan would never speak ill of her, but Gentry might surprise you. She's actually pretty good at this PR stuff. She lives on social media, and she's funny and fresh. Honestly, I think she's got a ton of potential, if she could lose the chip on her shoulder."

"What's the deal with that? Who has an easier life than her?" He bugged his eyes. "I don't get all the anger."

"I know you think Mom is clingy, but at least she was present for big and small milestones, and took us on fun adventures. Gentry had nannies. Maybe Gentry envied our 'normal' life."

"In high school, my summers were spent working at CTC. Hers consisted of pool parties and shopping sprees." He grimaced. "I doubt she's envious."

"We had each other, but she was more or less an only child over there. I think she's jealous of our relationship." She forced Hunter to acknowledge her point. "You and I need to do better by our sister. I worry that her life could run off track. We need to keep her busy and involved."

For the second time, he stared at her, his brain working overtime.

"Colby." He sighed. "I know no matter how often I say otherwise, you'll always feel like you failed Mark. But you can't save people. People have to save themselves. Mark, Gentry, whomever. Don't run yourself ragged trying to prevent people from making bad choices."

Hunter's words bothered her, but before she could respond, their burgers came. The mammoth sandwich and heaping pile of breaded onion rings almost made her troubles disappear. Alec's food may be beautiful and complex, but for Colby, little could beat diner food. Her mouth watered in anticipation of that first bite.

As if reading her mind, Hunter snickered. "I know. Alec and Sara would be horrified, but this is the bomb."

Now that they'd moved away from discussing the CTC situation, Colby decided to probe about Sara.

"So tell me, how can I help with Sara?"

"I don't know. I get that she's thirty-four and getting nervous about the kid thing, but it's become an obsession. Her quitting work has only made it worse, as I'd predicted. She was insistent that less stress would make getting pregnant easier, but she's only become more stressed, and more needy. She forgets how tiring the workday can be. My only downtime now is my morning bike ride. She's bored at home and needs stuff from me that she never needed before. If she doesn't get pregnant with the next IVF round, I don't know what she'll do." He frowned and bit into his burger. He didn't sound angry, just confused, depressed, and maybe a little powerless. That probably bothered him most of all, because one thing Hunter had never been in his entire life was powerless.

"I'm sorry."

"We're waiting another month to start the shots, then it'll be a few weeks until harvest and implantation. I hope it works. I really do. I hate seeing her depressed, but with this new threat at work, I don't have time to hand-hold."

"Well, when it comes time for shots and the posttransfer bed rest, ask Mom to help."

"Oh God!" He shook his head. "Mom?"

"Mom's happiest when she feels needed. She'd love for *you* to need her for *anything*, Hunter. I swear, just ask and you'll see. She'll keep Sara company and take care of her, so you'll have more time to focus on work." Colby savored a greasy onion ring. *Heaven.*

"Maybe you're right. Sara likes Mom, and I'm going to need to stick closer to the office in order to fend off Jenna's attempt to sell my birthright."

Colby thought about the situation with Gentry and about her dad's age and health. "I'm not defending Jenna, but do you think she might want to sell because she wants Dad to slow down? He hasn't looked so good lately. Have you noticed? Perspiration, exhaustion, and his knees have been bothering him."

"He's never said anything to me." Hunter shrugged, although a hint of concern edged his features. Like a typical guy faced with the idea of a nonemergency medical issue, he then waved his hand dismissively. "I'm sure he's fine."

"Men." Mark had never followed doctors' orders. Of course, her father was nothing like Mark. "Would you like me to talk to Dad about this sale?"

"I'm not above offering you anything you want if you can convince him to ignore Jenna." He smiled, and she knew he was mostly teasing. "Let's change the subject so I don't get heartburn. So . . . Alec. When we were young, I thought you might end up with Joe. Then you brought Mark home. But Alec? Never saw that coming. Of course, he's the best of the lot."

Not to mention the only one alive. That fact made her a little heartsick.

"Guess I had to grow up before I could appreciate him." She set her chin on her fist, thinking about the fresh tulips he left on her desk each Wednesday. "I wish his father weren't so bitter, though."

She'd been letting herself daydream a little about what her future could look like with Alec, but his father could come between them. So could the business matters they didn't agree upon and his inability to fully control that temper. She wouldn't rush into any relationship again like she'd done before, so she kept her daydreams to herself.

"Frank Morgan has always been hard on him. For a while I thought Alec had stopped caring about that. But since Joe died, he seems determined to forge some relationship with his dad."

Colby didn't mention Alec and Joe's fight or Alec's guilty conscience. "When you lose someone close, you want to hold on extra tight to anyone who's left. I get why Alec wants to fix his broken family. I only wish I could help."

He reached across the table and tugged at her hair. "You're always the cement that binds people. Eventually, you'll find a way to help. That much I know."

"That's the nicest thing you've said to me in ages." She smiled and stole the last onion ring from his plate.

"I'll try to sneak in another compliment before Christmas." He smirked, looking much more at ease than when he arrived. "I'd better get back to the office. Let me know if I can do anything for this fundraiser. I've got a lot of people who owe me favors, so we can lean on them for donations."

"Send me the list!"

Hunter threw down forty bucks. "Lunch is on me. Thanks for listening and for the advice. I'll talk to Sara about having Mom help, and I'll think about how to reach out to Gentry."

She mockingly placed a hand on her chest. "See, deep down beneath that cold, all-business exterior, you have a good heart."

"Don't tell a soul!" He winked and walked out the door.

◆ ◆ ◆

"Why are you waking me at this ungodly hour?" Alec murmured when Colby tried waking him for the third time. "It's Monday, our sleep-in day."

"I have a surprise." She kissed his shoulder. He was half-tempted to pull her into bed again, but exhaustion won out.

"It's five thirty," he griped, eyes still closed, defiantly *not* a morning person.

"Hurry." She drew back the blankets, showing no mercy. "We've got to be there by six thirty."

"Be where?" One eye popped open.

"Get up if you want to find out. Throw on some layers because it may be chilly."

"I need a shower." He propped up on his elbows, moving at the speed of molasses.

"No time." She grabbed his wrist and tugged. "Let's go, sleepyhead."

Alec groaned but got out of bed and washed his face. He slipped into jeans and a jersey and grabbed his jacket. "Is this okay?"

"It should be." She clasped his hand and raced to his car. Twenty minutes later, they arrived at an open field where he spied a seventy-foot-long multicolored balloon. It lay spread out on the ground while a crew pulled out the wrinkles and dealt with the other equipment.

"Are you surprised?" Colby clapped her hands together and bounced on her toes. "I thought we'd start our bucket-list adventures with a hot-air balloon ride."

"I can't believe you planned this behind my back." He lifted her off her feet and kissed her, consumed with joy that she'd finally done something whimsical and fun for herself.

"Just a few weeks ago, it wouldn't have occurred to me. I'd been locked in a place of grief and regret for so long, just hoping that a career change would somehow jolt me forward. When Hunter hired you, I worried it would set me back. Instead, you've pulled me through. Thanks to your support, I'm feeling more and more like myself. Like maybe I deserve to be happy again. And that even after my mistakes and so much sorrow for both our families, there is hope and forgiveness. So this is partly for you, too. A thank-you for helping me rediscover myself."

"I'm touched." He kissed her again. "And happy for this gorgeous morning, too."

It took roughly thirty minutes for the crew to inflate the balloon and right the basket. Once he and Colby climbed over its side to join the pilot in the basket, she clutched his arm and whispered, "I'm a little nervous."

When the ropes were released, the balloon lifted into the air. Not with a jerk, as he'd expected. It simply floated upward, as if gravity no longer existed. A singular experience, reinforced by Colby's delighted giggle.

She'd positioned herself in one corner, clutching a rope and looking over the edge as they climbed higher into the sky. Aside from an occasional instruction, the pilot focused on his job and left them alone.

The sunrise bathed the earth beneath them in swaths of warm golden light. Colby's nose and cheeks were pink; her eyes twinkled. Seeing her awed made Alec feel like a king because she wouldn't have planned this without his encouragement.

"I feel like a bird." She surveyed the miles and miles of countryside. "My heart's racing. I wonder if this is how Mark and Joe felt on all of their adventures."

"They were fearless," Alec admitted. Both men had other traits he hadn't respected, but they *were* brave.

"Mark feared things, but he pushed through it. I usually liked that about him." Her wistful tone reawakened the remorse he'd suppressed. The letter. The damned letter he wished he'd never opened. Guilt filled his lungs like the hot air inflating the nylon balloon.

Alec didn't want to share this experience with Mark or Joe. This moment was his and Colby's. He wanted to be the only man with her as she rediscovered herself and embraced excitement, life, and even love. His love. God, he wanted her to love him.

He stepped closer and pulled her back to his chest, wrapping his arms around her waist. "I'm glad you're enjoying this experience as much as you'd hoped."

"And I'm glad I'm sharing it with you." She settled her head on his shoulder and continued observing the scenery while he kept a tight hold on her.

"It's so quiet," he said after several minutes spent drifting across the sky.

"Dead quiet," she agreed. "Except for when the pilot turns on the gas."

"The whole world looks different from up here. Reminds me that life is full of infinite possibilities."

She turned her face toward his, wearing a broad smile. "'Infinite possibilities' sounds great. Do you forgive me for forcing you out of bed so early on our day off?"

He chuckled and kissed her. "Yes, although I hope not all of our adventures will require predawn departures."

They drifted along for forty minutes, occasionally speaking with the pilot, until he glided them to a fairly smooth landing. The basket butted against the ground once or twice before the crew members waiting for them got involved.

After settling the bill, they climbed into the SUV to catch a ride back to where they'd originally parked. Once they parted from the crew, she hugged him. "I love that we did that. Next we should work on that Adam Levine wish."

He jokingly frowned. "If he weren't married, I might get jealous of your infatuation."

She chuckled. "I'm still a teenager at heart when it comes to rock stars."

Alec mockingly grabbed his chest as if stricken, and she kissed him and got in the car.

A mile or two later, she pointed at a run-down diner. "Let's grab breakfast here. We can talk about the foundation."

Sketchy diner aside, he'd rather go home and laze around on their day off, but they had too much to do. He repressed a shudder at the thick film on the diner floor and led Colby to a booth in the rear of the restaurant. "I can't believe how much you've accomplished already."

Colby snorted. "Your mom's a force of nature! I'm surprised your dad hasn't complained about all the time she's put into planning the party."

So was Alec. In fact, he suspected his dad didn't know. "She's committed. It makes her feel closer to Joe."

"It was an inspired idea, yet you shy away from taking credit and a more prominent role." She then wrinkled her nose and teased, "Quite a change from the egomaniac who runs the kitchen."

"I've been restraining myself somewhat and doling out praise like you asked." He couldn't help himself and added, "Honestly, they'd be further along if you let me handle them my way."

"Without *any* encouragement I think they'd all quit to avoid those times when the whole restaurant feels like an earthquake zone." She paused. "You sort of become like your dad when you're in the kitchen."

That was *not* a compliment, and he knew it. "My job is to require perfection."

"It's not your job to demean the other cooks." She pressed her lips together in what he guessed was an attempt to stave off more lectures.

"I'm not demeaning, just demanding." He frowned. "Have they complained?"

"No, but given our relationship, I doubt they'd feel comfortable coming to me now."

"My style may be exhausting, but you'll all be proud when we win awards."

Instead of beaming, Colby fidgeted with the saltshaker. She did this—sighed and averted her gaze—whenever she was gearing up to say something he wouldn't appreciate. The anticipation only heightened his anxiety.

"I wish you believed that we could be happy and create a restaurant people love even if A CertainTea never earns a single award. That adding a couple of normal options on the menu wouldn't ruin the restaurant. Gab-n-Eat is a town favorite, and it's far from perfect." Colby stared at him, her eyes filling with concern. "When you flip out over wilted chiffonade, I worry that you can't be happy *without* an award."

Acclaim wasn't a goal he was willing to concede. "I've lived and breathed this industry my entire adult life. Paid my dues in ways you can't conceive. Earned a reputation people dream of, only to have lost it. I'm not in this for 'happiness,' Colby. I'm in this because it means something to me. It defines me. Being the best at it is my goal, and I'll give it everything I have. I'd think you'd like that about me, considering how assertive Mark was."

Colby sat back as the waitress brought her short stack of blueberry pancakes and Alec's coffee—bitter coffee that had obviously been burning in an old pot. Meanwhile, Colby merely pushed her fork at the short stack rather than attack it like he'd expected.

"What's wrong?"

Colby looked up. "I don't want to re-create my relationship with Mark. And I certainly don't want you to emulate him."

"What *do* you want?" To date, most of their time and effort revolved around work and the foundation. She'd hardly confided anything personal. He had no clue of the depth of her commitment to him, if any, even as he continued to put his career and family on the line for her.

"I want peace."

"Doesn't the fact that I'm on top of things at work give you peace of mind about your investment?" He leaned forward, trying to read her thoughts. "I've made compromises for you, but don't ask me to give up my dreams, Colby."

"That's not what I'm saying." She looked around as if the words she needed would pop out from behind another booth. The only thing she'd likely find behind a booth in this joint was a cockroach. "There are lots of things that define you, Alec, not just this job. When you think your entire worth rests on being 'the best,' I worry that this quest for perfection is actually some way of proving something to your dad. If his opinion never changes, can you accept that?"

She looked sincerely concerned, so he shouldn't be insulted. He shouldn't be, but he was. Perhaps his dad's respect played some role in that goal, but it wasn't the only one, and he didn't need her psychoanalyzing him, either.

He held up his scarred hands. "You think I've spent the last fifteen years earning these scars just to win my dad's love?"

"I know it's not *that* simple. I'm just wondering . . . wishing your dreams . . ." Her voice trailed off. She raked her hands through her hair and shook her head as if she could shake away her doubts. "Never mind. If you need awards to feel successful, then I'll do whatever I can to help you get them."

"Don't diminish those awards. Athletes train for the Olympics to win medals. Actors vie for Oscar nods. Musicians yearn for Grammys. I earned that James Beard Award, and it was as important in my profession as any of those others."

"This is all coming out wrong. I only want you to be happy." Her voice dropped. "You got so depressed after losing Une Bouchée . . . you took off for months."

"I *was* depressed, but not just because of the restaurant. It was everything with Joe." He stopped talking before Mark's name fell from his mouth.

"I've been reading about chefs who get obsessed with their ratings, like Chef Violier or the old speculation surrounding Chef Loiseau . . ."

"Suicide?" He scoffed without thinking. When her eyes got misty, he felt like a shit. Suicide would never be outside the realm of possibility in her mind. Softening his tone, he said, "Colby, I'm not them, or Mark. I swear I'd never do that. Not to you or my mother."

"Let's drop it, okay." She smiled weakly and poured a pint of syrup on her plate. She smothered her pancakes in butter and sliced them into uniform, bite-size pieces. Despite the bacon she inhaled and strawberry she dipped in her syrup—normal behavior for her—he saw her retreating. Felt a distance that hadn't been there earlier.

Reaching across the table, he clasped her hand in his and squeezed. "Remember, in the balloon, we talked about unlimited possibilities? That's what we can have. I want recognition, I want my family to be happier again, and I want you. I'm going to make all three of those things happen. And as long as you're by my side, everything is possible."

She sucked down her orange juice before responding. "Everything except for my ideas about the menu, right? I still think we could introduce one or two new menu items for the common palate. For people like me, who like burgers and bacon."

Burgers and bacon? Good God, how did she expect him to make that work? If A CertainTea were his, he wouldn't have to entertain this discussion. Wishful thinking didn't help, though. It wasn't his restaurant. It was hers, which meant he couldn't ignore her wishes.

"Alec?"

Her voice yanked him back to the filthy diner, where she, oddly, looked perfectly comfortable. "I'll give some thought to an item or two that aren't strictly haute cuisine."

A grateful syrup-glossed smile stretched across her face. "You'll see. People will *love* that!"

In that moment, he didn't care about what other people loved. Only that she might come to love him.

Chapter Seventeen

"You're a miracle worker, Julie. If Alec and I didn't work weekends, I'd bid on this hotel-and-spa package in Cannon Beach." Colby scanned the list of silent-auction items Alec's mom had accumulated in a few weeks' time. When Joe had been alive, Colby and Julie had routinely greeted each other with a hug. Now Julie kept her hands safely clasped together, warding off contact. "Come sit. Everyone else will be here soon."

"Actually, I came early because I hoped we could talk." Julie's sober expression sent up a red flag.

Had Alec hidden something more from Colby? Had his father gotten drunk again? Or was it something related to another compromise Alec had made for her? The tea-braised double-fried chicken he'd added to the menu this past week had drawn positive reviews from a few customers, but she'd been suspecting Alec still hated the concept.

"Oh?" Colby braced herself.

"I want to apologize for my cool attitude toward you these past two years. I don't hold you responsible for what happened to Joe."

Colby held her breath, waiting for the flood of relief she expected from the absolution. She and Julie silently stared at each other while the harsh truth settled in. No pardon would bring Joe back or fill the void he'd left behind.

Colby swallowed the lump in her throat, steadying herself by clutching the back of a dining chair, her nails biting into the velvety fabric. "Please don't apologize. I understand. I still blame myself sometimes. I loved Joe. I miss him. And I hate how rash he and Mark were that day."

Through her own blurry vision, Colby saw ocean-deep pain in the pool of tears shining in Julie's eyes.

The woman's voice emerged hollow and cracked. "Every once in a while, I wake up and forget, for just a second, that Joe's gone. When it hits me, the pain's *so* fresh. I hate those mornings almost as much as I hate waking from dreams where Joe's still with us. But I can't live every day holding on to grief." She dabbed the corner of her eye and cleared her throat. "Now Alec's back, and I'll do anything to keep him here. Thank you for giving him this job, and for giving him a special place in your life. He's had a spring in his step these past few weeks."

Colby's chest filled with satisfaction. She couldn't claim Alec struck her like a thunderbolt, considering how long she'd known him. But even though she'd been taking things slower so as not to repeat her past mistakes, she couldn't deny being smitten.

"Thank *you* for raising such a considerate, loving man. Alec's special." It dawned on Colby that the second anniversary of Mark's suicide was on the horizon. She hadn't visited his grave in weeks—the longest stretch since he'd died. A twinge of guilt nipped at her conscience, but she resisted the urge to twist her wedding band in front of Alec's mother.

"Is he in the kitchen?" Julie asked, having reclaimed her composure.

"No. He went to Oregon Blues for berries, and then maybe to the lavender farm, too. He had some idea for a special he wants to test-prep today."

Before Julie replied, Colby's mother breezed through the door, waving a sheet of paper. "I got Harrington's to donate pavé diamond earrings!"

"That's excellent, Leslie," Julie praised.

Colby contrasted Julie's refined bob and conservative navy dress to her mom's unkempt wavy locks, flowing pants, and frenzied persona. They were a female Odd Couple, yet they worked well together.

"Fantastic, Mom," Colby said just as Todd strolled in, briefcase in hand, and smiled at her. She'd grown accustomed to chef coats, so Todd's pinstripe suit caught her unawares. What different life and work environments she now had.

"Three lovely ladies and more to come." He shook hands with her mom and Julie before greeting Colby with a slight hug. "This will definitely be my favorite board appointment."

"Thanks for squeezing us in today," Colby said.

"I brought more paperwork for you to sign." He raised his briefcase.

"Perfect." She then informed her mother and Julie, "I'm kicking in five thousand dollars to get the fund started."

"There goes my garden's stone fence," her mother sighed.

"Mom."

"I'm kidding." She sniffed.

Before they were seated, Sara walked in with Alec, surprising Colby. She'd been waiting to tell Todd about Alec in person—and in private. Now he'd get blindsided.

Her pulse skipped. She tried signaling Alec with her eyes, but he was too busy kissing his mom hello to notice. He eventually sidled over to her and kissed her hello—a kiss intended to send Todd a message. To his credit, Todd's wide grin barely faltered.

"I thought you were busy," she muttered to Alec.

"Finished up early." He grinned.

"Where's Gentry?" Sara glanced around anxiously, tossing her purse on the table. "I have an appointment at three."

Another vague "appointment" reference. Colby replayed her recent conversation with Hunter and wondered, for the first time, if Sara's appointments had nothing to do with fertility. "Never fear. We're starting on time, with or without my sister. Todd needs to get back to work, too."

"Don't rush me off so quickly," Todd joked, his face full of good humor as they all took seats. "I know I missed the earlier meetings, but

I've been thinking about the broad mission and urge you to reconsider. While it's laudable to try to help everyone, it might end up creating more problems than it solves."

"I like Colby's idea. It gives us flexibility," Alec challenged. His spine was straight as a ruler, and his right leg bounced beneath the table.

"In my experience, most people support pet causes. A diverse mission could hinder your ability to retain loyal donors," Todd replied.

"Or we might attract more donors because we'll be helping a wide range of causes," Alec countered, his strained grin barely masking his tension.

Colby jumped in before Alec lapsed into the kind of meltdown she'd seen when anyone on the staff challenged his opinion. "Todd, is there a compromise that would work? Perhaps we could pick a theme, like "helping families" or something, that would allow us some flexibility while giving donors a clearer picture."

"That might work," Todd conceded.

"But then we'd be eliminating environmental issues, which are what Mark and Joe loved most." Alec tilted forward, his gaze locked on Todd. "We already drafted a mission statement, which my mom and Leslie have been promoting to get the donations we've already received. We can't change course now."

"I'm not suggesting a wholesale change, Alec. Just a refinement." Todd smiled politely, like Colby had seen him do many times with belligerent clients. She resisted the urge to sneak a peek to see if his legs were also jostling under the table.

She set her hand on Alec's thigh, hoping to uncoil whatever had him ready to pounce. "We'll give it more thought. For now, let's focus on what needs to be completed before the party."

"Fair enough," Todd conceded with his usual pleasantness and slouched deeper into the dining chair.

Colby opened her notebook. "By the way, thank you for writing off your fees for preparing the organizational documents."

"Anything for you." Todd winked.

Beside her, Colby saw Alec's jaw clench.

"How generous," her mother added, which did nothing to wipe the sour look off Alec's face.

"A great friend." Colby hoped her words eased Alec's ridiculous jealousy.

The group discussed the nitty-gritty planning details for the next thirty minutes, when Gentry finally showed up. She sat beside Todd and adjusted her skimpy skirt with a smirk. "Sorry."

"Just in time for the last item." Colby refused to give Gentry the satisfaction of having annoyed her by being so late. "Sara, I assume you've been keeping track of the donations and sending out tax letters?"

"Yes," she replied.

"Hunter was planning on contacting some friends. Has he mentioned anything to you?"

"No. He's been preoccupied."

Looking at Sara now—serene and collected—one would have no idea that she and Hunter were struggling. Like Colby had done, Sara hid her marital problems from the family. Having learned the hard way what a mistake that had been, Colby wanted to reach out. Then again, Hunter and Sara weren't Colby and Mark. Whatever rough patch they'd recently hit, they'd work it out.

She had to believe that, because if Hunter and Sara couldn't make love last, no one could.

"If that's it, how about we get the photos out of the way," Gentry said. "I'll take some of the whole group, then the board. Lastly, I'll shoot Alec and Colby, the proud parents."

Sara's head snapped toward Colby, as did everyone else's, in a tense moment of silence. If a pin dropped ten blocks away, it would've been audible in the room.

"Is there news?" Julie's face filled with so much hope it broke Colby's heart to disappoint her.

"No!" Colby perspired even as Gentry laughed.

"Parents of this idea, people. Jeez, why does everyone always have babies on the brain?" Gentry shook her head, pulled out her Nikon, and pointed toward the wall where the ironwork artwork had been hung. For a split second, Colby fantasized that Gentry was somehow trapped behind that metal, until she learned better manners. "Everyone, over there."

Gentry arranged them in a variety of positions. When it came time for the board photograph, she sandwiched Colby between Alec and Todd. Alec possessively linked his arm around her waist. If Todd had any feelings about that, he didn't show them.

After the photography session, people gathered their things and left for the day. When Alec started to follow her and Todd outside, she shot him a do-not-follow-me look. Thankfully, he stayed behind, allowing her a few minutes to speak with Todd.

Once alone in the parking lot, Todd said, "Looks like you decided to dip your toe back in the dating pool."

"Todd," she started, but he cut her off with a quick wave of his hand.

"No need, Colby. I'll survive." He set his briefcase on his back seat and closed the door. "We've always been friends. Nothing will change that. If Alec makes you happy, that's what matters."

"Thank you." She hugged him goodbye. "For everything."

"See you at the event!" He got into his car and returned to Portland. To the office where they'd become friends. To the life she'd mostly left behind.

She turned and studied A CertainTea. The flower beds were in full bloom. The grass between the pavers was neatly trimmed, and the lake twinkled in the sunlight. Tomorrow evening the restaurant would be bustling again, having a full slate of reservations on the books. She'd even received her first inquiry for a private party—a golden wedding anniversary in October. Little by little all her plans and hopes were coming to fruition. *"If Alec makes you happy, that's what matters."* He did make her happy . . . when he wasn't acting jealous.

She found him sprawled out in a chair in some kind of power pose. He'd appear relaxed if she didn't notice his white knuckles fisted on the arms of the chair, or the tilt of his chin.

"What was that?"

"What?" He sat up now, alert and ready to battle. Well, if he thought to intimidate her into silence, he'd thought wrong.

"You were supposed to be at those farms, not here staking your territory."

"Isn't my presence welcome at the foundation *I* suggested?" His cool tone slid right through her, coating her bones in ice.

"That's not what I meant, and you know it. I told you I'm not interested in Todd, so you had no reason to rub his nose in our relationship or pick an argument over his perfectly reasonable advice."

Alec narrowed his gaze, head tipped to the side. "Would you be comfortable if I hired Colette?"

"That's completely different." A vision of the sex siren flashed, making her imagine Alec's body intertwined with Colette's. Had he looked at her the way he looked at Colby? Had he held her close at night and whispered in her ear? Had he brought her flowers at work? "I've never had sex with Todd."

"So what? I had sex with Colette, but there were no real feelings."

His admission filled Colby's heart with something resembling helium but didn't stop his chaotic emotions from rolling off him.

"You *care* about Todd. You trust him, you confide in him. You have a real connection with that man. Sex is nothing compared with those things."

"You're being irrational."

He winced, then grew thoughtful, tapping his palm against the table a few times. At the moment, she didn't know which scared her more, explosive Alec or quiet Alec. In a soft voice, he muttered, "Well, maybe I wish you'd be a little *less* rational."

"Meaning what?" she ventured.

"Meaning I've risked a lot, compromised, and pretty much laid my heart bare to you, yet you keep a part of yourself closed up." He shot out of the chair, raised her right hand, and pinched her wedding band. "I'm sorry to bring up Mark, but he's the ghost between us I don't know how to fight. It's easier to pick on Todd, because he's here, and it hurts to see you so carefree and chummy with him when you never share how you feel about me." Following that outburst, he stepped back and raked his hands through his hair. Like an accordion, he folded up on himself. "Sorry. I need a minute."

He stormed across the room and out the glass doors, heading toward the gazebo.

Colby stood in the middle of the empty restaurant, her body vibrating from shock. An array of images and memories sparkled to life—tulips and silly videos, the reporter's interrogation, the space Alec had given her after their second "first" kiss, the time he spent with her mother, his confiding in her about Joe, his compromises here at the restaurant. He *had* laid his heart bare, every day and in every way. All the while, she'd been holding back.

Alec didn't understand her reticence, because she'd never been honest with him about her marriage.

Without another thought, she trotted through the dining room, spotting him in the gazebo staring out across the lake, like he'd done that first day. Stoic, assessing, hurting. If he heard her coming, he didn't turn around.

She rested her hand on his back, causing his muscles to flinch. "Alec."

He turned, his face flushed, eyes downcast. "I'm sorry."

She shook her head and brushed his cowlick with her fingers. Her heart pounded in her chest from how much she had to say and how scared she was to say it. "*I'm* sorry I've hurt you. I promise, my reserve has nothing to do with you. It's self-preservation. Todd's safe because I'm not invested in him. But the closer *we* get, the more afraid I am that something will go wrong, so I withdraw. I don't mean to, but after everything I've been through, I can't promise I'll ever be able to give my *whole* heart to anyone again."

She let her hand drop and then eased away, shaken by her own admission.

Alec didn't stir. He didn't make the moment easier for her by quickly accepting her confession or offering the warmth of his embrace. If anything, he seemed to withdraw further, gazing back out across the lake. Finally, he uttered, "Because of how Mark left you."

"Not the way you mean." How could she explain that her reservations were more than a response to Mark's suicide? That they had to do with not trusting herself. And maybe no longer trusting in love.

When she closed her eyes, Mark's face surfaced—his young face. "I met him in the quad outside the law school one April afternoon. He was only there to meet a friend—pure happenstance. If I'd lingered an extra five minutes in the lounge that day, my life would be entirely different today."

A shiver ran through her. She opened her eyes and gripped the wood railing. Staring at a kayak on the lake, she continued. "Our attraction was instantaneous and blazing hot. You know we eloped three months later despite my parents' objections. Nothing else mattered to me. I'd just *known* we were meant to be together. How ridiculous, now, to think that, at twenty-four, I'd been so confident—and careless—with such a life-altering decision."

Alec looked at her expectantly, waiting for the rest of her story. To some, this might have been easy, but her breathing strained as if she were climbing a wall. She'd never spoken of Mark's illness to anyone. Truthfully, it hadn't been just because he'd pleaded for secrecy. Ultimately, she'd been ashamed, too, of how poorly they'd managed it.

Of how she'd withdrawn and given up. She stared at Alec now, knowing she had to trust him. Mark hadn't kept his promises to her, so maybe she wasn't awful for finally breaking her silence. "I loved Mark, but . . ." She paused, her body heavy with a new doubt. "Honestly, you might think less of me when I tell you everything."

"That could never happen." His decisive response came swiftly, even as he kept some distance between them. "You can trust me."

She eyed him from the side without facing him directly. Tucking a lock of hair behind her ear, she said, "I have so many regrets. Things I wish I would've done differently."

"So do I, Colby."

She hadn't meant to make him think of Joe. "Mine often make me question my judgment, because most of my marriage was a lie."

He blinked, slack-jawed. Apparently, she'd struck Alec dumb.

She leaned her butt against the railing and cleared her throat, hoping to keep her voice from cracking. "Mark knew I was thinking about divorce."

Alec's eyes widened. "Because of the dare?"

"No. Before that." She pressed her palms to her forehead and sensed Alec step closer, as if at war with himself about whether to press her for details or pull her close and hush her. "Life with Mark was difficult. He . . . he was bipolar."

She recognized Alec's preternaturally impassive expression as his intent way of listening. Oddly, that calmed her. She recited the facts of Mark's first manic episode, of how they eventually got a diagnosis, and of how they'd hidden it from everyone—even when he'd failed to control it—as dispassionately as if she were reading a teleprompter.

Inside, however, retelling the sordid details of her marriage and first love ravaged her. Colby hung her head. "He wanted a family, but I wouldn't bring kids into that chaos unless he completed eighteen consecutive months of therapy. He couldn't do it. Over time, the cycles and lies broke me down. Made me wary and suspicious. Exhausted.

Angry." She looked up at Alec. "I envied other couples I'd read about who managed that illness and made the relationship work. But I didn't know what else to do or how to be a better wife. When Mark couldn't be loyal or promise to be a stable father, I looked into divorce.

"My doubts took away the one stable thing in his life." Her nose tingled. "I think it made it easier for him to give up after Joe died. I failed him when he was sick. Sometimes I think I don't deserve to find love again after being willing to walk away from it before. And then I worry that even if I take that leap, it will all turn to ash, just like before." She looked at him now. "I want to love again, Alec, but I'm afraid."

Listening to Colby's story chilled Alec more than if he'd just been thrown into the frigid lake. Her gorgeous eyes, swollen with misery and shame, pricked his heart and conscience.

She deserved the truth about Mark's suicide. God help him, he didn't know how to dive in. "I understand how keeping secrets can drive you crazy and make you feel unworthy of anything."

"I know you do."

"Not just with Joe, Colby." For a few short weeks he'd had her in his arms at night. Tasted her kisses. Seen her passion-weary. Savored the weight of her leg across his in the middle of the night. The scent of her skin and hair. Now, he worried he'd have to miss those things for the rest of his life. Maybe that was twisted justice, seeing that Mark never got to live the rest of his life thanks to him.

"Secrets and lies. A habit I don't want to repeat again." She swiped a stray tear before wrapping her arms around his waist and tucking her head against his chest. "No matter what mistakes you've made before, or how we disagree about stupid things like the menu, you've brought joy back into my life. You've reawakened the part of me that wants to love and trust. I can never, ever repay you for that, Alec. I want to give you what *you* need. Tell you what you want to hear. Believe that this happiness I feel again won't scatter like dandelion fluff. Please be patient. And don't be jealous of Todd or any other man, because there isn't anyone more important to me than you."

"Colby, I—"

"Shh. Just kiss me." She rose onto her toes and kissed him.

If only a kiss would erase his guilty conscience. But how could he confess now, after she just expressed her fears about this fragile trust and joy vanishing. If she lost faith in her judgment again, she might retreat so deeply into herself she'd never find happiness with anyone. Neither solution to this puzzle had a good outcome. He didn't like not knowing how to complete the picture . . . or even what the picture would look like when finished. Uncertainty convinced him to keep quiet. "I wish I had known about Mark's illness before. I'm sorry you were so alone."

"Not as alone as Mark."

"I should've been a better friend. I'm sorry you've suffered for so long." He hugged her so tight she coughed. He loosened his hold just enough to make her comfortable, but couldn't quite let go.

When she sighed, the weight of her solemnity resonated in his chest. "Mark and I had started out planning for our lives to be a grand adventure. When I think about my future now, I just crave peace. I've done love the hard way. Now I want simple. Dependable. And no more looking back."

He raised her chin and kissed her. No matter how perfect his kisses, they alone couldn't offer her an uncomplicated life and an effortless relationship. Given his situation, he didn't know how to manage that, but he sure as hell would try. No more wasting time on bullshit like jealousy and menus.

"You deserve love you can count on, Colby. Let me give that to you. I swear, I'll do everything I can to make your life simple." Even cheat, steal, and lie, which was pretty much what his continued silence amounted to. Hopefully karma would give him a pass for his good intentions. Then again, that road to hell . . .

Chapter Eighteen

Colby clipped the newspaper article about the Maverick Foundation's upcoming fund-raising event that Gentry had submitted. The piece, she thought, should cause a few folks to look up the website and click on the "Donate" button. She stared at the grainy photograph of the executive committee. The one in which she'd been uncomfortably sandwiched between Todd and Alec. Her mother, blissfully unaware of any awkwardness, had smiled broadly for the camera. Julie, like Alec, remained inscrutable. To strangers, Sara's smile probably looked welcoming, but Colby knew the difference between her forced and genuine smiles.

Miraculously, despite the fractures in the ragtag group, all their plans were coming together. Thanks to Alec's initiative, something good would finally come out of the tragedies. The peace she'd been craving seemed just within her grasp. In fact, she'd been enjoying the foundation work more than running the restaurant and dealing with customers. If her finances weren't tied to A CertainTea, she could see herself committing fully to a nonprofit career.

While she placed the clipping in a frame for her embarrassingly sparsely decorated office walls, Chris knocked on her door. Although the lines in his face had deepened since she'd first hired him as sous chef, his shoulders remained proudly thrown back. "Alec hasn't returned. Has he called you?"

By the time she'd arrived at work this afternoon, she'd learned that Alec had left suddenly without explanation. She'd tried calling him, but it had gone straight to voice mail. Initially, she'd assumed the urgent matter had something to do with a supplier. Now she wasn't sure.

A quick glance at the clock warned that the doors would open in twenty minutes. "Guess you're in charge of the kitchen tonight."

A grin spread across Chris's face.

"Is there anything else?" She kept her gaze locked with his, her voice calm and steady, showing none of the turmoil gnashing her stomach lining.

"No." Chris nodded and left the office.

She stared at the framed news clip with the dawning realization that it might have something to do with Alec's absence. Colby impatiently tapped her pen on the desk and then dialed Alec again. Voice mail. *Of course.*

Why hadn't he called? Then again, she'd told him she wanted easy, and his family didn't exactly fall into that category. Mr. Morgan's temper dwarfed Alec's. A rising dread slowed her movements. What if Alec needed her and she didn't get to him on time? Alarm triggered memories of Mark's final moments.

She was getting ahead of herself. If something had happened to Alec, surely Julie would let her know. She texted him again.

WHERE ARE YOU? I'M WORRIED.

When no response came, she called Hunter without thinking it through. When he answered, she blurted, "Have you heard from Alec today?"

"No. Why?"

"He left work suddenly before I arrived, and I haven't heard from him."

Hunter paused. "If he needs you, he'll call. Otherwise, let him sort out his own family emergency."

Family emergency. The words she'd used when calling off work the morning Mark jumped. At the time, she'd been in shock, locked in a hazy sort of limbo, unable to voice the screaming in her head. Horror had consumed her. She'd acted on instinct, with monosyllabic replies to voice mails and texts. Now her body trembled at the memory.

"Sis?" Hunter's voice shook her back to reality.

"What family emergency?" she asked, her pulse fluttering irregularly now. "Tell me what you know."

"Only that Alec wouldn't leave someone else in charge of his kitchen for anything other than some kind of family emergency."

No, he wouldn't.

"Please call me if you hear anything," she said.

"I will."

She tossed her phone on the desk and tapped her foot incessantly. Every pore in her body decided to perspire. Hunter was right. Nothing less than a serious emergency would pull Alec out of the kitchen on a Saturday night.

Drawing a deep breath, she picked up her phone and called Julie. That call also went to voice mail. Apparently Alec had learned his cell phone habits from his mother.

Holding her breath, Colby called the hospital. Her breathing settled when she confirmed that neither Alec nor Frank Morgan had been admitted to the ER. Then it caught. Julie Morgan was a patient, but no further information would be given.

She sat, frozen by indecision. Mr. Morgan would lose his shit if Colby showed up, which would only increase Alec's stress. If he'd wanted her there, he would've called. He mustn't think she could handle it, which didn't make her feel better. Nor did the fact that, once again, he'd chosen not to share important, if unpleasant, news.

Each time her mind wandered—practically every ninety seconds—
she refocused on the tasks at hand. Outside her office, they'd be servic-
ing a full house on this Saturday night. She knew she should be happily
checking on customers instead of pacing in her office and checking her
phone for messages.

Attachments were complicated. How had she thought she could
have a simple, fresh start with Alec? She fingered the white tulips Alec
had placed in the vase on her desk on Wednesday. A reminder of exactly
why she'd fallen for him.

After four yoga breaths, she forced herself to return to the dining
room. Clyde, her most experienced waiter, rushed over, surreptitiously
pointing toward table eight. "Ms. Baxter, I think that's the Trib's food
critic, Gordon Jeffers."

Tonight? She'd been overwhelmed with foundation work these past
weeks and had forgotten all about Gentry's gossip. This was not good!
Alec wasn't even on the premises. "Are you sure?"

"Not one hundred percent, but I'd bet on it."

"Please inform Martha, so she'll be extra attentive. I'll let Chris
know." Colby beelined to the kitchen. As usual, the flurry of frenzied
activity and bursts of noise and heat made her want to run in the other
direction. She much preferred the casual elegance and relative serenity
of the front of the house.

Carefully, she picked her way over to where Chris was supervising
the lines. "We think Gordon Jeffers is seated at table eight with a guest,
so pay particular attention to that order, okay?"

"No word from Alec?" Chris's expression remained unflappable.

"No." Colby pushed that worry aside for the moment. She couldn't
lend her support at the hospital, but she could protect this aspect of
Alec's life. A good review would be a crucial step in his comeback plan.
She'd make sure the staff did everything in its power to earn an outstanding one. "This is it, Chris. Your chance to shine. I trust you'll be
on top of it?"

"Of course." He kept working at a steady clip, which reassured her.

"Excellent. We're counting on you." Colby left the kitchen and methodically worked the room until she arrived at table eight. Gordon Jeffers—at least, that was his pen name—didn't look like she'd imagined. His name and position implied a certain power that his long, narrow face and nose, thinning blond hair, and, as Gentry might describe it, boring navy blazer failed to convey. At present, his "date"—a middle-aged woman of similar nondescript appearance—sampled Alec's twist on a French onion soup gratinée.

With her warmest smile, Colby greeted them. "Good evening. Welcome to A CertainTea. I'm the manager, Colby. Is this your first time with us?"

"Yes." The man smiled.

"Wonderful. Are you a local?" She feigned polite interest while trying not to overplay her hand.

"Close enough. Portland."

"Well, we'll make sure it's worth the journey."

"So far, so good. The ambience is outstanding." His smile loosened the knot in her stomach. With a little luck, this could turn out well. They'd been open several weeks—long enough to work out the major kinks—and the cooks had worked with Alec even longer. Alec's absence didn't need to be a disaster. In fact, a good review might give him more faith in his staff and make things easier on everyone going forward.

"Thank you." Colby nodded. "Please let me know if you need anything. Enjoy your meal."

Rather than hover, she meandered through the crowd. As the evening progressed, she barely recalled a single conversation with any customer. With each minute, she grew more concerned about the Morgans. If she was the impetus for another family tragedy, how could she and Alec stay together?

◆ ◆ ◆

Alec was in hell. Why did a CT scan take so long? He paced the waiting room, avoiding his father—the asshole who'd clocked his wife in the head with a vase thrown in anger after reading the newspaper. If it hadn't been for that photo, his dad would've likely skimmed right over an article about a local charity.

"I didn't mean to hit her." His father drummed his fingers on the chair arm. "She practically jumped into the line of fire."

"So it's her fault she didn't duck?" Alec muttered, keeping his back to his dad.

"I wouldn't have thrown anything if she hadn't been sneaking around working on *your* damned foundation, for chrissakes." His father shifted noisily in the chair.

"Stop talking." Alec stood in the doorway, muscles pulsing with quiet rage. He glanced up and down the hall, hoping to catch a doctor or nurse. No luck. He couldn't sit still in the cramped waiting room, with its plastic chairs and months-old magazines. He needed to put more than a few feet of space between his father and him, or one of them might also end up needing X-rays. "What's taking so long?"

"Red tape." His dad cleared his throat twice. "We'll be here forever."

"We wouldn't be here at all if you weren't such a bully." Alec finally looked his dad in the eye. "Considering how many things you've smashed in my lifetime, it's a wonder this is our first visit to the ER."

"Don't start with me." His father stood, crossing his arms. For most of Alec's life, he'd found that posture intimidating. Today he almost itched to take the man down. "If anyone's at fault, it's you, for bringing Colby back into our lives and starting this blasted foundation."

No point in arguing with him, because crazy never listened to reason. Alec's failed plans to reunite his family brought back unpleasant memories of the way he'd lost Une Bouchée, too. Not that *that* mattered at this point. His priority now would be keeping his mother safe. "Mom's coming home with me tonight."

"Like hell." His father's face darkened.

"Look around, Dad. You're in no position to argue. And if you try to stop me, I'll press charges."

His father peered up at him, his eyes filling with something other than disdain for a change. Alec recognized that look, actually, because he'd envied it whenever his dad had bestowed it upon Joe.

Respect.

It figured that the first time Alec earned it—something he'd sought for years—it didn't thaw one bit of his ice-cold feelings for his father.

"*You* can't press charges. I didn't do anything to you. Besides, your mother knows it was an accident."

An ironic justification.

"Funny how that works," Alec snorted, forcing his father to meet his gaze. "Hitting Mom with a vase was an accident, but Joe's taking a dare was homicide?"

"Dammit, Alec." His father jutted out his chin, the vein in his temple pulsing visibly. Alec thought his dad's head might actually explode like a potato in a hot oven. "Don't start defending Mark Baxter."

"Just calling it like I see it. Mark's not the problem. You are."

"Me?" he huffed.

"Yes. And since you're so intent on assigning blame for Joe's death, then you ought to take a look in the mirror."

"You want to blame me?" His brows rose so high on his forehead that they looked like part of his hairline. "If it weren't for your girlfriend and her husband—"

"Mark made an idiotic dare. One he quite obviously regretted. But that isn't the whole story." The day's events had pushed Alec beyond reasoning. "Actually, you and I *both* share some blame."

"What the hell are you talking about?"

They were in a hospital, possibly the safest place for Alec's confession. With everything falling apart, the time had come to man up and get years of pain and guilt off his chest.

"When I was little, Joe thought I was funny and smart. He used to follow me around. Even sat and did puzzles with me. I'm sure you must remember that."

He couldn't tell if his dad had tuned him out or just become lost in his own memories. He wasn't screaming, so Alec continued. "We were friends, but the older I got, the more it bothered you that I wasn't athletic or aggressive. Instead of accepting me, you tried to bully me into being more like you. When that didn't work, you teased me until it became a bad habit. *You* taught Joe to disrespect me as being weak, and *that* drove the wedge between him and me."

His dad's menacing-cop face surfaced. Alec should've been afraid, but calmness settled over him. It was almost as if Joe had stepped into his body as he recited the events that took place with Joe and Beth that night two years ago. With each word, his dad's face turned deeper shades of purple, but he pressed on. "For two years I've felt guilty because of that fight. But as awful as I behaved that night, none of it would've happened if you hadn't rewarded Joe with affection every time he teased me. Joe learned how to avoid your disdain by distancing himself from me and being the kind of tough guy you wanted for a son. So if my lie that night emasculated Joe, that's only because Joe took all his cues on masculinity from you.

"And even if that fight had never happened, Joe probably still would've jumped off that cliff knowing how cool you'd think it was when he came home and told you about it. Let's be honest. If Joe had survived, you would've been bragging about that dare. So, in a way, I can trace Joe's death right back to you and your inability to appreciate me for who I am."

Alec watched his dad blink as if *he'd* been the one clocked by the vase. For a split second, he wondered if one of them would throw a punch. Then the doctor walked in. Doctor? Hell. Dr. Kang looked younger than Alec, and even more exhausted, if that were possible.

"We've looked at the scans. There's no skull fracture, so your wife's fall won't require any intervention other than stitches to close the gash. She has a mild concussion, so she should be cocooned for a week—no stimulation, TV, radio, reading. Just rest and dim lighting."

Her fall? Not even a doctor that young could buy that story. Alec clenched his jaw to keep from calling his dad out. The only thing stopping him was the fact that it would make things worse for his mom.

"Thanks, Doc. When can I see her?" Alec's father asked, still appearing out of sorts, which meant he was still processing Alec's tirade.

"The nurse will be in with release paperwork and care instructions. If you need anything, call this number." The doctor handed him a card. "If you notice symptoms like vomiting, dizziness, or double vision, bring her back."

"Okay, thanks." His father shook the doctor's hand. After the doctor left, he raked his hand through his hair.

"Give that to me." Alec reached for the card.

"*I'll* be taking care of your mother. Once she finds out about how you treated your brother, I doubt she'll want to see you for a while."

That might be true, but that would be her choice, not his father's.

"I don't trust you with her." Alec glared at the man he'd forgiven so often throughout the years. "Honestly, maybe I'll file a restraining order on her behalf. If you won't get counseling to deal with your grief, that's your choice. But I already told you, I'm not going to sit by while Mom's safety is in doubt."

A plump, elderly nurse disrupted their stare-down. She crooked her finger at Alec's dad. "Your wife's ready to be released. I just need to go over this paperwork with you."

Alec ducked out of the waiting room while they spoke, sneaking back to find his mom sitting at the edge of the bed, slipping on her shoes. She hesitated to make eye contact with him, as if she should be ashamed of what her husband did.

He crouched down, setting one hand on the mattress. "Mom, I want you to stay with me for a while."

She sighed. "Where's your father?"

"With the nurse, signing your release papers."

"I don't know, Alec." She touched her bandaged stitches. "I just don't know."

"Be honest with me. Has this happened before?"

She shook her head. "I promise, he's never hurt me. I'm not afraid of him, I'm just tired."

"*I'm* afraid *for* you. We're lucky that blow didn't do more damage. How many chances will you give him?" Alec stood and rubbed her shoulder. "He'll never change if you don't take a stand."

His dad walked in then, worried smile fixed in place. "Let's get you home. Doc says you can't do anything, so I'll be your handservant for the next week. You should like that for a change." His lame joke fell flat as he moved awkwardly around the room, trying not to spook her.

The three of them waited in silence, listening to the sounds of shuffling feet and bleating equipment coming from the hallway. Alec held his breath, awaiting his mom's decision.

"Frank, I'm going home with Alec." She slid out of the bed, keeping one hand on the mattress to test her balance.

"Julie—" His dad stepped toward her.

"No, listen to me." She held up a hand. "I've warned you about the anger and bullying. Joe left a bottomless hole in our hearts, but I'm tired of living in mourning. I've begged you to try to move on, but you can't or won't, so now I need to think about my future."

When his father's jaw slackened, Alec realized he'd never seen his father shell-shocked.

"What are you saying, Julie? Are you leaving me?" His dad's wide eyes and slumped shoulders almost made him look sympathetic. Lost, even. At the very least, that bombshell stopped his dad from blurting out Alec's fight with Joe, which meant Alec would be able to tell her on his own.

"Thirty-five years of marriage doesn't entitle you to assume that you can run our lives however you want without consequence. If you want me back, you need to make some changes, and not just with me. We lost a son, but we have another one right here. One who's been willing to forgive you for years of hurtful parenting, yet you continue to push him away. I'm not going to lose another son because you think you're the only person whose feelings matter." Her eyes watered, but her voice didn't waver. She linked arms with Alec. "I need to stop at home to pick up a few things."

"Okay." Alec wrapped an arm around her waist to steady her shaking.

"Julie, for God's sake." His dad drew a deep breath. "Come home and we'll talk about this, but don't go to Alec's."

"I have to." She didn't even look sad so much as she looked defeated.

"What do you expect me to do now?" His dad's hands went out, palms up. "Take a knee and beg?"

"I don't expect anything. All I know is that I'm not happy with the life we've been living. I don't deserve to be standing here in this hospital room, either."

If his dad looked lost, his mother looked detached. Alec took no joy in this moment, but he did feel safer knowing she'd be with him for the night, maybe a little longer.

"Let's all take a deep breath and talk tomorrow," Alec suggested. "Hand me the instructions and get some rest. Nothing permanent is being decided here."

Alec's mom laid one hand on his father's chest. "I love you, Frank. I just can't live this way any longer."

She strolled out of the room without looking back.

"Alec, don't think you've won." His dad's voice was low and lethal.

"No one's winning anything, Dad. If you can't see that, I don't know what else to say."

"Go on and go. I can't stand the sight of you right now."

"Trust me, the feeling's mutual." Alec shook his head, having nothing left to say, and followed his mother.

Confessing his fight with Joe and argument with his dad to her on their way home hadn't been easy. She seemed more sad than angry, which he regretted. Still, a burden had lifted by telling the truth. Even as his family crumbled around him, he knew a certain sense of freedom from having finally stood up to his father.

It wasn't until he had his mother settled in his apartment that he'd even thought about work, or Colby. When he plugged in his phone, it lit up with a dozen messages and texts. He dialed the restaurant and waited for Becca to pull Colby off the floor.

"Where are you?" she asked without preamble. "When I couldn't reach you, I called the hospital. Is your mom okay?"

"For now. I'm getting her settled."

"You're still with her?"

"Yes. She'll be staying at my place for a while."

He heard Colby suck in a breath. "Where's your father?"

"At home. She's threatening to leave him." He sighed and began reciting the details of his afternoon.

Colby listened to Alec describe his traumatic day, her heart sinking with each sentence. "I'm proud of you for telling the truth and standing up to your dad."

"Little good it did. Both my parents are hurting and disappointed in me, and it doesn't change the fact that my mom ended up in the hospital because of me and our foundation."

Colby repeatedly stabbed her pen into the notepad on her desk. Once again, she'd been a catalyst for trauma in the Morgan family.

"I'm sorry. I would've kept her name out of the article if I'd known her involvement was a secret."

"It's not your fault. She posed for those photos." Alec sighed. "Maybe she wanted to shock him."

A huge risk, considering how that vase could've caused much more damage. An image of Mark's cracked skull flashed, turning her stomach. Why couldn't she escape violence and tragedy? Her thoughts circled that question until Alec's voice brought her back.

"How'd Chris handle the dinner rush?"

"I think well." She pictured Gordon Jeffers sampling his entrée—flared nostrils, impeccable table manners. The enigmatic man had given no sign of his opinion. Her stomach dropped at the thought of telling Alec the news, but better he hear it from her than someone else. "Clyde thinks Gordon Jeffers was here tonight. I warned Chris, and the waitstaff was on top of the service end, so I'm confident it went well."

After a pregnant pause, Alec asked, "Are you sure it was Gordon?"

"I didn't ask, but we think so. He was with a woman, and they paid with cash."

"Fuck!"

Silence.

"Alec?" Had he put down the phone? "Alec?"

"I'm here."

She envisioned him sitting alone in the dark, stabbing his hair with his fingers. No doubt this would go down as one of his worst nights in recent memory. She hated feeling so powerless. "Please don't worry. Everything went fine."

"Fine," he grumbled. "That's probably true. But it wasn't exceptional, I'm sure of that."

She heard a rattling, as if his fist had pounded against some object. "Don't overreact."

"Overreact?" A strangled laugh followed. "I think I've earned the right to some anger tonight. Everything I've done to rebuild my reputation has been sideswiped. Trust me, Chris can't do what I do yet. Dammit, I'm screwed."

A mix of anger and anguish, so raw it hurt her heart, tore through his voice.

"I'm sorry, Alec. About your family, about the bad timing tonight. But getting worked up now won't change anything. My finances are wholly tied to A CertainTea, and yet I'm not ranting." *We still have each other.* Even as she thought the words, she knew not to say them. Not now, when they'd sound trite—even condescending—given his current state of mind.

"I told you before, the executive chef gets all the credit and *all* the blame. You can fire me and get a new chef. A CertainTea will go on, with or without me. My reputation follows me wherever I go." Alec fell silent, so she waited, listening to the sound of his breath through the phone. "I can't talk about this now. My mother needs me."

"Should I stop by after closing?"

"Thanks, but I'm exhausted, and I doubt my mom wants company." Alec sighed. "For all I know, my dad may come storming over later to drag her home. Seeing you wouldn't help. I'll call you in the morning."

Heaviness bunched up in her chest. He might not have meant for his offhand remark to hurt her, but it had. "This wouldn't have happened if you weren't involved with me."

When he didn't respond, she let out a long sigh, hoping the release would ease the ache in her lungs.

"I don't regret the time we've spent together." Alec's words might've been reassuring if his voice hadn't sounded so hopeless.

"Take tomorrow off to help settle your mom." They needed time to regroup, and she didn't want Alec taking out his frustrations on the staff. "We'll manage brunch without you."

A sour laugh came through the line. "Guess the damage is already done." After another muttered curse, he said, "I'm sorry. I know it's not your fault."

Would he think that if he knew that she'd ignored the rumor? Now would be the worst time to tell him, though. "Alec, maybe the review will be fantastic, and you'll see that you've got a whole team to count on. That you're not alone."

A beat of silence passed. "Let's just talk tomorrow. My family has to be my priority right now."

Colby hung up and cradled her head in her hands. The navy-blue fund-raiser invitation, edged with silver glitter, lay on her desk, taunting her. The Maverick Foundation and its potential for good had inadvertently caused irreparable harm.

Two years later, the aftershocks from their families' tragedies were still wreaking havoc. What would they claim next?

Chapter Nineteen

Anyone familiar with award-winning Executive Chef Alec Morgan would expect a select yet ambitious seasonal menu at A CertainTea, a new restaurant located on the east shore of Lake Sandy. Surprisingly, its menu lacked cohesion—the first sign that his much-anticipated return would not fulfill the promise of his former glory.

Colby set the paper down again, unable to read the full review a third time. Statements like "time off left him rusty" and "inconsistent presentation" ping-ponged inside her head and would be like a knife to Alec's chest. That bit about the menu lacking cohesion—totally her fault. Alec had only added that fried-chicken dish to please her. Now he'd suffer public humiliation, because that review was not at all what he would've hoped for, or what he'd be proud for his peers to read.

She stared out her living room window at the foggy skies. For the past few weeks, Monday mornings had involved waking up wrapped in Alec's arms, fabulous breakfasts followed by reading while he worked on a puzzle, like the partially finished one taking up half her dining table now, maybe a stroll to Powell's or along the Willamette.

This one, gray and silent, seemed lonelier than the years of Mondays sandwiched between Mark's death and her new relationship with Alec. He'd barely spoken with her yesterday, so she'd given him and his mother space to recover. Doubtful he'd be more interested in speaking with her today after he read the review.

She ripped the newspaper in half, crumpled it into balls, and tossed it in the trash. No use focusing on things beyond her control. Time to take action where she could, beginning with A CertainTea's response to that damn critic. She'd need Gentry's help with that. Fortunately—or not, depending on one's perspective—Gentry was mere minutes away at Jake's apartment.

Colby grabbed her keys and ambled through several blocks of heavy fog to meet her sister at a park bench on West Burnside. She cooled her heels while waiting for Gentry, who apparently believed clocks were invented as a mere curiosity. When her sister finally arrived, she'd tossed a Voodoo doughnut in Colby's lap as a peace offering.

Sugar typically did the trick, but even a Lemon Chiffon crueller doughnut didn't much lift Colby's spirits this morning.

"Chill out, Sis. It wasn't a *terrible* review. In fact, it might even get some people to come see if they agree or not." Gentry flicked the fallen purple sprinkles from her Grape Ape doughnut off her skirt. "Even if it had been shitty, one crap newspaper review isn't going to tank your business. Look at Yelp and TripAdvisor. In less than a month, you've racked up almost a hundred reviews, with an average of 4.4 stars."

"Alec cares about *real* critics' opinions." Jeffers's review likely tanked Alec's wish to be in the running for another James Beard Award this year and next. If only she hadn't convinced him to change the menu, or altered his management tactics. If she'd just warned him that the critic might show up that very night.

If, if, if. If she hadn't interfered on so many levels, might Chris and the others have performed better on Saturday? Or had Alec's original tactics caused the problem? More confounding what-ifs that would never be answered. "His reputation means everything to him. He's worked *so* hard. His personal involvement with me and the foundation are basically why he wasn't there Saturday night. I should've warned him about the rumor."

"Stop." Gentry slapped Colby's leg. "You're more important to Alec than some stupid critic and awards from anonymous people."

"Don't be sure. Those 'anonymous people' make and break careers. Alec's self-esteem is tied to his talent and reputation. Losing Une Bouchée broke him before. I could throw up from thinking about how he'll handle another perceived failure."

"We'll spin this stupid Jeffers review. Alec wasn't even working."

"That doesn't matter. It's *his* kitchen, and we'll look desperate if we try to blame the problems on his absence."

"Everyone who's eaten there knows the restaurant rocks." Gentry scowled, licking the last bit of icing from her fingertips. "We're not going to let one turd with an attitude have the final word."

Colby couldn't help but laugh. Humor felt oddly out of place yet wonderful given the past couple of days. "Before you put anything out there, I want to see it. We need to be tactful."

"You think I can't be subtle?" Gentry's brows rose.

Colby eyed her sister's lime-green sneakers and neon multicolored paisley top. "Not usually."

"Just because I don't work in a cubicle—*and* I dress with a bit of flair—doesn't mean I didn't learn anything from Dad and my mom. Trust me. I've got your back." Gentry crossed her legs and lazily turned her top foot in small circles. "The problem is that the critic expected A CertainTea to be a carbon copy of Une Bouchée."

"It might've been if I hadn't insisted on something a bit more casual. Now Alec's being penalized for that compromise."

"It's *your* restaurant, and nobody forced him to work there."

"It's more complicated than that, and you know it. He never would've lost Une Bouchée if Mark hadn't made that stupid dare."

"Again, not your fault. Besides, we can't fix the past." Gentry flicked her wrist, waving the history away as if it didn't matter. "I say we go with the angle that the critic just didn't get it. You and Alec weren't trying to re-create Une Bouchée. You're going for something hip, designed to appeal to a broader base, not a narrow band of critics."

Colby conceded it was their best option. "Run with that, but don't directly reference the review. Do it more like a promo piece."

"See, I'm not an idiot." Gentry grinned.

"I never said you were an idiot."

"No, just 'too intimidated' to try."

"I already apologized." Colby squeezed Gentry's thigh.

"I know. I'm just giving you a hard time."

"I've had a hard enough time this weekend."

"Sorry." Gentry put on her futuristic-looking Dior sunglasses. Colby grinned because Gentry always looked like she jumped out of an editorial shoot in *Vogue*. "Well, I should get going."

"Jake's waiting for your return?"

"Yeah." The lack of enthusiasm surprised Colby. "I'm not sure how much longer he'll be in the picture. I'm a little bored."

Colby refrained from clapping. "Oh?"

"Like I've said all along, I'm just out for a good time. At first it was fun to hang out all around the city and meet tons of people. The extra cash was nice, too. But it's becoming ho-hum now. My friend Melanie wants to take a trip to Napa, and I'd like to be single for that. *Soooo*, time to break up with Jake."

"Heartless!" Colby almost felt sorry for Jake.

"Better to leave than be left." Gentry stood suddenly, as if she didn't want to discuss that theory. "I'll post something *discreet* to deflect attention from the review."

"Thanks." Colby hugged Gentry. "Let me know how it goes with Jake."

"It'll be anticlimactic. He's no more invested than I am." Her sister shrugged. "That's what made him the perfect guy."

"I don't understand that, but I suppose it's your life."

"That it is, and now I'm off to live it up." Gentry waved goodbye, her layered top flouncing in the breeze as her long legs ate up the pavement in lengthy strides.

For a brief moment, the appeal of living life without strings tugged at Colby. She'd sworn off complications after Mark's death but somehow ended up inviting them into both her personal and professional lives. Worse, she'd tied those two together. Now, even if she wanted to change one, she couldn't do it without affecting the other.

◆ ◆ ◆

Wearing a smug smile, Colby's mom picked another ripe tomato from the vine and set it in her basket. "And you thought I'd quit gardening by the end of summer. I love these fresh vegetables. Now I'm thinking instead of a stone fence. I should enclose it all in a greenhouse so I can garden year-round."

"I stand corrected." Colby clipped a squash from its vine, wondering what a greenhouse would cost her. Depending on the damage that review did, she might not be able to afford it at all. Shrugging off that concern, she held up the sunny vegetable. "These look amazing, Mom. What can we whip up for dinner with them? Pasta?"

Alec would be more creative, but she didn't know when—or if—she'd hear from him again. Colby yanked a weed.

"I'd rather have dessert. Can Alec make something sweet with squash and tomato?" Her mom chuckled. "If anyone could, it would be him."

Alec had attempted the oddest creations throughout his years of playing around with foods, textures, spices, and herbs—like the weird Cheetos broccoli dish last month. That memory prompted a bittersweet grin, because Colby sensed her relationship with Alec was poised for upheaval.

"Colby, what's wrong? You look like you haven't slept, and you've barely said four words in the past hour. Is it that stupid Gordon Jeffers?" Her mom set the basket aside.

"He didn't help."

"Alec's taking it hard? I left a message for Julie, but she hasn't called me back."

Colby hadn't told anyone about Frank and Julie's troubles, so she hedged. "That review won't send droves of customers through our doors. As for Alec . . ." They'd barely discussed it. He'd shut her out. Whether that was because he needed to lick his wounds, blamed her for interfering with the kitchen, or had simply been too busy with his mom, she couldn't guess.

Her mom patted her shoulder. "Men's egos are delicate, no matter how tough they act. We women—our skin may be softer, but it's much thicker. *Fairer sex*, my ass. We can shoulder far more pain and disappointment than men, so be strong for him now. You've already proven that you can survive anything."

Normally Colby shied away from compliments, but she'd earned that one. She had survived some gut-wrenching experiences. The kind of life lessons that put other disappointments in perspective. She'd help Alec learn to do the same.

"Thanks, Mom. Let's change the subject and talk about something fun." Colby lifted the basket of squash and followed her mom back to the house, hoping her mother's special kind of kookiness might jar her out of her funk.

"Well, since we're talking about men, I met a nice one this week. Thanks to you, actually." Her blue eyes twinkled like a starry-eyed schoolgirl's.

"Me?"

"Indirectly, yes. I went to Lamont's Wines to rustle up some last-minute donations. I figured I could strong-arm Franny, of course. Well, Franny wasn't there, but her brother, Rusty, was."

Franny Lamont was a wiry mother of six. Her daughter, Angelica, had been in Colby's grade, but that girl's personality hadn't matched her name's promise.

"Franny has a brother?" Colby scoured her memory but couldn't come up with a single one involving a Rusty Lamont. Of course, *his* last name wouldn't be Lamont. "How have we never met him?"

"He just moved here from Sebastopol. His wife died about six months ago. His kids are grown and scattered, so he moved here for the less expensive cost of living."

She, Alec, Rusty, her mom . . . seemed everyone was looking for a fresh start these days. "He told you all of this in the wine store?"

"I'd arrived just before his lunch hour. We were talking about the foundation, so he invited me to join him for lunch over at Lakeside Deli."

Colby recognized that sparkle of interest in her mom's eyes. The same look she'd had when first describing her poet warrior, Richard. "Do you think he'll be different from Richard?"

"Who knows? You found Alec." Her mom set the bucket of tomatoes on the table. "Maybe I'll get lucky, too."

Colby had originally thought she'd been lucky to meet Mark. She'd also thought she'd lucked into something special with Alec despite their complicated history. Now she might've inadvertently hurt his professional reputation and splintered his family. At this point, "lucky" didn't exactly seem like the best cornerstone for a relationship.

"I hope Rusty appreciates your uniqueness, Mom."

"We'll find out soon. We're going out on Thursday to a Portland Pickles game. He's a huge fan."

"Do you like baseball?" Colby grimaced.

"I like Rusty. Or I like him so far." Her mom shrugged. "As for baseball, I don't hate it."

Colby sighed. "Maybe luck has nothing to do with good relationships. *Maybe* it comes down to honesty. Do me a favor. Don't pretend to like baseball if you don't actually like it. Better to end things early with the wrong man than try to force it to work."

Instead of answering, her mom bent to retrieve a colander and then handed it to her. Colby was rinsing vegetables and thinking about her own situation. A pity party wouldn't change one thing. She needed to confront Alec, even if that thought made her feel like someone tossed a lit match in her belly. "Mom, sorry to dash, but I need to find Alec."

"Oh? I thought he'd come cook and talk about last-minute fund-raiser matters."

"Not tonight. Maybe tomorrow." The fund-raiser. One week away and currently the last thing on Colby's mind. Her mother, however, had no idea about the Morgans' recent separation. "See you later."

She kissed her mom's cheek and went to Alec's apartment.

He answered the door looking ashen and exhausted. Worry lines bracketed his mouth. Even his cowlick looked defeated, sagging instead of springing from his forehead. "What are you doing here?"

Not the hugs and kisses she'd become accustomed to, but she stepped past him and into his apartment, anyway. "Checking on you. You weren't returning my calls, and I'm worried about you and your family."

He kept his hand on the doorknob and rested his forehead against the door. "My mom went to meet my dad for coffee in town, so I'm preoccupied. This isn't the best time to talk, Colby."

"Because of your parents or because of something else?"

He must've sensed she wasn't leaving, so he finally closed the door. "If by something else you mean the review, then yes, that hasn't helped."

"It's just one review, Alec. And Gentry and I have a plan—"

Alec waved his hands. "It's too late. There's no fixing it. The only way to overcome it at this point is to work twice as hard and hope maybe in another year you catch a break. But that review ambushed any chance that A CertainTea might've gotten any acclaim this year."

"You're angry." She reached for him, but he didn't reciprocate.

"Livid." He stepped back and turned away, cracking his knuckles.

"With me?" She tensed, awaiting his response.

He faced her now, expression rigid, voice blade-sharp. "I'm angry with myself for going against the formula I *knew* would work."

"I'm sorry about the menu, Alec. Maybe I shouldn't have pushed you to include anything, but it *is* my restaurant." She looked down. "I should've warned you about the rumor . . ."

His chin came up sharply. "What rumor?"

If he'd been livid before, he'd be murderous now. "Gentry had mentioned that she'd heard 'through the grapevine' that the Trib's reviewer might be coming that night."

"When did she tell you that?" His eyes widened with betrayal.

"A couple of weeks ago." Colby shrank back a bit in order to dodge the surge of contempt rolling off his body.

"Why didn't you tell me? If I'd known, I would've—"

"Would've what?" She regretted that decision now, but she wouldn't be bullied, either. His temper had been the reason that she hadn't trusted him with that information, and that was his fault, not hers. "Ridden the staff even harder? Been anxious and overbearing every day? Why *would* I tell you about a *rumor* when I knew it would only force the staff to deal with your temper?"

"I could've made the menu perfect for the weekend. And maybe if you'd let me 'ride the staff' harder, they'd have been better prepared." He shook his head, dismissing her rationale. "I can't believe you think that you made the right decision. This is my career, Colby. You know how important it is to me, yet you hid information that might've helped me."

His fists balled at his sides as he stared straight through her, clearly unable to comprehend her motives.

"I'm sorry, but I thought I was *protecting you* from yourself. It was right after your dad's drunken night weeks ago, and Gentry couldn't confirm it. I didn't think you needed more stress when it seemed your attentions were better served helping your family." The words sounded stupid and arrogant as they fell from her mouth. "Then we got busy with planning the fund-raiser, and it slipped my mind. Ultimately, you weren't in the kitchen Saturday, anyway, so it didn't really make a difference, did it?"

She braced for a major tantrum and almost fainted when, instead, Alec barked a laugh.

Colby gaped at him as if he'd lost his mind. Maybe he had. Two days of caring for his mom and walking a tightrope with his dad were bad enough. Then that review dealt a killing blow. Un-fucking-believable.

He cringed thinking about his colleagues reading it. Those chefs who'd once wanted to be him would now pity him for a second time. Would be convinced he'd lost his edge. In a way, he had. He'd let Colby influence how he did his job even though she had no experience in a kitchen or the industry.

He'd led with his heart, and now nothing was right. Not his family. Not his career. Not his relationship. Maybe his dad had a point about him lacking some essential element of manhood—courage. Courage to be honest about his mistakes, about who he was.

"Alec." Colby reached for him again, but he couldn't comfort her. Not now.

"Don't." This was a sign. A sign that he'd reached for too much too soon. "We need to take a step back, Colby."

"Step back?"

None of his goals—his reputation, his family, Colby's happiness—were viable. He'd been dishonest with everyone, and now they were all paying the price. It had to end, and he had to be strong enough to do it. "I went to the cemetery this afternoon."

"What?" Her eyes flew open. "Why?"

He'd visited Joe's headstone numerous times throughout the past two years, but today he'd gone to Mark's. Something he'd avoided until now. He'd apologized for his lack of mercy and admitted part of his dislike had been due to jealousy. Jealousy that Mark had married Colby before Alec ever had the chance to show her what kind of man he could be. A pointless wish, seeing as Alec had failed to be that guy, anyway. "To make some decisions."

"Decisions about your family?" She frowned, her face filled with confusion.

"I've given up hoping that anything between my dad and me will change." He still felt numb when considering the confrontation they'd had at the hospital and its long-term consequences.

"Don't give up." She laid her hands on his chest. Unrelenting in her effort to soothe him. Another irony, really. He'd wanted her to reclaim the pieces of herself that she'd shut away. That brave spirit that would wade into murky emotional tides in order to help someone. He just hadn't wanted to be that someone who'd needed her help.

He raised her hands to his lips, wishing he could hold on to her without being a selfish prick. He couldn't. Not if he wanted her to have the kind of carefree life she'd asked for. He'd been torn for weeks about doing the right thing and making excuses in order to avoid the fallout. No more. Now he faced the woman he'd wanted forever, unsure of how, exactly, to take the sledgehammer to his heart. "Sometimes walking away is the best choice."

"You can't walk away from family." She wrapped her arms around her waist. "Do you blame me for what's happened with your parents?"

Seeing her guilt wiped away any doubts about what he needed to do.

"You've got it backward, Colby. Before I showed up, you were on your way out of mourning, ready to open a new business. A nice, carefree guy wanted to date you. The past seemed to be shrinking in your rearview mirror. Then Hunter called, and I stepped smack into the middle of your happiness, bringing bad memories and trouble along with me."

"Alec," she started.

"No, listen." He backed farther away from her, needing distance. Needing air. "I need to tell you something, so please let me finish."

"I don't like the finality in your voice." She kept her gaze even with his.

"I love you, you know. I think I always have. You're kind and beautiful and brave, and you deserve a man who's your equal. If you believe nothing else when I'm done, believe that." His throat continued its fight against him, swelling as if trying to choke off what he planned to say. "Sadly, I'm not that guy. You kept a secret from me about the critic, but I've been far more dishonest. All I can hope now is that owning up to all my sins might eventually set us all free."

"Free from what?" She sank onto the sofa almost as if her legs had given out.

"Free from pain. From regret. From settling for less than we deserve."

He sat beside her then; despite everything, he wanted to be close to her one last time. He clasped her hand and placed her palm against his cheek, like some masochistic reminder of how much he liked it when she touched him. "I need to confess something to you."

"Me?"

"Yes." He closed his eyes for a second. "You've spent endless hours wondering how you could've prevented Mark's suicide. Endured nightmares and PTSD from witnessing it. And then you let me in, even with your reservations. Even with the complications of our families and our work relationship. Shamefully, I let you turn to me while knowing that I could've prevented all of your suffering."

"Alec, Mark's choices had nothing to do with you. I told you he was bipolar. Suicidal thoughts are somewhat prevalent in those afflicted."

"I still had a hand in it."

He stood and crossed the room, which would be the only way he could finish. He couldn't face her now, so he stared at one of the photos his mom had brought with her. The one of Hunter, Joe, Colby, and him hanging from the tree-house ladder. An innocent time before egos and puberty and jealousies corrupted the love and friendship they'd all shared.

"About a week before Mark jumped, he sent me an apology note, begging my family for forgiveness. He said he couldn't go on without it. I didn't take that threat seriously, and I wasn't ready to forgive him, or myself, for anything, so I ignored him. Obviously, I never even warned you about his state of mind."

He didn't glance over his shoulder. He couldn't. He doubted he had enough strength to see the disgust or anger he knew would be reflected in her eyes.

In the distance, the faint sound of a train floated through an open window. The droning of its engine ushered him back to the memory of Mark's funeral.

"The day you buried Mark, I watched from a distant spot in the cemetery. In all the years I'd known you, you'd never looked so vacant and frail. So spooked. I hated myself. I hated Mark and Joe. I hated the powerless feelings that consumed me. I wanted to fix it for you, but I didn't know how.

"I told myself the best thing I could do was stay away from you. That seeing me would only remind you of Joe and Mark. That confessing couldn't bring Mark back, anyway. But the truth is that I was a coward. I couldn't face you and your pain, knowing that I might've prevented it. When you'd tried to reach out to me in sympathy about Joe, I ran from you so you wouldn't see everything vile and worthless in me."

His voice cracked, but at this point weakness hardly mattered. "I never wanted to believe that my dad could be right about me, but that kind of cowardice sort of proves that he was, at least a little."

He hated himself for hurting her, but he'd also just lost ten thousand pounds by shedding the burden of that secret.

Colby's small voice emerged. "So Mark's jump and all the consequences of it might've been avoided if you had forgiven him or spoken up."

And there it was . . . the sickening truth he'd hoped to ignore for the rest of their lives.

"Since coming back to town, I've done everything possible to make you happy in some twisted attempt to make amends to Mark and you . . . to redeem myself. Yet none of this tiptoeing around to keep the peace—to keep things easy and simple—has made us strong. It hasn't helped my family or the restaurant. Any progress I thought we were making wasn't real, because we haven't been honest with each other." He slouched onto a chair, unable to stand on weakening legs. Shame and regret wedged their way into his voice. "Everything I've touched since my fight with Joe gets destroyed. I should've never touched you, but I couldn't resist."

He didn't glance up. Couldn't. He knew he'd see disgust reflected in her eyes, and he couldn't really blame her.

"So has this *all* been a lie? Sleeping with me and telling me you loved me was some kind of penance?" Her words were choked, her cheeks red-hot with shame. "Making me fall in love with you was some plan to 'fix' me?"

"No, Colby. None of that was a lie. I love you. So much so that I couldn't stay away even when I knew I should. Giving you up hurts more than cutting my heart out with a butter knife." He rested his elbows on his knees and hung his head for a moment. "We can tell ourselves and each other that we were hiding things for the right reasons, but the fact that neither of us felt safe being honest with each other proves this isn't working."

"I came here expecting to come up with some plans to deal with the review and your dad. I didn't expect all this." Her eyes glistened, but she stood tall and proud. That made his heart ache even more. She paced, lost in her thoughts, and he wished he could read her mind. Then she said, "I opened up my heart to you, and you're tossing it back all bruised."

"I never wanted to hurt you. I wanted to make you laugh and see you smile. I'm sorry . . ." He couldn't take it anymore. He needed to touch her, so he stood and weakly clasped her hand. "You want easy. Uncomplicated. That's obviously not me. And our visions for the restaurant aren't aligned. Let's admit all this and let it go before we hurt each other more."

"You're right about one thing. After all the lies I lived through with Mark, I *knew* how important honesty was, and yet I fell back into patterns of managing things like I did with him."

She withdrew from him and hugged herself.

"You deserve a better, easier guy. Someone like Todd." He closed his eyes to block the image of her and Todd hand in hand, hoping it would staunch his nausea.

"How nice that you've already picked out your replacement. Should I give him the good news, or would you like the honors?" Again with the sarcasm, but he preferred her anger to her tears.

"Let's not hurt each other more. I just want to see you happy, Colby. That's all I've ever wanted for you." He didn't know what else to say, so he said the next thing that flitted through his pea brain. "We should talk about what you'll do about my job."

"Hell if I know, Alec. I can barely think right now," she cried. He'd obviously said the wrong thing. Then again, he doubted there was a right thing to say at this point. "This is exactly what Hunter thought would happen, isn't it—personal problems making it uncomfortable to work together? Chris can manage the kitchen in the short run, but I need you to help me pull off the gala. Can I count on you for that much?"

"Of course." Walking away from her just about brought him to his knees, but this was the right decision. He knew it, even as his soul rebelled against it. "In the meantime, if you want, I'll compile a list of chefs that would happily carry out *your* vision for A Certain Tea."

"Thoughtful to the end." It might've been a compliment if she hadn't injected those words with sarcasm.

Colby turned to leave, but not before he saw her lip quiver. Everything in him wanted to wrap her in his arms and beg her for a solution that would fix everything they'd broken. But that'd be selfish, and he'd been selfish long enough.

"I guess grown-up dreams don't last any longer than children's, do they?" She drew a tired breath. "I hope your parents work things out so one decent thing comes from all this pain."

Before he responded, she turned and sprinted toward her car, crying. That gutted him. But she'd fought her way back from a worse loss before.

She'd survive this, too, even if he didn't.

Chapter Twenty

The last time Colby had called her entire family to a meeting at her mother's house, she'd announced her elopement. Mark had popped champagne corks, and her family swallowed their shock with several glasses of Veuve Clicquot.

If they'd expected something similar today, they'd been sorely disappointed. She'd spent last night thinking about how she'd ended up in this situation. Why she'd ignored the signs that Alec was more broken than she'd realized and also capable of deceit. Why, like Mark, he'd promised her the moon and sworn his devotion only to then leave her without giving her a choice. And how she'd patch the gaping hole in her chest where her heart used to be.

Crowded together in her mom's small living room, her family looked at each other with concern. The kind of worried, tentative looks she and Mark had avoided by keeping their problems a secret. Secrets hadn't worked out well then or now. Too bad it had taken so long for her to learn that sharing her troubles wouldn't make her weak; it would make her strong.

Still, she'd only had enough energy to explain what had happened with Alec—and her whole history with Mark—once. Hence, the group powwow.

Now everyone knew everything. Thankfully, they were preoccupied with sending silent signals to one another, which kept them from gawking at her.

She donned a brave mask, even though picturing Alec's face, or thinking about going to work without him, wrecked her. Logically, everything he'd said—all of his reasoning—made sense. But the problem with perfect kisses that make someone fall in love is that the heart isn't logical. Now hers was broken again, and all the reasoning in the world wouldn't make that pain disappear overnight.

Her mother remained uncharacteristically quiet. Colby suspected having Gentry, Jenna, and her ex in the house had set her on edge. But her mother had also been her and Alec's most fervent supporter, which meant her heart might be just a little bit broken now, too.

Colby's father spoke first. "Honey, I'm sorry you went through so much and I never had a clue."

Gentry snorted, but bit back whatever snarky remark had popped into her head. Fortunately, her sister had the sense not to turn this into a moment about *her* childhood disappointments.

Colby shrugged. "You've got a lot of responsibilities, and I was actively hiding the truth."

"My first responsibility should be to my family, not a balance sheet." He frowned. "I promise things will be different in the future."

Jenna laid her hand on his thigh and squeezed, wearing an approving grin. Colby glanced at Hunter in time to catch him bristle. She had to talk to her dad before her family ended up falling apart like the Morgans.

Colby looked at Sara sitting beside Hunter. The wrinkles at the corners of Sara's warm eyes proved she understood the fact that life doesn't always work out as you hope. She'd suffered through enough of her own disappointments to know that sometimes there was no easy answer. "I'm sorry, Colby. *Really* sorry. If you need anything, please let me know."

"Thanks." Colby took comfort in the fact that Sara and Hunter seemed more relaxed today, nestled on the sofa, his arm slung casually over her shoulder. Her experiences had made love seem as fragile as a soap bubble, but Hunter and Sara inspired hope.

Gentry was biting the inside of her cheek like she was clamping down on the words bunching up in her mouth, so Colby said, "Spit it out, Sis."

"This is exactly why I don't want a serious relationship." She raised one shoulder. "I mean, if you can't trust someone like Alec, who can you trust?"

"Don't," Hunter warned. "We're not going to trash Alec. He's been through as much as Colby, and he's just as hurt."

"Colby's your sister," their mom said. "Loyalty lies with your family."

"Loyalty lies in your heart. In your gut. In looking at people's intentions, not just judging their actions." Hunter rubbed his hand over his face before looking at his wife. "Babe, I'll meet you at home. I need to talk to Colby alone."

His authoritarian tone went unquestioned, as usual. They all took advantage of the chance to escape their discomfort with one another by taking off after hugging Colby in a final show of love and support.

Of course, their mom just stared at Hunter when he bugged his eyes at her to demand a little privacy.

"Hey, this is *my* house." She crossed her arms.

He shook his head before grabbing Colby's hand and dragging her onto the deck, where he stood for a minute, looking at the hedgerow separating their mom's yard from the Morgans' house.

Some might fight his tyranny, but Colby knew he loved her, and that he would eventually say something wise. For all his flaws, his strength of mind and purpose had always helped refill her tank when she let him in.

"Come with me." His voice had softened, so she followed him to the back of the yard, through the bushes, and to the old tree house.

She hadn't wandered back here in ages. The strip of woods separating her mom's street from the one behind it had seemed as dense and vast as Mount Hood National Forest when she'd been small. And the fort had been a castle in the air—a place of laughter and tears, secrets and wishes.

Hunter stared up at it for a moment before he spoke, although his gaze seemed unfocused. A rarity. "Lots of memories."

"Yes."

"Not all of them good, especially not for Alec."

Colby didn't reply. Alec had never talked to her about his problems back then, although she'd witnessed him with his dad often enough to feel sorry for him.

"I have to be honest," Hunter continued. "I didn't like Joe much once he hit puberty. The only thing that kept me from kicking his ass was the fact that he always watched out for you."

"Hunter!" Colby didn't like disparaging the dead. Especially not one who'd been her friend.

"Listen." Hunter held up a hand. "When you two were little, Alec always fought to let you up there with us, even when I didn't want you guys around. He'd never hurt a living thing in his life. Hell, he'd remove spiders from the fort rather than kill them. I watched him turn the other cheek with his dad and Joe time after time, and, trust me, Joe could be every bit as nasty as Frank Morgan. To be honest, it pissed me off. But Alec always believed in taking the high road. And dammit, the *one* time he didn't has now bitten him in the ass."

"What's your point?" Colby crossed her arms, wondering if Hunter blamed her for the situation.

He gripped her biceps. "My point is that I love you, but I love him, too. You haven't asked, but I'm telling you now I'm not going to take sides."

"I'm not asking you to, Hunter. I don't think Alec's a bad person, although if I'd known about the letter . . ."

"Then what?" Hunter released her in order to raise his hands heavenward. "What possible difference does that letter really make? You knew about Mark's illness. You knew he was depressed about Joe. I'd bet everything that he probably made similar comments to you throughout those weeks following Joe's funeral. Would some rambling words in a letter he sent to Alec honestly have changed anything you did before the morning he jumped?" Hunter cocked his head, barely giving her time to keep up with his thoughts. "If *I'd* have received that kind of letter from Mark, I'd have ignored it, too. Remember, none of *us* knew about his illness because you chose not to confide in your family or friends. You can't blame any of us for writing off his moods as melodramatic. And Alec didn't owe Mark his forgiveness. But you have to know that if Alec had had any real concern about Mark's state of mind, he would've warned you."

"Even if that's all true, Alec lied about it all this time. He wasn't honest with me. He didn't trust me."

"Maybe he just didn't see the purpose now that so much time has passed. Even if he'd come to you right afterward, it wouldn't have erased what you saw or lost. It wouldn't have alleviated your own sense of responsibility for Mark's state of mind. Nothing in this whole situation is that clear-cut. You, Alec, Joe, and I have a lifetime of history, but we're not those little kids anymore, playing Truth or Dare and arguing about who has to clean up the fort. We're grown-ups, which means we have to be willing to deal with messy shit. We have to look at the big picture instead of getting hung up on a small detail."

He glanced back up at the tree house. "Here's something else to consider. All these years you stayed friends with Joe and never once stood up to him when he'd insult Alec, yet I don't see Alec holding that against you. How many times did Joe openly refer to Mark as his brother in front of Alec? Maybe that never registered with you, but, trust me, it registered for Alec. You were in a position to make a difference with those two, but you didn't even try."

"Why are you attacking me? I'm heartbroken, too, you know. I thought all the pieces of my life were finally coming together. *Alec* blew it all up. He walked away, just like Mark, without giving me a choice or trying to fix our problems."

"Don't compare those two. Mark checked out and left you holding the cards because *he* wanted to escape *his* pain. Alec left because he's dumb enough to think someone else might be better *for* you. And the only reason he thinks that is because he's so used to being told he's not man enough—he just assumes it's true. He's never had anyone fight for him, including you. So don't tell me you have no choice. We all have choices. The only real question is whether you think he's worth fighting for."

He sucked in a breath after that emotional tirade. Abruptly, he bear-hugged her and kissed her forehead. "I love you. I'm sorry for everything you've suffered. Like I said before, I'm not taking sides, just playing devil's advocate. Despite what it might sound like right now, I'm here for you, whatever you need. Just remember you're not the only person hurting."

She wished being wrapped in his solid arms would somehow infuse her with a bit of his strength, but when he released her, she knew that wish hadn't been granted.

He banged a hand against the tree-house ladder before turning to go. "You coming?"

"Not yet." She needed some time alone before she could subject herself to her mother's hovering.

Hunter blew her a kiss and wandered through the trees until he disappeared in the brush.

Her brother's passionate arguments still rang in her ears. She stared up at the tree house, dim memories circling the periphery of her mind. She reached for the ladder, tested a rung, and then climbed up into the old fort.

Alec was right: animals had nested and eaten through a lot of the things they'd left behind, like the old coffee can where they'd stuffed bags of candy. A rusty, crushed beer can lay in the corner . . . probably Joe's. Wax stains still colored one corner of the floor from all the times they'd hung out at night and lit candles and told stories. Told secrets.

"I thought you were leaving today?" Colby asked, surprised to see Alec pop up the steps.

"I want this for my dorm room." He nodded toward the blue-and-gray tie-dyed tapestry on the wall.

"It'll be so weird without you and Hunter around. I'm jealous you guys are getting out of here and going to such big cities."

"You'll get your turn soon enough."

"Do you think you'll ever be back?" Seeing him now and saying goodbye made her stomach hurt a little.

"School breaks."

"No, I mean, like, where do you think you'll be in ten years . . . ?"

"I don't know. That depends on how well I do in school, but I hope to go to France or stay in New York when I graduate."

"So you won't be back."

"Will you miss me?" He teased her now, but at the same time, he almost looked like he was holding his breath.

"I guess I always thought we'd all be friends forever. Maybe even that our kids would be friends like us. That kind of thing."

"Why do girls think of marriage and kids so young?" he asked.

She stood and helped him take down the tapestry, now curious because he'd never really had a serious girlfriend in high school. "Don't you want to get married?"

"Sure, one day."

"And what will your wife be like? Another chef, or just a taste tester like me?" She laughed, again feeling another pang, this time for all the yummy food she'd miss sampling.

He paused, averting his gaze. "If I'm lucky, she'll be someone exactly like you, Colby."

"Whoever she turns out to be, I hope she'll let us stay friends."

Colby shook off the bittersweet memory. She climbed down the ladder, thinking about what silly ideas young girls could spin, whether plucking the petals from daisies or daydreams about the future. Maybe Hunter was right. Had Colby never let go of childish fantasies about life and love?

She'd gone off to college, planning to become a nurse because she liked to help people. Who would've predicted she'd become a transactional lawyer or run a restaurant? If anything, the foundation seemed a better fit for her skills and temperament. Especially if the right temperament for running a restaurant required Alec's relentless drive for perfection.

The sky warned of rain as she wandered back through the shrubs, past the garden, and up the steps of the deck. Once she reentered the living room, her mom handed her a full glass of Cabernet.

"Here you go, honey," she said, patting Colby's shoulder.

"I don't need this," Colby protested.

"Everybody needs wine once in a while, especially to relax. I'll make some lunch. You go take a hot shower." Before Colby could lodge another protest, her mom disappeared.

She didn't need a shower, but she meandered back to her room and lay on her bed, her mind still swimming in nostalgia. Rolling onto her side, she picked at the comforter while watching the sky turn dark gray, like her mood. Stitch meowed from the doorway, staring at her forebodingly. "Go away, Stitch."

Of course, he didn't listen. Obstinate, taunting old beast.

Colby closed her eyes and pictured Alec's face from yesterday. She couldn't decide if knowing about Mark's letter would've made a difference. Truthfully, Mark had said he couldn't "live like this" many times throughout their short marriage, usually when he was coming out of a depression. Those were the worst of times—the climb out of that hole, with its mix of good days and bad—when he'd lose hope then that he'd ever break through the clouds. He'd want to end his suffering, but she'd always found a way to keep him going until that day.

Had Alec alerted her, she might've confronted Mark, but ultimately she couldn't say that it alone would've prevented what had happened. And even if Alec had forgiven Mark then, Mark might have eventually slipped into some other depression that ended the same way.

Truthfully, the only silence to blame for Mark's suicide was her and Mark's choice to hide the truth about his illness. To isolate themselves from the support of family and friends, whose help might've actually made a difference in his treatment and prognosis. Those decisions she and Mark made together made that horrible day inevitable.

Yet even as she recognized herself repeating those same patterns with Alec, she hadn't spoken up—about the critic, about her life with Mark, about Alec shielding her from his dad. In her own way, she'd sabotaged their chance at happiness as much as Alec had.

She sat up, irked that she'd let him call the shots yesterday. Maybe they couldn't work everything out, but she should've demanded more than thirty minutes to make life-changing decisions.

She grabbed her keys and raced through the house. "Mom, I've got to run. Sorry about dinner."

When she arrived at Alec's apartment, his car was nowhere in sight, so she decided to surprise him by waiting. She still had her key. He could ignore her calls, but he couldn't ignore *her* if she was sitting at his table.

She parked at the curb, cursing the fact that the skies had opened up. After running through the downpour, she used her key to get inside, surprising the hell out of Julie Morgan.

"Colby?" Julie sat up on the sofa, where she'd been resting.

"Oh, I'm sorry to barge in." She wiped her wet hair off her face, embarrassed that she'd trespassed. "Is Alec home?"

"No." Julie froze, apparently stunned by the intrusion.

"Will he be back soon?"

"Let me get you something to dry off with." Julie went into Alec's bathroom and returned with a bath towel. It smelled similar to his clothes, thanks to his fabric softener, but was missing the essential element of *him*.

"Thank you." Colby began drying her hair and then wrapped the towel around her shoulders. "So where's Alec?"

"He went out."

"Has he said anything to you about . . . things?"

"Just that things aren't working out, and he might need to go to LA or New York to find work."

"I didn't ask him to go, Julie. He made all these decisions. I wish he wouldn't have hidden his feelings about so much for so long."

"Alec learned how to hide his feelings pretty young." Her expression turned grim again. "His father can take the blame for that."

Blame. Such a useless word. People flung it around when they were mad or hurt. Or they carried it like a cross until it destroyed any chance at redemption or happiness. Blame never solved one problem or changed a single outcome. A pointless, unproductive, ultimately destructive concept, really.

Looking around, she saw that destruction, too. Lives, marriages, businesses all laid to waste thanks to misplaced blame. Now she had to hope that they could pick up the pieces and start over.

Hope—another useless concept if not backed by a plan. Hoping for things never worked out well for her. It was time for action.

"You're still coming to the gala, right?" she asked Julie.

"Yes." Julie surprised Colby by giving her a quick hug goodbye. "Maybe things will sort themselves out before then, too."

Colby left Alec's, her thoughts turning as sharply as the winding road around the lake.

For months she'd told Alec she was finished looking back, but he'd been right. She couldn't move forward until she confronted her past and laid her demons to rest. Doing so would require two more stops, neither of which would be easy.

Chapter Twenty-One

The gates to Queen of Heaven were just ahead, shrouded by mist now that the rain had slowed to a drizzle. For the first time, the sight of those iron gates didn't cause her body to quake or nausea to churn. Purpose kept those things at bay.

She turned in to the cemetery and parked near Mark's headstone, undeterred by the rain and mud. After grabbing a yellow windbreaker from her back seat, she crossed the soggy ground to where he lay buried. She laid her jacket down and sat, cross-legged, on his grave, staring at his name on the marker.

At twenty-nine, she'd been a young widow. It seemed as if she'd aged a decade since she'd buried him almost two years ago to the day. Now she sat, twisting her wedding band around and around.

Fears born from that unhealthy marriage contributed to the failure of her relationship with Alec. She'd told him she wanted *easy*. She wanted *peace*. He responded by telling half-truths and keeping secrets.

In their own ways, they'd both been running from the past— sacrificing open communication for peace. Only now did she recognize that peace couldn't exist without honesty.

To find peace, she needed to forgive and be forgiven.

Drizzle continued to fall from the sky—fitting for the misty sort of sadness in her heart. She picked at the grass and started talking to her husband.

"Before you, I'd never met anyone whose energy and enthusiasm poured out of him like sunlight. Our love was wild abandon, partly because I hadn't yet learned that when you throw your heart in the air, it hurts like hell when it lands.

"I've spent a few years telling myself that we were a mistake. But that isn't fair. I wish I'd been better able to love you in spite of the problems your illness caused us both, and I'm sorry that our mistakes ended with me sitting on your grave.

"I know you loved me, even when you strayed, even when we fought, even when I no longer loved you the same way. And I'm so sorry for the way I hurt you. I think you understand what I mean, because I doubt you wanted to hurt me, either, even though you did.

"You'll always be a part of me. In that way, you'll live on as long as I do. I'll honor the best parts of you with the Maverick Foundation. I'll stop looking back with remorse and blame. When I will think of you, I'll remember your bright blue eyes, hear your deep laugh, and even smile at the memories of some of your zanier bursts of 'creativity.'

"I don't regret loving you, Mark, because you taught me how deeply a person could love and be loved. I hope you're in heaven, surrounded by love, and finally at peace. I forgive you for making me watch you leave this world. I know, in my heart, that it was the illness, not a choice, that made you jump. And I hope you forgive me for all my mistakes."

She reached out to trace Mark's name. Cold carved granite abraded her fingertips, but she traced his full name tenderly as if she were touching his face.

"I've found love again, with Alec. It's not anything like it was with you. Maybe the fact that it snuck up on me in a quiet way—so different from you—is what made it possible for me to let him in when I was convinced I'd never let anyone in again. I thought I wanted something simple and instead chose the most complicated person in my life. I see now that simple *isn't* what I want. Honesty is. Honesty you and I lost along the way with the choices we made. I can't believe it's taken me all this time and pain to understand that I can't 'manage' other people. Alec and I may not be able to fix what we've broken, but I'm going to try."

She took a flat rock and dug a six-inch-deep hole at the corner of the headstone. She could barely see what she was doing because of the tears clogging her eyes, but she removed her wedding band and placed it in the hole, then covered it with soil.

"Wish me well, Mark."

She wiped the tears streaming from her eyes and swallowed the lump in her throat. She should have been shivering from the cold, but her body warmed from the surge of emotion. Hoisting herself off the ground, she shook out her jacket, glanced across the narrow road to Joe, and sent up a silent prayer.

I loved you, too, Joe, but you were far from perfect. I wish I would've been a better friend and helped you see what an amazing brother you had. Maybe someday we'll all be reunited, and we can laugh like we did as kids. Until then, watch out for Alec now. He still needs you.

She looked at her hands, now devoid of any trace of her life with Mark. A clean slate, she thought with a slight shiver. It was cold and dusky, but that wouldn't keep her from making one more stop.

◆ ◆ ◆

Mr. Morgan opened his door, nostrils flared, eyes wide, looking almost constipated. Then again, Colby probably also looked frightful, muddied and wet, standing in his doorway in the dark.

"What do you want?" he grumbled, no more polite than when they'd crossed paths in his driveway two months ago. Of course, everything that transpired recently had probably refueled his hatred of her.

"To speak with you."

"I've got nothing to say to you." He waved her off.

"Please." She fought the shiver tickling down her spine. She'd hoped for a more civil conversation, but given all the circumstances, she should've known better.

"Get off my porch, Colby." He started to close the door, but she blocked it with her arm.

"If any part of the man who used to like me still exists, please give me five minutes." She raised her chin. "Joe wouldn't want you to treat me like this, would he?"

Narrowing his eyes, he opened the door to let her inside. He barred her from going farther than the entry by standing legs wide, arms crossed.

She hadn't been in their house in years. The familiar scent sucker punched her, calling forth childhood memories. Video-game marathons with Joe on rainy days. Talking with Alec while he worked on a puzzle or cooked. Hide-and-seek in the old basement, with its spooky equipment rooms, storage area, and multitude of odds and ends no one knew where to put. She fought against the dizzying images and brought her focus back to the burly man in front of her, who now glared at her like she was a delinquent he might haul off to juvie.

On closer inspection, he looked exhausted. She reminded herself that Frank Morgan had been shattered by grief. That his wife had walked out on him, and his son had reopened old wounds and caused some new ones, too. She also tried to recall him as a younger man. The one who'd built that tree house. Who'd stepped in to help her family after her dad had left.

But the good in this man seemed to have been buried with his son.

"For chrissakes, Colby, haven't you caused this family enough trouble?" He didn't bark at her this time. In fact, he sounded resigned.

"For a long time I thought so. But I've had a change of heart." It may have been too little, too late to stand up for Alec now, but better late than never. Her throat still ached from her graveside chat, but she dug deep for the energy needed to finish what she'd started. "I know Joe's death devastated you. And now you feel betrayed by your wife and son because of their involvement with the foundation and me. If you need to be angry, keep directing it at me. I can take it." She softened her voice now, hoping to appeal to his better nature. "But please don't take it out on Alec or your wife."

Mr. Morgan stared straight through her. She couldn't tell if he'd tuned her out or had become lost in his own memories. He wasn't screaming or kicking her out, so she continued. "If we're all being as honest as Alec has been lately, we should each take ownership for our roles in how things stand today."

Mr. Morgan's menacing cop face surfaced. His voice turned low and lethal. "You have no right to stand there and judge me."

Colby should've been afraid—alone with an angry ex-cop whose face looked like an overinflated balloon. But her purpose kept her going. "Maybe not. But tell me, what good is *your* judgment doing you or your family? Instead of lashing out and hurting each other, can't we pull together? If you don't want to be involved in the foundation, could you at least consider coming to the gala next week? Come see what your wife, son, and I have done for Joe. If you watch Alec at work, you finally might appreciate the talented, good, strong man he is."

Instead of being persuaded by her plea, Mr. Morgan spat back. "I see Alec for exactly who he is. Do you? He's hiding behind your skirt now, just like he hid behind his mother's forever. I love him, but that doesn't mean I have to like everything about him. And I don't have to pretend he's stronger than he is."

"Alec doesn't know I'm here. I don't even know where he is. But I do know how much he wants to reunite your family. And, like it or not, he's stronger than *you* because he understands how to manage his own disappointment without becoming a bully."

Mr. Morgan crossed to the door and flung it open, sending it crashing against the wall. "I'm done listening to you. Out. NOW!"

Her insides quaked in the face of his outburst, but she managed to get her legs to cooperate without her knees buckling. She got in her car and parked in her mom's driveway, chest heaving, tears stinging her eyes.

In hindsight, she wasn't sure whether that was the bravest or dumbest thing she'd ever done. Alec might even be pissed at her for interfering. Hopefully he'd understand that she'd been trying to fight for him. Now she just prayed it would work.

The last card up her sleeve involved a favor from her dad. If his food-journalist friend, Rob Salvetti, could attend the gala, he might write something positive for one of those foodie magazines. Then A CertainTea and Alec would get the respect they deserved. She'd given Alec free rein over that evening's menu, and he would be running the kitchen. He was already motivated to make the night perfect for Joe, so if she could surprise Alec with this coup, surely that could make a difference. She didn't want to raise Alec's hopes, but rather than manage his expectations, she'd simply inform him of the possibility. No more secrets.

Chapter Twenty-Two

Colby lugged a box of tea lights into the restaurant Tuesday morning. Yesterday she, Sara, and her mom had met here to decorate for tonight's gala. Now A CertainTea shimmered with silver-and-navy accents. Hundreds of balloons with shiny streamers had arrived early this morning, and flowers would be delivered any minute.

The warm, dry weather meant she could throw the glass doors open and allow the party to wander onto the flagstone patio. A gorgeous sunset on the lake would provide a perfect backdrop for the event.

Guests would arrive at seven. She should be thrilled for having pulled it all together in such a short time. She would have been, too, if it didn't also mark the last time she and Alec would work together.

All week she'd hoped Alec would change his mind, but he'd restricted their discussions to the gala. Neither he nor Julie had mentioned her confrontation with Mr. Morgan. Either the man hadn't told them, or it simply hadn't done any good.

Her Hail Mary didn't pan out, either. Her dad had promised to contact his writer friend, but to no avail. Although disappointed that she wouldn't be able to salvage Alec's reputation, Alec didn't seem surprised that Mr. Salvetti hadn't committed to coming. Alec's ennui suggested he'd given up on being a chef that drew any notice.

She set the tea lights on a dining table before going into her office and flicking on the light. When she draped her wrap over her chair and flung her purse on the desk, she noticed her empty bud vase. She lifted it to her chest, then laid it in her desk drawer.

A knock at the door caused her to look up, right into Alec's cautious gaze. "We're in good shape in the kitchen. Just checking to see if there are any last-minute items you need help with."

"Nothing for you to worry about." She sighed. "You must be thrilled to get tonight over with so you can leave this all behind."

Chin tucked, he closed his eyes and shook his head. "I wouldn't say that."

"You know, reservations are up this week. Our TripAdvisor and Yelp ratings are fantastic. Real people love your food, no matter what Jeffers says. You could stay and save me the trouble of hiring someone new." Stay and give us a chance to rebuild.

He tucked his hands in his pockets, like usual. "I appreciate the pep talk, but I can't stay here and work with you every day."

"I don't care about Mark's note. You're not the reason he's dead. His illness is. And as far as honesty goes, you were right. We both made mistakes, but we can learn from them. They don't have to mean the end of everything."

All week she'd fantasized that a speech like that would end in a passionate kiss. When it didn't, she simply hung her head.

"I'm not good for you." He sounded so certain he almost convinced her. "Look around. My mother lives in my apartment. My family is in shambles. My career is in neutral. None of that makes me happy, or fun. I want you to be happy. I want you to have fun."

"I'm not having fun now."

"You will soon enough. And if we're being completely honest, until I come to terms with my new reality, I can't be a good partner for anyone. Not in *any* way. I don't want you waiting around, or spending your time trying to fix me. You've spent enough of your life trying to fix people. You should be with someone who makes your stomach hurt from laughing, not from stress. But I can't stick around and watch you fall in love with someone else, so I have to go."

She thought to shove her right hand at his face and show him that she'd taken off Mark's ring. To tell him how she'd gone to his dad on his behalf. How she'd missed him and would happily "wait" or help him get back on his feet. But looking at the resolve in his expression, she knew it wouldn't matter. He'd made up his mind, and nothing she said now would change it.

"You say you love me, but apparently not enough." She turned her back to him, chin to chest. "I accept your resignation."

He stood there in silence. When she didn't turn around, he finally left, dragging her heart on the floor behind him.

◆　◆　◆

Two hours later, the din of the vibrant crowd drowned out the music. Large platters of hors d'oeuvres passed by, looking elegant and tasty. A festive celebration ensued, just like she'd envisioned when this building had been crumbling to the ground. Yet the happiness she'd imagined eluded her.

Colby set aside her hurt feelings and mingled with the patrons, thanking them for coming. She occasionally glanced toward the kitchen, fighting the urge to march back there and punch or kiss Alec. Either one might break him out of his self-imposed prison.

Her father appeared beside her, putting his arm around her shoulder and kissing her temple. "Smashing success, honey. I'm so proud."

His warm smile helped a little, just not enough.

"Thanks, Dad."

"How are you holding up?"

"I've been better."

"I know. I wonder if this restaurant idea isn't exactly the fix you'd hoped it would be. You've never lit up over it the way you do anytime you talk about the foundation. Maybe you ought to reconsider your career path and focus more on what makes you really happy."

"I'd need to win the lottery so I could repay CTC before I'd be free to make that change."

"You never know. Maybe the lottery is coming your way."

Colby thought of Hunter, who'd politely been steering clear of Jenna and their dad all night. She'd made him a promise she hadn't yet kept. "Hunter mentioned a rumor about Pure Foods. I have to say I can't believe you'd consider selling the family business."

"I'm not getting younger. If I had less responsibility, I could be more focused on what my kids need. I could be a better father." He shrugged.

"You're not a bad father, Dad. Besides, we're all grown up. And what about all the promises you made to Hunter? How can you take all that away from him, especially after he walked away from other opportunities? If you want to slow down, retire and let him run things, but don't sell out."

"Let's not get into this here." He patted her shoulder. "Nothing's even on the table yet . . . just whispers and rumors. Besides, we're at a party, and this night is about celebrating you and this wonderful idea. Speaking of which, I have a little something for you."

He handed her a generous five-figure check. "Dad, this is amazing. Thank you."

"Think about what I said. If you have the right people in charge here, you could dedicate more time to the foundation."

"It's ironic that the foundation was Alec's idea." She sighed, glancing at the kitchen again.

"I hear he's back there tonight."

"Yes, but only for the party."

Her dad kissed her temple. "I'm sorry, honey. But remember, it's never over until you quit. And, on that note, I need to introduce you to Rob."

Mr. Salvetti showed up? "He never RSVP'd!"

"He texted me two days ago, didn't I tell you? Sorry. I would've sworn I passed that along. What's one more, right? You got what you wanted."

Her father walked her over to a dark-haired man who was taking a flute of champagne from a waiter. "Jed, good to see you."

"So glad you could come." The men shook hands. "I wanted to introduce you to my daughter, Colby. This place and the foundation are hers."

"Nice to meet you," she said, also offering her trembling hand. He'd come! She should tell Alec as soon as possible. Maybe this was a sign of things turning around.

"You as well. This is a beautiful space, and the Scallop Carpaccio with Ginger Chive Pesto is amazing."

"That's all Alec Morgan. I'd be happy to introduce you if you'd like."

"Perhaps later. I'm sure he's busy now," Rob chuckled.

"True." Now wouldn't be a good time to interrupt him.

Todd walked over, unaware of his poor timing. "Hello, Mr. Cabot."

"Todd." Her father shook hands and then looked at Colby.

"I'll let you two catch up," Colby said to her dad and Mr. Salvetti. She could barely think, torn about whether or not to race back and tell Alec now. But Todd tugged at her arm.

"How does it feel to be a successful entrepreneur *and* philanthropist?" He winked.

"I think you may be jumping the gun on both—" She broke off when she noticed Frank Morgan stroll through the doors. Before she could draw a breath, her mother rushed to her side.

"This is a surprise." She laid her hand on Colby's back.

Todd followed their gazes. "A big donor?"

"Alec's father." When Todd frowned in confusion, Colby added, "His estranged father. Excuse me, please. I need to warn Alec."

Her mother held her arm. "Maybe you ought to first see what the man wants before you get Alec worked up."

By then, Julie had made her way to her husband, while the rest of Colby's family subtly closed ranks around her.

Frank surveyed the Cabot group, jaw set, avoiding making direct eye contact with Colby. He didn't look as threatening as he had at his house. But this was *her* turf. He murmured something to Julie, and then, together, they crossed the room.

"Jed." Frank reached for her father's hand. "Leslie. Hunter." Then finally he met Colby's gaze. "Colby."

"Mr. Morgan, thank you for supporting the cause." She wished her voice sounded stronger, but anxiety strangled it to something thready.

He drew a breath and looked at Julie. "You're welcome."

"I'm sure your family appreciates it." Colby smiled at Julie, seeking some assurance that her husband wasn't going to cause trouble.

"Contrary to what some people think, I love my family." Frank kept his voice as level as his gaze.

Too aware of their audience, Colby merely said, "The only people whose opinions matter are your wife's and son's."

"Where *is* Alec?" he asked.

"Busy in the kitchen." Colby wondered then if inviting him back to the kitchen so he could finally see his son's gift would rattle Alec. Her gut told her to do it, and, sick of doubting herself for so long, she decided to go with it. "I'll take you to see him, although he won't be able to speak with you now."

"Understood." His eye twitched, making obvious his discomfort at being the center of the Cabot family's attention. "Well, let's get on with it."

"Polished" would not be a word anyone attributed to him, but she had to give him points for guts.

"Follow me." She led him through the crowd.

Along the way to the kitchen, he muttered, "You had no business storming into my house and dressing me down"—he cleared his throat—"but you weren't entirely wrong."

She chose not to respond. It didn't matter if he liked her or she liked him. He was here for Alec, and that was all that mattered.

When they reached the kitchen, she held out her arm to keep Frank back for a moment. She wanted him to see Alec as others did: as a man completely in charge. A maestro conducting a grand orchestra of activity. The timing. The chaos. All of it coming together to produce exquisite, elegant food.

They watched for a full two minutes before Alec noticed them. He was so stunned he nearly dropped the plate he'd been inspecting.

He approached them quickly, panic on his face. "What's wrong?"

"Nothing." Mr. Morgan cleared his throat again.

"What are you doing here?" Alec looked at Colby, but she shrugged.

"I came to see what all the fuss is about." His father cleared his throat. "To apologize to your mom and you."

She'd done all that she could, and now she'd bow out. Perhaps she'd helped these two men rebuild some kind of relationship. Her time with Alec had taught her that real love is about focusing on what the person you love needs rather than what you need or want. That's what Alec was trying to do for her by leaving, except he didn't realize that what she needed was him.

"Alec, Rob Salvetti showed up and already fell in love with the scallops. If we play our cards right, this could be a coup!" Before Alec could say anything, Colby turned to Mr. Morgan. "I'll give you a minute alone, but then I'm sure Alec needs to attend to the kitchen."

She turned and tried to sneak to her office unnoticed, but Todd followed her, tissue outstretched.

"What's wrong, Colby?" He clasped his hands in front of his body.

"Everything and nothing."

"Riddles?" Todd leaned against her desk.

"It's complicated. Things with Alec look grim."

"You don't have to confide in me, but just remember, I'm here for you. And I'm about as uncomplicated as you can get." He grinned in his friendly way, and she knew he meant well.

"That's exactly what Alec said about you when he ended things. He thinks I'm better off with someone less encumbered than him."

"He's smarter than he looks," Todd teased, and then turned earnest. "He must be a good man to be willing to walk away for your sake."

"He is a good man." She looked at the empty spot on her desk where the bud vase had been.

"And you love him."

She nodded. "I do."

Todd patted her shoulder. "It sucks to be me. But I hope you get your happy ending, Colby."

She hugged him. "You are a dear, dear man and friend."

"Like I said, sucks to be me." Todd nodded toward the door. "We should get back to our foundation party."

"Yes. Let's fire up the auction and raise some money." She didn't know where the foundation would lead, or what would happen with Alec in the long run, so for now, she would simply take one step at a time.

◆ ◆ ◆

Alec couldn't clean the kitchen fast enough. He wanted everyone out so he could speak to Colby.

He'd watched her negotiate resolutions for most of her life, yet he'd never have thought she'd be the one to broker peace in his family. She'd done it, and now he wondered why he'd ever doubted her. On top of that, her machinations might've taken a step toward salvaging his reputation. He'd met with Mr. Salvetti at the end of the evening, who'd offered some much-needed and effusive praise.

Alec tossed his hat and coat aside and shut off the lights. Colby's office was dark, and only one set of sconces remained on in the dining room. The crew would come through in the morning to finish cleaning and set up for Wednesday's dinner service.

She'd gone. Of course she had. He'd given her no reason to wait.

Maybe it was for the best, because he didn't quite know what he'd say if she were here. He glanced around the front of the house, remembering the hope he'd experienced the first time he'd walked through its doors. The breathtaking beauty of the space. The pristine kitchen. The calming effect of the lake views.

For a while, he'd almost had everything he'd ever wanted. He should've trusted himself more, and trusted her. Instead, he'd resigned.

When he finally returned to his apartment, he found his mother zipping her suitcase.

"You're going home?"

"It's time." She set the suitcase on its wheels. "I've imposed on you long enough. I know it was only a small step, but it took a lot for Frank to swallow his pride and to show up tonight. He's never been one to gush, but he's apologizing the best he can at this point, and I have to hope it will get easier. Somewhere in there is the man I married, so I need to take a step, too. That's how marriage works. How love works. You have to forgive. You have to remember that it isn't always easy. And you have to fight for love, too."

"Not too subtle."

"Maybe not, but I don't think Colby would've confronted your dad if she didn't love you." She reached into her purse for her keys. "You have a chance to make every one of your dreams come true. Don't let pride or doubt get in your way." She hoisted her luggage off the floor.

"I'll get that."

"No. You sit and make some decisions about your own life. I can take care of myself, Alec. You don't need to worry about me anymore." She kissed his forehead. "Stop living in the past and dwelling on mistakes. We've all made them. And now we're all trying to heal. It'll take a lot of patience and compassion, but we'll get there. Don't let history define your future. Think about your priorities. What, or who, is most important to you? Answer that question and then make a plan. I love you, and I'll be with you every step of the way."

"I love you, too." He hugged her tightly, then closed the door behind her.

He stared at it once she'd left him alone. He'd spent most of his life fairly comfortable in his loneliness, but now the silence rang loudly in his ears and wrapped around him like an icy blanket. He wandered to his room and stretched out on his bed. The picture Colby had given him months ago stared at him accusingly. *What, or who, is most important to you? Answer that question and then make a plan.* The answer was obvious; he'd be an idiot to even pretend it was a close call. But he'd blown it, and he knew it. The only way he deserved another chance was if he came up with a plan.

◆ ◆ ◆

Colby opened the door to the restaurant, determined to run through the list of chefs Alec had given her before the gala three nights ago. Chris had steered them through the past couple of evenings, but she couldn't put off those calls any longer, especially if she wanted to dedicate more time to the foundation.

As soon as she stepped inside, she stopped. A dozen tightly packed vases of white tulips and pink peonies were scattered throughout the small entry. Her hands went to her cheeks as she took several hesitant steps toward the dining room. "Alec?"

No one answered. She continued her slow journey to her office, her heart beating a little faster with each step. Her door was closed, as usual. She opened it, wondering what surprise might be waiting inside. The aroma of additional flower arrangements nearly knocked her over, but what weakened her knees was seeing Alec in the middle of the room.

"You look tired," she said without thinking.

"You look beautiful." He fidgeted with the pencil he'd been twirling. "I hear the gala raised a bundle."

"Not too shabby for a first try." She couldn't keep the pride from her voice, even though it wasn't really what she wanted to discuss.

"There's never been anything that you couldn't do once you made a commitment."

"We both know that's not entirely true." But she was done dwelling on her failures. "I hope you didn't raid our donations to buy all these flowers," she teased.

"Not to worry. This is all me." He gestured around at the arrangements. "I wanted to surround you with things you love."

She wished he wouldn't say things like that if he didn't plan to stick it out with her. "I'm surprised you're here bearing gifts. If anything, I thought you might be angry."

"Angry?"

"About the way I interfered with your family."

"Grateful, Colby. Not angry."

"It's the least I could do. I should've been a better friend to you a long time ago. Maybe I could've helped you and Joe. But if I made some small difference with you and your dad, then that's something."

"More than something." He pitched forward, as if he wanted to get closer, then straightened again. "We've called a truce. It's strained, but better than it was a week ago. It won't be easy, but it's my family, so I'm willing to try. With time, who knows?"

It felt odd to talk about such intimate things while standing so far apart, but she didn't want to presume anything. The flowers might not be a romantic gesture at all, but just a show of deep gratitude. That thought made her heart sink. "I was planning to go through the list of chefs you gave me. Is there anyone in particular you think I should call first?"

"Yes." He hesitated. "Me."

"Is this also part of your plan to surround me with things I love?"

"Or, in this case, things that love you." He stepped closer, breathing a little heavier, or was that her?

"You said we couldn't work together because of our different visions. You said you couldn't make me happy. You said—"

"I know what I said. And now I'm admitting that I was an idiot. We started this relationship off with one hand tied behind our backs by grief and guilt. I know we can do better. *I* can do better. Will you let me try? I love you, Colby. You're more important than any of the rest of it. Maybe Salvetti will write a nice piece for *Saveur*, maybe not. Everything that went down with my dad, Joe, us—well, let's say I've revised my perspective on accolades. I'll still strive for them because I like the competition, but if I have to choose between my career and my heart, I choose my heart and fried chicken."

She fought the smile trying to reveal itself. "You don't have to choose."

His shoulders slumped. "I'm too late, then."

"Sort of." Then she placed her hands on his chest. "These past weeks I've realized that A CertainTea doesn't give me the intrinsic rewards that delivering that check to the Burnside Shelter did. When I think about how much good the foundation might do if I focused more of my energy there, I get so excited. So you don't have to choose because I'm no longer wedded to my vision for this place. I'll be happy to let you take charge and make your dreams come true with less interference from me so I can spend more energy on helping our community."

His arms snaked around her waist. "So I'm rehired?"

She nodded and he kissed her, finally. Another perfect kiss that went a long way toward filling up all the emptiness his absence had created.

He pulled away and smiled. "Guess I didn't need my backup plan."

"Now I'm curious."

He tossed an envelope on the desk and grinned. "Something to sweeten the pot."

She eyed it and him, then lifted it up for inspection.

"Unless you have X-ray vision, you might want to open it," he suggested.

She tore into it to retrieve two tickets to a Maroon 5 concert in LA in six weeks.

"It's not exactly meeting Adam Levine," he began, "but it's as close as I could get to that particular bucket-list item. I still have six weeks, and I'm leaning on a pal who might be able to get backstage passes."

"Really?" She grinned.

"I can't promise that part." Then he turned serious, his thumbs brushing her cheeks. "I can promise that I'll never quit on us again. Of all the bad ideas I've had and lies I've told, telling you I could walk away was the biggest of them all. Now we have no secrets or half-truths between us. Every day from now on, I promise to share everything with you."

She dropped the envelope on the desk and kissed him again, letting the rush of heat race back into her heart after a week of being in a deep freeze.

"I'm sorry," he said between kisses. "I'm sorry I let you down."

"No more apologies." She kissed him again while straining to unbutton his shirt. An ill-timed knock at the door interrupted their reunion.

"Go away!" Alec barked at the closed door at the same time she called out, "Come in."

Chris peeked into the office, eyes widening with surprise at finding Alec. "We've got a problem with the halibut."

Colby looked at him and smiled with a shrug.

"I'll be there in a minute," Alec replied.

"You're back, then?" Chris asked.

"I am," Alec said. "But thank you for keeping things going in my absence. It won't go unappreciated."

"Sure thing." Chris nodded and left them alone.

Alec squeezed her to his chest. "Thank you for not giving up on me. I was worried I'd taken too long to wise up."

"I love you, Alec. And some wise women have convinced me that it's never too late for love."

ACKNOWLEDGMENTS

I have many people to thank for helping me bring this book to all of you, not the least of which are my family and friends for their continued love, encouragement, and support.

Thanks, also, to my agent, Jill Marsal, as well as to my patient editors, Chris Werner and Krista Stroever, and the entire Montlake family for believing in me and working so hard on my behalf.

A special thanks to Susie and John Day, who hosted me in their city and offered an insider's peek at life in that gorgeous area of the country.

My Beta Babes (Christie, Katherine, Suzanne, and Tami) are the best, having provided invaluable input on various drafts of this manuscript. Also, thank you to Erika Kelly, Megan Ryder, Laura Moore, and Lisa Creane for your thoughtful feedback and insight into what wasn't working with the early drafts.

And I can't leave out the wonderful members of my CTRWA chapter. Year after year, all of the CTRWA members provide endless hours of support, feedback, and guidance. I love and thank them for that.

Finally, and most important, thank you, readers, for making my work worthwhile. Considering all your options, I'm honored by your choice to spend your time with me.

ABOUT THE RECIPES

The delicious dishes Alec prepared in this story are attributed to the following restaurants and chefs with gratitude:

1. White Gazpacho Soup (Dovetail, NYC)
2. Salmon Confit with a Brown Butter Hollandaise, with Young Asparagus and Beetroot, and Daylilies (TWG Tea, Singapore)
3. Pink Lemonade Lavender Thyme Sorbet, with Mint and Violet Garnish (*Boulder Locavore* blog)
4. Kingfish–Osetra Caviar Tartare with Smoked Crème Fraîche Emulsion (Le Bernardin, NYC)
5. Poached Marron on Crab Pillow with Truffle Emulsion, and Warm Artichoke Panaché with Vegetable Risotto and Lemon Emulsion (Le Bernardin, NYC)
6. Pan-Roasted Lobster with Stuffed Zucchini Flower and Tangy Persian Lime Sauce (Le Bernardin, NYC)
7. Grilled Pistachio and Chocolate Mille-Feuille (Rockpool Bar & Grill, Melbourne)
8. Broccoli Cheetos with Red Pepper Flakes (variation on a dish by chef Matt Farrell)
9. Chili-Lime Mango (*The Chew*, ABC Studios)

10. White Chocolate Mango Cheesecakes (Bertha Cherie Santoso, *Gourmet Baking* blog)

11. Scallop Carpaccio with Hand-Cut Ginger-Chive Pesto (*Food & Wine* magazine)

12. Wild Hibiscus Prosecco Cocktail (Paula Jones, *Bell'allimento* blog)

13. Tea-Brined and Doubled-Fried Hot Chicken (chef Joseph Lenn, Blackberry Farm, Walland, Tennessee)

An Excerpt from *All We Knew*
(Book Two of The Cabots)

Editors' note: This is an early excerpt and may not reflect the finished book.

The course of true love never did run smooth.

—*William Shakespeare*

Chapter One

Certain moments in a man's life are engraved on his memory in twenty-four-karat gold leaf. Hunter Cabot recalled several, including his first kiss (Tina Baker) and his father's proud hug when he'd graduated from college summa cum laude. But the shiniest memory of all involved the jolt he'd felt the instant he'd laid eyes on his wife, Sara, right here in Memorial Glade on Berkeley's campus.

He'd been comparing Microeconomic Analysis notes with two classmates in the shadow of Doe—the university's massive granite neo-classical-style library—when Sara exited the building and skipped down its stairs. Unlike most harried students, her miles-wide smile had radiated something other than stress. That smile and her bouncing honey-colored hair, which were both warmer than the California sun, had shone like a lodestar.

Mesmerized, he'd sprung off the ground, grabbed his backpack, and, without so much as a goodbye to his friends, chased her down before she could slip away. Luckily, his intensity hadn't scared her off, and she agreed to dinner that night. They'd been together ever since, marrying by the age of twenty-five and living that happily-ever-after dream most people only see in the movies.

Or at least he'd thought so, until recently.

Now he stood at the edge of the glade, having returned for alumni homecoming activities, hoping the faint aroma of eucalyptus and pine would trigger Sara's memories of what they'd once been and the promise of what still could be.

"Hey, Hunter. I was glad to see your name on the attendee roll." Greg Maxwell approached and sat on one of the new teak benches Hunter had recently underwritten.

"I know. It's been too long since we've been to one of these weekends." Hunter traced the plaque that bore Sara's and his names affixed to the back of the bench.

Smiling, he glanced around at the other seven benches now flanking the glade. He'd routinely donated thousands of dollars to his alma mater, but this year he'd wanted to do something specific. Something that gave Sara and him a permanent toehold on this particular ground. Not that she knew it yet. He planned to surprise her today, but Greg's unexpected presence meant he'd have to wait until later.

"Where's Sara?"

Hunter nodded toward the library. "Pit stop."

Sara had been complaining about headaches and bloating thanks to the daily course of shots and medications she was taking to coax her ovaries into producing more eggs.

"She still looks great." Greg crossed one loafer-clad foot over his knee and casually stretched an arm across the back of the seat. "You got lucky with that one."

"Luck's got nothing to do with it, buddy." Hunter chuckled, although he knew he'd been damn lucky. Lucky no one else had been smart enough to scoop her up before he'd swooped in. Then again, from the start he'd known they were soul mates. No one and nothing could have come between them back then. Even with the recent tension, his faith in their destiny had not been shaken.

Coeds were crisscrossing the campus all around Greg and him now, weighed down by backpacks and academic pressure. Hunter wished he could tell them life got easier, but he'd never lied to anyone for any reason.

"Were we ever this young?" Greg shook his head, his inky black hair now graying at the temples.

"Speak for yourself." Hunter patted his own trim waist in jest. "I'm still young. Just wiser and wealthier."

Avid cycling kept him fit, and his sandy-brown hair had yet to gray. But some days he felt every second of his thirty-four years, especially lately.

"That's true. I'm no longer invisible to women these days, either. Too bad you can't join me in playing the field." Greg glanced over Hunter's shoulder, raised his chin with a smile, and stood. "Here comes your wife."

Hunter turned in time to catch Sara descending the library steps. Unlike the first time he'd seen her there, her signature smile remained hidden behind a shallow grin. Her thick hair had been pulled into some kind of twist that didn't glint beneath the sun.

A cool autumn breeze tickled the back of his neck as she crossed the walkway and came to his side.

He captured her hand in his and kissed her knuckles—an intimate gesture he enjoyed. She had such soft hands, and he liked seeing his ring on her finger. "Feeling better?"

"Sure." She nodded, but he suspected she was faking it for Greg's sake. She leaned forward and pecked Greg on the cheek. "Hey, you. Long time."

"To look at you, I'd guess no time had passed whatsoever," he replied.

Hunter knew Sara wished she were still that girl, or at least that her reproductive organs were ten years younger. Still, she laughed at the compliment. "Since when did you become a flirt?"

"Better late than never. It's good to practice on married women. They seem to appreciate the flattery more than others." Greg gestured toward the pathway that led to the student union, where the alumni party was taking place. "I suspect most husbands take their good fortune for granted after the honeymoon."

"Savvy hypothesis," Sara teased, but didn't refute him.

"I take it back, Greg. I *did* get lucky. Luckiest guy on campus, actually." Hunter draped his arm over Sara's shoulder as they walked along the paved pathway. He liked the feel of her against his side, her floral perfume hovering around them.

Familiar. Warm. *His.*

They entered Pauley Ballroom in the student union. Soaring ceilings and floor-to-ceiling glass walls framed the space now crowded with alumni of all ages—a diverse group of people from around the globe. Hunter had been a star in high school, but amid the collective brain trust in this room, he was average. Normally he eschewed that lame designation, but he also didn't fight battles he couldn't win.

"I need a drink. Can I get you a glass of wine?" Greg asked Sara.

"No, thanks," she said.

"Not drinking?" Greg cocked his head, then his eyes widened and his gaze dropped to her midsection. "Any particular reason?"

"Just my headache." Sara's nonchalance fooled Greg, but Hunter felt her tense beside him.

"Sorry." Greg looked at Hunter. "Beer?"

"You go ahead. We're going to make the rounds for a bit." Hunter nodded goodbye to his friend and then turned to his wife. "Sorry."

"We're in our thirties and have been married almost nine years." She smoothed the front of her skirt, conveniently avoiding his gaze. "It's bound to come up. That's why I wasn't psyched to come."

So far his plan to rekindle that spark that had thrown them together hadn't been working out as he'd hoped. Rather than concede defeat, he shifted the conversation. "Did you notice the benches outside Doe?"

"I did. A nice addition, actually."

"I'm glad you approve, because we donated them." He stared at her, hoping for her wide smile to emerge. The expansive, joyful smile that always filled him with heat and happiness.

"*We* did?" She chuckled with exasperation. "I don't recall discussing it or writing a check. Maybe I've got Alzheimer's on top of everything else."

He pulled her to him and kissed her temple, inhaling the sweet scent of her skin. "You know why I did it?"

She shook her head against his chest. He eased his hold and looked directly into those intelligent sky-blue eyes that he'd never grow tired of waking up to each day. "Because of all the good things that came from my four years at this school, *you* are the very best."

"But what's that have to do with benches . . ." Her brow furrowed. Then her face relaxed, and, for the first time all day, a real smile stretched across her face. "You pounced on me in that glade."

"Pounced is an exaggeration," he scoffed.

She cocked a brow.

"Okay. I pounced." He tipped up her chin with two fingers and lightly kissed her. "I'm not ashamed or sorry, either."

"Hunter." She hugged him, sighing deeply. "Just when I'm feeling uncertain of everything, you say something that reminds me of why I love you."

He held her tight, his own muscles relaxing upon hearing that affirmation. Things might have been rocky lately, but she still loved him. He could work with that.

ABOUT THE AUTHOR

Photo © 2016 Lorah Haskins

Jamie Beck is a former attorney with a passion for inventing realistic and heartwarming stories about love and redemption, including her bestselling St. James and Sterling Canyon series. The Romance Writers of America Honor Roll author has seen her work translated into multiple languages. In addition to writing novels, she enjoys dancing around the kitchen while cooking and hitting the slopes in Vermont and Utah. Above all, she is a grateful wife and mother to a very patient, supportive family. Learn more about her at www.jamiebeck.com, where fans may also sign up for updates on new releases and giveaways, and interact with her on Facebook at www.facebook.com/JamieBeckBooks.